P9-CQA-197

The Portrait of Doreene Gray

Also by Esri Allbritten

Chihuahua of the Baskervilles

The Portrait of Doreene Gray

A CHIHUAHUA MYSTERY

Esri Allbritten

Minotaur Books
A Thomas Dunne Book New York

This is a work of fiction. All of the characters, organizations, and events portrayed in this novel are either products of the author's imagination or are used fictitiously.

A THOMAS DUNNE BOOK FOR MINOTAUR BOOKS.
An imprint of St. Martin's Publishing Group.

www.thomasdunnebooks.com
www.minotaurbooks.com

Library of Congress Cataloging-in-Publication Data

Allbritten, Esri.
The portrait of Doreene Gray : a chihuahua mystery / Esri Allbritten. — 1st ed.
p. cm.
"A Thomas Dunne book."
ISBN 978-0-312-56916-7 (hardcover)
ISBN 978-1-250-01151-0 (e-book)
1. Chihuahua (Dog breed)—Fiction. 2. Parapsychology—Investigation—Fiction. 3. Twins—Fiction. I. Title.
PS3601.L415P67 2012
813'.6—dc23

2012005478

First Edition: July 2012

10 9 8 7 6 5 4 3 2 1

To Angel Joe

and the 'rents,

and to

the people of

Port Townsend, Washington

Acknowledgments

Humongous thanks to Jennifer Unter, my agent—you're a star. Thanks to Marcia Markland, editor; Kat Brzozowski, assistant editor; Sarah Melnyk, publicity manager; and all the other folks at Thomas Dunne Books. Big thanks to Susan Schwartzman, for her great publicity work.

Thanks to all the people who gave such nice reviews to *Chihuahua of the Baskervilles.* Bless you.

Special thanks to Dominick Sekich, who introduced me to another "Doreene" and sparked the whole book. I'll miss having you next door.

Thanks to Chihuahua mavens Nikki Figular (ObsessiveChihua huaDisorder.com) and Ada Nieves (AdaNieves.com), and all the other Chi lovers out there (Fawn Frazer, Jan Sugden, Gail Hansen, Debra Gilbert, and I know I'm missing some), for your support of this series. I couldn't write for a better group of people. (P.S. In my mind, Gigi looks just like Nikki's Chico.)

Big thanks to Rhonda Beytebiere, of the Point Hudson Marina, and Walt at PT Outdoors, for help with boating questions, and Kate Burke, Fort Worden Parks Manager, for her help with those big trees! Thanks to Terolyn at the Blue Moose Café.

Thanks to fantastic mystery author Catriona McPherson, for her help with Angus's Scots-speak.

Thanks to Angel's Joe's whole fam-damily, especially Bonnie-mom, for medical info. Extra thanks to Bonnie and Dan French and Kim Graber. Thanks to supportive friends: Red Leather Heather, Poker Jeremy, Thanksgiving Sheila, Phil Brown, Uncle Dennis, and many more. Thanks to writing friends Lynda Hilburn, Karen Lin Albright, and Betsy Dornbusch.

Doreene Gray's house is inspired by the Ann Starrett Mansion in Port Townsend, Washington. Go see it. The Wooden Boat Festival is a real, very wonderful event. My apologies for the various inaccuracies I have included, unknowingly or for plot convenience, when describing Port Townsend. I'd move there in a minute.

The story of the sinking of the S.S. *Valencia* is true. Wikipedia has the goods.

My apologies to the International Fainting Goat Association for the joke I tell about the breed. It's probably physically impossible, but the gag got such laughs, I couldn't let it go.

And finally, thanks to all the dog-rescue organizations out there. You put more love into the world.

You can find me at EsriAllbritten.com. I hope to hear from you.

The Portrait of Doreene Gray

One

Outside the darkened windows of Doreene Gray's second-floor bedroom, a squall buffeted the house and whistled across the gingerbread trimming. A mile away, it sang through the rigging of ships in the harbor of Port Townsend, Washington, whipping the black water into whitecaps, then speckling the foam with rain.

Doreene slid out of bed, grimacing slightly at a twinge in her lower back. At fifty-eight, she could avoid many of the signs of age, but not all.

The young man beneath the sheets stretched one tanned arm across the bed. *"Princessa."* His drowsy voice was further thickened by a Brazilian accent. "You can't sleep?"

"Don't have a panic attack, Reynaldo. I'm just going to the can."

"What?"

"Banheiro."

He muttered something and subsided.

Doreene felt her way across the darkened room, but instead of going to the bathroom, she found the door to a small adjoining bedroom that had been turned into a closet. Under her fingers, the old-fashioned lock plate slid aside to reveal a computerized keypad. Doreene silently tapped a code onto the faintly glowing keys.

Once inside, she shut the door and locked it from the other side. The sound of the storm disappeared, muffled by the surrounding racks of clothes. Still in the dark, Doreene pulled what felt like a coat off a hanger and arranged it at the foot of the door before switching on the light.

A cluttered dressing table sat in the middle of the room, its mirror supported by two upright posts. Doreene sat in the matching chair and leaned close to the mirror. She might have been nearing sixty, but she didn't look a day over thirty. Blond hair curled gently over her shoulders, and her wide hazel eyes looked out from unlined skin.

"Eyebrows might be getting a little thin," she murmured, running a finger against the fine hairs and then smoothing them back down.

The dressing table had space behind it. Doreene grasped the top edge of the oak mirror frame and rotated it downward. The back side swung into view, revealing a stretched and mounted canvas.

She winced a little at the sight of the hideous portrait. The original oil painting was almost hidden beneath pasted-on bits of paper. Tiny lines of writing served as the furrows that ran from nose to chin. Blotches of red and brown paper, torn from magazine pages, marred the cheeks with an impressionist collage of age.

Doreene pulled open the drawer of the table and removed a newspaper clipping.

Famous Portrait for Sale
Maureene Pinter's painting of identical twin sister
to be sold at auction.

The photo below the subtitle showed Doreene's sister, Maureene, one hand raised too late to hide her haggard face. She looked every bit of her age, and more.

Doreene gathered cosmetic-smeared tissues from the table and threw them in a nearby trash can until she uncovered a pair of nail scissors.

Trimming carefully, she cut the picture of her sister's face from the article, then looked from it to the artwork in front of her. "Neck, I think."

She lay the trimmed photo down and found a bottle of foundation. After rubbing some of the makeup between finger and thumb, she carefully shaded the scrap of paper, holding it up to the portrait occasionally to check the color.

Next she uncapped a bottle of clear nail polish and brushed a few strokes on the back of the photo. After positioning it at the base of the portrait's throat, she carefully pressed it into place.

Doreene studied her sister's expression on the drying newsprint. "Didn't expect me to put the painting up for sale, did you? And you have one more shock coming."

As she leaned back, the newly applied photo merged into the impression of wattled skin. Doreene stroked the smooth column of her own throat and smiled. "If I do say so myself, I've become quite the artist."

Two

Two weeks later

In the Boulder, Colorado, offices of *Tripping* magazine (Your Guide to Paranormal Destinations), two-thirds of the staff were having a fight.

Michael Abernathy, *Tripping*'s main writer, had the sardonic look of a Greek faun, with the addition of gold-rimmed glasses and blue jeans. He was arguing with Angus MacGregor, editor and cofounder of *Tripping.* A tall, rangy Scot in his early fifties, Angus had the warm smile and twinkling eyes of a kindly uncle, which was only slightly misleading.

Michael raised his voice another notch. "Leaving aside the question of intrinsic value, astrology columns are everywhere. What's going to set ours apart?"

Angus thought for a moment. "We'll couch all the advice in terms of how it affects travel."

Michael looked over the top of his glasses. "So next to the article on 'Best Haunted B&Bs,' you're going to say October is a good month for Virgo to stay home?"

Angus ran a hand through his iron-gray hair. "Maybe we can focus on the paranormal aspect somehow."

"How?" Michael adopted a girlish tone. " 'March is not the time to change your hairstyle, Sasquatch. If you need a pick-me-up, focus on those big feet and get a pedicure.' "

Angus burst out laughing. "Perfect! Come up with eleven more and we'll have the first batch done."

Michael groaned but made a note on his laptop. "All right, but I'm using a pseudonym."

Suki Oota, *Tripping*'s photographer, wandered into the office carrying an iPad and a file folder. In a city where yoga-toned college students inflated the standard of looks, Suki still turned heads. Tall and half-Japanese, she wore her black hair in a short, spiky cut and favored red lipstick. Today she wore torn jeans over black leather boots with an array of buckles. A faux snakeskin tank top in red and black revealed her perfectly toned arms.

Michael looked up. "What's up with all the eyeliner? That's not very steampunk."

"I dropped the steam," Suki drawled in her Los Angeles accent. She tossed the folder on Angus's desk and slouched in the other chair. "Can we work on what features to do next?"

"Certainly." Angus pulled the folder toward him and smiled benignly. "What are these?"

"Suggestions I got through e-mail." Suki hooked one leg over the arm of her chair. "I don't know what you guys already have."

Michael opened a document on his computer. "Somebody caught a giant squid with a tennis shoe on one of its tentacles. Oh, and there's a new twist on those goats that faint when they hear a loud noise."

"What kind of twist?" Angus asked.

"Apparently some of them crap themselves, too."

Suki rolled her eyes. "Can't wait to take those pictures."

Angus looked skeptical. "I'm not sure there's anything paranormal about crapping goats."

"Depends on *what* they crap," Michael pointed out.

Angus raised his eyebrows questioningly.

Michael shrugged. "Sorry. It's just regular crap."

Angus shuffled through the printed e-mails. "Let's see what we have here. Ghost, turtle with an image of an alien on its shell, talking tree . . ." He read silently for a moment. "Looks like only one person can hear it. That's a shame. Oh, here's something. Mystery painting. Portrait of Doreene Gray to be sold."

"It should be 'picture'," Michael said.

Angus looked up. "What?"

"Oscar Wilde's original title was *The Picture of Dorian Gray*. People are always getting it wrong."

Angus stared at him. "It must comfort your friends, knowing you're always there to correct them." He tapped the paper. "Considering this is an auction and not a book, and the *portrait* is of *Doreene* Gray, I think Mr. Wilde is not under discussion."

"I bet Doreene Gray isn't her real name," Michael said.

Angus scanned the e-mail. "It has been ever since she married Mr. Gray. When the portrait was painted, she was Doreene Pinter. Bit of a lucky break there."

Suki heaved a sigh. "What's the deal with the picture?"

"It ages but she doesn't, or at least not much." Angus swiveled his chair and began to type on his laptop's keyboard.

"Who painted the picture?" Michael asked.

"Doreene's sister—*twin* sister, Maureene, who ages normally." Angus turned his computer so they could see the screen. "Here's a photo of the two of them, taken eight years ago."

Suki and Michael leaned forward and studied the photo. There was a strong resemblance between the two women, but they looked more like mother and daughter than twins.

"She's probably had work done, but it's really good," Suki said.

Michael rolled his eyes. "Of course she's had work done. Do you think she owns an actual magic picture?"

"Michael . . ." Angus waved a hand around the office, gesturing to the framed covers of *Tripping* magazine that decorated the walls. "May I remind you of our audience? Our mission is to present the uncanny for the public's entertainment." He picked up the e-mail and waved it. "We have a picture that changes over time, a woman who doesn't, and best of all, we have twins. Twins are always interesting."

"That's true." Suki gave a languid smile.

"What about the location?" Michael asked. "Do the sisters live in the same city? Is it a place people will want to go?"

"Absolutely." Angus turned the laptop so he could type in a search string, then hit enter and turned it back to show them a harbor full of masted boats and a Victorian-era downtown. "Port Townsend, Washington. The land that time forgot. At least, it forgot for about seventy years."

"Does that mean they don't have an airport?" Suki asked.

Angus shrugged. "I understand the drive from Seattle is beautiful."

Three

Maureene Pinter lived in a frame cottage separated from the main house and her twin sister by a quarter acre of overgrown woods.

Inside, sunlight slanted through windows clouded by dirt and rain spots. Dust floated on the air, settling on the Scottish terrier that lay, belly-up, on the sofa. The dog snorted and twitched a paw in its sleep.

Maureene sat hunched on a stool in front of her easel, rolling a stick of charcoal between two fingers. Her short salt-and-pepper hair stuck out on one side of her head. The canvas in front of her sported two curved lines. They could have represented anything or nothing.

Someone knocked on the door. The terrier barked sleepily, then twisted to its feet and jumped to the floor. Its claws clicked on the scarred linoleum as it followed Maureene to the door.

She pulled aside a curtain covering the door's window, then swiveled the dead bolt and opened it before going back to her stool.

Maxwell Thorne stepped inside. A broker for Rothwell's auction house, he wore at least three thousand dollars' worth of clothes. The charcoal suit wasn't showy, but the material hung perfectly. His shoes were slightly interesting, his watch deceptively simple, and his tie a work of art.

He reached down and spoke to the dog while scratching its head. "Hilda, it's good to see you again. You, too, Maureene."

Maureene didn't turn from her canvas. "What do you want, Max?"

Max strolled along the perimeter of the room, tilting his head to look at the titles in a dusty bookcase. "I'd like to take you out to lunch. What do you say?"

"I'd say I haven't showered and my hair looks like roadkill."

A trio of carved elephants sat on one shelf. Maxwell touched the tusk of the smallest. "Put a hat on. Hats are expected of artists."

Maureene rubbed a finger across one of the charcoal marks, softening it. "Who else would be coming to lunch?"

"No one, if that's what you want."

"What do *you* want?"

"What do *I* want?" Max straightened. "I want your portrait of Doreene to sell for so much that the rest of your existing paintings bring in seven figures apiece. I want your renewed fame to cause gallery owners to camp on your doorstep, begging you to paint more. I want museum curators to rend their clothes when they can't afford a Pinter for their *Great Portraitists of the Twenty-first Century* installations." He smiled. "In short, I want you to come out to a nice lunch with two very gentle members of the press and talk about yourself and Doreene's portrait."

Maureene shook her head slowly. "She can't sell that painting."

Max put his hands in his pockets and came over. He glanced at the canvas, then at the back of Maureene's neck, where charcoal streaked her weathered skin. "Are we talking about legalities? Because Doreene has a letter from you, giving her the painting."

Maureene looked up at him, her face bleak. "That portrait is a part of me. If she sells it, I don't know what will happen."

Max frowned. "This is not something people in my profession usually say, but *it's just a painting.*" He smiled suddenly. "Are you playing the eccentric-artiste card? It's true that a little tasteful insanity can add to a painter's caché, but you shouldn't waste it on me. I'll have Elizabeth arrange a TV interview if you like."

Maureene looked at the canvas again. "Go away, Max."

"I'll come back in an hour, all right? Is that long enough for you to shower and dress? Then we'll have a nice lunch."

Maureene stood and faced him. "I mean it. If you won't help me change Doreene's mind, then get out."

Hilda, who had been busily nosing at the corner of an area rug, looked up and growled, her teeth bared.

Maxwell backed toward the door. "Maureene, tell me what's wrong. Do you need a change of scene? Maybe there's something I can do to help."

"There is. Don't sell the painting."

"If I don't, Doreene will just find someone else. It's going to happen, Maureene."

Hilda gave a sharp bark.

"It can't," Maureene said. "It just can't."

Four

Seventy miles separated Port Townsend from the Seattle-Tacoma airport. The *Tripping* crew landed in early morning darkness and rented a minivan to accommodate the photography equipment. Suki drove to the Seattle Ferry Terminal, where they caught a ferry to Bainbridge Island.

Suki and Michael ate pastries in the ferry's café for their breakfast. A boy of about three stared at Suki, his gaze traveling from her studded leather bracelets to her face. She puckered her lips at him and he smiled delightedly.

Angus drank only tea. While his staff went out on deck, he sat inside and stared into his teacup, avoiding any view of the bobbing horizon.

Halfway through the trip, Michael came back in and took a moment to stand in front of Angus, swaying to the boat's movement.

"Sit down if you're going to stay," Angus snapped.

Michael switched to swaying in counterpoint. "What's the matter, Angus? I thought most Scots had Viking blood."

Angus swallowed thickly. "They learned you can only reproduce if you get off the boat and stay put."

"That's ridiculous," Suki said, joining them. "The motion adds to the experience." She raised the camera that hung on a strap around her neck and snapped a picture of Angus's face.

He groaned and turned away.

Michael sat on the bench opposite Angus. "What's the plan? Get settled today and do the interview tomorrow?"

Angus put his cup on the table. "We're seeing Doreene Gray today, but it's not exactly an interview."

Suki sat next to Michael. "What is it, exactly?"

"An invitation-only press conference," Angus said, "and we don't have an invitation."

"I wish you'd told me," Suki said. "I didn't pack any clothes for crashing press conferences."

"I'm sure you'll figure something out."

Michael held up a hand. "Wait a minute. Did you even *ask* for an interview before deciding to just show up? How do you know she won't talk to us?"

"Because Doreene Gray comes from money, and she's trying to sell a painting to moneyed people."

"Ah." Michael nodded. "So she won't want the tone of the event compromised by our piddling magazine."

"Piddling *paranormal* magazine," Suki corrected. "I thought the painting's big selling point was that it was spooky."

Angus gave a wry smile. "A mystery is only mysterious if you don't overpromote. Also, the sale is being handled by Rothwell's, and they'll err on the side of tasteful. Don't expect to see signs that say, THIS WAY TO THE POSSESSED PAINTING!"

Suki rested her camera on the table. "If this press conference is invitation-only, how did you find out about it?"

"I subscribe to a Web site that leaks that kind of information," Angus said. "It's run by personal assistants and gophers. Poor things, they have to make a living somehow."

Michael took off his glasses and rubbed the bridge of his nose.

"You're telling me we flew all the way out here on the off chance that we can get into an event?"

Angus tapped a finger on the table. "A journalist makes his own opportunities. At the very worst, we'll have photos of the house and Port Townsend and there's a boat festival going on right now. *Tripping* is a travel magazine, too, don't forget."

"What about the portrait itself?" Michael asked. "How are we going to do an article if we don't have a photo of that?"

Angus's eyes slid away. "I imagine there will be photos available online after the press conference."

"Oh, no," Suki said. "I draw the line at taking someone else's work."

Angus smiled at her. "I would never ask you to do such a thing, but don't photographers ever share work? You might be able to chat someone up and come to an arrangement."

Suki considered that. "Do I get a drinks allowance?"

"Naturally."

"Then I'll see what I can do."

Angus folded his hands on the table. "If all else fails, Suki can get a photo of Doreene Gray as she leaves to do her shopping, and we'll use that to make our own version of the painting. We'll put a wee label underneath—ARTIST'S RENDERING."

Michael laughed. "That's pretty funny, actually."

Five

Once off the ferry, Suki stopped at a filling station, where she got rid of her black eyeliner and studded bracelets and exchanged her torn jeans for polka-dot leggings. Only close examination revealed the dots to be tiny skulls. Her torn T-shirt was hidden beneath a worn leather jacket.

They arrived in Port Townsend. Suki followed the automated voice of her smartphone's navigation system and parked the minivan at the end of a long line of cars in front of Doreene Gray's home.

A fine mist spotted the windshield. In the backseat, Michael leaned close to the car window and bent his head so he could see the building's top story. "Another Victorian mansion. What is it with Victorian mansions and weirdness?"

Angus unbuckled his seat belt. "The style is actually Carpenter Gothic—note the pointed arches over the windows. But it was built in 1889, which is still the Victorian era. As for the weirdness, I have a theory that the Victorians were so repressed, they couldn't work out their issues during one lifetime, so their spirits tend to stay on."

Michael frowned. "Or maybe the upkeep on a place like this drives people crazy."

Suki turned in her seat and pointed at the pile of equipment in the back. "Michael, hand me that black bag with the red zipper pull." She looked at Angus. "This isn't another ghost story, is it? I'd hate to run two ghost features in a row."

"This painting business could be anything," Angus said. "We'll leave it as open-ended as possible. It should generate a lot of reader mail."

Michael looked at Angus. "Don't you have any angle in mind? Deal with the Devil, maybe?"

"I was toying with the idea of vampiric object," Angus said. "The painting gives youth but takes the soul."

"Isn't that the same thing as deal with the Devil?"

"No, because my theory uses the word 'vampiric,' and anything with vampires in it sells."

"How about a sidebar on possible causes, with vampiric object at the top?"

Angus nodded. "Good idea."

Suki hung a camera around her neck and put the bag's strap over one shoulder. "Don't you think Ms. Gray will object if *Tripping* says she's sold her soul to the Devil?"

Angus shook his head. "We'll talk about the subject hypothetically, in terms of other situations."

Michael nodded. "Involving people who are now dead."

"And who don't have rich relations still living." Angus pulled on a brown tweed sport coat and glanced at his watch. "The press conference started at ten-thirty. It's ten-forty now, and I'm hoping no one is manning the door. If all goes well, we can wander in and take up positions at the back of the room. Ready? Let's go."

They got out of the car and trotted up the drive, Suki with the camera tucked under her leather jacket, Michael holding one hand above his glasses to keep the mist off.

"If anyone asks, *Tripping* is an international travel magazine," Angus said.

"Since when?" Michael asked.

"Since we ran that sidebar on giant beavers and picked up a couple of Canadian subscribers." Angus pushed open the front door to the house.

They stepped into an opulent foyer. Suki walked to the foot of a huge spiral staircase and looked up. "Dude," she said, raising her camera.

The others joined her and looked at the distant ceiling, where painted cupids cavorted with nude women clad in wisps of fabric.

"I'm thinking these particular Victorians weren't that repressed," Michael said.

Angus raised an eyebrow. "Well, it was pretty late in the period. I suppose they were ready to bust out."

At the sound of a door closing, they turned.

A twentysomething woman wearing a gray suit and heels walked toward them, carrying a clipboard. "Can I help you? I'm Elizabeth Canter, Ms. Gray's publicist."

Angus thrust out a hand. "Sorry we're late. Angus MacGregor, *Tripping,* the international travel magazine. I take it we're supposed to be in there?" He walked toward the door she had exited. The murmur of a crowd could be heard behind it.

She blocked his way. "I'm sorry, but access to the press conference is restricted, and I don't recall your publication being on the list."

He smiled graciously at her. "We might be listed under our parent corporation. I'm sure you recall Condé Nast."

Her brows rose, and she looked at the clipboard uncertainly. "Um, there are several people from—" A sudden roar of voices behind the door made her turn.

"I think perhaps we'd better see what's happened, don't you?" Angus said kindly.

She didn't respond, just trotted toward the door. Angus and the others slipped in behind her.

More than thirty journalists and photographers jostled inside a space large enough to serve as a ballroom, shouting questions and taking pictures. Most of the questions seemed to be "Why can't we use a flash?" and "Will you have pictures available online?" On the far wall, a velvet rope and two uniformed guards kept photographers a good fifteen feet from the famous painting. The canvas measured twenty-four by thirty inches without the frame, and was poorly lit.

"See what you can do," Angus muttered in Suki's ear.

She disappeared into the crowd.

Michael craned his neck to see over the people in front of him. "I assume the retired *GQ* model behind the podium is Maxwell Thorne?"

Angus nodded, and inserted a shoulder between two men. "Excuse me," he said to their outraged stares. "My photographer is having an asthma attack and needs her medication." He held up his hand, clasped as though he held something.

They parted reluctantly and let him through.

Michael leaned against the wall and sighed. That trick wouldn't work twice.

At the podium, Maxwell Thorne succeeded in getting the crowd to quiet down. "I understand your frustration, but Ms. Gray feels that every painting has aspects of its personality that should be made available only to the eventual owner."

A murmur of confused speculation greeted this statement.

Max smiled. "I know it's unusual, but this is not your typical art auction. And after all, there is no question of this painting's provenance."

The door beside Michael opened, and a woman in her late fifties slid through. She wore a canvas jacket, splotched with paint, over baggy jeans. Despite gray hair, wrinkles, and thirty extra pounds, she was clearly Doreene's twin, Maureene Pinter.

Maureene stood on tiptoe and stared at the front of the room. After a moment, she sagged, blew out a breath, and opened the door to leave.

Michael followed her. In the foyer beyond, he spoke to her retreating back. "I'm a great admirer of your work, Ms. Pinter, especially *Girl in an Apple Tree.* The colors are so joyous, yet there's something wistful there, too. Maybe it's the little scratch on her face."

Maureene turned.

"Also, the apple she's holding has a bruise on it. You can see the brown at the edge of the bite she's taken," said Michael, who had made good use of Wikipedia and Google.

Maureene smiled slightly. "You have good eyes. Are you with an art journal?"

"A travel magazine, but I'm a fan." He shrugged and gave a half-smile.

Maureene put her hands in the pockets of her canvas jacket. "Are you an artist yourself?"

"I'm working on a novel, but this job pays the bills." Michael took a step forward. "Ms. Pinter, have you modified your sister's portrait since you first painted it?"

"I'm not answering any questions about the portrait." She turned on her heel and stalked toward the front door.

It opened before she reached it and a young man of exceptional beauty came in. "Maureene! Has she sold it yet?" he asked, taking her hand. His musical voice had a strong foreign accent.

She pulled free. "Today isn't the sale, Reynaldo, it's just the gathering of the vultures."

His large, dark eyes squinted slightly. "The what?"

Michael waved to get his attention. "May I ask who you are?"

Reynaldo stuck out his hand. "Reynaldo Cruz. I am *Senhora* Doreene's man, from Brazil."

"And how do you feel about the sale of the painting?"

"She *should* sell it! It is an evil thing—" Reynaldo broke off and touched Maureene's arm. "*Perdoem-me, senhora.* I am sure it is not your fault."

"Thanks for that," Maureene said dryly.

"Some things, they are so beautiful, they invite evil." Reynaldo dropped his voice. "My uncle had a wooden bowl, a work of art. But a demon possessed it and kept him up at night, telling him to kill his wife and children. Finally the priest came and burned the bowl, speaking the correct words."

"Are you talking about an exorcism?" Michael asked.

"Yes, *um exorcismo,*" Reynaldo said eagerly.

Maureene snorted. "I doubt the painting talks to my sister."

"She talks to it," Reynaldo said. "At night, I hear her."

Maureene's frown deepened. "That's weird."

"Right? I am telling you so!" Reynaldo nodded so hard, a lock of hair fell across his bronzed forehead.

Michael tapped his arm. "When you say she *talks to it,* do you mean casual conversation, or are we talking about chanting?"

Maureene gave Michael a pointed look. "Thanks for being such a fan." She turned to go.

"I'm sorry, but it's my job."

Maureene glanced over her shoulder as she headed toward the door. "Good luck, Reynaldo. I assume you have a word for *paparazzi* in Brazil."

Reynaldo's brow furrowed. "Yes. We call them paparazzi." The front door closed behind Maureene, and he turned back to Michael. "Excuse, but I want to see my *princessa* talk. Already I am late."

Michael followed him back into the press conference.

Behind the podium, Maxwell Thorne said, "Since then, Maureene Pinter has painted the crown prince of Dubai, Freddie Mercury, and Elizabeth Taylor, among many other notables. And now I'd like to introduce the subject of this portrait, painted some thirty years ago, Ms. Doreene Gray. She'll be happy to take your questions."

A door behind the podium opened, and Doreene entered, carrying a cream-and-white long-haired Chihuahua. Elizabeth Canter, the publicist, joined her as she made her way to the microphone.

Doreene stepped onto the temporary dais and took her place behind the podium. Her rose-colored dress revealed youthful-looking arms and excellent legs. Her golden hair was swept up on one side and held with a decorative clip.

Elizabeth stood beside her and scanned the crowd. "Mr. Crawford," she said, pointing to a man in a blue shirt.

"Ms. Gray, the painting has clearly altered since your sister first painted it. Who is responsible for those alterations?"

"You could say the painting is a joint project of my sister and mine." Doreene looked down at her dog and stroked its head, a secretive smile on her lips.

Elizabeth pointed into the crowd again. "Ms. White."

"What did you use to make the changes?" the reporter asked.

"Time," Doreene said.

The reporter waved a hand. "I mean, what artistic media?"

"That's a secret." Doreene's mouth quirked. "I'm sure the new owner will be happy to tell you." She pointed to Angus. "The gentleman in the tweed jacket." Elizabeth murmured something in Doreene's ear, but Doreene shook her head impatiently.

"Ms. Gray, you're an extremely youthful and attractive woman," Angus said.

"Why, thank you." Doreene gave him a seductive smile.

"Do you attribute your youthfulness to the painting in any way?" Angus went on.

"Being an art lover has definitely helped keep me young." Doreene pointed to someone else. "The gentleman in the gray suit."

This reporter crossed his arms. "Ms. Gray, if you're not going to give a straight answer to any of our questions, why are we here?"

Doreene's smile faded. "To announce that the picture is for sale and give you a chance to see it."

The young woman quickly pointed to another journalist. "Ms. Chandler."

Ms. Chandler continued the attack. "If you want us to see it, why are there two guards keeping us away from it?"

Doreene turned to her publicist. Thanks to the lavaliere mike clipped to her dress, her irate whisper could be heard throughout the room. "Now would be a good time to earn your keep, sunshine."

Elizabeth reached toward Doreene's chest, only to have Doreene slap her hand. "I'm trying to turn off your mike, Ms. Gray!"

The dog gave a sharp bark, ending in a growl.

At the back of the room, Reynaldo jumped so he could see above the crowd and shouted, "Doreene, *meu amor*! Do you need help?"

Every camera in the room immediately swiveled in his direction.

"No!" Doreene shouted back. She put a hand over the microphone clipped to her dress, but her next comment was still audible. "Turn this thing off, and don't let him talk to anyone."

As reporters converged on Reynaldo, Michael put a hand on his shoulder and spoke in his ear. "You'll never get to Doreene through this crowd. Isn't there another way to get to that side of the house?"

"Yes!" Reynaldo said, and darted out the door to the foyer.

Michael went through as well, then slammed the door behind him and held it closed.

Reynaldo turned at the sound of the slam. His eyes widened as the reporters on the other side hammered and shouted.

"Go on!" Michael said. He kept the door closed until Reynaldo made it through the foyer and out the front door of the house, then he let go and pelted through the foyer and into a side room, calling, "Reynaldo, wait!" as he went.

The reporters pounded after him. He let them catch up, let them push him aside and pass. When he was at the back of the pack, he doubled back and went outside.

There was no telling which way Reynaldo had gone, so Michael turned left at random and ran around the corner of the mansion, entering a weedy, overgrown yard. A few volunteer saplings waved their branches ahead of him, as though someone had recently passed. He pushed their rained-on leaves aside, getting wet in the process, and followed the trail of moving greenery.

Two-thirds of the way along the house, someone rapped at a window on his left. Michael turned to see Angus and Suki waving at him from inside. He pointed toward the rear and got a nod from Angus.

Twenty feet and another thirty seconds later, they came out through a side door and joined him.

"Who's the looker with the accent?" Suki asked.

"Reynaldo Cruz, Doreene's Brazilian boy toy," Michael said. "And as long as none of the other reporters catch him, *Tripping* has an exclusive interview. I talked to him in the foyer."

Angus clapped him on the shoulder. "You've made me proud."

The sound of many feet crunching on the gravel drive came from around the front of the house.

"C'mon," Michael whispered.

As they neared the back of the house, they heard the sound of raised voices from inside.

"Tell me again why I paid you an outrageous amount to let things get completely out of hand!" Doreene shouted.

"She is right," Reynaldo said. "They would have torn me apart!"

"I very much doubt that." Elizabeth Canter's voice was tight with anger. "If you'll recall, Ms. Gray, I did tell you that reporters are happier with a concrete, fact-based approach."

"Don't be ridiculous. I'm doing their job for them—telling a story, building up interest and suspense. Max, I thought she was supposed to have a relationship with these people. Isn't that why you hired her?"

Maxwell Thorne's smooth voice was only slightly rattled. "Doreene, why don't I escort Elizabeth out so you and I can have a private chat?"

"Fine, but do *not* apologize for me, Max. She's the one who blew it."

As the sound of the publicist's protests faded, Michael turned to Angus and whispered, "Now what?"

"Now we turn on the charm as though our livelihood depended on it, which it does," Angus muttered. "You go first. You're checking up on Orlando, there."

"Reynaldo," Michael corrected.

"Right. Suki, ignore the boy toy completely and flatter Ms. Gray like she's the deciding judge at your own personal Olympics."

"Got it."

"Let's go." Angus gave Michael a little push.

Michael held back the branches of an overgrown bush and turned the corner of the house. "Reynaldo," he called quietly. "Mr. Cruz, are you back here?"

They heard Doreene hiss something, and then Reynaldo pushed open the back door and stood at the top of a flight of stairs, looking back over his shoulder. "But *princessa,* this is the man I told you about!"

"Oh, there you are," Michael said. "I'm glad to see you got away. Pretty crazy, huh?"

Angus came up beside him. "Michael just wanted to see that you were all right. We don't want to be a bother." He peered past Reynaldo, into what looked like a glass-roofed conservatory. "Is that Ms. Gray? Can I just say that you handled yourself beautifully? That press person should be shot."

Doreene appeared beside Reynaldo. "Thank you." Her flushed cheeks made her look even younger. "May I ask who you are?"

Angus went up the stairs and offered his hand. "Angus MacGregor, *Tripping* magazine. We're an international travel publication, here to do a story on Port Townsend, but I couldn't resist dropping by when we heard about the press conference." He dipped his head and gave a shy smile. "You are something of a star, Ms. Gray."

She gave him her hand. "Call me Doreene."

Angus, holding it in both of his, looked over his shoulder. "Oh, dear. I think I hear the other reporters. We tried to give them the slip, but they're a wee bit angry with Michael for keeping them away from Mr. Cruz."

"Please, come inside," Reynaldo offered.

Doreene gave him a look, but stepped back so they could come through the door. "I suppose it might be easier to leave through the house."

Inside, a golden-oak dining table with eight chairs took up the center of the room. A matching sideboard sat on one wall, and shelves of plants took up the other. A kitchen was visible through an open door.

As Suki came inside, camera around her neck, Doreene's mouth tightened. "This must be your photographer."

"Suki Oota." Suki shook her head wonderingly. "Wow. You are even more beautiful up close. I can see why the camera loves you."

"Why thank you," Doreene said, dimpling. "You're quite pretty yourself."

Suki went by Reynaldo, both of them avoiding eye contact with the other.

Reynaldo closed the door, then stepped close to Doreene and kissed her neck under her ear. "My *princessa* has had a difficult day. I will be glad when this painting is gone from our lives."

Angus nodded sympathetically. "If it causes this much trouble, I can see why you'd want to be shut of it." He sat down in a wicker chair and rubbed one calf. "I think I may have pulled a muscle."

Doreene made a sympathetic noise. "Reynaldo, would you be a dear and ask Lupita to bring some water and ibuprofen?" As soon as Reynaldo was out of hearing, she sat in the chair next to Angus and leaned over the arm, toward him. "Let's get one thing straight. I'm not giving you a story."

"Thanks to Reynaldo's earlier talk with Michael, we already have a story," Angus said.

Doreene gave a slight laugh. "I wouldn't put much stock in that. His English is terrible. What exactly did he say?"

Michael, who had been wandering the room, stopped by an orchid and turned the pot slightly. "That his uncle also had an evil, possessed item, and that you talk to the portrait." He looked at Doreene. "Maybe you'd like to give us your version?"

Doreene smiled grimly. "My version is that if you print a word of that, I'll sue your ass faster than you can say 'Rupert Murdoch.' "

Angus shook his head. "Doreene, you misunderstand us. What Michael means is that because of that silly girl's handling of the press, there's bound to be a lot of misinformation. *Tripping* isn't a tabloid paper. It's a travel magazine with a focus on special places and the fascinating people who live there. We're more interested in you and Port Townsend than in a painting."

Doreene gazed at him, her mouth pursed. "I'll look up your magazine and get back to you, okay?"

"Can I at least have a picture?" Suki asked. "It'll make up for any shots where you look like you have peanut butter stuck to the roof of your mouth and are trying to suck it off."

Doreene glared at her. "Why would I look like that?"

"Usually because you're saying a *G* or an *N,* but if you piss off reporters, that's the one they'll use. I'll even let you look at what I take, and delete anything you don't like."

Doreene considered a moment, lips pressed together. "All right," she said grudgingly, "but make it quick."

Suki looked around the room. "If you'll stand next to those little purple and pink flowers, I think the light will be softest."

"Just a minute." Doreene went to the doorway and whistled breathily, then yelled, "Gigi! *Gigi!*"

A few seconds later, the Chihuahua came in, its claws clicking on the floor.

Doreene scooped up the dog and stood where Suki had suggested. She smoothed her skirt.

"That's good." Suki reached over to adjust a swathe of the dog's silky fur.

Gigi growled and snapped the air next to her hand, causing Suki to gasp and jerk her hand away.

Doreene burst into delighted laughter. "Did my little-bitty girl scare the big, tough photographer?" She leaned down and kissed the top of Gigi's head. Gigi laughed up at her, pink tongue hanging out of her mouth.

Suki took a deep breath and looked through the viewfinder. "Hold that pose."

Doreene remained motionless as Suki took the picture. Then she plunked the dog on the floor and stretched out a hand. "Let's see it."

Suki showed her the camera's screen.

"It's not bad," Doreene said. "You can use it."

"Can I get a few more?"

"One is all you need."

Suki reached into her camera bag. "I need you to sign this release." She handed Doreene a card and a small pen.

As Doreene read the form and signed it, a Latina woman in her late forties entered with a tray. She had a black ponytail and wore an apron over her powder-blue skirted uniform. "Who wanted the ibuprofen?"

Angus raised his hand. "Thank you very much."

Doreene let Angus swallow the pill before getting up to stand by the door to the rest of the house. "I'll show you out. I have a lot of things that need to be done."

"Of course." Angus got up and took her hand again. "Thank you for your time."

Reynaldo smiled at everyone. "This has been a nice visit."

As promised, Doreene led them through the house to the front door, the dog trotting at her heels. Antique furniture and intricately woven carpets gave the house a luxurious feel. Custom paint picked up the colors in the rugs.

The walls were ornamented not with paintings, but with mirrors and large photographs of Doreene in exotic locales. In them, she stood next to one or more attractive young men. Although the settings and companions changed, Doreene looked roughly the same in all of them. Only her hairstyle and clothing changed with time.

As they went through the room where the press conference had been held, they heard Maxwell Thorne's voice in the foyer beyond. This time, he didn't sound calm, although the words were difficult to make out.

Doreene frowned and jerked open the door to the foyer. As it opened, they heard Maxwell say, "It'll only take a second. I know you can understand me!"

Inside the foyer, the two guards from the press conference stood at the bottom of the stairs. One of them carried what was presumably the portrait, draped in a white cloth. The other held out a hand to keep Maxwell Thorne back.

As Doreene and the *Tripping* staff entered, the guard holding the portrait turned, and the painting hit the banister with a dull smack.

"Be careful!" Doreene yelled. She wrapped both arms around her waist and groaned.

Gigi the Chihuahua looked up, her brow furrowed.

Reynaldo gripped Doreene's upper arms. "*Preciosa,* what is it?"

Maxwell Thorne trotted across the floor toward them. "What's wrong?"

"Reynaldo," Doreene said, panting. "Get the pills. In my nightstand drawer."

Reynaldo darted past the guards and took the stairs two at a time. Maxwell tried to support Doreene, but she gave him a venomous glare and pulled away.

“Should I call nine-one-one?” Michael asked, cell phone already in his hand.

“No.” Doreene raised her head and looked at the guards, who still stood at the bottom of the stairs with the painting. *“Anda!”* she croaked, waving at them to go on.

As the guards resumed their climb, she slowly collapsed.

Angus caught her and lowered her gently to the ground.

Behind him, Suki took a picture of their hostess as she lay sprawled on the floor.

Six

Fifteen minutes later, Doreene reclined on a love seat at the back of the ballroom, pale but apparently recovered.

"Cara," Reynaldo murmured as he knelt at her feet. He laid his cheek against her hand. "My angel."

"Are you sure we shouldn't call a doctor?" Maxwell asked.

Reynaldo looked up at Doreene. "Please, can we?"

She shook her head. "I already saw a doctor. He's the one who gave me those pills, and that's all I need. It's just a minor thing, nothing to worry about."

"It didn't look minor," Maxwell said.

"It was the shock of realizing I couldn't trust you," Doreene snapped. "I saw you trying to look at the painting."

Maxwell glanced at Angus and the others. "All right, if you want to discuss this now, let's discuss it. Yes, I think I should be allowed to see the portrait before the day of the sale. How am I supposed to appraise it, let alone—"

Doreene cut him off, grimacing. "You're making me hurt again."

At the sound of footsteps on the wood floor, they all turned toward the back of the room.

Maureene slouched toward them, hands in the pockets of her coat. "Lupita said you had some kind of attack. Are you all right?"

Doreene leaned over the love seat. "Where's Gigi?" She picked up the dog and clasped it to her chest. "I'm fine."

"I'm glad to hear it." Maureene frowned and jerked her head at Angus and the others. "You know they're reporters, right?"

Maxwell turned a professional smile on Angus. "What publication are you with?"

"*Tripping*, international travel magazine. We're doing a feature on Port Townsend."

Maxwell nodded. "There are a lot of artists in Port Townsend. Is that your focus?"

Maureene answered him. "Don't waste your time, Max. I looked them up online. *Tripping* is only interested in a town if it has a lake monster or a haunted graveyard. Their last story was about a ghost Chihuahua."

"And what's wrong with that?" Doreene looked down at Gigi. "Maureene prefers her dirty old terrier." She swung her legs over the edge of the love seat and got up.

"Where are you going?" Reynaldo asked, scrambling to his feet.

"Upstairs. I have to make sure those idiots put the painting away."

"You gave them the key code?" Max asked.

"Of course not. That's why I'm going up there." She left the room carrying the dog, Reynaldo trailing after her.

Maxwell took a business card from his suit-coat pocket and handed it to Angus. "This number is for Elizabeth Canter, Doreene's publicist. She'll advise you as to what you can legally print. I suggest you follow her instructions to the letter if you don't want Rothwell's coming after you."

Angus took the card. "I'm sure there won't be any problems."

"I'll show you out," Maxwell said. "I have to get back to my hotel anyway."

Maureene followed them back through the foyer and out the front door.

The line of cars was gone, leaving only *Tripping*'s minivan, a white car across the street, and a silver Volvo convertible with rental plates.

"I'll be in touch, Maureene," Max said.

"Unless you're going to help, don't bother," she said bitterly.

He shook his head wearily and walked toward the Volvo.

Maureene turned to Angus. "Was the owner of the ghost Chihuahua really named Baskerville? That seems too good to be true."

At the sound of Maureene striking up a conversation, Maxwell turned and gave her a surprised look.

She lifted a hand. "*Good-bye,* Max."

He raised a hand and continued on his way to the Volvo, albeit more slowly.

Angus smiled at Maureene. "The owner's last name actually was Baskerville. Charlotte Baskerville designed clothes for small dogs."

At the sound of Maxwell's car door closing, Maureene dropped her casual attitude and leaned forward. "If you'd like to interview me for your magazine, I'll do it."

Michael raised his eyebrows. "But I thought—"

"I know, but you heard what Reynaldo said, that my sister talked to the painting. Maybe there is something strange about the portrait. I don't have experience with that kind of mumbo jumbo. You do."

"That's very true," Angus agreed, just as Michael said, "Not exactly."

They stared hard at each other for a moment until Michael sighed and looked away.

"When would be convenient for you?" Angus asked Maureene. "Is now a good time?"

"Um, no. What about late tomorrow morning, say eleven? And come directly to my house." She pointed off to the left. "See that little path, with the mailbox? I'm just down there."

"Wonderful!" Angus said. "We'll see you then."

They watched Maureene go to the path, which was marked by a galvanized mailbox on a weathered post. She turned and waved once, then disappeared behind bushes and trees.

"There's an about-face," Michael said. "Earlier she called us 'paparazzi' and basically warned Reynaldo about talking to me." He squinted in thought. "I suppose she might have been jealous that I stopped talking to her and started talking to him, but she didn't strike me as that kind of person."

"Artists are weird," Suki said.

"Hey, as a novelist, I'm an artist," Michael pointed out.

"And I'm a photographer, so what's your point?"

"Whatever the case with Maureene," Angus said, "I'm more interested in Doreene's reaction when that guard knocked the painting against the banister. It's clear she and the portrait are connected in some way."

"Psychosomatic," Michael said dismissively. "She thinks they're connected, so she reacts."

"Would a doctor give her pills for a psychosomatic reaction?" Angus countered.

"Antianxiety meds, maybe. Anyway, we only have her word that she got them from a doctor. They could have been mints in an old prescription bottle. Trust me, it's all part of the show."

"It's more likely she has pain from some recent surgery," Suki said. "Did you notice all those photos of Doreene on vacation? Pretty much all of the locations—Costa Rica, Switzerland—are known for plastic surgery. Brazil is where you go for cheap boob jobs."

Michael smirked. "You think Reynaldo was a candy striper at the hospital?"

"Candy something." Suki looked at her watch, which featured a pink cat in pirate's garb. "It's after noon. Can we find somewhere to eat?"

Angus started toward the minivan. "Good idea. I got some recommendations from a very nice woman named Amy, online. I sometimes wonder how we wrote magazine articles before the Internet existed."

"There were magazines back then?" Suki asked, unlocking the car.

"Amazingly, yes, but the pages were made of wood, and they were printed with ink squeezed from seeds. It was all very awkward." Angus leaned over and looked in the rearview mirror. "Do you see the man in the white Impala, across the street and slightly behind us?"

Suki adjusted her side mirror until it showed the car in question. "Shaved head, dark glasses, killer tan."

"That's the one. He was there when we first came, but I didn't see him inside with the rest of the press. Did you, Michael?"

Michael looked out the rear window. "No, but I stayed at the back of the room."

Suki still had her camera around her neck. She lifted it slightly and took a picture of the man's image in her side mirror, then handed the camera back to Michael. "Put this in the bag, will you?"

They found the recommended pub on the waterfront, up a vertiginous flight of stairs. The place had the feel of a men's club crossed with an antiques market and installed in a rather nice attic. Upholstered and wicker chairs clustered around tables topped with wine-colored cloth. Gilded frames were much in evidence.

The waitress brought water and menus and left.

"What's our budget for meals? Michael asked. "Is Pendergast feeling flush?" Len Pendergast was the orthodontist who financed *Tripping.*

"We have a reasonable meals allowance, and it is part of the job," Angus said. "I think I'll have the crab cakes."

When the waitress came back, Michael ordered the cioppino.

Suki closed her menu. "Small Caesar, with salmon. Angus, are we walking around for a while after this?"

"I think so, yes."

Suki looked up at the waitress. "Then I'll also have an oyster shooter on a separate tab. Michael, you want one?"

"Okay, thanks."

The waitress looked at Angus. "And you, sir?"

"Iced tea, thank you."

She took their menus and left.

Angus leaned back in his chair and drummed the fingers of both hands on the table. "Well. This is certainly an interesting story." He pointed to the camera, which Suki had brought with her and placed on the table. "Let's have a look at the man in the white car."

Suki brought up the photo and zoomed in on the man's face. "I don't see anything new. Dark tan, shaved head, sunglasses—maybe expensive ones. Looks like he might be a big guy." She handed the camera to Angus.

Angus studied the screen with pursed lips. "Doesn't look familiar."

"Let me see," Michael said, hand hovering near the camera.

"You'll get your turn, Mr. Grabby." After a few more moments, Angus handed the camera to him.

Michael took off his glasses and peered at the image. "If that's his right hand just above the edge of the door, it looks like he's wearing a big ring. Maybe he's with the Mafia."

Suki took the camera from him. "Where?"

He pointed. "Right there. See the shiny bit?"

"That's the top of a phone. He's probably texting someone."

Michael leaned over and looked again. "Oh."

"They had two security guards there," Angus said. "Maybe he's the outside man."

"Speaking of the guards," Michael said, "Doreene yelled 'anda' at them. That's 'go' in Spanish."

"And in Portuguese," Suki said. "They could be friends of Reynaldo's or Lupita's, but either way, I don't think they spoke much English. When I got up to the rope around the painting, I asked one of them to move to one side, and his only response was to kick the leg of my tripod back when it crossed the line. When I told him what he could do with his foot, he didn't even blink."

"Did you get a picture?" Angus asked.

"Yeah, but the colors are pretty murky, and I couldn't get any real detail." Suki pushed the scroll button on the camera before handing it to Angus.

He studied the image. "Not exactly a flattering portrait, is it? Michael, did you research the sisters' background before we left Boulder?"

"Yeah." Michael took the camera and looked at the photo while he spoke. "All I could find on their father was his name, Sean Pinter. Their mother divorced him and remarried when the twins were pretty young. Then Mom died, leaving the stepfather in charge. He died in a boating accident when Maureene and Doreene were eighteen."

"What kind of boating accident?" Angus asked. "Any suggestion of paranormal activity?"

"He got drunk, went out in a boat, and drowned," Michael said.

"So we could say spirits were involved in that death."

Michael dropped his forehead to the table. "Please tell me you're joking."

"I'm joking." Angus caught Suki's eye and winked. "Go on, Michael."

Michael raised his head. "Apparently Maureene was pretty attached to her stepfather, because she went into a real funk after he died. Shut herself up in that cottage and wouldn't talk to anyone. Finally Doreene asked Maureene to paint her portrait, as therapy."

"Had Maureene painted before?" Suki asked.

Michael nodded. "She'd gone to art school and was starting to get some local attention, but I guess the portrait blew everyone away."

"So Maureene went on to become a famous artist and Doreene married Mr. Gray," Angus said. "Where's he?"

"Dead."

Angus raised his brows. "Another boating accident? Are we talking family curse?"

"Sorry. He fell off a mountain."

Angus smiled. "Still, you have to admire this family's capacity for dramatic death. Makes our job that much easier. Go on."

"Hank and Doreene Gray were big travelers," Michael continued. "They were mountain trekking in Argentina when Hank got too close to the edge. It crumbled, and Hank fell so far they had to leave his body there. Doreene came home a widow."

Suki took back her camera. "Did Maureene ever get married? If her husband died, too, my money's on *went hang gliding and was attacked by condors*."

"Maureene never married." Michael held up a finger. "But she does have a daughter. The rumor is that her agent at the time was the father, but she's never said, and he's not her agent anymore."

"Is he dead?" Angus asked eagerly.

"No. And before you ask, neither is Maureene's daughter, Lyndsay. She married an Englishman and moved to the UK. They own a chain of high-end lingerie stores."

The waitress brought the oyster shooters. "Here you go."

Angus smiled at her. "Thank you."

"Did Doreene and Hank have any children?" Suki asked when the waitress had gone.

"No," Michael said. "They were only married four years before he died, and Doreene never married again."

"Aw," Suki said. "How sad to have to console yourself with an endless parade of luscious young men." She tossed back the oyster shooter and licked her lips.

Seven

The next day, they went back to the house for the promised interview. Angus led the way along the path to Maureene Pinter's cottage. Suki carried one of her cameras on a tripod. A few birds chirped in the surrounding trees. Overhead, clouds threatened rain.

"Let's keep this interview friendly and nonconfrontational," Angus instructed, shooting Michael a glance.

Michael rolled his eyes. "I know. We're not here to debunk the story, we're here to . . . What was the rest?"

"Shed enough light to explore mysterious corners, but not so much that we fade the colors," Angus recited.

"The colors of what? Something that has corners?"

Suki swung her tripod clear of a dead branch. "I wonder why Maureene lives in a cottage where there's room for her in Doreene's big house. I thought twins were supposed to be super close."

"Maybe the cottage has better light for painting," Michael said, "or maybe, after fifty-eight years, they've had enough closeness."

Angus shrugged. "Perhaps the stepfather left Doreene the bulk of the estate, and that's why Maureene was depressed after he died. Best not to ask. Property is often a sore spot with families."

They came around a bend in the path and saw a single-story frame house painted gray with blue trim. As they approached the front door, a bark sounded from inside the house.

Angus knocked to the accompaniment of more barking. After a few moments, the door swung open and Maureene Pinter stood there, the Scottish terrier at her feet. Maureene's hair was wet. She wore cotton pants and a heather-green sweater with a smear of black paint on the cuff of one sleeve. "Come on in."

"Cute pooch," Suki said as they trooped inside.

"Thanks. Her name is Hilda."

Hilda trotted around them, sniffing shoes.

Maureene looked around the room uncertainly. The couch held a stack of magazines and unopened mail in addition to a fleece blanket covered with dog hair. "I guess we could sit at the table." She made a vague gesture toward a wooden kitchen table that sat beneath a wide window. The view outside was of trees.

"The table's good for me," Suki said. "You don't mind if I take pictures while we talk, do you?"

"I guess not."

"Great, and can you sign this photo release?" Suki handed Maureene a card and watched while she read it and signed the bottom. "Thanks," she said, taking it back.

"I'll just clean the table off," Maureene said, picking up a plate with toast crumbs. She took it through to a galley kitchen, visible through a doorway.

Michael picked up a cardboard box of paints from the table's top and set it on the floor next to his chair before taking his seat. Suki didn't sit, but unfolded her tripod.

Maureene came back, looked around, then spotted the box of paints and picked it up. "Gotta keep things off the floor. Hilda sometimes chews." She put it on the windowsill before sitting.

Michael took his digital recorder out of his pocket and held it up. "Do you mind if we record this interview?"

"That's fine." Maureene perched on a chair and ran her palms down her thighs.

Angus folded his hands on the tabletop and smiled. "Ms. Gray, did you know there was something special about the portrait when you first painted it?"

"I knew it was my best work. It was the first time I hadn't planned the life out of a painting, just did a few preliminary sketches and went for it." At the sound of Suki's camera powering on, her shoulders hunched slightly.

Angus gave Maureene a reassuring smile. "And how long was it before you or your sister noticed that the portrait had changed?"

Maureene put her hands on the table as if to rise. "I forgot to ask, do you want anything to drink?"

"No, thanks," Angus and Michael both said.

"I'm good," Suki said, eye glued to her camera's screen.

Maureene pushed back her chair. "I need a glass of juice or something. Talking makes my throat dry." She got up and went into the kitchen, where she could be seen taking a glass out of the cupboard and opening the fridge and freezer doors.

Michael switched off his recorder and raised his brows at Suki, who shrugged.

Finally Maureene came back, ice tinkling in a glass of orange juice. "Sure you don't want anything?"

Angus shook his head. "We're fine."

Michael switched the recorder back on. "Ms. Gray, I understand that you painted the portrait as therapy, to deal with the death of your stepfather."

Maureene took a long drink of her juice, then rubbed her thumb along the sweating glass. "Yeah."

Angus took up the questioning. "Do you think the emotion you were feeling at the time might have imbued the painting with its unusual qualities?"

"I don't know. Maybe."

The others waited a moment, but she didn't say anything more. In the silence, Suki moved the tripod.

"Why do you think the portrait changes?" Michael asked, his tone significantly less diffident than Angus's.

Maureene looked up from drawing trails in the condensation on her glass. "I assume Doreene changes it. Why, I have no idea. She's always been a little obsessed by the painting, and now Reynaldo says she talks to it." She leaned forward in her chair. "What do you think is going on with the painting?"

"We were kind of hoping you could tell us," Michael said drily.

Angus gave him a quelling look. "There are several possibilities that spring to mind. Doreene might be performing a ritual, designed to maintain her youth. Or perhaps she feels the painting has developed its own spirit, and she is communing with it." He eyed Maureene intently. "Ms. Gray, would you say either of those things is possible?"

Maureene shrugged, then turned in her chair so she could see Suki. "Don't take any photos of artwork in progress, okay? No sketches or anything."

"You got it."

Behind Maureene's back, Angus lifted his hands in a frustrated gesture.

Maureene checked her watch, an antique man's timepiece with a paint-specked crystal. "I'm having lunch at the main house today. Do you want to come? You might be able to ask Doreene some of these questions."

Angus perked up. "If you don't think it would be a problem."

"It shouldn't be." Maureene stood. "Let's go."

They collected their things and headed toward Doreene's house, with a slight delay while Hilda milled around outside and Maureene encouraged her to do her business.

Finally Maureene shut the dog inside and led the way down the path. She took a narrow shortcut through the woods that led to the side of the house. They went up the stairs and into the conservatory.

Doreene and Reynaldo sat at the oak dining table. As the staff from *Tripping* entered, Doreene gave her sister a look made of equal parts disbelief and anger.

Reynaldo's face lit up. "It is my new friends!" he said, tossing his napkin onto the table and getting up. He came around and clasped Michael's hand, then patted his shoulder. "Come in, sit down!"

Doreene raised her voice to be heard over Reynaldo's enthusiastic greetings. "I hate to be rude, Maureene, but were your friends planning on having lunch? I don't want to inconvenience Lupita with extra people."

"It's okay," Maureene said, as Reynaldo kissed her cheek. "I told her I might have guests. I'll go check that everything's okay." She went through an open door at the back of the room.

Reynaldo shook Angus's and Suki's hands, then waved them into chairs. "Are you liking this weather? I tell my *princessa* it's a good thing she is my sunshine, or I could not have moved here with her." He laughed gaily.

"Oh, so you're planning on staying in Port Townsend?" Michael asked.

Reynaldo took Doreene's hand and kissed it. "Why would I go?"

Angus cleared his throat, but Doreene spoke before he could.

"So, Mr. MacGregor," she said. "How long are you staying in Port Townsend?"

"Please, call me Angus. We're here until after weekend."

Lupita entered with a tray of extra dishes and put place settings in front of the newcomers.

"I imagine you'll spend most of your time at the Wooden Boat Festival," Doreene said over the clatter of china.

Maureene returned from the kitchen with a handful of cloth napkins, which she passed to Angus and the others. "Have you been to Fort Worden yet? There's a nice lighthouse there. Reynaldo, I've been meaning to ask if you'd like me to take you there."

"*I'll* take Reynaldo, if he wants." Doreene ran a finger down Reynaldo's cheek.

He gave her a smoldering look. "I will let you take me."

Lupita muttered something as she put the last fork on the table.

"What did you say, Lupita?" Doreene snapped.

"Nothing." Lupita coughed. "Something in my throat." She disappeared through the door to the kitchen.

"Pay her no attention, *cara,*" Reynaldo murmured. "In Brazil, we have a saying—*one man's happiness is another man's sadness.*"

"We have a saying in Boulder," Suki said. *"Always lock your bike."*

Reynaldo looked confused.

Lupita entered with a tureen, steam trailing from the surface. "Chicken noodle soup." She put it on the sideboard and took Doreene's bowl to fill.

Angus looked around. "Where's the little dog? Gigi, wasn't it?"

"Upstairs," Doreene said. "I don't like it when she begs." She watched Lupita ladle soup into her dish. "Lupita, I'm expecting someone important this afternoon. Make sure you find me when she comes."

Lupita set the bowl in front of Doreene and took Reynaldo's dish. "What's the name?"

"Rita Ledger. She's a Realtor. I'm selling the house."

The ladle clattered against the side of the tureen.

Maureene leaned toward her sister and spoke in a low, tense voice. "What do you mean, you're selling the house?"

Doreene smiled at her. "Someone will give me money, and in return, I will give them the house."

"But you can't do that!"

"Of course I can. It's my house."

"And where will I live?"

"You should do what I do and just . . . travel." Doreene lifted her arms luxuriantly on the last word. "It would do you good to get out of the country."

Maureene gaped at her for a moment. Then she rose abruptly, napkin falling from her lap to the floor, and left.

Doreene turned to Angus. "Have you traveled much, Angus? Apart from coming to the United States, obviously."

Angus smiled tentatively at Lupita as she put a bowl in front of him, but her face remained rigid. "Um, I toured Europe as a young man."

"Oh, you should do it again. I'm sure things have changed radically since then." Doreene glanced around the table. "Is everyone served? Then *bon appétit*!"

Silence descended, except for the clink of spoons on bowls. Reynaldo darted nervous glances at Doreene. Michael, Angus, and Suki exchanged looks.

Michael coughed slightly, then held his napkin to his face and removed something from his mouth. A moment later, Angus did the same thing.

Doreene took a mouthful of soup and chewed determinedly. Reynaldo poked suspiciously at the noodles in his bowl.

Suki, not bothering to cover her face with her napkin, pulled something long and skinny from her mouth and held it up. "What the hell?"

Doreene spat something into her hand and yelled, "Lupita!"

"It's paper," Suki said, laying the strip flat on the table. She picked up an end and tore it experimentally. "Or vellum, because paper doesn't hold up that well." She picked up her camera from the floor near her chair and stood to take a picture of the strip.

"Lupita!" Doreene shouted again.

Angus and Michael opened their napkins and investigated the contents while Reynaldo fished a strip of paper out of his soup with his spoon.

Lupita came running into the room. "What?"

Doreene held up a scrap of paper and shook it. "You're fired!"

"*Que?* Why?!"

"This has writing on it." Michael took off his glasses and held a strip up to the light. " 'Soul, night, lost . . .' "

Suki turned her strip over. "Oh, hey, look at that." She took another photo.

Doreene's face was red. "Why is there *paper* in the soup, Lupita?"

Lupita squinted at her in apparent incomprehension. "There's no paper. It's noodles."

Angus squinted at the faded writing on his strip. " 'Satan, Beelzebub, *El Diablo* . . .' "

Lupita and Reynaldo crossed themselves simultaneously.

"Dios mio," Lupita moaned.

Reynaldo closed his eyes and rocked back and forth, murmuring rapidly in Portuguese.

"Lupita, get your things and get out," Doreene ordered.

"But I didn't put paper in the soup!" she wailed.

"Then who did?!"

"I don't know, but it wasn't me, I swear!" Lupita clasped her hands to her chest.

Doreene stared at her, breathing heavily, then crumpled the bit of paper in her hand. "Maureene must have done it. She went into the kitchen."

Angus spoke to Lupita. "How long has the soup been in the kitchen?"

"Since this morning. Miss Doreene told me yesterday that she wanted chicken noodle soup."

"And who else has been in the kitchen today, besides Maureene?"

Lupita bit her lip in thought. "Mr. Reynaldo came in and asked where we put the scissors."

Doreene turned on Reynaldo. "It was you?"

"*Cara,* no! I had a thread on my sleeve I wanted to cut." He raised his forearm.

"That's true," Lupita said. "He showed it to me."

"Anyone else?" Angus asked.

Lupita looked at Doreene, one shoulder hunched. "Miss Doreene did, to tell me not to put too much salt in."

"I wouldn't put paper in my own soup," Doreene said scathingly.

"No, ma'am."

"Was the back door to the house locked?" Michael asked.

Lupita shook her head. "I'm supposed to leave it open during the day, for Miss Maureene."

"I never told you to do that!" Doreene said.

"She did, a long time ago. You're not here a lot, so I thought it was okay."

"And were you in the kitchen all the time the soup was cooking?" Angus asked.

"No," Lupita said. "When the soup was cooking, I went to clean the rooms." She sniffed wetly. "Please don't fire me, Miss Doreene."

Doreene stared into space and heaved a sigh. "I suppose you can stay on until I sell the house, but I'll be watching you." She glared at Lupita.

"You want the rest of the food?" Lupita asked, voice quavering.

"No." Doreene waved her hand in a shooing motion.

Lupita left the room, head bent. A moment later, the sounds of muffled sobs could be heard from the kitchen.

Reynaldo put his hand on Doreene's arm. "*Cara* . . . It is the painting doing this. You have to get rid of it."

Doreene rolled her eyes at him. "I *am* getting rid of it."

"No, I mean now." He gripped her wrist. "Take it out and burn it."

Doreene jerked away. "Don't be stupid. It's worth a fortune."

Reynaldo gazed at her solemnly. "What is your soul worth, *princessa*?"

Doreene's lips twitched, and then she laughed. "Oh, Reynaldo, you provincial little boy." She patted his cheek, and he turned his face away. "This isn't the Devil, it's just someone with a grudge."

"A what?"

"Never mind." She tapped her fingers on the table, then looked at Angus. "You say you're in Port Townsend through the weekend?"

He nodded.

"Why don't you stay here, at the house? Maybe you can figure out what's behind this."

"We're not paranormal investigators," Angus said.

Suki nodded. "They'd probably get paid."

"All right, here's the deal," Doreene said. "Stay here and be nosy. You're good at that. In return, you can write whatever story you like, as long as it's not in print until after the painting is sold."

"And when is that?"

"A month from now."

"I'll need to confer with my staff," Angus said, pushing his chair back.

"Go ahead." Doreene waved them away.

Angus, Suki, and Michael went outside and stood at the bottom of the steps.

"What do you think?" Angus murmured.

Michael glanced back at the conservatory. "Considering *Tripping* only comes out bimonthly, I don't see a problem with waiting that long to publish."

Angus frowned. "Aside from the fact that she's a right old bitch and I hate to help her. Is there anything else we can get out of the deal?"

"Meals?" Michael asked.

Angus and Suki gave him a look.

"Okay, maybe not. Permission to interview Reynaldo?"

"Also, some good photos of the painting," Suki suggested. "She might as well give us that if we're not going to publish until after it's sold."

"Those are both good ideas." Angus stood up straighter. "All right, let's go back."

In the conservatory, the table was mostly cleared, and the clatter of dishes came from the neighboring kitchen.

Reynaldo leaned close to Doreene, whispering urgently. Doreene pushed him away as the others entered the room.

"We'll stay," Angus announced, "on two conditions."

Doreene narrowed her eyes. "Conditions? I don't think so. You need the story."

"We have enough for a story. In fact, it's not in our best interests to hang about and debunk your uncanny artwork. So our conditions are, first, that we are allowed to take some good, close-up photos of the painting."

"No."

"It shouldn't matter, since we're not going to publish—"

"Forget it," Doreene said. "You can leave right now, as far as I'm concerned."

Angus took a deep breath through his nose. "All right, then how about an interview with Reynaldo?"

Reynaldo shook his head infinitesimally.

Doreene smiled at him. "Why not? Reynaldo, you don't mind playing host, do you?"

Reynaldo shook his head, his expression was miserable.

"And now I have to call Max and arrange some things." She got up. "Make yourself at home."

Reynaldo watched her go. Then he pushed a folded napkin along the table, toward Angus. "She said to give you the paper from the soup. Lupita found the rest, so they are all here."

Angus took the napkin. "Did Doreene look at them? Did they mean anything to her?"

Reynaldo shook his head. "She said it was nonsense." He looked at Angus with something like despair. "She doesn't see that the painting is evil."

"Maybe it would help to talk about it. Would you like to do the interview now?"

"I would rather not." Reynaldo pushed himself to his feet. "We have another saying in Brazil. *Words will not pollute the soup.* But I am not in Brazil anymore." He smiled sadly.

They watched him walk slowly from the room, his beautiful figure drooping.

"Words will not pollute the soup?" Suki said. "What the hell does that mean?"

Michael looked at Angus. "What do we do now? Get our stuff from the motel?"

"Soon," Angus said thoughtfully. "But first, I think we should find Maureene before she has a chance to cool down. We might get more out of her if she's angry."

But when they got to Maureen's cottage, no one answered the door, and no barking came from inside.

"Now what?" Suki asked.

Angus put his hands in his jacket pockets. "Let's wait a bit. She might have taken Hilda for a walk. If so, they shouldn't be gone long. Those wee terrier legs can't go too far."

There was no lawn furniture, not even a stump to sit on, so they walked about aimlessly.

"Anyone have any guesses as to who put the paper in the soup?" Michael asked, kicking a fallen twig.

"Supernatural forces," Angus said firmly. "Remember who pays your salary."

"Pendergast pays my salary, and it's not a lot," Michael countered. "Suki, what do you think?"

"No clue. I did notice something odd, though. Reynaldo took a strip of paper out of his bowl but he didn't really look at it. I mean, he glanced at it, but he didn't study it the way we did. Maybe he already knew what was on it."

"He seemed pretty afraid," Angus said. "He could simply have not wanted to have anything to do with it."

"Or," Michael said, "maybe Reynaldo is trying to frighten Doreene into destroying the painting instead of selling it, although that seems counterproductive. Wouldn't he want his lover to have more money?" He thought for a moment. "How about this—Reynaldo is afraid Doreene is getting tired of him and will send him back to Brazil. So he's trying to scare her so she'll want a man around to protect her."

They considered the idea that Doreene might want Reynaldo to protect her.

"I'm not seeing it," Suki said.

Angus nodded. "Agreed."

Michael pointed a finger. "I know! *Doreene* put the strips in the soup to enhance the painting's supernatural reputation, so it would sell for more."

"But Doreene told us we couldn't publish a story until *after* the sale," Angus said. "So how is that going to help?"

"Lupita and Reynaldo were there. They could spread the word."

Angus shook his head. "If Doreene wanted that kind of publicity, she'd be better off having Max to lunch." He rubbed his chin. "If we were the intended audience, surely it was Maureene who put the paper in the soup. Doreene didn't even know we'd be coming. I think

Maureene must have wanted us there. She's the one who agreed to give us an interview, after all."

Suki huffed in disgust. "Yeah, the lamest interview ever. I think you're right, and it was just an excuse to get us to lunch."

"Shhh . . ." Angus waved a hand to quiet them. "Someone's coming."

Maureene came stumping down the trail toward them, Hilda trotting in front of her. At the sight of Angus and the others, Hilda broke into excited barking.

"Quiet, Hilda." She picked up the dog and spoke to Angus. "What do you want?"

"I realize now may not be the best time," Angus said, "but we still have an interview to do with you."

"I gave you an interview."

Michael tapped his chin. "Was that the part where you asked what we thought about the painting or the part where you asked if we wanted a drink?"

Angus gave him a look. "Forgive my colleague, Ms. Pinter, but there are still a lot of things I'd like to ask you about. For instance, can you think of any reason there would be strips of paper in the soup at lunch?"

Maureene stared at him blankly. "What on earth are you talking about?"

"After you left Doreene's house, we found bits of paper in the soup." Angus took the folded napkin out of his pocket and opened it.

Maureene came closer as he took out one of the strips. "Are those words written on it? I don't have my reading glasses with me."

"They are. Words like 'devil,' 'lost,' and 'soul.' "

Maureene took a step back. "It must be getting stronger," she whispered.

"What's getting stronger?" Angus asked.

Her eyes focused on him. "Nothing. I can't think about an interview right now." As Maureene turned toward her cottage, Hilda leaned over her arm and uttered a final bark.

They watched Maureene clomp into her house and slam the door.

Michael blew out a breath. "Is there an online database that tells which families have insanity? 'Cause that would be really handy."

"Why the glum face, Angus?" Suki asked. "A story this freaky, you should be rubbing your hands with glee."

Angus shook his head. "That woman is in a lot of pain." He gave the cottage one last look before heading down the path, toward the main road and their van.

Eight

They had lunch at a tiny café that featured art for sale, closely packed tables, and a bohemian vibe.

Suki took a few photos of the interior before they sat. "It's like we never left Boulder."

They picked a table in the corner and ordered.

Michael rested his crossed arms on the table. "You know, this story doesn't need paranormal elements to be creepy. What do you think it's like for Maureene to see her lost youth whenever she looks at Doreene?"

Suki put her napkin in her lap. "I like how the portrait originally showed young Doreene, but now it essentially shows current Maureene. Maybe Doreene sticks pins in it." She made little jabbing motions.

Michael took a small notebook from the inside pocket of his leather jacket. "Possible sidebar on voodoo objects. What do you think, Angus?"

"Definitely." Angus put the folded napkin from Doreene's house on the table and opened it. The paper strips were yellow and slightly greasy from chicken broth. "I suppose we should wash these if we want to keep them."

Michael slid a strip between two fingers to straighten it. "This one has tooth marks."

When all the strips were roughly flat, Angus lay them on the napkin. "Nine strips of three words apiece. Doomed evil destruction, Satan *el Diablo* Beelzebub, damned devil darkness, Hades hell horned . . ."

"Nice alliteration," Michael said, tilting his head so he could see the scraps better.

"Lost fallen night," Angus went on. "Sin sold soul, destroy decay death, persecute eternal torment, flames pay debt."

"It's like fridge-magnet poetry for Goths." Suki pressed down the curling end of a strip before standing to take a photo of them.

Angus waited until she was finished and arranged them into a different order. "I wonder if they make better sense if you read them top to bottom? Doomed Satan, damned Hades, lost sin destroy persecute flames."

Michael crossed his arms over his chest and leaned back. "If you're looking for an actual message, forget it. There's nothing concrete."

"How do you know?" Angus asked.

"Because words are my life."

"Maybe the first letters spell something," Suki suggested.

"Twenty-seven letters, three vowels," Michael said. "All *E*s."

"Maybe the last letters spell something," Angus said.

"There are only three vowels in the last letters, too. *Y, E,* and *O.*"

Angus pushed the scraps around some more. "Huh. I think you may be right."

"Of course I'm right. This is just a generic message of occult doom, designed to scare someone."

Angus flipped the corners of the napkin over the strips. "It certainly scared Lupita and Reynaldo, but I don't think Doreene was frightened."

"Pretty impressive, considering you could interpret it as a death threat." Suki stretched her legs under the table.

Michael grimaced. "That's my shin you just kicked."

"Sorry." She withdrew her feet.

Angus stared into space, tapping a gentle rhythm on the table with one hand. "She may not show that she's afraid, but why sell the painting—"

"And the house," Michael interjected.

Angus nodded. "And the house. Why sell both of those right now? Is she trying to get away from something?"

Suki shrugged. "Maybe she just needs money."

"For what?" Angus pondered. "What's changed recently in Doreene's life?"

"Reynaldo seems to be a new addition," Michael said. "Maybe he wants her to buy a big ranch in Brazil and move there with him."

Angus nodded slightly. "That's a possibility. Of course, he says he wants her to destroy the painting, not sell it."

"Maybe the new thing is a fight between the sisters, and Doreene is trying to punish Maureene," Suki said. "So she's selling the portrait and the house."

"What we need is a good source of local gossip." Angus spotted their server approaching with the food. "After we eat, I think we should take a tour of Port Townsend's art galleries."

Port Townsend's main street had no fewer than five art galleries. They were in the fourth when Angus paused before the portrait of a young man. "Henry Gray, by Maureene Pinter," he murmured, pointing to the small placard below the painting.

"As in Hank Gray, Doreene's dead husband?" Michael wondered. He leaned in to see the card. "Fifty-seven thousand dollars."

Angus put his hands in his jacket pockets and studied the portrait. The subject's curly brown hair was ruffled by wind. One hand gripped a rope, and more rigging and the sea were visible over his shoulder. His blue eyes seemed to look directly at the viewer. "This is very good."

"I hope so," Suki said. "That's a chunk of change for two square feet of canvas." She studied the portrait. "He looks kind of familiar, but maybe it's just the setting. I had a really good time at the America's Cup one year."

A smiling woman in a linen pantsuit approached. Somewhere in her midfifties, her round face was weathered and pink cheeked, as though she might be a sailor herself. "Isn't it wonderful? In addition to being a superb work of art, that painting should be a very good investment. One of Maureene Pinter's other works is about to be auctioned through Rothwell's. The value of her work should rise significantly."

Angus beamed at her. "It's exciting, isn't it? We're staying at the house."

The woman's smile remained, but uncertainty tinged her voice. "Maureene's house?"

"Well, it won't be hers for long, with the property being put on the market."

The woman looked flabbergasted. "Maureene is leaving Port Townsend?"

"I don't know what her plans are. Doreene is the one selling the place." Angus shook his head sadly. "Between you and me, Maureene isn't very happy about it."

"But . . ." The gallery owner seemed overwhelmed by this information. "I thought their stepfather left everything to Maureene."

"I don't understand it myself," Angus said confidingly. "First the painting, now the house." He leaned down and dropped his voice further. "What do you think Doreene needs all that money for?"

Her expression turned frigid. "I'm sorry, I didn't catch your name."

He offered his hand. "Angus MacGregor, *Tripping* magazine. Do you have any opinion on what powers the portrait of Doreene Gray has?"

She pulled her hand from his. "I don't. Excuse me."

They watched as she walked the length of the gallery and disappeared through a side door.

"Not the hot gossip you hoped for, huh?" Michael asked.

"You never know until you try." Angus tilted his head in the direction the gallery owner had gone. "That's interesting, though, that she thought the stepfather left everything to Maureene."

"Doreene probably told people that to drum up sympathy," Suki said. "I wouldn't put it past her."

Michael shifted impatiently. "We should get settled in Doreene's house *right now.* What do you bet the gallery owner is calling Maureene to tell her we're being nosy?"

Angus made an impatient noise. "Ach, she already knows. This story's moving too slow. We need people to start talking, so that real gossips know to approach us. Anyway, Maureene can't kick us out. Doreene is the one who asked us to stay, and she seems to call the shots."

"I wouldn't mind going back to Doreene's place," Suki said. "If I can't photograph the portrait, I can at least photograph the house, and daylight is better for that." She yawned. "Plus, there are only so many pictures of boats I can look at."

"Not a fan of nautical art?" Michael asked, already moving toward the door.

"I prefer pictures of people," she said. "Preferably without so many clothes."

They went back to the hotel, packed up, and checked out before heading to the Gray mansion. As Suki drove the last block to Doreene's, Angus pointed to a car parked across from the house. "Look. There's that white Impala again."

In the back of the van, Michael unbuckled his seat belt and leaned forward between the two front seats. "And there's the guy, just sitting. He must be with security."

"Let's find out." Suki pulled over to the curb, directly behind the Impala.

The man's tanned, bald head turned as he looked in his side mirror to observe them.

"Suki, why don't you have a go at him?" Angus suggested. "Michael and I will go around the back and get the bags."

Suki looked in the rearview mirror and tidied the line of her lip gloss with a finger. "No problem."

They got out, Angus and Michael going to the rear of the van, Suki strolling forward.

When she reached the side of the Impala, she tapped on the window with two knuckles.

It rolled down with an electric whir, and the man looked up at her.

From this close, Suki could see that he shaved his head. She put his age at around fifty, but with that tan, it was hard to tell. The jacket of his charcoal suit was folded neatly over the back of the passenger seat. In addition to the matching pants, he wore an expensive-looking shirt in a sheeny slate blue, with no tie around his thick, muscular neck. Sunglasses hid his eyes. "Are you with security?" she asked. "Doreene asked us to stay at the house, but do we need to show you some ID?" The corners of her lips curved. "Or anything else?"

He smiled back. "No, you're fine." His voice was husky, with some kind of accent.

Angus and Michael joined her, carrying an assortment of luggage.

"Hello," Angus said cheerfully. "I'm Angus MacGregor, from *Tripping* magazine. This is Michael Abernathy, one of our writers, and I see you've already met our photographer, Suki Oota."

The man nodded by way of greeting. "Enrico Russo. I wonder if you can help me. I need to talk to Ms. Gray, but I don't want to disturb her if she has company. After you've been inside, could you come out and tell me if she's busy?"

"Can't you just call her?" Michael asked.

Enrico lifted a shoulder. "As I said, I don't want to disturb her. It's not urgent."

"I'll find out for you," Suki offered. "Hey, are those amber lenses in those sunglasses? I've been wondering if I should get some while I'm up here. It's always clouding over." She held out a hand. "Could I try them on?"

"Of course." He took them off and gave them to her. Behind the glasses, deep crow's feet bracketed his eyes, which were brown and flat.

Suki put the glasses on and gazed around. "Nice." She handed them back. "Thanks. I'll go see if Doreene is free."

He didn't put the glasses back on, but held them loosely in the hand he had draped over the steering wheel. "I appreciate it."

Angus raised a hand. "Pleasure meeting you."

They walked across the street to the house.

"Do you think he's a stalker?" Michael muttered.

"He might be a member of the press," Angus said quietly. "Enrico Russo is an Italian name, isn't it?"

Suki nodded. "Yeah, but his accent didn't sound Italian to me."

"Italy's a big place," Angus said mildly.

Michael snorted. "Europeans don't know big. Scotland is only the size of North Carolina."

Suki shook her head. "I swear I've heard that accent before, and I don't think it was Italian. It's something subtler."

"Brazilian?" Michael asked. "Although that guy didn't sound like Reynaldo to me."

"Brazil *is* a big country, but I don't think it's that, either." Suki shook her head. "I don't know."

At the front door of the house, Michael reached toward the handle, but it swung inward before he could grasp it.

Maxwell Thorne stood in the doorway. "Can I help you?"

Suki gave him a wide grin. "Honey, we're home!"

He smiled uncertainly.

"Doreene invited us to stay with her." Michael lifted one of the bags he held, by way of illustration.

"Is Doreene with you?" Max craned his neck to see past them.

"She's not home?" Suki asked. "Because there's this guy . . ." At the sound of a car starting up, she turned. ". . . who wanted to see her, and now he's driving away. Weird."

Max watched the Impala accelerate down the street. "What guy? Who was that?"

"Enrico Russo," Angus said. "I don't suppose he's part of your security detail, is he?"

Max looked disgruntled. "Doreene hired two of Lupita's relatives to guard the painting at the press conference. She never mentioned anyone else. Maybe I should call the police. Did anyone catch the license plate number?"

The others shook their heads.

"Make sure you tell her about this," Max said. He held the door open wider. "I suppose you may as well come in. Doreene isn't answering her cell phone, so I dropped by to see if she was here. Presumably Lupita knows where to put you. Lupita!" he called.

They trooped inside as Max held the door for them. Lupita came clattering down the stairs.

"I'm sure I'll see you later," Max said, and left.

Angus smiled at Lupita. "Did Doreene mention that she asked us to stay at the house?"

Lupita nodded. "The bedrooms are all upstairs."

She took them to the second floor and down the hall a little, where she gestured to an open door. "Here's one. This used to be the parlor."

Suki looked inside. "Do Angus and Michael need to share?"

Lupita shook her head. "There are a lot of bedrooms. Miss Doreene sometimes throws big parties."

Angus set the bags he carried just inside the door. "I think I'll take this room, if that's all right."

"Do you think Doreene is selling the house because she wants a smaller place?" Michael asked Lupita as they continued down the hall.

"I don't know." She shook her head. "I've worked for this family since I was seventeen and my aunt brought me over from Mexico." She took a tissue from her apron pocket and blew her nose. Then she straightened her shoulders and went farther down the hall.

They all followed.

"This used to be the drawing room," Lupita said, going through another doorway.

"I wonder why they call it a *drawing* room," Suki said.

Lupita looked around. "All I know is, it's the only guest room with its own bathroom."

Suki put her bags down. "I'll take it."

Michael cleared his throat. "*Drawing room* is short for *withdrawing room*. Members of the household entertained guests in it."

"I thought that's what the parlor was for," Suki said.

"It is," Michael said, looking uncertain.

"Does Maureene have any say in whether the house is sold?" Angus asked Lupita. "Someone told us their stepfather left everything to her."

Lupita shrugged. "I don't know about that. All I know is that Maureene has always protected her sister, always done everything for her, even above her own daughter."

"How so?" Michael asked.

Lupita went to the door, looked into the hallway outside, then closed the door and spoke quietly. "Lyndsay is Maureene's daughter.

She was mostly a good girl until high school, and then it was lots of yelling about wanting a car, wanting to go to a fancy college. The last thing they argued about was her wedding, and that was the worst." She shook her head. "Screaming and crying about how Maureene wouldn't pay for her to have it in Tahiti and must not like the man she was marrying."

"What did you think of the guy?" Suki asked.

Lupita shrugged. "He seemed okay. Anyway, it got so bad in the house that Doreene decided to go on one of her trips, and that was the last straw."

"How so?" Angus asked.

"Doreene went on a round-the-world cruise, starting in Tahiti."

The others groaned.

Lupita nodded. "Lyndsay went back to England and got married with only her boyfriend's family there. Maureene has only seen her daughter a few times since then." She shook her head sadly. "I never saw someone get old so fast. It broke her heart."

"And Doreene?" Michael asked.

Lupita's sorrowful expression hardened. "She came back two months later, looking younger than ever, with some Italian boy who wouldn't drink anything but wine and fizzy water." She snickered. "Every time I brought him a glass of water, I put a little bit of sleeping pill in it. Finally Miss Doreene got rid of him, he was so drowsy all the time. He said it was the weather." She bit her lip. "Please don't tell anyone. That's the only time I ever did anything like that, but she made me so mad."

Suki nodded. "Next time, try laxatives."

Lupita smiled slightly. Then her smile disappeared, and she rubbed her arms. "Last night, I went to close my bedroom window and I saw lights in the woods. Maybe *el Diablo* is finally coming to take her away."

"What kind of lights?" Angus asked eagerly.

Lupita turned her head and rubbed her chin on one shoulder. "Spirits of the dead, crawling across the ground."

Angus and Michael both whipped out notebooks.

"Actual crawling figures?" Angus asked. "Did they have ragged clothing? Long, straggly hair?"

"Angus!" Michael said. "Quit leading the witness."

"More like glowing bones," Lupita said. "I closed the curtains and prayed half the night, I was so afraid."

"Glowing bones," Angus murmured, writing furiously. "Brilliant."

"I assume you live here," Michael said. "Where's your bedroom?"

Lupita pointed at the ceiling. "I have a suite, upstairs. It's just me on the third floor."

Angus nodded. "And where is Doreene's room, so we know not to go in there?"

Lupita pointed. "Master suite, at the very end of the hall."

Nine

The staff of *Tripping* spent the rest of the afternoon doing Internet research on the family, the portrait, and the town. Michael also searched for the name Enrico Russo, but was unable to find any information on the man in the car.

By six o'clock, Doreene still hadn't returned. Angus ordered a pesto pizza, and they ate it in the conservatory.

"This was a good idea, Angus," Suki said, pulling a slice onto a plate. "The smell was driving me crazy the whole time we were walking around this afternoon."

"They probably vent it out specially," Michael said, before taking a bite.

They ate in silence for a while. Then Angus dabbed his mouth with a paper napkin. "*Spirits of the dead, crawling across the ground.* That's a hell of a quote."

"Lupita's got a vivid imagination, that's for sure. You should offer her a job at *Tripping,*" Michael said.

"I wish I could, poor woman." Angus tossed his napkin in the lid of the pizza box. "Doreene has a lot to answer for. That was a terrible thing she did, going to Tahiti instead of offering to chip in on her niece's wedding."

"Not to take away from Doreene's horrible behavior, but Lyndsay sounds like a spoiled brat to me," Michael said.

"Oh, I don't know," Suki said. "If Maureene's paintings were selling well at that time—"

"They were," said Michael, who had done the bulk of the research.

"Then why shouldn't Lyndsay have gotten a car, or gone to the school she wanted?"

Angus lifted a finger. "We don't know Maureene's financial situation. Maybe she was loaded with debt."

"Then her sister should have helped, instead of taking round-the-world cruises," Suki said. "It's hard for a girl to see her aunt living that kind of lifestyle when she isn't getting what she wants. They were family, after all."

Michael snorted. "The kind of family that keeps therapists in business."

They heard voices approaching.

"Speak of the devil." Michael wiped his mouth with a napkin. "I think Doreene might be home."

Sure enough, the sound of Doreene's chatter came closer, interspersed with Reynaldo's laughter. Doreene appeared in the door, carrying Gigi. Behind her, Reynaldo carried glossy shopping bags, several to a hand.

Doreene looked particularly lovely in a dress with a pleated skirt. Printed morning glories decorated the black fabric, and her heeled sandals matched the blue color. "I see you've made yourselves at home."

"Thank you for your hospitality," Angus said. "We'll be sure to wash our dishes."

"You can leave them for Lupita." Doreene turned to go. "Come on, Reynaldo. You can give me a fashion show with all your new clothes."

"Doreene," Angus said. "A man came to see you today. Enrico Russo."

She turned back, an irritated look on her face. "Who?"

"He was sitting outside your house in a white Impala," Michael said. "We thought you might have hired him as part of the security for the painting."

Doreene shook her head impatiently. "I didn't hire anyone to sit outside in a car. Is he there now?"

"Not unless he came back," Michael said. "He drove off a while ago."

Reynaldo set down the bags he held. "I will look." He trotted away, admirable backside flexing beneath sleek trousers.

Suki wiped her hands on a clean paper napkin and reached for her camera, which sat on a plant stand beside her. "I got a picture of the guy. You can take a look and see if you recognize him."

"At least one of you was thinking," Doreene said, coming to stand next to Suki.

Suki brought up the picture.

Doreene squinted at the screen. "Is that the best you could do?"

"Hold on, let me magnify it for you," Suki said. She pushed a button several times, then tried to retain her grip on the camera as Doreene pulled at it. "I'd rather you let me hold it," she said, just before Doreene wrested it from her hands. "Fine, but if you break it, you're buying me the newest model."

Doreene angled the camera's screen to avoid the late light that slanted through the window. Then her eyes widened and her jaw tensed.

"So you do know him," Angus said.

"What did he say his name was?" Doreene asked.

"Enrico Russo."

"I might know him." She pressed some buttons on the camera.

"Don't do that." Suki pulled it from her hand. "If you need . . . Hey! You deleted it!"

They heard Reynaldo's returning footsteps.

Doreene made her way around the table. To Angus, she said, "If Enrico comes around again, I'd like to speak with him. I meet so many people in my travels, it's hard to keep track."

Reynaldo came back, panting slightly. "I ran up both sides of the street, but didn't see anyone." He bent to pick up the shopping bags.

Doreene swatted his rump. "That's all right, sweetie. I'm sure it's nothing. Let's go try on your new clothes."

He leaned in quickly and kissed her cheek. "I will start with the bathing suit." They left, chatting merrily.

Suki slowly lifted her gaze from her violated camera. "The nerve of that unholy, surgery-addicted, Botoxed bitch of a—"

"Steady, lass," Angus broke in. "I've never seen you this upset."

"I've never seen her upset at all," Michael said.

Suki clenched and unclenched her jaw. "I'm okay."

"You didn't happen to back up that photo, did you?" Angus asked carefully.

"When would I have done that?" she snapped. "We've been out all day. My laptop is in a bag upstairs."

"That's all right," Angus said soothingly. "I'm sure Enrico will be back, and you can get another picture. A better one."

Suki glared at him, breathing heavily through her nose. "Sure. Photographers are always saying that. Don't worry if you miss a shot, there's always another chance."

"Really?" Michael asked. "Because you'd think—"

"Hush, Michael," Angus said.

After they cleared the table and washed their dishes, Suki insisted on going up to her room so she could back up all her photos.

Michael wandered into Angus's room carrying his laptop and sat down in a chair by the window. "I think all our windows look out on the woods. If there's something glowing out there tonight, I should be able to see it." He opened the laptop and pushed a button. "Here are my notes on the article. So far, we're doing sidebars on possible causes for the portrait's mysterious powers, and also voodoo objects. I wish the portrait wasn't connected to a living person. We're going to have to be careful if we don't want Doreene to sue us."

"I'll have my pet lawyer look everything over before we go to print," Angus said.

Michael looked up from his screen. "You have a pet lawyer?"

"He's a lawyer, with pets, which I take care of from time to time. I'm sure he won't mind checking the article for obvious problems." Angus draped a shirt over a hanger, then froze at the sound of muffled voices coming through the wall next to him. "Hear that?"

Michael left his computer on the chair and was halfway across the room when a door opened in the hallway and the voices became quite audible.

"I never promised to buy you a boat!" Doreene said.

"You said that if you had your way, I would captain my own boat!" Reynaldo said.

"Well, I don't always get my way."

"How is this not getting your way?" Reynaldo shot back. "We met on a boat, you knew I wanted a boat, you told me you lived in a place where everyone had a boat, but I have no boat."

"I have other expenses right now, Reynaldo." The door slammed.

Reynaldo's feet thumped toward Angus's room. He passed the open door, apparently oblivious to their presence.

They heard his feet stomp down the staircase, followed by the slam of the front door.

"Sounds like that lad could use a confidant," Angus whispered to Michael. "You go after him. I'll get Suki and we'll call you."

They went into the hall and separated, Angus continuing toward Suki's room, Michael running downstairs.

. . .

Michael hung back until Reynaldo was about a hundred feet away, then strolled down the street behind him.

The evening was mild and clear. Here and there groups of people walked to or from the boat-festival activities.

When Reynaldo descended the municipal stairs that led downtown, Michael hurried forward to keep him in sight.

As they neared the waterfront, the crowds thickened. Deciding there was no reason to be stealthy, Michael trotted along the sidewalk until he caught up. "Hey, Reynaldo!"

Reynaldo turned and gave a halfhearted smile. "Hello."

"I'm out covering the festival," Michael said. "Are you interested in boats?"

Reynaldo nodded sadly. "I love boats."

"Oh, so you have some experience?"

A spark of animation lit Reynaldo's face. "In Brazil, people hired me to captain many, many sailing boats. I am very good. When Doreene said she would . . . When she invited me to live here, she made it sound as if we would always be sailing in Port Townsend, but I have yet to get on a boat." He glanced longingly in the direction of the pier, where a forest of masts could be seen between buildings.

"Well, let's go fix that," Michael said heartily. "I'm sure people will be happy to invite a Brazilian captain aboard."

Reynaldo's bronze complexion flushed slightly. "I think there is an admission fee and I, uh, did not bring my wallet."

"I'll buy your ticket, and you can pay me back when it's handy," Michael offered.

Reynaldo looked at the ground. "Thank you."

Angus rapped urgently on Suki's door.

"Come in!" she called.

He came in and shut the door carefully behind him.

Suki had her open suitcase on the bed and was unpacking clothes.

"Grab a camera and come with me," Angus said. "Michael's following Reynaldo, who just stormed out of the house after a fight with Doreene."

"At least I get plenty of exercise on this job." She tossed a pair of lacy red panties into an open drawer and bent to rummage through a camera bag on the floor. "Although I'm starting to think you have an unhealthy attraction to drama."

"What part of being a reporter do you not understand?" Angus asked. "Now pick a camera and let's go."

Suki chose an assortment of equipment, then finally slung a camera around her neck and a bag over her shoulder. "All right, let's go track the wild Brazilian."

As she followed Angus down the stairs, Suki asked, "Do you know where Reynaldo was going?"

"We'll call Michael once we're out of the house and can't be heard," Angus said, cell phone already in his hand. He pushed open the door to the tiny foyer and stopped dead. "Look," he whispered, pointing out the glass pane of the door. "The white Impala."

"Now you're talking," Suki muttered, camera already in her hand. "Where is he? I don't see anyone in the car."

Angus pushed the door open as quietly as he could. They stepped onto the porch, both looking from side to side.

"There," Suki whispered, pointing.

The back of Enrico Russo's shaved head was just disappearing behind a rhododendron bush as he walked down the track to Maureene's cottage.

Suki and Angus kept well back as they followed. As they neared the cottage, they heard Enrico knock on the door. Suki took a few careful steps and hid behind two closely spaced pines. Angus stood close behind, looking over her shoulder. They peered carefully between the tree trunks.

Enrico stood on the doorstep, waiting. From inside the cottage came the sound of Hilda's barking.

The door opened, and Maureene stood there, looking suspicious.

Enrico said something too quiet to hear.

A look of astonishment dawned on Maureene's face, and then she gave an inarticulate cry and threw herself into Enrico's arms. They rocked back and forth for a moment, hugging, while Hilda sniffed around their feet. Finally Maureene pulled him into the cottage by the hand.

"Well." Angus took a step back and pulled a pine needle from his hair. "That was intriguing."

Suki put her bag on the ground and unzipped it feverishly. "If they sit at that table near the window, I might be able to get a picture of his face. Depends on what light she turns on inside."

"You can't possibly sneak up to that window without them seeing you," Angus said.

Suki pulled a lens the size of her forearm from the bag and grinned up at him, her teeth showing white in the dusk. "Telephoto." She lifted something that looked like an assemblage of black sticks. "Tripod. Let's find a spot while they're busy saying hello."

They picked their way through the trees until they were parallel to the house and about forty feet away, shielded by another rhododendron bush.

"Bingo," Suki said, pushing some leaves aside. She placed the camera on the ground at her feet and assembled the tripod.

Angus stood on tiptoe and looked through a gap in the bush. Maureene's window looked like a well-lit stage. Enrico stood beside the table, talking to an unseen Maureene, who was apparently in the kitchen. In a moment, she appeared, holding two cups. They sat down, the light illuminating Enrico's face.

"Move," Suki whispered to Angus.

He stepped carefully aside and watched as Suki pushed herself and the tripod-mounted camera almost a third of the way into the bush. "Careful," he said. "They might see the branches moving."

"They can't see much out here with that light on," she muttered, attaching a cable to the camera. She checked the viewfinder, then took her eye from the camera and pressed the cable attachment, humming quietly and cheerfully.

"Did you take a picture?" Angus whispered. "I didn't hear anything."

"Digital cameras don't have to make noise. I just took ten pictures." She pressed the cable attachment again. "Ten more. Take that, Doreene."

Ten

The Port Townsend pier hummed with activity. People strolled between the rows of anchored boats, admiring masts decorated with lights. Musicians played under a large tent, people chatted, and a few vendors still sold food and souvenirs.

Reynaldo heaved a happy sigh, his shoulders visibly relaxing. "This is good. Perhaps I will see someone I know."

"You mean someone on a boat?" Michael asked. "Is that likely?"

Reynaldo shrugged. "I have heard people talk about this festival before. It's very popular, and the number of long-distance sailors is not that large."

"But I thought people hired you as a captain for rental boats. Surely the people here own these boats and don't need a captain."

Reynaldo resumed walking. "For the last few years, yes, I have rented myself as a captain, often to people who own a share in a boat. But I have worked on the sea since I was nine. I have fixed boats, helped build boats, and sailed boats from the old owner to the new one. Once, I worked on a research boat."

"What did it research?"

"Sailing."

"Fair enough," Michael said.

Reynaldo laughed. "They were testing a new hull material."

"And how did it work?"

Reynaldo raised his eyebrows pensively. "Not good. Two weeks out, the boat developed leaks and rolled over. We had inflatable dinghies, of course, but there were some very aggressive sharks in the area, and it took a few minutes to get under way. Luckily, the boat was owned by a couple, and the woman had brought a pair of very expensive shoes for dancing. She insisted on saving them, and I used the heel of one to hit the biggest shark on the nose, many times, until it went away."

"*Wow,*" Michael said. "Were you not wearing shoes?"

"Of course I was, but it is a well-known fact that sharks respect the blow from an expensive shoe more."

Michael laughed. "That's a great story."

Reynaldo grinned in the darkness. "It was a valuable voyage for me. Whenever I told that story, my tips went up."

"So is that how you met Doreene? On a boat?"

Reynaldo's grin faded to a wistful smile. "Yes. It was a weeklong trip, part of the vacation package she was on. She was very fragile, very vulnerable . . ."

Very postoperative, Michael thought uncharitably.

Reynaldo shrugged. "Anyway, we fell in love, and I came here with her."

"And do you think you'll stay?"

Reynaldo frowned and didn't answer.

"Sorry," Michael said. "That was a very personal question. Oh, there's a boat with nice lines. What kind is it?"

Reynaldo looked to where Michael was pointing and his face lit up. "The *Rachel Diana*!"

"Seriously?" Michael said. "We've been here, like, five minutes."

But Reynaldo had already trotted ahead.

Three people sat in deck chairs on board the *Rachel Diana*. The glow of a lit cigarette bobbed in the dusky light.

"Sissy! Paul!" Reynaldo called, and the shadowy figures rose to their feet.

"Oh, my God! Reynaldo?" a woman's voice asked.

By the time Michael reached the boat, Reynaldo had climbed aboard and was receiving enthusiastic hugs.

Some kind of safety netting surrounded the sides of the cruiser. Michael touched it hesitantly, unsure how to maneuver around it.

One of the two men came over. "Put one hand on the shroud, that's this wire here, and swing your leg over."

Michael gripped, swung, and found himself on the boat, clutching the shoulder of his helper. Noticing that the boat was more or less motionless, he let go. "Thank you."

"No problem. Watch where you walk."

They picked their way across the deck to the rest of the group. In the dim light, Michael saw that they were all somewhere in their fifties, with the weathered, competent look of people who work outdoors and are completely at home in their environment.

"Paul, Sissy, this is my friend Michael," Reynaldo said.

"Good to meet you," Paul said, gripping Michael's hand with one that felt like tough leather. "And this is Daniel," he said, introducing the man who had helped Michael. "We picked him up in San Francisco and gave him a lift here."

"Have a seat, guys," Sissy said.

Several chairs surrounded a small table with a collection of beer bottles and one ashtray. They sat.

"Reynaldo, my little sun bunny, who are you working for this time?" Sissy asked.

"No one," Reynaldo said, "I'm staying in Port Townsend." He hesitated. "With my girlfriend."

"Excellent!" Paul said. "Which boat is hers?"

"She doesn't own a boat."

There was a small silence, as if someone had mentioned the death of a friend.

Sissy broke it. "Well, you're certainly the man to help her find one. Do we know her?"

"I don't think so," Reynaldo said. "Doreene Gray?"

"Never heard of her," Paul said, "but the best ones are often kept secret." He chortled. "Does she sail at all? Because we're looking for more crew for a trip after the festival. You interested?"

"I won't be able to," Reynaldo said.

"That's too bad," Paul said. "We'd have been glad to have you. How about you, Mike?"

Michael raised his hands. "Strictly a landlubber, but I wonder if you can help me a little."

"Possibly." Paul looked wary, and Michael wondered how many people asked for free sailing lessons.

"I'm here with *Tripping* magazine. We cover destinations of paranormal interest, and I wonder if you've heard any stories of that nature, about this area. You know, sea monsters, haunted lighthouses—that kind of thing."

"I'm pretty sure all lighthouses are haunted," Sissy said. "It comes with the territory."

Daniel chipped in. "You mean the territory of living alone for months on end and drinking a fair amount?"

She laughed. "That's the one. Although I think most lighthouses are completely automated now, so the ghosts are on their own."

"How about ghost ships?" Paul asked. "Are you interested in those?"

"Absolutely." Michael reached for his digital recorder and pocket notebook.

"Are you thinking of the S.S. *Valencia*?" Sissy asked Paul.

He nodded. "You tell it."

Michael set his recorder on the table and leaned forward expectantly.

"It was January of 1906," Sissy said. "The S.S. *Valencia* was an iron-hulled passenger steamer traveling from San Francisco to Seattle. The weather was clear when she set off, but as she passed Cape Mendocino, she found herself in the grip of strong winds and currents, with very little visibility. Unable to see land, the navigator passed the entrance to the Strait of San Juan de Fuca. Shortly before midnight, the S.S. *Valencia* struck a reef on the coast of Vancouver Island."

Paul broke in. "You see, when you get to the coast, you're in an area that's called the Graveyard of the Pacific, because it's so dangerous."

Michael looked up from making a note. "This isn't the coast?"

"No, this is the Sound."

Sissy went on. "The captain of the *Valencia* ordered the ship reversed, and when it did, the crew saw water pouring into the ship, which had only a single hull. So they ran it aground again."

"Why would they do that?" Michael interrupted.

"If it was stuck on the reef, it couldn't sink," Paul explained.

Sissy continued. "Only about a hundred and fifty feet separated the *Valencia* from shore, but the waves were so great that when passengers came on deck to see what was happening, many of them were washed overboard. The crew panicked, and six of the seven lifeboats they launched were lost almost immediately, along with their passengers. On the ship, husbands lashed their wives to the rigging, above the waves, where the women held their children and hoped for rescue."

Michael realized that his hand was sweating on his pen, and loosened his grip.

"By morning," Sissy continued, "four ships had tried to help the *Valencia,* but none of them could get close. The *Valencia*'s remaining crew launched the last two lifeboats, but most of the passengers chose to remain on board, thinking they would be rescued. Instead, the ship began to break up, and waves washed the *Valencia* off the rocks, drowning all the remaining passengers. The last view many of the survivors had of the ship was of the women, still tied to the rigging, singing 'Nearer My God to Thee.' A hundred and thirty-six passengers died, including all the women and children. Thirty-seven men survived."

As she fell silent, Michael heard the lapping of waves on the hull, and the laughter of nearby sailors.

"What a terrible tragedy," he said, shaking his head.

She raised a finger. "That's not the end of the story. Sailors began seeing a ghostly steamship off the coast of Vancouver Island, and twenty-seven years after that shipwreck, an empty lifeboat was found floating in Barkley Sound. Its nameplate showed that it belonged to the S.S. *Valencia.*"

Michael shook his head. "Incredible. These days, of course, the passengers' families would sue the company."

"Oh, the government launched an investigation," Paul said. "President Teddy Roosevelt even got involved, but it was determined that even though the crew hadn't carried out lifeboat drills, they weren't particularly at fault. The S.S. *Valencia* mostly had a lot of bad luck."

Michael nodded. "What does 'S.S.' stand for, anyway?"

"In this case, *sunken ship,*" Sissy said.

Daniel laughed. "It stands for *steamship.*"

Michael smiled. "Has anyone here had otherworldly experiences while sailing?"

"I had a close encounter with tequila that was pretty otherworldly," Daniel said. "Does that count?"

"That depends," Michael said. "Did you throw up anything you don't remember eating or drinking?" Over their laughter, he asked, "Sissy, can I have your full name and some way to contact you?"

"Sure. "Penelope Thacker." She spelled out an e-mail address while he wrote.

Michael wrote it in his notebook. "Why are you called *Sissy,* out of curiosity?"

"That's by way of being an ironic nickname," Paul said. "She once steered the ship through a gale while I was down in the cabin, laid up with stomach flu."

"Oh, it was just a little breeze," Sissy said.

Paul raised his brows at her. "Let's just say that, one of the times I woke up, I was resting comfortably on the wall instead of the bunk."

Michael suddenly realized that Angus hadn't called. He checked his cell phone but saw no messages. "Thanks for the story. I should probably get back to the house." He found a business card and gave it to Sissy.

Reynaldo rose as if to accompany him, then sat back down, saying, "I will stay a little longer."

"Sure. If I see Doreene, I'll tell her you ran into some friends."

Angus's phone rang while he and Suki were still watching Maureene and Enrico from their place behind the bush. He fumbled the phone out of his pocket and silenced the ring. "Just a sec," he whispered, looking nervously at Maureene's window. Inside, she and Enrico talked on.

Angus crept farther into the woods, until he could barely make out Suki and the lighted window beyond. "Hello?" he whispered.

"What's going on?" Michael asked. "Where are you?"

"Outside Maureene's cottage, with Suki. Maureene is in there with Enrico. Apparently they're old friends. Maybe more than friends."

"Interesting!"

"Isn't it? We should probably leave before he comes out. Where are you?"

"Downtown, by one of the piers. Reynaldo ran into some boating buddies. I got a reasonably local ghost-ship story."

"Good work. Listen, we'll meet you back at the house, all right?" Angus looked toward where he thought Suki was. "Bloody hell, I can't see the cottage anymore. Hold on." He pointed his phone at the ground, using the light to check for things that might trip him, but the ground at his feet appeared to have been swept clean of leaves. In addition, several long gouges marked the soil next to the nearest tree. He put the phone to his ear. "Michael? What was it Lupita said she saw out in the woods?"

"Spirits of the dead, crawling across the ground."

Angus stared at the gouges. "Right. See you back at the house."

When Michael returned to the house, he found Angus in Suki's room, looking over her shoulder while she uploaded photos of Enrico and Maureene to her laptop.

Michael shut the bedroom door and joined them in looking at pictures. "Those two look cozy."

Angus nodded. "Maureene hugged Enrico like she hadn't seen him in years. They were still talking when we left."

"I know it's a long shot," Michael said, "but do you think he's the mystery father of Maureene's daughter?"

"I was wondering the same thing," Suki said. "If only Maureene had brought out a box of baby pictures while they were sitting there."

Angus took a seat on the bed and leaned back on his arms. "If Enrico and Maureene are such great friends, why did he tell us he wanted to speak to Doreene?"

Suki clicked to a new picture. "Oh, Doreene knows him, too. I could tell she recognized him. Why else would she delete the photo?"

Michael bent to get a better view of the laptop, where Suki zoomed in on the lighted window of Maureene's cottage. "She looks so happy. I didn't see much resemblance between the sisters before, but now it's clear."

Suki cropped the photo and saved the new version. "Show him the picture you took, Angus."

"Right." Angus stood and dug in his pocket for his phone. "It was while I was talking to you, Michael, that I looked down and saw this."

Michael squinted at the phone's screen, which showed a rather overexposed flash photo. "Looks like dirt, and the base of a tree. What am I supposed to be seeing?"

"If you'll notice, there are no leaves on the ground in that area." Angus pointed. "Also, see those two grooves in the dirt?"

"Uh-huh."

"Those could be the marks left by a skeleton dragging itself across the ground, scraping leaves as it went. *Spirits of the dead,* Michael."

"Wouldn't there be ten grooves, in that case?" Michael asked. "One for each skeletal finger?"

Angus made an impatient noise and put his phone away. "Maybe it's missing some finger bones, or these are from its knees."

"Pelvis," Suki said absently. "That's the heaviest, and it has sharp edges."

"Regardless," Angus said, "I clipped a pen to the nearest bush. We'll go back tomorrow and take pictures during the day. I hope we can find the place. It was a nice pen."

"We should get some of that stretchy plastic ribbon people tie around trees and stuff," Michael said. "Wonder what that's called?"

"Flagging tape," Suki said.

"Let me guess, you dated a hunter once," Michael said.

"Surveyor."

Angus looked at his watch. "I'm going to my room. We did some good work today."

Michael followed him out. "Wait until you hear this shipwreck story, Angus. It's really tragic."

"I look forward to it."

Suki got up and shut the door behind them. Then she went back to her laptop and pulled up one of the best photos of Enrico, where he had momentarily turned toward the window. "I swear I've seen this guy somewhere else," she muttered.

Eleven

Angus woke sometime in the middle of the night. He lay in the dark room with the vague notion that he had heard a thump. Then he got out of bed and went to the window.

The sky was dark, probably with clouds, and showed no hint of moon or stars. The outline of a tree, black and very still, showed against a neighbor's security light.

Angus felt for the window's latch and opened it. Cool, damp air chilled his face and hands, but there was no wind. He closed the window and went to his bedroom door, where he briefly looked into the hall. Yawning, he closed the door and went back to bed.

The next time Angus woke, it was to the sound of a woman's scream, high and shrill. He froze for a moment, then threw back the covers and found his boxer shorts on the floor. From the amount of light coming through the windows, he guessed it was about six in the morning.

The scream came again, and he heard the skitter of Gigi's claws as she ran past his door and down the hallway. She began to bark.

Angus left his bedroom and trotted down the hall. Gigi stood upright against Doreene's door, barking. In the pauses between, Angus heard Reynaldo's voice, alarmed and questioning.

Angus pounded on Doreene's door. "Is everything all right? Do you need me to call nine-one-one?"

The door opened a bit, and Reynaldo stood there, in much briefer and tighter underwear than Angus's. "I don't think so, no." An overhead light showed that his lithe body was corded with muscle.

Angus felt the hardwood floor vibrate with footsteps and turned to see Suki, wearing a silk robe patterned with peacock feathers and holding a camera in her hand.

Michael was close behind, wearing jeans and glasses, his chest bare. "What's going on?"

Suki looked Reynaldo up and down and gave a barely audible whistle.

He smiled shyly.

The door jerked open farther and Doreene stood there, wearing a long, elegant nightgown of cream satin and clutching a wadded tissue in her hand. "Did you do this?!" She shook the tissue at them, panting with rage.

"I don't think so, but what are we talking about?" Angus asked cautiously.

She flung the door open and gestured to the room. "This!"

Dead leaves littered the carpet. At first Angus thought some of them had somehow stuck to the wall, but then he realized that those were Washington's infamous banana slugs. They moved sluggishly across the floor, their glistening trails crisscrossing the hardwood floor and leaving strands of mucus on the Oriental rug. One hung halfway off the shade of a bedside lamp, its questing horns waving gently.

Gigi ran around the room, sniffing busily.

Doreene leaned against the door frame. "I got up to go to the bathroom and *stepped* on one." She opened the hand that clutched the tissue and they saw the sad little corpse.

Suki raised her upper lip. "Ew."

Lupita came running down the hall, a terry cloth robe cinched around her waist. "What happened?"

The others stood aside so she could see.

Doreene made an angry gesture around the room. "Get a bucket and a broom or something," she snapped.

Lupita's eyes widened. "Spirits of the dead," she whispered.

"Don't be stupid." Doreene gave her a little push. "Go on, get something to clean this up."

As Lupita scurried away, Doreene turned back to Angus with a glare. "Admit it. You did this to drum up interest in your little magazine."

Angus drew himself up. "I assure you, we did nothing of the sort."

"Princessa," Reynaldo said hesitantly, "don't you usually lock the bedroom door when we have guests?"

"That's right, I did lock it." Doreene's angry expression faltered, but then she turned on Reynaldo. "Did you unlock it? Maybe you did this!"

"No! I swear." Reynaldo raised both hands in denial, causing his pecs to jump.

"Can I take a look?" Michael asked. He pushed his way past the others and went inside the room, where he got down on his hands and knees and tilted his head this way and that.

Doreene folded her arms across her satin-clad middle. "What are you doing?"

"Looking to see if the slime trails lead back to any one point," Michael said.

Suki took advantage of Doreene's inattention to take some pictures.

Michael sat back on his heels and stared at the ceiling. "There's a vent up there. Could someone have gone into the attic and dropped slugs into the room from up there?"

"There's another floor above us," Doreene said.

"Oh, right. Lupita sleeps up there." He resumed crawling across the floor.

Angus crossed the room and gripped the top of Michael's head, stopping him. "The explanation is pretty obvious to me."

Michael slapped at Angus's hand. "Let go!"

Angus grabbed his wrist and tugged Michael to his feet. "Lupita said that, night before last, she saw spirits of the dead crawling through the woods. Last night, they must have reached the house."

Reynaldo crossed himself. "*Cara,* you have to get rid of the painting!"

Doreene rolled her eyes. "I'm selling the damn painting, Rey. Would you rather I put it out by the curb?"

Michael headed toward the windows that looked out on the front lawn, evading Angus's reaching hand. "Two of these windows are unlatched, and there are no screens. What do you bet someone just opened one and tossed in leaves and slugs?"

"On the second floor of the house?" Angus asked.

"Ever heard of ladders?" Michael asked drily.

"These leaves are pretty spread out," Suki said. "Wouldn't someone have to come inside the room to do that?"

Michael picked up one of the leaves. Another one followed, dangling several inches below it on an almost invisible thread of mucus. "I think the slugs are responsible for distributing the leaves." He dropped the leaves and wiped his hand on his pants.

Angus went to the window and looked out. "Wouldn't Doreene or Reynaldo have heard something? A bunch of slugs hitting the floor must make some noise. And if someone used a ladder, that wouldn't be exactly silent." He thought of the thump he had heard during the night.

"I take sleeping pills," Doreene said. "I wouldn't have heard a thing. And Reynaldo sometimes pulls the covers over his head."

"Because it is cold," Reynaldo said. "But I did wake up last night."

He looked at Michael thoughtfully. "I thought I heard a door closing in the hall. Then I went back to sleep." His frightened look eased.

"It'd be an awful risk," Angus pointed out. "What if Reynaldo had got up and looked outside?"

"I'm sure they waited a while after putting the ladder up to see if any lights came on," Michael said.

"Also, that window is on the street side of the house," Angus said. "Anyone might have seen them and called the cops."

"He's right," Reynaldo said, looking frightened again. "It would be very risky."

Michael rolled his eyes. "So you think it's more likely that *actual skeletons* put slugs in the room than that someone propped a ladder against the house in the middle of the night?"

Reynaldo bit his lip. "But why would someone do that?"

"Why would skeletons scatter gastropods across the carpet?" Michael countered.

"Because they are messengers from the Devil," Reynaldo said.

Doreene pointed a finger at him. "I swear, Reynaldo, if you start yapping about the Devil one more time . . ." She went to a side chair and grabbed a robe from the back of it. "I never did get to pee." She passed Lupita, who had returned in her uniform, carrying an empty bucket and a whisk broom. "*Finally.* Make sure you check under the bed and on the curtains, Lupita. And we'll be eating out today, so don't get any bright ideas about slug soup."

Michael came out of his room wearing his jacket and found Angus leaning against the wall, arms crossed.

"I've a bone to pick with you," Angus said.

"Finger or knee?" Michael glanced toward Doreene and Reynaldo's room. The sound of slugs hitting the bottom of a bucket came from beyond the open door.

Angus pushed away from the wall. "Do you or do you not work for a paranormal magazine?"

"I've never seen the pages turn by themselves or felt cold when I picked up a back issue, so no, I don't. If you mean, do I work for a magazine that covers paranormal topics, then yes, I do." He crossed his own arms. "Do you have a problem with my writing?"

Angus frowned. "Your writing is fine. It's your interview technique that needs work."

Followed by Angus, Michael started downstairs. "Reynaldo is determined to believe in walking skeletons, no matter what I say. If I weren't here for him to argue with, we might not have that quote about skeletons being messengers from the Devil."

They reached the ground floor, and Michael turned. "And in case you've forgotten, Doreene asked us to stay because she hoped we'd find out what's behind all this, starting with the paper strips in the soup. If we had been all for demonic warnings this morning, she might have kicked us out."

"Maybe," Angus said.

Michael opened the front door, and they went out. "Anyway, we both know that it doesn't matter what rational explanations I come up with, because you'll edit those out of the finished article." He paused on the walk and took a small digital camera from his jacket pocket.

"I'm glad you brought that," Angus remarked. "We need better pictures of the ground where those gouges were. I knocked on Suki's door earlier, but she didn't answer."

"She was probably in the shower. I could hear a hair dryer going when I left my room."

Angus watched Michael fiddle with the settings on the camera. "I clipped a pen to the bush, so we could find the spot."

"We can search for your pen, but first I want to look around the outside of the house."

"What for?"

"A ladder." Michael turned left, walking around the corner of the mansion. He led the way past the side door to the conservatory and continued to the back of the house, where a small greenhouse stood, moisture clouding the windows. Beyond it was a medium-sized shed of weathered wood. "Aha!"

"Bet it's locked," Angus said.

"Nope." Michael gave him a triumphant look and pulled the slightly rusty hasp back. Metal squeaked against metal, and the sagging door opened. He peered into the dusky interior, making out a lawn mower and a selection of pruning tools. Then he pointed. "If I'm not mistaken, that's a ladder."

Angus stood next to him and peered inside. "It's awfully dark in here. Are you sure it isn't a bookcase?"

Michael ducked his head and moved cautiously into the shed, then backed out, making spitting noises and pawing at his mouth. "Yech. Spiderweb."

"If there's a spider's web, I'd say this ladder hasn't been used in a while," Angus said smugly.

"Or the spider made a new web after the ladder was returned. It's had a few hours, after all." Waving his hands in front of him, Michael edged inside the shed, grabbed the end of the wooden ladder, and dragged it out. "Hmm. Stepladder. That doesn't seem like it would be tall enough."

Angus looked at the ladder's feet. "And I'd expect the feet to show a little moisture, or grass." He rubbed his finger across the wood. "Dry as a bone."

Michael shoved the ladder back into the shed and latched the door.

Angus stood behind him, hands in his pockets, breathing the damp morning air appreciatively. "Can we look for my pen now?"

"In a minute. I want to check the ground underneath Doreene's windows."

They made their way back to the front of the house, Michael

studying the ground the whole way. "I'm not used to grass that's this lush. Would it stay down for a while or spring right up?"

"You'll have to ask someone local, but remember, we're not in the debunking business, Michael."

Michael stopped and turned to look at him. "Aren't you remotely interested in the truth?"

Angus smiled. "Truth changes constantly, but a good story lasts and lasts."

Michael resumed walking. "Ah, aphorisms. The spray cheese of wisdom." He looked up and pointed. "Those are Doreene's windows, and those two on the end are the ones that weren't latched. If I were going to put a ladder up, I would put it right . . ." He took a step back, then several to the left. ". . . here." He pointed at the lawn. "What does that look like to you?"

Angus squatted and brushed at two indented spots in the grass. "I suppose it's possible someone put a ladder here." He stood, and watched while Michael took several photos of the marks. "Or it could be from something completely different."

"Like what?"

"Like a skeleton with several other skeletons on his shoulders, putting slugs through the window."

Michael shook his head and looked at the sky. "You never give up, do you?"

"I've a magazine to put out," Angus said. "Now can we go and find my pen?"

They were still looking for the pen when Suki joined them in the woods around Maureene's cottage. She had topped her jeans and buckled boots with a faded Velvet Underground T-shirt. As usual, she had a camera around her neck. "Did you find the place?"

"No," Angus said grumpily.

Suki walked a little back way back, keeping Maureene's cottage in sight. "Okay, I'm pretty sure this was the bush we were standing in at first."

Angus joined her, then turned around and mimed the events of the previous night. "I took out my phone, I walked this way a little, I turned . . ." He glanced around. "There it is!"

The others joined him.

Angus unclipped his pen from a branch and put it in his jacket pocket, then studied the ground. "See how there aren't many leaves in this area?" He took a step toward the nearest tree and pointed. "And there are the two gouges."

Michael squatted and stared at the spot. "It looks to me as though someone dug through the leaves with a stick, looking for slugs, then scooped some up, leaves and all. If they used a flashlight, that would also explain the light Lupita saw in the night."

"Could you lie down on the ground and really look at those marks, Michael?" Angus asked.

"What for?"

"It's just that you look very *investigative reporter* down there. I'd like Suki to take a few pictures of you for the magazine."

Michael looked pleased. "Okay." He lay on the ground and fixed the marks with a serious look.

Suki raised her camera.

"Hold on," Angus told her. He bent and positioned Michael's arms so they were on either side of the marks. "Fire away."

Suki circled Michael, taking pictures as she went.

"Excellent," Angus said. "We'll use these as a re-creation of a skeleton dragging itself along the ground."

Michael scrambled to his feet. "Did you listen to anything I said?"

"Slug gathering with a flashlight. It's a possibility." Angus turned and looked at Maureene's cottage, barely visible through the bushes and trees. "I wish we had a better interview with Maureene."

"Want to see if she's home?" Suki asked. "We could tell her about the slugs and see what she says."

"Good idea."

They went to Maureene's cottage, their feet rustling through the dead leaves.

Angus rapped on the door. No one answered, and no barking came from inside. "Probably gone out to get breakfast. Michael, where are you going?"

Michael had walked down an overgrown path of concrete pavers that led along one side of the cottage. "I'm just looking around." He disappeared around the back of the cottage. "Well, would you look at this!" he called.

Angus and Suki trotted to join him. "What?"

Michael pointed to a shiny aluminum extension ladder, neatly folded and leaning against the back of the house. He checked the bottom of the feet and pulled a fresh blade of grass from one. "Looks like Maureene and the Slug Fairy could be one and the same."

Angus held up a finger. "*Or,* the skeletons forced her to do their bidding. I don't imagine you get good purchase on these rungs with bare bone."

Michael flicked the blade of grass away. "I like my explanation better. The question is, why would Maureene throw slugs into her sister's bedroom?"

Twelve

They returned to the house to find Reynaldo on the front walk watching Doreene drive away. Enrico's white Impala was nowhere to be seen.

Reynaldo smiled as he turned back toward the house.

Suki raised a hand in greeting. "Morning, Reynaldo. You look pretty happy for a man who recently had a close encounter of the slug kind."

"My *princessa* has gone to talk to Max about shipping the painting to New York," he said, walking to meet them. "I would be happier if she destroyed it, but this is very good."

"So what are you going to do this morning?" Michael asked.

Reynaldo looked blank. "I don't know. Perhaps I will go back to the festival."

"Come and have breakfast with us," Angus invited. "We're going to a restaurant in one of the shipyards."

Suki drove the minivan along a winding asphalt road, through industrial outbuildings of corrugated metal. The buildings petered out and were replaced by ships propped on their keels as they underwent maintenance. A lone man used a long-handled roller to apply a layer of blue anti-fouling paint to the towering hull of his ship.

In the front seat of the minivan, Reynaldo pointed and made little exclamations of excitement.

At last they found the café. Inside, the warm smell of baked goods greeted them. The closely spaced dinette tables were packed, and a cheerful buzz of conversation mixed with the clink of forks and glasses.

A waitress hurried over. "It's gonna be about five minutes, okay?"

"That's fine," Angus said.

They crowded close to the front door to stay out of the way.

A few minutes later, the waitress came back. "Some seats just opened up at the counter, if you want to sit there."

Angus nodded, and they followed her. "Do you have any recommendations?" he asked, as they sat down.

"Oh, it's all good," she said, taking a plate from the outstretched hands of the cook. "Excuse me." And she was off and running.

A weathered man was seated on the stool next to Angus. "You might want to try the French toast. They dip the bread in custard."

Suki put her menu down decisively. "Sold."

Angus smiled at the man. "Do you live in Port Townsend?"

"I live on a boat." The man wore a nylon windbreaker, a battered ball cap, and faded jeans. He looked to be in his midseventies. "Jem Michaels. I'd shake your hand, but mine's got bacon grease on it."

Angus laughed. "Angus MacGregor."

"You folks here for the festival?" Jem asked.

"We're here to write a story about Maureene Pinter's portrait of her sister, Doreene."

Jem's expression turned solemn. "There's a family with bad luck."

"How so?" Angus asked.

Beside him, Suki and Michael leaned forward. Reynaldo, seated beyond them, appeared not to have heard.

Jem shook his head. "I don't know the twins personally, but I went to high school with their mama. Her second husband used to beat the tar out of her. Everyone in town knew, but back then there weren't all these social service people to talk to. She had family back East, but she stuck it out until cancer got her. Sad." He took a sip of his coffee.

"I'm surprised the daughters stayed with their stepfather after their mother died," Suki said. "If he was abusive, why didn't they live with their relatives?"

"By then, they were probably used to hiding what was going on, and I doubt their mama told her family what was happening." He shook his head. "The whole town was glad when that sonofabitch drowned, but Maureene seemed pretty broken up about it. Maybe he treated them better than he treated his wife, although you wouldn't think so, since it was the booze that made him mean."

"How did he drown?" Michael asked.

"He liked to get drunk and take his little sailboat out from the pier at Fort Worden. He went out late one evening. It was a calm night, but when he wasn't back by ten, Maureene got worried and called the cops. They found him floating about fifty feet offshore, next to the boat. Just one of those dumb, drunk-guy accidents."

The waitress came over in time to hear the last part. She gave Jem an uneasy look. "You aren't gossiping again, are you, Jem?"

He grinned up at her. "Only because you won't sit and talk to me, darling."

She smacked his arm and turned her attention to the others. "You folks know what you want?"

Michael ordered the breakfast burrito, but the others all asked for the French toast and coffee, a locally roasted brand. Reynaldo was the last to order.

The waitress smiled as she took his order. "That's a nice accent. Where are you from?"

He smiled back. "Brazil. Near São Paulo."

Jem leaned close to Angus and whispered, "Shit. That's not the man living with Doreene, is it?"

Angus nodded slightly.

Jem grimaced. "I'd have never said all that if I'd known."

"He might not have heard you," Angus said. "And anyway, if people talked more about that sort of thing, maybe it wouldn't happen as often."

"I suppose." Jem smiled wryly. "Well, that's one good thing about living on a boat. When you screw up, you can just sail away."

After breakfast, they went back to the house and followed Reynaldo upstairs to the second-floor bedrooms.

Doreene's door was open, and she could be seen sorting through piles of clothing on her bed. Gigi looked into the hallway, then wandered out of sight.

Angus stopped at his room. "Wait out here a sec," he told Michael and Suki. "I need to find our schedule."

"We have a schedule?" Suki asked.

Angus tipped his head toward Doreene's room and mouthed the word, *listen*.

"Oh. That schedule." Suki leaned against the door frame.

While Angus puttered around his bedroom, Reynaldo went to meet Doreene.

He gave her a kiss. "*Cara,* what are you doing?"

"Going through my clothes. I couldn't stand the thought that some of those slugs might be in the closet, and then I thought I might as well get rid of things I'm not wearing. Plus, some of it doesn't fit anymore."

"Don't get too skinny, *cara*. A man doesn't like that."

Doreene gave a little yelp and then giggled.

Angus gave up his pretense of looking for something and hovered just inside his doorway.

"Is Max going to take the painting away today?" Reynaldo asked.

"He's coming later to measure it," Doreene said. "Rothwell's will send a special packing case, and it'll be gone before you know it."

"Good," Reynaldo said. "Can I help you with the clothing?"

"You can help me by making a coffee run," Doreene said.

Angus waved Suki and Michael inside his room and shut the door. "Damn it! We still haven't gotten a good picture of that portrait."

"I took pictures at the press conference," Suki said. "They're just not very detailed, from that distance, and with that light."

Angus shook his head. "I was hoping for something better."

"Still," Michael said, "We have enough material for an article, what with cryptic alphabet soup, lights in the woods, and unexplained slugs."

Suki looked thoughtful. "Unexplained Slugs would make an excellent band name."

"And let's not forget Doreene collapsing when the guards banged the painting on the railing," Michael continued.

"I suppose." Angus sighed. "I was counting on getting a photo at some point."

"Would Maureene have a photo?" Suki asked.

"Probably of the original," Michael said. "I don't know if she has a picture of what it's become. She more or less told me that she wasn't responsible for the portrait changing, but it doesn't hurt to ask."

"Let's go to the cottage," Angus said. "If Maureene doesn't have a photo of the painting, she might at least give us that interview she promised. I have a new tack I want to take on that."

"What tack?" Michael asked.

"You'll see."

They went outside and down the path to Maureene's cottage, where Angus rapped on the door.

From inside, Hilda started to bark. No one came to the door.

"What do you bet Maureene is hiding behind the couch?" Michael muttered.

Angus raised his voice to be heard over Hilda's barking. "Let's go back to the house and find out exactly when the painting is leaving."

They had gone perhaps ten feet down the path when the cottage door opened and Maureene stood there. Hilda stood at her feet, front paws coming off the ground with each bark. "Sorry," Maureene said, picking up the dog. "Couldn't get to the door right away. Come on in."

They trooped inside the cottage.

Maureene gestured to the couch. "Have a seat. I'll get us some water."

When she was out of earshot, Michael rolled his eyes. "Here we go with the drinks again."

"At least she's being friendly," Angus whispered back.

Maureene returned in a few minutes, carrying what looked like a pizza pan with four glasses on it. She set it carefully on the table in front of the couch and took a glass. "Help yourself."

Angus and Michael sat on the couch with Maureene while Suki took a side chair.

"What's up?" Maureene asked.

Angus gave her a warm smile. "We were wondering if you had a photo of Doreene's portrait as it is now, or during any point in its transformation."

Maureene scowled. "No."

"Do you know if anyone else has one?" Michael asked.

Maureene's eyes narrowed. "To my knowledge, no one has a photo. Did someone tell you they did?"

"Um, no." Michael took out his recorder. "Can we do your interview now?"

"I suppose." Maureene tucked a strand of hair behind one ear as Suki powered on her camera.

Angus turned sideways on the sofa so he was facing Maureene more squarely. "Have you heard about the plague of slugs that appeared in Doreene's bedroom last night?"

"Slugs? In her bedroom?" Maureene's forehead wrinkled. "How on earth did they get in there?"

Michael opened his mouth to say something.

Angus cut him off. "No one knows. The door was locked and the windows closed, but Doreene and Reynaldo woke up to dead leaves on the floor and slugs climbing the walls. It's quite the inexplicable phenomenon." He fixed Maureene with his most sincere look. "Ms. Pinter, you painted this portrait shortly after your stepfather's boat accident. Is it possible that the changing image in the painting isn't your sister, but your stepfather trying to come through? Could his spirit be haunting the portrait?"

Maureene reached for her water and took a drink before replying. "My stepfather had his problems, but he had no reason to haunt anyone."

"Sudden and untimely death often results in a restless spirit," Angus said gently. "He might have something he needs to tell someone, or—"

"It's not my stepfather." Maureene looked at her watch. "I just realized that I have somewhere to be. I mean, I'm meeting someone for lunch."

One corner of Suki's mouth lifted. "Hot date?"

Maureene flushed. "Just a friend." She stood and put the glasses back on the tray. "I'm sorry if you got the impression there's something supernatural about the painting. The only power it has comes from my sister's unhealthy obsession with it."

"Then you'll be glad to hear this," Michael said. "Maxwell Thorne is going to measure the portrait today. It'll be out of here as soon as Rothwell's sends a shipping container for it."

Maureene picked up the loaded tray, then put it down again and looked at her watch. "Really, I have to go." She went to the door and held it open for them.

"Can we finish your interview after lunch?" Angus asked, getting up.

"I don't know. Maybe." Maureene opened the door wider. "Bye."

They filed out and she closed the door behind them.

"Talk about the bum's rush." Michael took out his pocket notebook as they started down the path. "I swear she told me there was something supernatural about the painting." He flipped pages, squinting at his scrawled notes. "Here it is. She said, 'Maybe there is something strange about it,' and also that we had experience with 'mumbo jumbo,' while she didn't."

" 'Mumbo jumbo' covers a lot of ground." Suki said. "It's a Caribbean restaurant in Toronto, for starters."

Angus put his hands in his pockets. "When we told Maureene about the paper strips in the soup, she said, 'It must be getting stronger.' "

"That could refer to Doreene's obsession," Michael said, putting his notebook back. "Our article's premise took a hit today."

"Nonsense," Angus said. "There's no law that says we have to quote everything Maureene says."

When they reached the place where the path came closest to the street, they saw Reynaldo coming from the direction of town, a lidded paper cup in each hand.

He lifted one cup in greeting. "Hello again, my friends!"

They waved back and waited for him at the front door.

"Let me get this for you." Angus turned the knob and pushed it open.

"Thank you," Reynaldo said as he went in.

"Angus!" Suki whispered, still outside.

Angus and Michael both turned.

Suki jerked her head toward the other side of the street. The white Impala sat there, empty.

"Enrico," Angus murmured. "I'm surprised we didn't pass him on the way back from Maureene's."

They went inside.

Reynaldo had waited in the foyer for them. "Did you know that

Brazil is the largest grower of coffee in the world? And of course it is the best." He started up the stairs.

"That's true, actually," Michael said, following. "The Bourbon Santos cultivar is particularly good."

Lupita came running down the stairs, interrupting their conversation. "Mr. Reynaldo, a man came to see Miss Doreene, and now they're in her bedroom, fighting!"

Reynaldo handed her the cups of coffee without a word and went up the stairs two at a time. Lupita pressed herself against the wall and closed her eyes as the *Tripping* crew ran after him, the stairs bouncing slightly under everyone's combined weight.

They heard raised voices as they entered the hallway. Gigi ran back and forth in front of Doreene's closed bedroom door, barking.

"Why now?" Doreene shouted, from inside the room. "Is it because you finally have some money of your own? You're guilty of abandonment, at the very least, and think of the child support you owe!"

"I would have paid if I'd known!" Enrico shouted back. "It's too late for that. Give me the painting and I'll go away. No one has to know."

Reynaldo tried Doreene's door, then banged on it with his fist, causing Gigi to dart away. "*Cara,* are you all right?"

"Go away, Reynaldo," Doreene yelled, sounding both angry and weary.

Angus, Suki, and Michael clustered at the halfway point of the hall.

Inside the room, Enrico pitched his voice to carry. "Shall I tell your boyfriend what you're capable of?"

"Me?!" Doreene sounded livid. "How can you take her side? Do you know what that painting is?"

Lupita crept up next to Michael, still carrying the lidded cups of coffee.

Reynaldo pounded on the door again. "Doreene, let me in!"

Inside the room, Enrico went on. "I know what the painting is, Doreene, but it's turned you into a parasite. You're like a vampire, sucking the life out of your sister with your endless quest for youth."

"Dios mio," Lupita whispered.

"I'm coming in!" Reynaldo took a few steps back and hurled himself at the door, shoulder first.

"Stop it, Reynaldo," Doreene yelled.

Gigi ran back toward the stairs, tail tucked between her legs.

Suki picked up the dog and held her small, trembling body.

Reynaldo stepped back, then slammed into the door again.

"I told you to go away," Doreene screamed. "This has nothing to do with you!"

"Open this door!" Reynaldo hammered on the door with both fists. "Doreene, do as I say! I am your husband!"

Silence fell in the room beyond.

Reynaldo pounded twice more, then tried the handle. "Doreene, are you all right?"

The door opened, and Doreene gave Reynaldo a look of such fury that he took a step back.

Her gaze fell on the others. *"Marvelous."*

Enrico appeared behind her, a triumphant smile on his face. "So this is your husband, Doreene? You should have introduced us."

Reynaldo took a step forward. "Who are you?"

Doreene shoved Reynaldo in the chest. "Idiot!"

He grabbed her arm, but she raised her other hand and hit him clumsily across the face. Reynaldo staggered back against the wall, holding his jaw.

Enrico's smile disappeared. He shouldered Doreene aside and put a hand on Reynaldo's shoulder.

Reynaldo shrugged it off in a quick, violent gesture and squared up to the larger man. *"Fudi a tua mãe quando ela estava gravida de ti!"*

"Oh, wow," Suki muttered.

Enrico gave Reynaldo a sardonic look. "You'll probably thank me someday." He glanced at Doreene. "This isn't over."

He stalked past them and down the staircase.

The sound of the front door opening and closing was immediately followed by the slam of Doreene's bedroom door as she shut herself inside.

Reynaldo looked at the closed door for a moment. Then he walked rigidly past the others to the stairs, the mark of Doreene's hand livid on his face.

Angus took the coffee cups from Lupita. "I don't think they need any more caffeine."

Lupita shook her head slowly, her eyes wide. "You can't hit a man like that and not be punished."

"Sure you can." Suki put Gigi down. "You have a stronger legal position if no one sees you do it, of course."

Lupita shook her head. "God will punish her." She turned and went downstairs, Gigi following her.

Angus jerked his head toward his room. "Staff meeting."

Michael and Suki followed him, Michael closing the door after they were inside.

Angus set one of the coffees on the dresser and removed the plastic lid from the one he still held. He took a cautious sip. "Perfect. Anyone want the other?"

"Not me," Suki said. "I'm wired enough from that scene." She flopped into a brocade-covered armchair.

"What was it Reynaldo said to Enrico?" Michael asked, taking the other coffee.

" 'I screwed your mother while she was pregnant with you,' " Suki said. "Them's fighting words."

"And also impossible, from a strictly chronological standpoint."

Angus kicked his shoes off and lounged on the bed. "So Doreene and Reynaldo are married. Why keep it a secret, I wonder?"

"So Maureene doesn't find out?" Michael suggested. "She probably wouldn't be happy to learn that the house and any money goes to Reynaldo if Doreene dies first."

Angus shook his head. "I don't think Doreene cares if she upsets Maureene. If anything, she goes out of her way to do it."

Suki took off one of her boots and adjusted a buckle. "Ten bucks says Doreene put one over on Reynaldo and it isn't a real marriage."

Michael looked at Angus. "I'm not going to take that bet."

Angus nodded. "It sounds all too plausible. Reynaldo might not have come here without the assurance of marriage."

Suki dropped the boot on the floor and took off the other one. "Looks like we were right about Enrico being the father of Maureene's daughter, too. All that talk of child support and abandonment."

"Then there was that bit about the painting," Michael said. "'Do you know what the painting is? I know what the painting is.' What the hell is it?"

"I told you, vampiric object. Enrico even called Doreene a vampire." Angus smiled in satisfaction. "If we don't pick up a dozen new advertisers from this story, I'll be very surprised."

"I wonder what the blackmaily part was about," Suki said.

Michael nodded. "'Give me the painting and no one has to know.' Know what?"

They both looked at Angus, who shrugged. "I've no clue."

"So where are we going to stay tonight?" Suki asked.

"What do you mean?" Angus asked.

Suki put her boots back on. "You don't think Doreene is going to want us hanging around after we saw her smack Reynaldo and get threatened by Enrico, do you?"

"What's that got to do with us?" Michael asked.

Suki looked from him to Angus, who appeared similarly baffled, and laughed. "Well, maybe you're right, and the next time Doreene meets us in the hall, she'll say, 'I'm not at all embarrassed. Feel free to stick around and watch my life go down the crapper. Oh, and make sure to write it all up in your little magazine.' "

Michael sucked in a breath. "You have a point."

Angus frowned. "I wish people wouldn't call *Tripping* 'little.' Our last issue was twenty-eight pages. Still, I see what you mean." He swung his legs off the bed. "Get whatever equipment you need for the day, quietly, and let's get out of here before Doreene comes out of her burrow and sees us. If we keep away for a while, maybe it'll be more embarrassing for her to bring it up than to let us stay."

Thirteen

They sneaked out of the house without seeing Doreene. Michael carried his laptop bag over one shoulder, Suki had a bulging camera case in addition to the camera around her neck, and all of them carried umbrellas. They wandered around downtown Port Townsend, taking notes and pictures.

Suki lowered her camera from a shot of the Haller Fountain. "Hey, there's Max Thorne."

Angus and Michael both looked around.

"Where?" Angus asked.

Suki pointed. "He just went into that art gallery."

They walked down the street and went inside.

Dressed impeccably in a blue-black suit and snowy shirt, Max Thorne stood out among the tourists like a magpie surrounded by chickens. He stood, hands clasped behind his back, gazing at an impressionist painting of a fleet of sailboats on a steel-colored sea.

"Hello, Mr. Thorne," Angus said, coming up beside him.

"Mr. MacGregor," Max said. He nodded at the other two.

"Thinking of buying a souvenir of your time here?" Angus asked, tilting his head toward the picture.

"I thought I might get it for my daughter. She sails."

Michael tilted his head and studied the picture. "A robust use of impasto."

"Indeed," Max said, smiling at him. "Very painterly. Almost aggressively so."

"What's your expert opinion on the properties of Doreene Gray's portrait, Mr. Thorne?" Angus asked. "We've been considering the possibility that it's haunted by Doreene and Maureene's stepfather. I understand he may have been a difficult parent."

Max sighed. "Mr. MacGregor, Rothwell's is a professional auction house. I can discuss Maureene Pinter as an artist, but I can't gossip about her private life."

"Then let's gossip about the painting," Angus said.

Max laughed, briefly and mirthlessly. "I wish I could. She hasn't let me get any closer to it than anyone else."

"But you *will* get close, when you measure it," Angus said. "When is that going to happen?"

"Two-thirty."

"Can you talk to us about it after that?"

"I really can't."

Angus shook his head in frustration. "I don't understand. You'd think Rothwell's would want every bit of publicity they could get."

"It's not Rothwell's that responsible for my vow of silence," Max said.

"Did Doreene have you sign a nondisclosure agreement?" Michael asked.

Max smiled. "I can't tell you."

"If you can't give us any specific information, perhaps you can help with something general," Angus said. "What great works of art are reputed to be haunted or cursed?"

"None of them, to my knowledge."

"You're kidding," Angus said.

Max laughed. "Artists and art lovers deal with enough illogic without looking for more." His voice took on a confidential tone. "The industry of art exists by putting a price on beauty and strangeness, which is impossible. Art lovers demand dedication to craft, then reward people for ignoring it. If an artist hustles, we call him crass. If he doesn't, we say he's naïve. The ideal artist has the eye of a camera, the brain of a lunatic, and a funny hairstyle or moustache, women included. He should paint prolifically for fifteen years, then die infamously just as he's becoming well-known. With all that to deal with, do we really need to make up ghost stories?"

Angus tilted his head. "Perhaps not, but would Maureene Pinter be as famous if her sister's portrait weren't somehow mysterious?"

Max smiled. "I see your point, but Maureene Pinter is still a very good artist. Also, this portrait represents something epic and unusual—a dialogue between a painter and her subject, twin sisters, represented on a single canvas. The reason for that dialogue is a secret, and only the eventual owner will have a chance of figuring it out."

Michael raised his brows. "Nice phrasing. Is that from the catalog copy?"

"It's good, isn't it?" Max said. "The intern who wrote it is getting dual degrees in art history and literature. I have to stop her from using 'numinous' in every other paragraph, but other than that she's working out well."

A well-dressed woman eased up next to them. "I don't want to interrupt, but can I answer any questions for you?"

Max gestured to the boat painting. "I'd like to buy this."

"It's a wonderful piece." She ran a hand down the frame. "This wood is from the hull of an old sailboat."

"What a little bonus."

The woman grasped the painting's frame and carefully lifted it from the wall. "Do you live locally, or would you like us to ship this for you?"

"If you could package it for shipping, that would be wonderful," Max said, "but I think I'll take it with me on the plane. I want to be there when she opens it." Max turned back to the others. "Well, it's been a pleasure. Good luck with the article." He gave them a wave as he followed the woman toward a counter at the side of the store.

Angus leaned forward and read the card next to where the painting had hung. "Three hundred dollars. What a nice father."

"I think he bought it to get out of talking to us," Suki said.

At two o'clock, Angus decided they should go back to Doreene's house. "She might not give us the push if Max is there, and I want to see his reaction after he gets a close look at the painting."

They walked back toward the mansion. When they were about a block away, a white car pulled up to the curb at the next intersection.

"Get over here behind this bush." Angus tugged at the straps on Suki's and Michael's bags. "Is that Enrico's car?"

Michael squinted through the leaves of a rhododendron bush. "It looks like it, but I'm not certain."

Suki unzipped her camera case and removed a telephoto lens.

Angus reached out a hand for it.

"Just a sec. This isn't a telescope, you know." She attached the lens to the camera, powered it on, and looked through it. "Oh, I don't *believe* this."

"What?" Angus reached for the camera.

"You break it, you bought it," Suki said, handing it to him.

Michael, staring through the bush, made spitting noises as he got rid of a gnat that had flown into his mouth. "That's Reynaldo getting out of the car."

Angus stared through the camera at the interior of the car. "I'm only getting a silhouette of the driver," he murmured. The car drove out of sight and he lowered the camera, then looked at it regretfully. "I should have taken a picture."

Suki took it back from him. "That'll teach you to be so grabby."

"C'mon." Angus walked quickly back to the sidewalk. "In journalism, timing is everything."

Michael followed him. "I've always heard that credibility is everything."

"Don't be ridiculous."

"Hold on!" Suki hung the camera around her neck, then picked up her bag and ran to catch up with the other two. "Ow. You know, a really big camera doesn't feel good smacking against your ribs."

"Help her out, Michael." Angus began to jog toward Doreene's house.

Michael took Suki's bag, and they trotted after him.

Ahead, Reynaldo walked with his hands in his pockets, head slightly bowed.

When they were perhaps fifty feet behind him, Angus slowed to a walk, panting. "Somebody get his attention," he gasped.

"Hey, Reynaldo!" Suki yelled.

Reynaldo turned and waited. When they had caught up with him, he gave Angus a look of concern. "Are you well?"

"Fine." Angus put a hand to his ribs and massaged them. "We saw you getting out of Enrico's car. Did you work out your differences?"

Reynaldo looked at his feet. "Um, yes."

"That's good, since Enrico seems to be an old friend of Maureene's. He's Lyndsay's father, isn't he?"

Reynaldo turned and walked away. "Leave me alone. I don't have to answer your questions."

Suki trotted to get beside him, holding her camera with one hand to keep it from bouncing. "Listen, Reynaldo. We're the only people who don't have a stake in how any of this turns out. We want to know what happens, obviously, but we don't care who it happens to."

Reynaldo shot her a glance. "Is that supposed to make me want to talk to you?"

Suki looked at Angus and Michael. "Would one of you word guys help me out here?"

Michael spoke first. "Reynaldo, if you need help, just ask."

"Really?" Reynaldo stopped suddenly. They were at the curb. Across the street, Doreene's house loomed beneath a gray sky. He turned to Michael. "If I wanted to go home, would you buy me a plane ticket to Brazil? Is that the kind of help you mean?" Reynaldo watched as Michael opened and closed his mouth. "No? I didn't think so." He stepped off the curb and crossed the street.

"Wait!" Angus called. "Maybe we can—"

Reynaldo lifted a hand without turning around. "Don't worry. Everything is fine." He jogged the rest of the way to the house and went inside.

Angus looked at his watch. "It's twenty-five past two."

As he spoke, a silver Volvo passed them, crossed the intersection, and parked in front of Doreene's house. Max Thorne got out and waved at them before going up the walk.

"Let's go," Angus said, trotting across the street.

Lupita opened the door for Max as they reached the porch. Max gave the *Tripping* crew a polite smile as they followed him inside.

"Miss Doreene says to go on up," Lupita said to Max. She turned in the direction of the kitchen.

Angus touched her arm and whispered, "Is Reynaldo upstairs with her?"

Lupita shook her head. "He's in the kitchen, getting a drink."

"Double shot of vodka?" Suki asked.

Lupita smiled faintly. "Excuse me, I have to cook dinner." She left.

Angus started up the stairs. "Guess we'll go see what's happening."

"Good idea," Suki said. "Let's go beard the loony in her den."

They heard a chuckle from the top of the stairs and looked up to see Max's back as he disappeared down the hallway.

When they reached the second floor, Doreene's door stood open, and she could be heard chatting to Max.

Angus strolled toward the sound. "She sounds happy enough," he murmured.

"Are we going to just walk in?" Michael whispered.

At the sound of footsteps on the stairway, they turned toward the end of the hall.

Maureene came toward them, Reynaldo behind her. Maureene's skin was the color of putty, and the skin under her eyes had drooped into bags. She leaned over and murmured something to Reynaldo. His expression, already haunted, grew more anxious.

Maureene stopped when she reached Angus. "Is Max in there with her?"

"I believe so."

"Anyone else?"

"Not that I know of."

She nodded briefly and walked on, Reynaldo at her side. They disappeared into Doreene's room.

"Once more unto the breach," Angus said, following.

When they reached Doreene's bedroom, Angus knocked very quietly on the frame. Suki and Michael looked over his shoulders.

Inside, Doreene stood with her arms wrapped around Reynaldo and her face pressed to his chest. Gigi stood at their feet, looking up.

Doreene pulled away enough to look up at Reynaldo. "I'm sorry I yelled at you, Rey. You're absolutely right about that painting, it's making me crazy. I know I'll feel better when it's gone. Can you forgive me?" Her lower lip pouted prettily.

He kissed her. "Of course, *cara*."

Maureene headed toward the closet door, which stood open.

Doreene pulled away from Reynaldo and darted in front of her sister. "Leave Max alone while he's working." Poking her head inside the closet, she said, "I'm closing this so you won't have any interruptions,

Max. Just knock when you're done." She closed the door and turned back to her sister. "Sit down and relax, Maureene." Doreene looked at the bed, which was covered with piles of sorted clothes, including a fur coat and a satin ball gown. "Or just stand. He won't be long."

Maureene shook her head, the wrinkles on either side of her mouth deepening. "Why are you doing this?"

Doreene laughed gaily. "Because it's my painting. You gave it to me, remember?"

Reynaldo spoke. "Doreene, I have something to ask you."

"What is it, sweetie?" Doreene went to him and wrapped her hands around his bicep.

"As your husband, I am asking you to get rid of that painting," he said solemnly.

Doreene smiled more brightly. "I *am* getting rid of it. That's why the nice man is in there, measuring away."

Reynaldo gathered her hands in his. "It needs to be burned, *cara.* Until it is, I'm afraid you won't be free."

Doreene's smile tightened. "No one's free, angel. You should know that better than anyone." She looked past him and seemed to notice Angus and the others for the first time. "Have you found out who's responsible for the slugs or the soup? No? Then I think you'd better leave."

"We won't be able to find a motel," Michael said, "with everyone in town for the boat festival."

Doreene tossed her head irritably. "I suppose you can stay tonight, but I want you gone tomorrow—in the morning."

A knock came from inside the closet. Doreene went over, slid the lock plate aside, and punched a code on the keypad beneath.

Max came out, rolling a fabric tape measure around one hand. "All done." He saw Maureene. "I commend you for using a standard canvas size, Maureene. It makes shipping that much easier."

Maureene's face seemed even grayer. "When is it leaving?"

"Rothwell's will overnight a shipping case to me. I'll pack the painting and send it off the next day. So . . . day after tomorrow." He looked at the piles of clothes on the bed. "Going on another trip, Doreene?"

"Just cleaning house. See anything your daughter might like?"

He chuckled. "I've given up trying to figure out her tastes. My intern would go crazy over that fur coat, though. She's into vintage glamour."

Doreene looped her arms under the folded coat and offered it to him. "Take it. I get dirty looks every time I wear it in Port Townsend."

Max raised a hand in protest. "Oh, I wasn't seriously suggesting . . . Anyway, your sister should have first dibs on something that nice." He turned to Maureene.

She shook her head. "I don't want the damn thing."

"Take it, Max," Doreene said. "You'll save me having to find someone who'll actually wear it."

"If you're sure." He took it from her. "You've made a poor little New York girl very happy." He leaned over the bundled coat and kissed her cheek, then turned. "Maureene, can I take you out to dinner? I'd love to run some catalog copy by you."

Maureene left the room without a word.

Max grimaced slightly. "Artistic temperament. All the great ones have it." He nodded at Reynaldo and the others. "I'd shake hands, but they're full of fur. Take care, everyone." He left.

Reynaldo turned back to Doreene. "*Cara,* I'm telling you, there is still time."

Doreene gave him a sultry smile. "Before dinner? You bet there is." She looked at Angus and the others. "Close the door on your way out."

Michael and Suki followed Angus back to his room.

Angus shut the door and turned, shaking his head. "I'd love to know what's going on with that painting. Is it voodoo? Demonic possession?" He sat on the edge of his bed.

"Blackmail?" Michael suggested. "Hidden microchips? Some Old Master stolen by the Nazis that Maureene painted over?" He slouched in an armchair and straightened his long legs. "Doreene is certainly good at spin. I love the way she said, 'Sorry I yelled at you' instead of 'Sorry I smacked you hard across the chops.' "

"Maybe she's not sorry about that part," Suki said. She poked through Angus's plastic bag of toiletries, which sat on his nightstand. "Don't you use sunscreen?"

"I'm too old for sunscreen."

"No one is too old for sunscreen."

Angus ignored her. "It might pay for us to keep in touch with Reynaldo. If he and Doreene split up, he might feel the urge to tell his side of the story. We can at least give him our phone numbers and offer him a place to stay."

Suki raised a hand. "Dibs."

"What are we going to do now that Doreene is kicking us out?" Michael asked. "Try to find a motel tomorrow or just go home?"

Angus ran a hand through his hair. "I'll call some motels and see if we can find something reasonably close for tomorrow night. In case we can't, tonight would be a good time to look at Fort Worden. I found a few people online who said the old gun batteries are haunted."

"And if you have your way, a lot more people will think that after reading our article." Michael put his hands behind his head. "Don't you ever get tired of being a fright monger?"

"On the contrary," Angus said. "I'm providing a public service. Humans crave a certain amount of danger in their lives. If we don't give them a few harmless shivers, they'll risk their lives jumping out of planes or driving too fast."

Suki looked at Michael and raised her brows.

"What?" Michael said.

"No rebuttal?"

"Actually, there is evidence that humans thrive on a certain amount of fear. Although you'd think that paying attention to world affairs would do the trick."

Angus smiled and shook his head. "Oh, Michael. Where's the fun in that?"

Fourteen

The staff of *Tripping* drove to Fort Worden State Park, about ten minutes away.

"So what's the deal with this place?" Suki asked as she navigated the minivan past tidy houses and green, green grass.

Angus consulted a book in his lap. "This fort, as well as Fort Flagler and Fort Casey, was constructed to protect Puget Sound from attack by sea. Together, they were called the Triangle of Fire. Construction on Fort Worden began in 1897, and it was decommissioned in 1953." He flipped some pages. "The army built it, and the government created the coast artillery to man it. That branch of the military doesn't exist anymore."

"Did the fort see any action?" Michael asked.

"No. Soon after it was built, the navy began mounting big guns on ships, and the fort was rendered obsolete from a defensive standpoint. But I'm sure lots of valuable training took place here, and they built a balloon hangar when the military started experimenting with air reconnaissance and attack."

Suki drove through the main gates and past a rhododendron garden, its blooms a riot of color. "Pretty."

In the backseat, Michael gazed out the window as they passed rolling lawns and well-kept frame buildings. "Are those the barracks? Those look like pretty nice houses. Where's the corrugated metal?" He scooted across the seat and looked out the other side. "I don't know, Angus. A place this pleasant doesn't seem like fertile ground for ghosts."

Angus waved his book. "After the government sold the fort property, but before it became a state park, it was a facility for troubled youth."

"Ah." Michael nodded. "Now we're talking."

The car reached an intersection. On the other side of the road, a beach flanked the slate-blue water. Long, sere grass waved in a steady wind.

"That's Admiralty Inlet ahead of us," Angus said. "Take a left here. We'll do a loop before we go to the gun battery."

They passed a weathered wood building with a dock, labeled the Port Townsend Marine Science Center. Boats bobbed in the water next to it.

"RV park," Suki said as she drove past an army of campers on the left. Adults sat at picnic tables while children and dogs ran around.

Angus waved at an adorable little girl as they passed. She lifted a tentative hand. "It's a well-used facility. They rent out the barracks and officers' quarters as well."

The coast curved to the right, and they left the campers behind.

"Hey, a lighthouse!" Suki said. "With a whole house attached to it."

Angus nodded. "The Point Wilson Lighthouse was built in 1913, and is the tallest on Puget Sound. As with all the best lighthouses, it's reputed to be haunted."

Michael looked thoughtful. "I'd probably drink a lot if I lived all alone with nothing to watch but sinking ships. You sure it wasn't the booze making them see things?"

"Ships aren't supposed to sink when there's a lighthouse," Suki said. "That's the whole point."

"And the lighthouse keepers weren't alone," Angus added. "They had families, which is why that nice house is attached to the place. Of course, it's all automated now, so no one lives there. They have tours, but I think it's past time."

As they got closer, they saw a fenced yard around the house. A swing set stood in the dry grass, its chains twisting slightly in the wind.

Suki pulled over. "We're losing light, but I should be able to get something with a tripod."

They got out of the car and stood, zipping jackets and hunching their shoulders. The temperature wasn't that cold, but a damp wind blew. Suki went to the back of the minivan and rummaged for equipment.

"You said the lighthouse is haunted?" Michael prompted Angus.

Angus put his hands in his jacket pockets and rocked on his feet. "A wandering woman in white. It was the wives of the lighthouse keepers who mostly saw her. They thought it might be a woman whose daughter was lost in one of the many shipwrecks in this area."

"So why doesn't the woman haunt the wreck?" Michael asked. "Do ghosts need an audience? Someplace to sit down, maybe—take a break from all that moaning and chain rattling?"

Angus gave him a sour look. "People have also heard the sound of someone rummaging through the bathroom cabinets, even though no one else was in the house."

"I'd be looking for Valium if I had to spend my afterlife out here on the edge of nothing." Michael blew on his hands.

"It wasn't just the bathroom," Angus said. "Some wives also saw a woman's shadow and heard a female voice in the keeper's quarters."

Michael gave a bark of laughter. "I can hear Mr. Lighthouse Keeper, as he's frantically buttoning his trousers. 'Woman's voice? What woman's voice? Must have been a ghost, honey!' "

Suki came around the back of the van with a camera mounted on a tripod. "Anything in particular you want me to get, Angus?"

"Anything that looks good. And afterward, how about some video for the Web site? Michael can stand in the foreground and talk very convincingly about ghosts."

"Aw, come on," Michael protested.

Angus straightened the collar of Michael's coat. "And make it good."

After taking photos and video, Suki and the others got back in the minivan.

"Where to next?" Suki asked.

Angus studied his map. "The road loops around. We'll park in the lot next to the RVs and walk to Battery Kinzie. There are about a dozen gun batteries, but Kinzie looks like the most accessible. Some of them are hidden in the forest above the bluffs."

Suki steered the minivan along a road that curved through the dunes before heading back the way they had come. The light had dimmed considerably, and the wind had picked up.

"Turn right here," Angus said as they approached a parking lot.

Suki parked on the cracked concrete, and they got out.

Before them, a path led up a sandy rise. The bluffs to the east were thickly covered with trees, but here, only a few towering fir trees stood silhouetted against the gray sky. Their sparse crowns looked like tattered umbrellas, torn by the wind.

Black birds, crows or ravens, called harshly from the treetops, jumping from branch to branch as the pecking order dictated.

Suki stood with her hands on her hips. "This is some photogenic shit."

From somewhere behind them, a woman's voice called, "Dinner!"

"Coming, Mom!" Two children of about ten appeared over the rise and ran down the sand toward the RVs. "Hi," they said breathlessly as they passed Angus and the others.

"Nice kids," Angus said. "Suki, why don't you take whatever pictures you want here, and then meet us at the battery. You can see the top of it over that hill."

Angus and Michael climbed the short slope that led to a plateau dotted with scrubby grass. Battery Kinzie stretched in front of them—two wide stories of gray concrete with square pillars on the bottom and staircases crisscrossing the front.

"Are there supposed to be ghosts in here?" Michael asked as they approached it.

"Why do you care, Mr. Skeptic?" Angus asked grumpily.

"I may not believe in ghosts, but I'm still interested as to why most cultures have some level of belief in them."

"There's a catchy title for an article. Try selling that."

They stepped onto a walkway that ran along the front of the building, their footsteps suddenly loud on the concrete. In the front wall, a massive iron door stood slightly open, its surface traced with orange rust.

Angus grasped the vaultlike handle and pulled on it. It swung open with a grating, metallic moan. "Hollywood sound engineers probably come here to record that." He stepped into the relative darkness beyond. "Empty."

Michael followed him into the dimly lit space and pointed at the low ceiling. "Look—iron tracks, set into the concrete. They hung something from the ceiling and moved it around by track."

"Ammunition, probably. The biggest guns could fire a thousand-pound shell ten miles."

"Holy crap!"

"That's the magic of gunpowder. Wonder what that doorway leads to." Angus turned and took a brisk step, only to smack his head on the cement archway. "Mother of . . . !" he said, holding both hands to his forehead.

"Are you okay?"

"F . . ." Angus sputtered, bending over.

"You can cuss in front of me. I'm not five."

"Could you . . . Just shut up, will you?" Angus said, his voice squeaky with pain.

A metallic squeal came from the front of the room.

Michael turned. "Suki?"

The heavy iron door slammed shut with a clang, plunging them into darkness. A rasping thump indicated that the latch had been lowered.

Angus raised his voice to a yell. "Very funny! Now let us out!"

"Hold on," Michael said. "I have an app for this." There was a rustle of clothing, and then the slightly blue illumination of Michael's phone came on, followed by a blinding white light.

"You could have warned me," Angus said, shielding his eyes. "I was looking right at it."

"Pretty bright, huh? It turns on the LED for the camera flash. Do you want me to call Suki?"

"Not yet." Angus ducked beneath the arch on which he had hit his head. "This is just another room, but without a door."

"There has to be a way out," Michael said, following, "doesn't there? Otherwise, kids would be locking each other in all the time. Don't you think it was probably a kid who shut us in?"

"That, or a ghost. Excuse me—*some level of belief common to most cultures.*" Angus looked around the room, then pointed toward an aperture in the back wall. It was the height of a door, but much narrower. "Maybe we can get out through that."

They walked to the back of the room, the light casting sharp shadows.

Michael stuck his phone through the doorway and peered into the space beyond. "Some kind of passageway. It's only about two feet wide, and the floor is wet. If I were writing this, I'd have a big hatch at the end, and when we opened it, the ocean would rush in."

"We should be quite a bit above the ocean. Give me that thing."

Angus took the phone and stepped inside, his shoulders almost brushing the walls. He moved forward slowly, pointing the light at the floor.

The stagnant water deepened until a quarter inch rippled around their feet. Angus gave a sudden kick and dislodged something sodden from the toe of his shoe. "Candy wrapper." He sighed in relief.

"In Boulder, it'd be condoms and rolling papers," Michael said. "The kids here must be really wholesome."

"Aye, it's like frickin' Brigadoon." Angus pointed the light to the right. "We've reached a corner." He covered the phone's screen with his hand for a moment. "It's brighter up ahead."

The floor became drier as they progressed. Another ten feet, and they emerged into a large room. Trees were visible through the doorless arch in the front.

"Thank goodness," Angus said, handing the phone back to Michael.

Outside, they heard voices from somewhere on the second level. Angus cupped his hands around his mouth and shouted, "Suki?"

"Up here!"

They climbed the stairs that led to the top. The second-floor walkway was a twin to the one on the ground below, with more empty rooms along it.

"Where the hell are you?" Angus yelled.

"Over here!" Suki called.

They backtracked, and the space suddenly opened into a large rooftop area indented by what looked like a small, shallow amphitheater. Five steps led down to a semicircle backed by a wall. A beach lay on the other side, and beyond it, water.

Suki stood at the wall, next to Maxwell Thorne. She waved when they came into view, then turned back to her camera.

Maxwell walked to join them, then gestured to the view. "You're looking out at the Strait of Juan de Fuca."

"Did you shut us in?" Angus demanded.

Maxwell grinned mischievously. "I thought it would be a thrill for you, since you're ghost hunters."

"We're journalists," Angus said, "and I smacked the hell out of my head thanks to your little stunt."

Maxwell's expression sobered. "I'm so sorry."

"Actually, he smacked his head bef—" Michael began.

"Apology accepted," Angus interrupted loudly. He looked around. "Nice view. I wonder what that semicircular hollow was for."

"That was where one of the big guns sat," Maxwell said. "The barrel measured a foot across, and each shot required almost three hundred pounds of powder."

"Cool." Suki joined them, carrying her tripod. "How'd you guys get out?"

"Through a narrow little tunnel," Michael said.

"Those passageways run throughout the battery," Maxwell said. "They provide ventilation, but they also buffered the rooms from the tremendous shock of the guns firing."

"What brings you here, Mr. Thorne?"

"I'm staying on the grounds." Maxwell pointed toward the main body of the park. "I don't know if you noticed a brick tower with a crenellated top."

"Alexander's Castle," Angus said. "It predates the fort and was built by the Reverend John Alexander in 1883, supposedly for his prospective bride. Unfortunately, by the time he finished it and went to Scotland to get her, she'd married someone else."

"Probably got tired of waiting for the kitchen counters to be delivered," Suki said.

Maxwell chuckled. "It was the only lodging I could get with the boat festival in town, and that was a cancellation. But Fort Worden runs a hostel in a neighboring building. I moved from the castle to the hostel today."

"Decided to save your company a bit of cash?" Angus asked.

Maxwell's lip quirked in an amused smile. "No. Rothwell's expense account is quite liberal, and the company expects me to make my success clear. It's more a matter of being bored, staying by myself. When I walked by the hostel last night, I could hear people laughing and singing inside. They have a piano, and I play reasonably well."

"Won't you feel a little out of place?" Michael asked. "You're not exactly a college student on a budget."

Maxwell smiled at him. "Isn't that what traveling is all about—being out of place?" He looked at his watch. "And now, I have to excuse myself. I offered to pick up some steak for the communal stir-fry. Have a good evening, and give my best to Doreene."

Maxwell left, and the others walked back to the view of the water.

"What a smarmy jerk." Michael leaned on the concrete wall. "Off he goes to grace the little people with his steak and piano playing."

Angus chortled. "What's the matter, Michael? Been out-condescended?"

Suki looked through her viewfinder. "Maybe he's trolling for someone young to visit the bicycle shed with."

Michael leaned forward and looked across Angus toward Suki. "Out of curiosity, how much of your time do you spend thinking about and or participating in sex? Just ballpark."

She looked at the sky thoughtfully. "Thirty percent?"

"You know, some people might consider that an addiction."

"It's not much when you compare it to the amount of time you spend trying to be better than everyone. And unlike your hobby, mine is enjoyable for other people." She pointed at the water. "Hey, look—seals."

Fifteen

They ate dinner at the boat festival's food kiosks, then sat under the music tent and listened to several bands.

By the time they returned to Doreene's house, it was eight-thirty. Lupita met them at the door.

"All quiet on the western front?" Angus asked. "Doreene and Reynaldo still getting along?"

Lupita shut the door behind them. "Miss Doreene had me pack all your things for leaving tomorrow." She dropped her voice to a whisper. "I'm sorry."

"Quite all right," Angus said. "We appreciate everything you've done for us."

She nodded and headed in the direction of the kitchen.

"I feel like we should tip her," Michael said quietly as he and Suki followed Angus up the stairs to their bedrooms. "Is that something you do?"

"Possibly," Angus said. "I'll call Len and ask if that's all right with him." Len Pendergast was the orthodontist who financed *Tripping.* "After all, we did save hotel expenses. We should check in with him anyway, to see if he wants us to stay on."

They followed him to his room, and Suki shut the door. She and Michael took the two chairs, while Angus sat on the edge of the bed.

Angus put his cell phone on speaker and dialed.

Len answered on the second ring, his New Jersey accent prominent despite years of living in Colorado. "Angus! What's going on with the creepy painting? Has Doreene with an *E* thrown any orgies or murdered anyone?"

"Not that I know of," Angus said, "but while we've been here, she's had cryptic messages in the soup, a plague of slugs in her bedroom, and we found out she's secretly married to her young Brazilian lover."

"Way to bring it, big guy!"

"Also, the housekeeper says she saw skeletons in the woods."

"Skeletons is *your* word," Michael corrected. "Lupita said 'spirits of the dead.' "

"And then she went on to say 'glowing bones,' " Angus shot back. "That sounds like skeletons to me."

Len's barking laugh came over the speaker. "Keeping him honest, Michael? Don't make a habit of it."

Angus went on. "Len, the painting is leaving town tomorrow, and Doreene is kicking us out of the house."

"You haven't done anything actionable, have you?" Len asked, his tone suddenly serious.

"No, no. It's just that we saw her smack the hell out of her husband, and I guess she's embarrassed about it."

"He ought to sue. What's the artist sister say about everything?"

Angus grimaced. "Very little. We've tried to interview Maureene Pinter several times, but haven't been able to get anything out of her."

"Tortured artist. Unable to speak of her pain," Len said.

Michael took out his pocket notebook and made a note.

Angus continued. "Our flight back isn't until day after tomorrow. The problem is, we may not be able to find a motel. Do you want us to come back a day early?"

Michael leaned toward the phone. "And can we tip Doreene's housekeeper?"

There was a pause. "Yeah, give her twenty bucks and submit it on your expenses," Len said. "Angus, it sounds like you have enough material. Drive to Seattle tomorrow and see if you can fly standby. If you can't, find a cheap place to stay and go on a ghost tour or something. I gotta go. I'm bidding on a marble fireplace mantle, supposed to be haunted. Haunted or not, I can at least set my friggin' drink down without a coaster."

"Marble's heavy," Angus said. "Make sure you check the shipping cost."

"What am I, twelve? Bye."

Angus disconnected. "Looks like we leave Port Townsend tomorrow."

"What time?" Suki asked. "Doreene said she wanted us out in the morning."

"Officially, that's any time before noon," Angus said. "We'll leave when we feel like it. I wouldn't mind a photo of the painting being taken out of the house in its special box. There's something very mysterious about a crate. Anything could be in there."

He glanced at his watch. "It's nine o'clock. That's a bit late to get anything significant done."

"We didn't look at the Fort Worden cemetery," Suki pointed out. "Flash photos of tombstones at night can be cool."

Angus considered a moment. "I don't think the stones are very interesting—just those military markers." He rubbed his jaw and sighed. "I suppose we could try to get an interview with Maureene one last time."

Michael groaned.

"I know it's not an inspiring thought." Angus got to his feet. "Still, I won't feel right if we don't make one last attempt."

Outside, the air was moist and chilly. Very little light reached the path beneath the overhanging trees. Michael took out his phone and used the LED to light their way.

Suki tucked her tripod under one arm and pulled her beret down over her ears. "Maybe I shouldn't come. It could be the camera that's putting her off."

"She signed the photo release without any fuss," Michael said. "Let's ask what kind of brushes and paints she likes. Most artists can't shut up about that. Then, when she's feeling talkative, we slip in an actual question."

At the end of the path, only one of the cottage's windows had a light behind the curtains. The subdued glow lit the last few yards of the path. Michael switched off his phone light.

Angus knocked on the front door. After a moment, the light inside the cottage shut off, leaving them in darkness.

"Oh, *come on,*" Michael muttered, taking his phone back out.

Angus knocked louder, then raised his voice and said, "Ms. Pinter, I realize it's late, but we found a hat on the sidewalk by the house. Can you tell us if it's yours?" He snapped his fingers at Suki and held out a hand.

She reluctantly pulled off her beret and gave it to him. "She better not claim this is hers," she whispered. "I stole it from a performance artist at the Prague Fringe Festival."

"You *stole* it?" Michael whispered.

"That was part of the performance."

The porch light came on, and the door opened a foot.

Maureene peered out, holding her flannel robe closed at the neck. "You got me out of bed. What's this about a hat?"

Angus held up the beret. "Is this yours?"

She took it from his hand and turned it over. "No, but it might belong to Lyndsay."

"Lyndsay?" Angus asked.

"My daughter. She flew in from London for a visit." Maureene started to close the door. "Thanks."

"Wait!" Suki said.

Maureene turned. "What?"

"It's just that . . . If that isn't Lyndsay's beret, I'd like to have it."

"If it's not hers, you can have it tomorrow," Maureene said.

"But we're *leaving* tomorrow," Suki said. "Can't you ask her now?"

"She's asleep. I'm not going to wake her for this. Good night." Maureene stepped back and shut the door.

Suki gave Angus a fulminating look.

The porch light shut off, leaving them in darkness.

"Be snappy with that phone light, Michael," Angus said. "I'm expecting to feel a tripod between the ribs."

Michael switched on the LED.

Suki stood glaring at Angus from a distance of six inches. "You gave away my beret."

"It was for a good cause." Angus started down the path.

Suki paced beside him, staring fixedly at his profile. "He's famous now, that performance artist."

"Did he sign the beret?" Angus asked.

"No."

"Then I'll get you another and no one will know the difference."

"*I'll* know."

Angus shoved his hands in the pockets of his jacket and walked faster. "How was I supposed to know Maureene's daughter had come for a visit?"

Michael caught up to Angus on the other side. "Hey, do you think Maureene asked Lyndsay to come and put pressure on Doreene?"

Angus shrugged. "From the story Lupita told about Lyndsay's wedding, it doesn't sound as though Doreene is particularly influenced by her niece, or even kind to her."

Beside him, Suki muttered, "If Lyndsay keeps that beret, Doreene is going to look like a freakin' fairy godmother compared to me."

They went back to the house.

. . .

Angus made calls, but was unable to find a vacant motel room within twenty miles. The staff of *Tripping* magazine retired to their bedrooms with the intention of leaving sometime the next day.

Angus brushed his teeth and stripped down to his reading glasses, then got into bed with his pocket notebook and jotted down stray thoughts. The portrait kept Doreene looking young. What would happen when it changed hands?

He drew a little skeleton on the edge of the page.

What if the portrait's youth-giving properties required some kind of sacrifice? Had Maureene already started painting it when her stepfather drowned? Doreene's husband had died falling off a cliff, and now Doreene herself was experiencing stabbing pains.

Angus doodled a little knife between the skeleton's ribs.

Had anyone actually *seen* Maureene paint the portrait? Perhaps it was a demonic family heirloom, hundreds of years old, that took on the appearance of family members. He gave a little hum of pleasure as he wrote.

In the bathroom down the hall, Michael thought about titles for the story, but of course they would call it *Picture* (or *Portrait*) *of Doreene Gray*. He spat toothpaste into the sink and drank out of his hand to rinse his mouth.

It seemed likely that Maureene had put the slugs in Doreene's room, given the ladder he had found, but one thing puzzled him: Doreene hadn't for a moment thought there was something supernatural going on. Surely Maureene would know that about her twin, so why bother with the pretense? Was all this fear and antagonism a ruse? Could the sisters be collaborating on stunts to drive up the price of the portrait?

Suki sat at the small desk next to her bed, transferring the latest photos from camera to laptop. As the files copied, she perused the shots she'd taken of Enrico Russo. Why did he look so familiar?

She brought up one of the photos of Reynaldo she had taken, most of them surreptitiously. Was there a slight resemblance between the two men? Suki chortled at the thought that Reynaldo could be Enrico's son. That would be *awesome.*

What if Doreene and Enrico were lovers first, but Maureene had lured him away and become pregnant with Lyndsay? Thinking of Lyndsay reminded Suki of her absent beret, and she glowered in the direction of Angus's room.

Angus woke to the sound of rain lashing against the house. He got up and looked out the nearest window. A strong wind blew, making wet, black branches dance crazily in front of the streetlights. Angus used the edge of the curtain to rub the fog of his breath from the glass. Was that a white Impala parked across the street? The rain streaming down the window made it impossible to tell.

Angus walked carefully back to his bed in the dark, stubbing his toe on the furniture only once, and peered at the red numbers on the clock radio next to his bed. It was a little after two A.M.

He went back to the window. The white car had gone. Angus leaned on the sill and chewed his lip. The thought of going outside in the wind and rain did not appeal, especially to look for a car that wasn't there anymore.

He found his boxers and pants and pulled them on, then went to his bedroom door and opened it a crack. The hallway was dark and quiet, except for a strip of light beneath Doreene's door.

Angus tiptoed across the cool wooden floor and carefully put his ear against the door, but heard nothing. After perhaps three minutes of listening, his adrenaline waned, leaving him tired and cold. For all he knew, Doreene always slept with a light on.

He tiptoed back to his bedroom, hugging his bare torso.

Sixteen

Angus was up and dressed by seven-thirty the next morning. At a quarter to eight, someone tapped on his door. He opened it.

Suki stood there, a symphony in black from her boots to the long-sleeved shirt that hung off one shoulder. A ragged strip of acid-green silk wrapped one wrist. She glared at Angus. "I want my beret."

"I understand that, believe me," he said. "We might have better luck if we wait an hour to roust Maureene."

"Half an hour," Suki countered.

"Lyndsay may still be asleep. I'm sure she has jet lag."

Suki stared at him.

"And after all, we haven't eaten breakfast yet."

Suki stared at him.

"I had a terrier who gave me that same look at the dinner table," Angus said. "It didn't work then and it won't work now."

Down the hall, Michael's door opened. "What's going on?" he asked, joining them.

"I want my beret," Suki said.

Angus rolled his eyes. "She's a wee bit possessive about her things."

"Remind me never to borrow a pen from you," Michael said. "Are we going to Maureene's cottage?"

"In a *bit.*" Angus led the way downstairs. "I want to talk to Lupita one more time. She gave us our best quote."

Down in the foyer, Gigi came running up to meet them, then raced over to the front door and jumped against it, looking back over her shoulder.

"It's a miracle that dog doesn't pee in the house," Suki said. "Give me a minute to let her out." She looked around the foyer. "Why is there no leash for this dog? Honestly, these people." She unfastened a studded belt from around her waist, slipped it free, and looped it through Gigi's collar. They went outside.

Michael took out his phone and checked *Tripping*'s e-mail. "Pendergast says he has our next story lined up. Reports of a feral pig in Florida's Ocala National Forest."

"Hmm," Angus said noncommittally. "I'm not a huge fan of pigs."

Michael read a little more. "Sorry, a giant prehistoric pig with huge tusks."

Angus brightened. "Might be something in that."

Suki returned and took the makeshift leash from Gigi's collar. "I wish that belt were longer. I had to stand right over her."

Freed, Gigi ran back upstairs.

They found Lupita in the kitchen, stirring something in a pot. She looked up as they came in. "Do you want some oatmeal? Miss Doreene says it is healthy."

"That it is," Angus said. "Are you sure there's enough to feed us?"

"Oh, yes. Miss Doreene told me to make it last night, but she must have gone out for breakfast." She opened a cabinet and stood on tiptoe to get some bowls.

Michael stepped forward. "Can I help you with that?"

"I'm fine," Lupita said, bowls already in her hands.

Angus watched as she ladled oatmeal. "That was quite a storm last night. Doreene's door had a light on under it, so maybe it woke her up, too. Do you know if she sleeps with a light on?"

Lupita shrugged. "I go to bed before her, and once I go upstairs, I stay there." She opened the refrigerator and took out a butter dish. "We have raisins and brown sugar. Do you want milk also?"

"Please," Angus said.

"Go ahead and sit at the table," Lupita said. "I'll bring everything in."

They went into the conservatory, where a watery sun came through the windows. The table was set with place mats and cutlery for two.

Lupita came in with the oatmeal and condiments on a large tray. She set it on the table and opened a drawer in the sideboard, from which she took another place setting, as well as cloth napkins.

"Did you know that Maureene's daughter is at the cottage?" Angus asked, taking a bowl of oatmeal. "Apparently she arrived yesterday."

Lupita looked surprised. "No one told me to expect her."

"And then there's Maureene's male friend," Angus went on. "Enrico Russo. They seem very close. Do you know if he's Lyndsay's father?"

Lupita shook her head and handed Suki a napkin. "No one knows who Lyndsay's father is."

"Well, presumably Maureene does," Michael said.

Suki reached for the dish of raisins. "Not necessarily."

Reynaldo came in, almost running into Lupita as she went out. "Has anyone seen Doreene this morning?"

Everyone shook their heads amid a chorus of "no"s.

Reynaldo rested his hand on the back of a chair and rubbed the wood absently with his thumb. "She was not in bed when I woke up, and her car is here."

"Perhaps she's with Maureene," Angus suggested. "Apparently Lyndsay arrived for a visit yesterday."

"Who is Lyndsay?" Reynaldo asked.

"Maureene's daughter," Michael said. "Didn't Doreene ever mention her?"

Reynaldo nodded slightly. "Oh, yes. I just forgot the name. I will call Maureene and ask if Doreene is there." He left.

"That's interesting," Angus said.

Suki swallowed a bite of oatmeal and looked up. "Is it?"

Angus glanced at the empty door and dropped his voice. "It was two in the morning when the storm woke me up. There was a white car parked across the street, and now Doreene is missing."

"You think it was Enrico's Impala?" Michael asked.

"I couldn't tell for sure with all that rain."

"Why didn't you wake me up? We could have gone out and checked."

"I went to look at the clock, and when I came back, the car was gone," Angus said.

Michael looked skeptical. "Are you sure it wasn't a dream?"

"Very sure. I stood outside Doreene's door for several minutes, listening. It was cold, and boring, and I was very much awake." At the sound of footsteps, Angus straightened and spoke normally. "And that's why I don't camp in the Himalayas anymore."

Reynaldo came back in, worrying his lower lip between his teeth. "No one has seen Doreene."

Maureene came in through the side door ten minutes later, with Hilda on a leash. She unclipped it, and Hilda ran into the kitchen. "Has anyone called Max?" Maureene took off her water-spotted canvas jacket and hung it over the back of an empty chair. "Maybe Doreene went out to breakfast with him and didn't tell anyone."

"I didn't know his number," Reynaldo said piteously. "I don't know anything in this place."

Maureene took out her cell phone. "Calm down, Reynaldo. Falling apart isn't going to help anything." She touched the screen of her phone a few times, then held it to her ear. "Max, is Doreene with you? Well, have you seen her this morning? For that matter, have you seen her any time since last night?" A pause. "No. I'm sure it's nothing, but we're a little worried. Right." She hung up. "He hasn't seen her today. Has anyone called Doreene's phone?"

Reynaldo shook his head, eyes glistening. "It is in the charger in our room."

Maureene absently tapped the phone against her palm. "I guess we should search the house."

"Can we help?" Angus asked.

Maureene frowned. "I suppose you can check the grounds."

Angus led the way outside. "Let's check around the house, and then we can make a quick search of the woods."

They fanned out slightly as they walked.

"I find it interesting that Maureene phoned Max and that was it," Angus said. "Does Doreene not have any other friends?"

"I get the impression Doreene spends most of her time away from Port Townsend," Michael said. "Her friends probably all live elsewhere."

Suki walked around a bush and rejoined them. "If she has any."

When they reached the back of the house, Angus pointed to the greenhouse. "Suki, take a look in there. Michael and I will check the shed."

While Suki headed for the greenhouse, Michael flipped the hasp on the shed's door and dragged it open, then turned and picked up a stick from the ground.

"Expecting to have to poke a corpse?" Angus asked.

"It's for the spiderwebs." Michael went inside, waving the stick before him. He shifted a stepladder, bags of potting soil, and miscellaneous tools aside until he reached the very back, then shone his light around.

Angus returned from inspecting the surrounding area and met Michael as he came out of the shed. "Nothing?"

"Nope," Michael said.

Suki joined them. "She's not in the greenhouse."

Angus crossed his arms and looked thoughtful. "We may be overlooking the obvious. What if she snuck out last night to meet Enrico?"

"And ran off with him?" Michael asked. "They didn't seem very friendly."

"But Maureene and Enrico *are,* and they both want the painting. What if Doreene got up early to let Gigi out—"

"Fat chance," Suki grunted.

"And Enrico and Maureene abducted Doreene so they could work on her in private."

Michael blew out a breath. "That seems a little over-the-top."

Angus held up a finger. "And yet, Doreene is missing. What do you say we search the area around Maureene's cottage—maybe even knock on the door and see who's really there? This Lyndsay thing might be a smokescreen to justify extra food and whatnot."

They went back to the front of the house, then took the lane to Maureene's cottage, making excursions into the woods as they went. The trees didn't extend very far before ending at the lawn of a neighboring property.

Once at the cottage, Angus tried to see in the front window, but the curtains were pulled. "I'm going to knock on the door," he whispered. "Suki, you go around the right side. Michael, you check the left. Maybe you can see something through the windows."

They nodded and split up, Suki walking casually, Michael sidling.

Angus knocked on the door and waited. No sound came from inside. He knocked again and tried the door, but it was locked. After waiting a little longer, he walked around the left side and found Michael.

"Anything?" Angus whispered.

Michael shook his head.

They found Suki on the other side, head cocked as she listened to something.

She pointed to the house. "Hear that? It's water running through the pipes. Somebody's taking a shower. What do you say I go inside and look around? Whoever it is won't even know I'm there, and I can get my beret while I'm at it."

Angus sighed. "Forget the damn beret, would you? It's not worth the risk. Anyway, the door's locked." He looked at his watch.

"Are we still planning on flying home today?" Michael asked.

"I don't know yet. Doreene's disappearance is definitely an interesting addition to the story." Angus put his hands in his jacket pockets. "Let's go back to the main house. If Doreene hasn't turned up, I say we have a word with Reynaldo. He can ask Maureene where Enrico is and demand that she prove Doreene isn't with him."

But when they neared the house, they saw the white Impala parked in front of it.

"I don't suppose there could be two white Impalas," Angus said drily.

Suki walked around the back and peered at the license plate. "That's his car."

They turned as a silver Volvo drove up, Maxwell Thorne behind the wheel.

He parked behind the Impala and got out, looking model-perfect in a pair of charcoal slacks and a burgundy cashmere sweater. "Have they found her yet?"

Angus shook his head. "We've been searching the grounds and are just now coming back."

"Let's go see if they've heard anything." Max started up the walk. "I'm sure it's nothing serious."

Angus followed him. "Of course, if she has disappeared, that can only drive up the price of the painting."

Max paused with one foot on the stair to the front door. He turned. "You think this is a publicity stunt?"

Angus shrugged. "It's been known to happen."

Inside, they found everyone in the kitchen. Maureene and Enrico leaned against the counter shoulder to shoulder, speaking in low voices.

Lupita stirred a pot of hot chocolate on the stove and murmured quietly to Reynaldo, whose eyes were pink-rimmed.

"Any word?" Max asked.

"Not yet," Maureene said. "We're wondering if Doreene went into the closet with the painting and fell asleep or passed out. She takes pretty powerful sleeping pills."

"I assume you've tried banging on the door," Max said.

Maureene nodded. "Doreene's lawyer has the code for the lock. We've called him, and he's on his way."

"Shouldn't you have an ambulance standing by?" Max asked.

Maureene looked at Enrico. "I didn't think of that. She might not even be in there." The doorbell rang, and she pushed herself away from the counter. "That must be him."

Reynaldo pushed Angus aside as he headed for the front of the house at a trot.

The others reached the foyer as Reynaldo shook hands with a short, trim man with mousy hair and a lively face.

He held an attaché case tucked under one arm. Wire-rimmed glasses magnified eyes that snapped with intelligence. "Mr. Cruz. I'm Harvey Baumgartner." He spotted Maureene. "Good to see you again, Ms. Pinter."

Reynaldo pulled him toward the stairs. "Please, you must hurry. Doreene may be sick, she may be hurt . . ." His voice broke.

"Of course. Lead the way." Baumgartner followed Reynaldo up the stairs, his highly polished shoes shining beneath the cuffs of his suit pants.

The others followed. Lupita brought up the rear, clutching the flap of her apron in both hands.

Inside the bedroom, Gigi raised her head from a padded bed in a corner of the room. She stood and shook herself, then turned around once and lay back down.

Baumgartner turned and spoke to everyone. "I have to ask you all to stand back so you don't see me enter the code. I don't have the authority to reset it."

They shuffled backward, bumping against each other, and watched as he took a piece of paper out of the attaché and consulted it, then held it in such a way as to block their view of the keypad.

Buttons beeped, followed by a substantial-sounding click. Baumgartner pushed the door. It opened about eight inches and then stopped, blocked by something. He peered around the edge. "Oh, no."

Reynaldo rushed forward. He pushed Baumgartner out of the way and looked inside. "Noooo!" he keened, falling to his knees so he could grope through the opening.

Startled, Gigi lifted her head, then ran out of the room as Reynaldo's wails increased.

Enrico joined Reynaldo at the closet's entrance. "Stop trying to pull her through. Push her to the side or we'll never get the door open." He shoved at Reynaldo's arm. "*That* way. Push her that way."

Maureene walked slowly up behind them, holding her clenched hands to her mouth and muttering, "Oh, my God. Oh, my God."

"I take it we should we call an ambulance?" Maxwell said.

"Yes, please," Baumgartner said, putting the paper with the code back in his attaché. He walked to Maureene and gripped her shoulder for a moment in a sympathetic gesture.

Enrico knelt by the closet, trying to help Reynaldo. "Keep pushing her shoulder that way while I open the door." He stood and slowly pushed it open while Reynaldo, sobbing, shuffled forward on his knees, one arm hooked around the door's edge so he could grip something out of sight.

When the opening was wide enough, Reynaldo crawled through it. *"Princessa,"* he sobbed, bent over. Beyond him, the others could see bare legs and feet below the hem of a lacy nightgown. A horizontal layer of dark red showed through the skin that lay against the floor.

"Is she alive?" Maureene asked.

Enrico bent and moved Doreene's foot gently, then stood and shook his head.

Baumgartner stepped forward and tugged on Enrico's belt. "Sir, I must ask you and Mr. Cruz to come away." He looked back at Max. "Call the police, please."

Maxwell looked startled. "Is that necessary? It seems pretty clear she locked herself in before she died. It might even be suicide."

Baumgartner shook his head. "It doesn't matter. My duty to my client is very clear. The situation needs to be investigated, and you are all in the way."

Max shrugged and took out his phone.

Baumgartner turned to Enrico. "Can you get Mr. Cruz out of there, please?" He stepped back.

"Come on, Reynaldo," Enrico said. "There's nothing you can do."

Reynaldo sobbed harder, but slowly let go of Doreene's body and allowed Enrico to pull him to his feet.

As he stepped out of the doorway and stumbled away, Michael let out a gasp and pointed to the interior of the closet, visible through the partially open door.

An oak dressing table stood inside, with a canvas mounted where a mirror would normally be. Doreene's face smiled out at them, looking as fresh and young as the day it was painted.

"Dude," Suki whispered.

Angus heard murmuring behind him and turned to find Lupita standing in the door, crossing herself repeatedly.

She looked up, her dark eyes huge. "Spirits of the dead. They came for her."

Baumgartner reached forward and pulled the door closed. It latched with a decisive click.

A woman's melodious voice came from behind them. "What's going on?"

Lupita gave a startled shriek, and the rest of them turned to look.

A lovely young woman stood in the doorway to Doreene's room. With her blond hair and large hazel eyes, she could have been the subject of the portrait they had just seen. She wore a black beret.

Seventeen

Baumgartner suggested that everyone wait in the conservatory until the police came.

Without extra chairs, the dining table couldn't accommodate ten people. Enrico stood behind Maureene, who occasionally wiped her hand under her eyes. Lupita hovered behind Reynaldo, who let out an occasional sob. Max and Baumgartner stood in the doorway to the rest of the house, speaking in low voices.

Angus pulled out the last chair for the blond woman who had appeared in their midst. "You must be Maureene's daughter, Lyndsay, but I'm afraid I don't know your last name."

Lyndsay smoothed the skirt of her black sundress before sitting. "Waring, until the divorce goes through, and then it's back to Pinter." She glanced at Reynaldo and shook her head slightly. "Poor man. Poor Aunt Doreene, for that matter. It looks as though she committed suicide, doesn't it?"

Baumgartner raised his voice. "I know it's difficult, but please don't discuss Doreene's death until the police arrive. Memory is a very unreliable thing. We tend to fall in line with what others say and forget or change details that don't fit the most likely scenario."

Enrico leaned down and muttered something to Maureene, then straightened and fell silent, arms crossed across his broad chest.

Lyndsay looked up at Angus. "I'm sorry. I didn't ask who you are."

"Angus MacGregor, of *Tripping* magazine." Faced with her blank, expectant look, he went on. "We've been doing a story about your mother's portrait of Doreene. Did Maureene not mention all of that?"

"There hasn't been much time to talk since I got here, and she didn't know I was coming." Lyndsay glanced at Enrico, and her smile turned wry. "If I had called, I'm sure she would have told me I'd be meeting my father for the first time."

Angus patted her shoulder gently. "That must have come as a bit of a shock."

"It's been interesting, to say the least."

The distant chime of the doorbell sounded.

"That will be the police," Baumgartner said.

The police detective interviewed the staff of *Tripping* last.

An officer led them through the house to the same large room where Doreene had given her press conference.

In the center of the room, a man in his forties or fifties sat hunched over a delicate antique table, typing on a laptop. Deep lines pulled his face down, giving it a weary look. His haircut was typical of a cheap, walk-in salon. Hair, skin, and suit were all gray.

Suki nudged Angus. "There's a trench coat draped over the back of his chair," she whispered. "An actual trench coat!"

"This *is* the Pacific Northwest," Angus murmured back. "He needs something to keep off the rain, and I don't think a poncho would inspire confidence."

Their police escort waved them into a few extra chairs someone had pulled in front of the little desk. "Detective Kroger, these are the people from the magazine."

The detective looked up and gave them a thin smile. "Thank you for coming."

"Did we have a choice?" Michael asked, sounding genuinely curious.

"Not really." Detective Kroger picked up a legal pad and a pen. "You've been in the house for how long?"

"A day and a half," Angus said. "Two nights."

Kroger made a note. "Did you know Mrs. Gray before this visit, either in person, or through phone calls or any kind of correspondence?"

"No. In fact, we weren't sure she would give us an interview, so we showed up for the press conference unannounced."

Kroger nodded absently. "What was your impression of Ms. Gray? Was she well-liked in her household?"

Angus cleared his throat. "Reynaldo seemed very devoted to her."

"All right, let's go through the events of your visit, starting from the beginning."

They spent the next hour painstakingly detailing their visit. Detective Kroger had an Officer Madison go upstairs with Angus to retrieve the strips of paper they'd found in the soup. He also sent Officer Madison outside with Michael to look at the ladder beside Maureene's cottage.

Once, Kroger excused himself, returning after ten minutes. While he was gone, a different officer came in and took extensive photographs before beginning a thorough search of the room.

Kroger came back and held a muttered conversation with the officer before resuming his seat and taking up his notepad again. "Mr. MacGregor, you said that after the storm woke you, you went into the hall and saw a light under Ms. Gray's bedroom door."

"That's right," Angus said.

Kroger flipped to a different page. "Mr. Cruz, on the other hand, said that his wife must have gotten out of bed in the dark, without waking him. In other words, he doesn't remember her turning on a light or he slept through it." He looked up at Angus. "Are you sure you saw a light under that door?"

"Absolutely," Angus said.

Kroger turned his attention to Michael and Suki. "Maybe Mr. MacGregor got turned around in the hall and only thought he was looking at Ms. Gray's door. Did either of you turn a light on at around two o'clock?"

Suki and Michael shook their heads.

"Do you think Mr. MacGregor could be mistaken? Maybe he was dreaming, or saw a light on a different night and thought it was last night."

"I'm not daft," Angus said.

"I'm not suggesting that," Kroger said calmly.

"I don't think Angus was mistaken," Suki said.

Michael nodded. "Or dreaming. He said he stood outside Doreene's door for several minutes, listening, and he got bored and cold. People don't stand around doing nothing in dreams. I wrote an article about it once."

Kroger turned back to Angus, a slight smile on his gray features. "You didn't mention listening at the door, Mr. MacGregor."

"I didn't think it mattered, since I didn't hear anything."

"How long did you listen?"

"Perhaps three minutes."

Kroger wrote a note. "Did the light beneath the door change in any way? Did you see a shadow, maybe of someone standing or walking inside the room?"

Angus shook his head.

"Did you look under the door or through the keyhole?" Kroger asked. "I'm assuming they have keyholes in a house this old."

Angus looked chagrined. "I never thought of it. There was no sound, so it didn't occur to me to try to see anything."

"Why did you listen at the door in the first place? Was there something that raised your suspicions?"

"I listened because I saw a white car across the street that looked like Enrico Russo's, and his behavior has been quite suspicious."

Kroger flipped back a page in his notes and studied them. "Right. You heard Enrico Russo demand that Doreene give him the painting."

"It also sounded as though he was trying to blackmail her," Angus said. " 'Give me the painting and no one has to know . . .' Any idea what he was talking about?"

"We're checking into that."

"Where was Enrico last night?" Michael asked.

Kroger stared at him for a moment before answering. "Maureene Pinter says he spent the night with her."

Angus frowned thoughtfully. "If Enrico stayed with Maureene, it probably *was* his car that I saw. Why did he move it?"

The detective flipped to another page. "Mr. Russo says the storm woke him. He got up and moved his car because he remembered seeing a weak branch in the tree above it, and he was afraid the wind would bring it down. He doesn't remember what time that was."

"Huh," Angus grunted, a wealth of skepticism in the syllable.

Kroger put his notepad down. "The three of you work for a magazine."

"We *are* the magazine," Suki said. "Except for the guy who pays the bills."

Kroger nodded. "Most cops don't like journalists, but I'm not one of those cops. You're observant, and that helps me do my job."

Angus gave him a regal smile. "That means a great deal, coming from a peace officer."

Kroger nodded. "Thanks. Would you be willing to give me copies of your notes on what you've observed in this household?"

Michael made a reluctant face. "That's kind of problematic—"

"Not at all," Angus said, interrupting him. "But it won't be now,

I'm afraid." He looked at his watch. "We need to leave right this minute if we're going to make our flight to Colorado, and then there's the drive back to Boulder, unpacking, typing up the notes—mine are handwritten and I doubt you could read them. But I'm sure we could get something to you by the end of tomorrow, or perhaps the next morning."

Kroger shook his head. "The first forty-eight hours of an investigation are the most important. Also, I'd like you to stay in Port Townsend longer. Not that you're under suspicion, but as witnesses, I'd like to have access to you."

Angus looked regretful. "There's nothing I'd like better, but we've been staying here at Doreene's invitation, and now that she's gone . . . The local hotels are full, you see, because of the Wooden Boat Festival."

Kroger stood. "Give me five minutes. I'll ask Mr. Cruz if you can stay longer."

Angus smiled. "That would make all the difference."

When the detective had left, Michael whispered, "No one in law enforcement likes the media, Angus. He just wants our notes."

"And I want to stay in the house. There's nothing wrong with a bit of mutual back scratching."

"You got that right," Suki said.

Michael ignored her. "What happens if Kroger gives an interview to some local reporter, using *our* material? We'll have lost the story."

"Don't be ridiculous," Angus said. "Police dislike the media because they think we release too much information, so why would he give a tell-all interview to someone else? Also, it won't hurt the article to say *Tripping* helped the police in their investigation."

Michael snorted. "In case you haven't noticed, a lot of our readers are paranoid anarchists—not the biggest fans of police."

"That's ridiculous," Angus said, "and I never want to hear you say it again. The last thing we need is some angry gun nut showing up at the office."

The cop searching the room answered his cell phone, listened for a moment, then came over to them. "Detective Kroger says he asked Mr. Cruz, and it's okay for you to stay over."

"Sounds like a slumber party," Suki said. "Let's order pizza and stay up late, talking and listening to CDs."

Angus gave her a reproving look before speaking to the officer. "Tell Detective Kroger we appreciate his help, and we'll get those notes to him right away."

"Will do. You're to wait with the others for now. Detective Kroger says it won't be for much longer."

The *Tripping* crew followed him. In the kitchen, Lupita was making roast-beef sandwiches. The cop ushered them into the conservatory and left.

Maureene sat at one end of the table, Max and Enrico on either side of her. On the far side of the room, Reynaldo hunched sideways in an upholstered chair, his face pressed against the seat back. Lyndsay was nowhere to be seen.

Angus, Suki, and Michael sat at the unoccupied end of the table. Lupita's sniffles could be heard through the open door to the kitchen, along with the clink of metal on glass as she scooped mayonnaise out of a jar.

Angus took out his pocket notebook, flipped to a new page, and scribbled something on it.

"Taking notes?" Enrico sneered. "I don't see how journalists can live with themselves, making money off other people's suffering."

Angus continued to scribble. "Actually, I'm jotting down a list of people I need to call to tell them we've been delayed." He looked down at his note, which read, *Did Doreene Gray fight the mysterious force that sucked the life from her even as youth returned to her portrait?*

Michael leaned over and glanced at what Angus had written. "Don't forget to call the orphanage where you volunteer."

"Right." Angus crossed out *mysterious* and wrote *malevolent* instead.

"Sorry," Enrico muttered. "The waiting is making me tense."

"Think nothing of it," Angus said graciously.

Suki folded an origami boat from a stray napkin and tossed it on the table with a heavy sigh. "So is that the original portrait of Doreene upstairs, or what?"

"I . . ." Maureene broke off and dropped her gaze to the table. "I don't know."

Max gave her a sympathetic look. "The detective had me examine the portrait and asked what I thought. It seems impossible, but I had to admit that it appears to be the original."

Maureene turned to him. "It does, doesn't it? I could hardly believe my eyes, but it has my signature, my brushstrokes, everything."

Max gave Angus a bemused look. "I hate to say this, but it seems almost . . . supernatural."

Michael rolled his eyes. "Or maybe Doreene removed the collage elements. We don't know what she put them on with, after all. They might have peeled right off."

Max shook his head. "I don't see how you could do that and leave no marks whatsoever. Oil paint would certainly be affected by any kind of adhesive."

"Maybe she covered the painting with cling wrap and pasted stuff on top of that," Michael said.

Max gave a bark of laughter. "Someone would have spotted a plastic covering over the painting."

"Are you sure?" Michael asked. "Have you ever wrapped a painting in cling wrap? Maybe we should do a test and see how obvious it is."

Max's smile faded. "Perhaps you've forgotten, but I got a good, close look at the portrait when I measured it for the shipping box. I've been in art for thirty years. Trust me, there was no plastic wrapping.

And today, when Kroger had me look at it again, I saw no marks from anything pasted on top. It's as if the collage elements vanished into thin air."

Michael gave a dismissive sniff. "Well, I don't think the police are going to settle for that explanation. They're searching the whole house, and I imagine they're looking for the missing collage pieces."

Lupita came in, bearing a tray of sandwiches. "The detective asked me if I found paper bits in the trash and threw them out. I told him I didn't." She put the tray on the table and got a stack of plates from the sideboard.

The sound of voices came from outside the room. Everyone paused to listen.

A police officer appeared in the doorway and ushered Lyndsay inside. "Won't be long now." He left.

Enrico cleared his throat and pushed out the chair next to him. "Lyndsay, would you like to sit down?"

"Sure, Dad." Lyndsay bent and kissed the top of his shaved head before taking her seat.

The skin over Enrico's cheekbones turned pink beneath his tan.

Lupita gaped at them, her hand pausing in the act of serving a sandwich to Maureene.

Maureene gripped the hovering plate and took it from her. "Lyndsay, would you like a sandwich?"

"No, thanks. I'm still on London time." Lyndsay smiled faintly. "It's nice of you to think of me."

"Lupita, wrap a sandwich for Lyndsay so she can have it later," Maureene said.

Lupita was still staring at father and daughter.

"Lupita!" Maureene snapped.

"Que?" Lupita wrenched her attention back to Maureene. "Oh, right. I will wrap a sandwich."

Max draped a napkin over his lap. "I wonder how long it will be before they release the portrait. It's an unfortunate part of human nature, but there will be three times as many people wanting to buy it after this."

"I hope the police give it back soon." Maureene picked up her sandwich. "I can't wait to get the damn thing sold and out of the house."

Lyndsay didn't look at Maureene as she said, "I don't think what happens to the painting is up to you, Mother. I imagine it will be left to Reynaldo, since he's Doreene's husband."

Angus wiped some mustard off his lip. "If I were you, Reynaldo, I'd get rid of it. Remember your uncle's bowl."

"Maureene can have it," Reynaldo said, his voice choked. "I don't care."

Lyndsay got up from her chair and went to where Reynaldo sat. She put a hand on his shoulder and spoke softly. "Poor angel. I'm going through a divorce, so I know a little of what it's like to lose someone you love. It's not the same as this, of course."

Angus leaned toward Michael. "I'll wager Reynaldo's experience is unique," he murmured.

"But you have to be practical," Lyndsay said. "I think my aunt had a couple of mortgages on this house, and Lupita has been on half-salary for months. You'll need the money from the sale of the portrait to make things right."

Reynaldo twisted in his chair and looked up at the face that was so eerily like Doreene's, his expression a mix of fear and longing.

At the far end of the table, Maureene said, "I'll take care of everything for him."

Lyndsay moved her hand to Reynaldo's head and stroked his hair gently. "It's good to have friends, but in the long run, I've found that you have to take care of yourself."

"That's true," Enrico said glumly.

Maureene gave him a sharp look.

"But you can trust Maureene to do the right thing," Enrico added quickly. "She knows all about selling art."

Max cleared his throat. "Although her experience is with dealers, rather than the general public. If you want to set up an auction, Reynaldo, everything is in place on my end. You just have to say the word."

Lyndsay gave Reynaldo's hair a final caress and returned to her seat.

Reynaldo resumed his hunched position. "Maureene can deal with the painting," he said quietly.

Everyone else looked up at the sound of a knock. A police officer stood in the doorway. "Ms. Pinter? Detective Kroger wants to see you again."

Maureene draped a napkin over her half-eaten sandwich and left with him.

Max sighed. "I wonder if this means a second round of questions for everyone?" He pushed his chair back. "I'm going to ask Lupita if she'll make coffee. Does anyone else want some?"

There was a chorus of agreement from everyone, even Reynaldo.

Angus dabbed his mouth with his napkin. "Congratulations, Mr. Russo, on your reunion with your daughter. How did you and Maureene first meet?"

Enrico's expression turned hard. "I don't talk about my personal life with strangers, especially reporters."

"I wasn't asking as a reporter." Angus smiled wistfully. "I don't have any family myself, so the idea of parents and children reuniting is quite touching to me." He turned his attention to Lyndsay. "Ms. Waring, are you planning to move back to the United States, to be closer to your mother?"

"For a while, at least," Lyndsay said. "I need to find a way to support myself. My husband and I had some business setbacks, unfortunately. Dividing assets isn't an issue when there aren't any."

Reynaldo stirred briefly in his chair. "A woman as beautiful as you should have a man to take care of her."

Lyndsay smiled. "That's sweet, Reynaldo, but I'm afraid I'll have to find a job."

Max came back from the kitchen as she was speaking. "If you want, I can ask if Rothwell's is hiring. The world of fine-art sales would break down completely without a steady supply of charming women."

"I appreciate that, Max," Lyndsay said. "I do have some education in art, even if it's a little informal." She looked at the door as her mother returned from speaking with the detective.

Maureene went to her chair, but didn't sit. Instead, she gripped the back, as if to steady herself. Her face contorted, contracting into an expression of grief.

Enrico got to his feet. "What is it?" He pulled out the chair and guided her into it. "What's happened?"

Maureene gripped Enrico's wrist and looked up into his face. "Doreene had stomach cancer. Her prognosis wasn't good."

Enrico and Maureene stared at each other in silence for a moment while shocked exclamations came from those seated around the table.

In the corner, Reynaldo put his hands on the arms of the chair as if to get up, then subsided and covered his face with his hands.

Enrico sat down slowly. "How do they know? Did she leave a note?"

Maureene took a gasping breath, but managed to speak without breaking into tears. "Doreene's lawyer called her physician, Dr. Wharton, and told him Doreene was dead. Dr. Wharton came here immediately and told Kroger what he knew. The three of them were still talking about it when I left." Maureene squeezed her eyelids shut. "Doreene was taking sleeping pills *and* painkillers, and it looks as though that's what killed her."

Reynaldo looked up, tears streaking his face. "I knew she took medicine, but I didn't know what kind."

Maureene nodded at him. "You didn't know about the cancer, did you?"

"No." His face contorted with anguish. "Why didn't she tell me?"

"My sister was basically a secretive person." Maureene rubbed a napkin beneath her nose. "If we'd known, we might have been able to help with her depression. The police aren't sure whether she got confused about the dosage or took too much on purpose. Either way, it looks like she went into the closet for some reason and just . . . fell asleep."

"Remember the day of the press conference?" Max asked. "When Doreene clutched at her stomach? She said it was nothing to worry about, just something minor." He shook his head sadly. "I noticed she'd lost weight, too, but I thought it was vanity. Poor Doreene."

Maureene nodded and seemed to compose herself. "Anyway, with this new evidence, they've decided to declare it an accidental death."

Michael frowned. "Even though they can't find the collage pieces?"

Maureene nodded. "I guess that will stay a mystery."

Michael turned to Angus. "Doreene did have some time after Max measured the painting and left. She could have peeled them off and thrown them away in someone else's trash, I guess."

"Or put them in a bottle and dropped them in the Sound," Angus said.

Suki looked thoughtful. "Or mailed them to someone."

Maureene had been listening. Now she looked across the table at Reynaldo. "What did you and Doreene do the evening Max measured the portrait?"

Reynaldo thought for a moment. "We stayed in the bedroom for some time, and I fell asleep. Doreene, she woke me at eight to go to dinner."

"And after dinner?" Maureene asked.

Reynaldo pulled his chair up to the table, next to Lyndsay, before going on. "After dinner, we took a walk down to the pier to see the boats. Then we came home, watched television in the room for a while, and fell asleep."

Maureene nodded. "So basically, Doreene had the time before dinner, while you were napping, to get rid of the collage pieces."

Lupita came in with a tray full of cups, saucers, and spoons and distributed them around the table.

"Does anyone know what all those bits of paper were?" Suki asked. "I could make out what looked like writing, and maybe some newspaper pictures."

Michael pointed at Max. "You saw the portrait when you were measuring it. What *was* all that stuff?"

Everyone looked at Max.

He lifted his shoulders and smiled. "There were definitely pictures of Maureene and Doreene. Some of them looked like they were cut from newspapers and magazines. And there were a lot of smudgy, handwritten words, but I couldn't make them out. They were very organic looking."

Angus nodded. "Ectoplasmic writing presents a very similar appearance."

Lupita, who had left after passing out cups and saucers, returned with a coffeepot, cream, and sugar.

Lyndsay spoke to the room at large. "I saw the portrait once, when I was a kid. It looked younger then." She leaned to one side as Lupita poured coffee into her cup and then smiled as Lupita added cream and two sugar cubes. "Thank you. I can't believe you remembered."

Maureene stared at her daughter. "Did Doreene show you the portrait for some reason?"

"No," Lyndsay said. "I went up to her room to ask her something and she had it out on an easel." Lyndsay gave a little laugh. "She told me to get out and slammed the door after me."

"Typical," Maureene muttered. She watched Lupita pour cream into her cup, nodding to tell her when it was enough.

Enrico leaned back and crossed his arms over his chest as Lupita poured his coffee and added one sugar. "Now that they know what happened to Doreene, did the lawyer say when everything will be settled as far as property is concerned?"

"Soon," Maureene said. "Baumgartner says Doreene left a very clear will."

Lupita put the coffeepot on the sideboard and leaned down to whisper something in Maureene's ear.

Maureene looked at Angus. "When are you heading home?"

Angus steepled his hands. "We were going to leave today, but Detective Kroger asked us not to." He turned to look at Reynaldo. "Thank you, by the way, for letting us stay."

Reynaldo nodded listlessly.

One of the police officers appeared in the doorway. "Detective Kroger says you're all free to go, but please don't enter Ms. Gray's bedroom yet." He started to leave.

"Sir?" Lyndsay called.

The officer turned back. "Yes, ma'am?"

"All of Reynaldo's clothes are in Doreene's room," she said. "Can he get some of his things?"

The officer gestured to Reynaldo. "Come with me, sir."

Reynaldo got up. As he passed behind Lyndsay, he bent down and murmured, "Thank you," before following the officer out the door.

As everyone pushed back their chairs and headed for the door, Enrico smiled at his daughter. "That was a nice thing to think of."

Lyndsay joined him and put her arm through his. "Thanks, Daddy." They walked out together.

Maureene watched them leave. Then she sat back down, took a sip of coffee, and stared into space as the rest of the group filed out of the room.

Eighteen

Angus gathered his staff in his room and shut the door. "Doreene is full of surprises, even when she's dead. It's very sad that she was ill, of course."

Suki lounged in a chair, legs straight and crossed at the ankles. "If I had cancer, I wouldn't marry a hot sailor. I'd marry a hot male nurse."

Angus shrugged. "She might have wanted to keep her love life untainted by worry over her health." He squatted by his carry-on bag, unzipped the front pocket, and removed his laptop. "Now let's write down what everyone said in there, while it's still fresh." He put the laptop on a small table, opened it, and pulled up a chair. "What was that word Max used to describe the writing on the painting?"

"Organic." Michael reclined on the bed, laptop on his thighs. "There's a strong underlying theme of secrets in this story. Doreene kept her marriage from her family. She kept her illness from her husband. She kept the secret of the painting from everyone."

Angus typed rapidly. "And she took any other secrets to her grave."

"Metaphorically," Michael said. "So far she's probably only taken them to the coroner's office."

"Doreene isn't the only one who kept secrets." Suki put two fingers in a hole near the hem of her shirt and tore it a little more. "Maureene didn't tell her daughter about Enrico, and Enrico and Lupita know each other somehow."

Angus looked at Michael. "You said there was speculation that Maureene's agent at the time was Lyndsay's father. If Enrico was the agent, then Lupita would know him that way."

Michael shook his head. "Her agent had an American name. Jackson, I think it was." He looked at Suki. "What makes you think Lupita knows Enrico?"

"She knew how he liked his coffee." Suki looked from one to the other of them. "What, you didn't notice?"

"Maybe you should explain it to us," Angus said.

Suki bent her knees and sat up. "When Lupita brought coffee around, she fixed it for some people but not others. Lyndsay was pleasantly surprised when Lupita remembered how she liked her coffee, and thanked her. Maureene was so used to it that she just nodded to let Lupita know when to stop pouring cream. And Enrico sat back and watched while Lupita put one sugar in his coffee."

"What about Reynaldo?" Angus asked.

"He took his black."

Angus shrugged. "Enrico must have spent some time here, and Lupita remembered how he took his coffee."

"Then why was Lupita so shocked when Lyndsay called him 'Dad'?" Suki insisted. "If he was a regular visitor around the time Maureene got pregnant, she must have had her suspicions. Anyway, I'm going by how Enrico acted as much as Lupita. He didn't reach for the sugar himself and he didn't thank her. He took it for granted that she would fix his coffee." She folded her arms and leaned back. "Trust me, those two have known each other a while, and it has nothing to do with Lyndsay."

Angus closed his laptop. "I think we should go talk to Lupita." He got up and opened the door to find Gigi out in the hall.

She skittered away, toward Doreene's room.

"Now that's just sad." Angus and the others followed the dog to the end of the hall.

Yellow crime-scene tape crisscrossed the closed door to Doreene's bedroom.

Angus squatted and held out his hand as though it contained a treat. "Is no one taking care of you?"

Gigi approached hesitantly.

Suki, leaning against the wall just outside the door, bent and scooped up the dog when she got close enough.

Gigi gave a startled yip and growl.

"No," Suki said sternly. She held Gigi up to eye level and changed her tone to one of encouragement. "We're going downstairs now. I'm going to take you outside, and then I'll make sure someone has fed you."

They went downstairs.

"It's awfully quiet," Michael said. "I wonder if the cops are all gone."

"We'll see if they're still parked outside," Angus said.

Suki headed toward the front door, then stopped and held Gigi out toward Michael. "Take her for a minute."

Gigi lifted her lip and growled at him.

"No," Suki said.

Michael put his hands behind his back. "I don't want to get bit."

"She won't bite you."

Michael reluctantly held out his hands. "Are you sure?"

Suki quickly handed him the dog. "Pretty sure."

Gigi's growl escalated to a snarl as she was handed off, but then she fell silent and licked her nose.

"You might want to pet her," Suki suggested.

Michael carefully scratched Gigi's silky neck.

Suki unwound the long green strip of fabric from her wrist. "This is one of my favorite accessories," she told Gigi, tying it to the loop on her collar. "Try not to get any bodily fluids on it."

Michael put the dog down and they went outside.

Angus gazed up and down the street. "No official police cars. Detective Kroger presumably drives something unmarked." He glanced at Gigi, who had squatted on the lawn, then looked quickly away.

After Gigi finished her business, they went back inside and trooped through the empty house until they found Lupita dumping canned green chilies into a large pot on the stove.

"What are you making?" Michael asked.

"Posole." She stirred the contents. "I don't usually make soup so often, but with all the people coming and going, it's easier."

Suki put Gigi on the floor, keeping a firm grip on the makeshift leash. "Who feeds the pooch?"

Lupita turned, wiping her hands on her apron. "She has dry food in Doreene's room."

"Her bowl is empty, and that room is still off-limits," Angus said. "I'd ask if we could go inside, but I don't know if any of the police are still around."

Lupita gestured to the closed door of the conservatory. "Detective Kroger is in there with the rest of the family."

Angus raised his brows. "Is there new information about Doreene's death?"

"I don't think so. The detective is calling it an accidental death." Lupita stood on tiptoe and opened one of the cupboards. "But the lawyer said he might as well go over the will while everyone was here, and the detective wanted to hear it." She pushed cans aside, clearly looking for something.

Michael furrowed his brow. "If they're going over the will, shouldn't you be in there, too?"

"He already told me what I got. It's not great, but I don't have to be so worried." She closed the cupboard and set a small can of dog food on the counter, then found a saucer and peeled back the lid of the can.

They watched her spoon brown glop onto the saucer while on the floor, Gigi danced in place. Lupita started to put the food on the floor, but Suki intercepted it.

"I want to see something," she said, taking the saucer.

Gigi pranced on her hind legs as she followed Suki to a corner of the kitchen.

"Sit," Suki said.

Gigi dropped to all fours, but continued to prance.

Suki looked at Lupita. "Doesn't she know how to sit?"

Lupita shrugged. "Miss Doreene either carried the Chihuahuita or ignored her."

Gigi gave an urgent bark.

"No." Suki stared down at the dog.

Gigi stared back and gave another, louder bark.

Angus leaned toward Michael. "Who do you think will win?"

Michael gave a huff of disbelief. "Please. Who do you think?"

Angus chuckled. "Don't know why I asked, really."

Gigi alternately stood on her hind legs or barked for another minute. Finally she stopped and milled around uncertainly. Then she sat.

"Good girl!" Suki put the saucer in front of her.

"You should keep her," Lupita said.

"I travel too much to own a dog." Suki watched Gigi wolf down food. "I'm sure someone in the family will want her."

"Or maybe they'll sell her to help pay creditors," Michael said.

"Hush, Michael." Angus gave Gigi a look of concern.

"What? She can't understand me."

Enrico's voice came from behind the conservatory's closed door. The words were indistinguishable, but there was no mistaking the angry tone.

"Why is *he* in there?" Angus whispered to Lupita.

She shook some salt in the pot and stirred it. "Maureene wanted him."

Suki leaned against the counter. "You and Enrico knew each other before he came for this visit."

Lupita raised the wooden spoon to her mouth and blew on the soup it contained. "I don't think so."

"You knew how he took his coffee," Suki said. "One sugar."

"Miss Maureene must have told me." Lupita tasted the soup, then added more salt.

The door to the conservatory opened. Enrico came through and slammed the door behind him, his expression furious. His gaze fastened on Lupita. "Bring me a drink. I'll be in the downstairs parlor." He glared at Angus a moment. "And I don't want to talk to anyone." He stormed out.

Lupita released a slow breath and pointed to a lower cabinet, behind Suki's legs. "Excuse me. I need to get in there."

"Sure." Suki moved out of the way. "That is one angry guy."

"Maybe he has reason." Lupita opened the cabinet and pushed liquor bottles aside until she found a bottle of gin. She stood and closed the cupboard.

"How do you know that's what he wants?" Suki asked.

Lupita looked at the bottle she held and bit her lip.

"Don't pester her," Angus said kindly. He rested a hand Lupita's shoulder. "If you ever need to talk someone, we'll respect your privacy."

Lupita scanned his face. Her mouth opened, then closed as the conservatory door opened again.

Maureene came out first, lips compressed. Reynaldo came next, his face still dazed and tragic. Lyndsay and Baumgartner, the lawyer, followed. Detective Kroger brought up the rear, trench coat draped over one arm, a briefcase in his other hand.

Gigi scampered across the room toward them, trailing her brightly colored leash. She looked from face to face and stopped, her tail drooping.

"Gigi," Suki said quietly.

Gigi looked over her shoulder at Suki, then walked slowly back.

Suki picked her up. "Who's taking care of the dog? I don't think she's been fed or taken outside today."

Maureene heaved a sigh. "I let her out this morning when I took Hilda for a walk, but I didn't think about food. Lupita, will you look after Gigi until we figure out what's going to happen to her?"

"I need to know . . ." Lupita stood up straighter. "I need to know who I'm working for now."

Maureene looked startled. Then she frowned, the lines on either side of her mouth deepening.

Baumgartner spoke. "Any contract you had with Doreene, written or verbal, is null and void. I will do my best to see that you're paid for any labor previous to her death. I can't speak to your future arrangements with other members of the household. That will be up to you and . . ." He glanced at the staff of *Tripping* and hesitated.

"Reynaldo," Lyndsay said. "It'll be up to you and Reynaldo, who owns the house." She looked at her mother. "And the painting."

Maureene brushed past her daughter and left the room.

Lupita wiped her hands on her apron and faced Reynaldo. "Do you want me to stay and work for you?"

"I . . ." He looked at Lyndsay.

She nodded slightly.

"Yes," Reynaldo said. "Please."

"For now, anyway," Lyndsay added. "Mr. Baumgartner, is it all right for Reynaldo to sell something quickly—furniture, perhaps—in order to bring Lupita's wages up to date?"

Baumgartner turned to Reynaldo. "You're free to do what you like with Doreene's estate. If you'd like me to serve as your legal adviser, since I am familiar with the house, et cetera, feel free to call and we can discuss your situation." He handed him a card.

Reynaldo took the card and gazed unseeingly at it. "Thank you."

"What about the dog?" Suki asked.

"Lupita?" Lyndsay asked. "Will you take care of Gigi for now?"

Lupita sighed. "Okay. But not for long. She bites."

"Has she actually bitten anyone?" Suki asked. "As in, teeth on skin, blood, etc.?"

They all looked at Gigi, who looked anxiously back from her place in the crook of Suki's arm.

Lupita made an unhappy face. "Well, she *acts* like she will bite."

"She growls at people, in other words," Suki said. "Because Doreene encouraged it."

Reynaldo made a small noise of protest.

Lyndsay put a hand on his arm. "Doreene thought it was cute because Gigi is so small. It's not as though she could hurt anyone."

Reynaldo gave her a grateful look.

"In that case," Suki said, "maybe you'd like to have her." She held Gigi out toward Lyndsay.

Gigi turned her head sideways and snarled, revealing surprisingly large teeth.

Lyndsay stepped smartly back.

"No?" Suki asked. She put Gigi down and unfastened the strip of cloth from her collar. "Lupita, do you know all the things a dog needs?"

"Food, and to be let out in the yard."

"Food and fresh water," Suki said. "Also, you need to go with her outside, and she needs to be on a leash. Otherwise she could run into the street or be attacked by a larger dog, a hawk—"

"Even a squirrel," Michael murmured.

Lupita frowned. "It sounds like a lot of work."

"It won't be for long," Lyndsay said. "I'll work on finding a place for her."

Reynaldo gave Lyndsay a wistful look. "You don't think you and the Chihuahuita will learn to love each other?"

"Um." Lyndsay went from startled to smiling. "It's just that I've never owned a dog. I wouldn't know the first thing about taking care of one." Her smile turned sad. "And of course, I don't know what I'm going to do or where I'll live."

Reynaldo dropped his gaze to the floor.

Baumgartner checked his watch. "I have to go." He shook hands with Reynaldo. "Good luck, Mr. Cruz. Feel free to call me if you'd like to set up a professional arrangement. In the meantime, I'll send you the names of several excellent financial advisers."

He sketched a wave to everyone else and left.

Detective Kroger set down his briefcase and put an arm through one sleeve of his trench coat. "Mr. MacGregor, do you have those notes for me?"

"We're almost done whipping them into shape," Angus said. "If you'd like to give me your e-mail address, we'll send them along shortly."

Kroger patted his coat pockets and came up with a card case. He wrote on the back of a card and handed it to Angus. "The sooner the better. I appreciate it." He turned to the others and handed out more cards. "I'm very sorry for your loss. I'll keep you informed of our progress, and please, if you come up with any more information, call me anytime. I'll let myself out."

They murmured good-byes as he left.

Lyndsay sighed and put her arm through Reynaldo's. "Would you like me to help you make a list of everything that needs to be done?"

He lay his hand over hers where it rested on his bicep. "You are an angel." They walked out together.

Lupita turned back to her soup.

Suki cleared her throat.

Lupita immediately turned. "Sorry. Did you want something?"

Suki put Gigi down and pointed to her. "Dog. Water."

Lips tight, Lupita got a bowl from a cupboard and filled it at the tap before setting it on the floor.

Gigi ran to the bowl and drank thirstily.

"Is that where it's going to stay?" Suki asked.

Lupita frowned. "The dog?"

"The bowl. It's going to be in your way there." Suki went to the conservatory door, looked inside, then came back. "There's a little space between the sideboard and the wall. I'll put it there." She picked up the bowl and whistled lightly.

Gigi trotted after her, chin dripping.

Lupita turned to Angus and whispered, "Can't you make her keep it?"

"You can't make Suki to do anything," Angus said. "And we're always traveling, you see."

Lupita crossed her arms. "Hopefully it won't be here long."

Suki came out alone. "She's drinking a lot. You might want to take her outside in another hour."

"Okay, I'll take her outside." Lupita gestured for them to leave the kitchen. "I have to cook now."

"And don't forget to find a leash," Suki said.

"Okay, I'll find a leash."

Angus tugged on Suki. "Come on. She'll be fine."

Suki shook herself loose and followed him out of the kitchen. "I know."

Back in Angus's room, Suki plopped into the chair she had occupied before. "See what I mean about Lupita knowing Enrico? She knew how he liked his coffee, and she knows his stress drink of choice."

"It certainly looks that way." Angus sat in the chair by the desk and looked over at Michael. "Shoes off, please."

Michael kicked off his shoes and resumed his place on the bed. "I want to know why she *lied* about the fact that she knew him. I mean, if you can't trust a Latina cleaning woman, who can you trust?"

Angus spread his hands like a film director. "Picture this . . . Maureene and Lupita are talking. Maureene says something about hating Doreene and wanting her gone, and Lupita says she knows someone who can kill someone at a distance *through supernatural means.*"

"An assassin," Suki said.

Michael groaned. "Not you, too."

"Not the supernatural part." Suki frowned thoughtfully. "But Maureene didn't want her sister to sell the painting, and now Doreene can't."

"Except that she left it to Reynaldo, and he can," Michael pointed out.

"Yeah, but it would reasonable for Maureene to expect Doreene to leave her the painting in the will. She's the artist, after all. *And,* the portrait isn't the same. The scraps of paper with writing on it are gone."

"There is that," Michael said. "I wonder what was on that stuff?"

Angus nodded emphatically. "An excellent question. We should make a list of possibilities for the article." He opened the lid to his laptop. "One, it was a spell for immortality, which evaporated when Doreene died."

Michael opened his own computer. "Isn't the body supposed to suddenly age, in that case?"

"Two," Angus continued. "When pieced together, the collage bits spell out the location of a hidden treasure."

Michael began typing. "I like the treasure idea. It could explain the lights in the woods that Lupita saw. Someone was out there searching."

"It was glowing skeletons," Angus said firmly. "Three, the collage pieces revealed some secret of Doreene's, like a contract with the Devil."

Michael typed more slowly, then stopped. "Are we sure it's a secret of Doreene's?"

Angus continued to type. "When Enrico and Doreene were fighting, Enrico said, 'Give me the painting and no one has to know.' "

"Yeah, but Doreene was willing to sell the painting, in which case her secret would be exposed. *Maureene* was the one who was so against the sale."

Angus thought for a moment. "Okay, but the collage pieces disappeared before the sale could take place. Possibly Doreene planned that all along, so her secret would be safe."

Michael shook his head in frustration. "None of that explains why *Maureene* was so determined to stop the sale of the painting."

Angus frowned. "Presumably Maureene knew about Doreene's secret, and wanted to protect her sister from exposure."

"*And* assassinate her?" Michael asked. "Not that I believe that part. Still, don't you think it makes more sense that the paper bits contained a secret of Maureene's? Enrico, who is clearly attached to her, came here to pressure Doreene into backing down from the sale."

Angus squinted. "But Enrico said, 'No one has to know' to *Doreene.* That's clearly a threat to expose *her* secret."

Suki stirred in her chair. "Why can't there be two secrets? Maureene's secret was in the collage, and Doreene had a secret that Enrico knew about. He threatened to expose Doreene if *she* exposed Maureene."

"That works," Michael said slowly. "I would love to know what it was all about."

"Doreene's secret might have been her marriage to Reynaldo," Suki said. "Why *did* she keep that a secret?" Michael asked.

"Seems obvious to me," Angus said. "Doreene didn't want her sister to know that Reynaldo would inherit. But that's not the kind of secret that's tied up with a mysterious painting. We're talking diabolical bargains and eternal youth, trust me."

"I agree that a secret marriage isn't a strong enough threat," Michael said. "Plus, if Enrico knew about the marriage and is on Maureene's side, why wouldn't he just tell her?"

"Doreene also kept her cancer a secret," Suki said. "Maybe that was it."

Michael shook his head. "I could see that if she had something contagious or hereditary, but she didn't." Michael raised both hands in a eureka gesture. "*Insanity.* Doreene defaced a valuable painting with who-knows-what gibberish, then overdosed in her closet. Maureene didn't want the painting to sell and reveal that her twin had a mental illness, and that's also what Enrico meant when he told Doreene, 'Give me the painting and no one has to know.' It all fits."

Suki sucked in a breath through her teeth. "I don't know . . . Artists usually don't care if someone in the family has a mental illness." She looked thoughtful. "Unless Doreene was going to become a more famous artist. But modifying one painting is a pretty limited portfolio." She looked at her watch. "I'm starving. Do you think Lupita's soup is ready?"

"Let's go out," Michael said. "I could use a break from this family's dysfunctional crap."

"Every meal we have here is another opportunity to add to our story," Angus said reprovingly. "We're going to go downstairs and observe the natives." He started to rise, then sat back down. "I suppose I should e-mail Kroger those notes first." He clicked through a couple of screens on his laptop. "There. Let's go."

When they reached the conservatory, they found only Lupita, eating a solitary dinner. She got to her feet, swallowing a mouthful of soup. "Would you like some *posole*?"

"Has everyone else already come and gone?" Angus asked.

"Mr. Reynaldo and Miss Lyndsay went out. I don't know about Miss Maureene and Mr. Russo." Lupita began to work her way around the table.

Angus held up a hand. "Stay and enjoy your soup. It smells delicious, but I think we'll explore the town a little more."

"You sure? It's no trouble."

"That's all right." Angus turned to go.

"Where's Gigi?" Suki asked.

Lupita's mouth lifted on one side. "Miss Lyndsay took her along. She asked me for some cut-up cheese, too."

Angus smiled. "Excellent. I'm glad to hear someone has taken an interest in the little mite." He turned and patted Suki's shoulder. "Looks like your wee friend will be fine."

"Yeah . . ." Suki said, her eyes narrow.

Angus waved to Lupita as he herded the others out the door in front of him. "I'm sure we'll see you again before we leave, but if we don't, thank you very much for all your help."

"No problem," Lupita said.

"So we are leaving tomorrow," Michael said as they walked through the house.

"If there's a suitable flight, yes," Angus said. "I suppose we should check now."

"I'm *hungry,*" Suki moaned. "I'll check flights on my phone while we eat, okay?"

Nineteen

After dinner, they walked back to the house. The evening was cool and dim.

"So what's the plan for the rest of the day?" Michael asked.

Angus took an appreciative breath of the greenery-scented air. "I'm wondering if we might be able to poke around the house a little. There must be something that will give us an insight into Doreene's relationship to the painting—newspaper clippings, a scrapbook, even a diary."

"Leaving aside the ethics of reading a dead woman's diary," Michael said, "what if we get caught?"

Angus waved a dismissive hand. "Unlikely. Reynaldo is the only one with authority, and he's in no shape to lay down the law."

"I don't know," Suki said. "Lyndsay could put her hand up his backside and make him talk like a puppet."

Angus smothered a laugh.

Michael snickered. "I suppose we can do a little poking around, if we're subtle."

"I'm not suggesting we dump the contents of drawers onto the carpet," Angus said. "I'm simply hoping to find something that will tell us what angle to take. Every family has secrets—this one more than most."

Michael nodded. "Just remember—we're not writing a tell-all on these people."

Angus patted his back. "Relax. We're only interested in family matters as they relate to supernatural events."

As they approached the house, Reynaldo and Lyndsay came out the front door. Lyndsay's hair was swept up on one side and fastened with a clip. She wore a striking black-and-pink dress and carried Gigi, who also wore a dress, in the crook of one arm.

"She's made herself look just like Doreene," Suki whispered. She surreptitiously pointed her camera at them and took several shots in succession.

"Out for a stroll?" Angus asked when they were in speaking distance.

"We're going to go look at the boats." Lyndsay stroked Reynaldo's arm with her free hand. "Get out of the house a little."

"Gigi is dressed for an evening on the town, I see," Angus said.

The dog wore a pink sundress with a flouncy skirt. Lyndsay tweaked it so the neckline hung straighter. "To tell you the truth, I've always been a little afraid of dogs, but this one is different. After spending some time with her, she seems almost familiar." Lyndsay stroked Gigi's soft fur.

Reynaldo's eyes took on a liquid sheen. "I remember when Doreene bought that dress for her. She said every blonde's wardrobe should have some pink."

"It's one of my favorite colors," Lyndsay said softly. She turned to Angus. "By the way, I keep forgetting to thank you for returning my beret. I wondered where I lost it."

"You're lucky," Suki said evenly. "So often, people just walk off with other people's things."

Angus gave a jolly laugh. "Very true. Well, have a good evening." He put a hand in the small of Suki's back and propelled her forward.

Once inside the house, he closed the door and heaved a sigh.

"Well done, Angus," Michael said. "I thought we might have to break out the squirt bottle and break up a catfight."

Suki shook herself and unclenched her fists. "I'm okay."

Michael gave her a slap on the back. "For the record, my money was on you. She's tough, but you have a longer reach."

Angus held up a hand to silence them. He listened for a moment. "It's very quiet in here."

"Maureene and Enrico are probably at her cottage," Michael said. "That leaves only Lupita."

Angus nodded. "If we're in luck, she's out grocery shopping, and we have the place to ourselves. C'mon." He headed toward the center of the house.

"Aren't we going to look around Doreene's room?" Michael asked.

"In a minute." Angus led the way to the kitchen. The pot of *posole* stood covered on the stove, cooling. He squatted and opened the cupboard doors beneath the sink.

Suki looked at Michael and shrugged. "It's not the most obvious place to search for family secrets, but maybe that's the point." She opened an upper cabinet, stared at the glassware inside, then shut it.

Angus shoved cleaning supplies aside until he reached the far back of the cupboard. He grabbed something with a crinkle of plastic, stood, and shut the cupboard. "Let's go upstairs."

Michael tossed a pot holder back in a drawer and closed it. "What've you got there?"

Angus waved an open packet of yellow kitchen gloves.

They went back through the house, up the creaking stairway to the second floor, and down the hallway to where yellow DO NOT CROSS tape zigzagged across Doreene's doorway. Behind the tape, however, the door stood open. They stopped a few feet away.

"Who do you think opened it?" Michael said.

"Lyndsay the accessory thief," Suki said. "I'm pretty sure the hair clip she had on just now is the same one Doreene wore at the press conference."

"The police declared Doreene's death accidental," Angus said, "so I'm sure it's perfectly fine to go in. They probably just forgot to take the tape down." He held out the bag of gloves. "Now put these on."

Michael made a reluctant face. "Maybe we should call Detective Kroger—just to make sure."

"And disturb the poor man's evening?" Angus shook the bag of gloves. "Here we go."

Suki took it from him and pulled out a pair. "I'll help you look. Michael can keep watch."

Michael sighed. "We don't need to keep watch. Those stairs creak enough to let the neighbors know someone is coming." He took a pair of gloves for himself. "There's not much of a gap in that tape, Angus. Are you sure you can fit through?"

"Don't be ridiculous." Angus pulled on his second glove with a snap of rubber before swiping the tape down with one wave of his arm. "If anyone catches us, we'll say it was off when we got here."

Doreene's room smelled faintly of perfume. Someone had pulled the curtains back. Dim evening light came through the windows, muting colors. The bed was unmade.

Angus stumbled over something on the floor. "Bugger. Go ahead and turn on your little phone light, Michael."

"Don't," Suki said. "It'll look like someone's robbing the place." She crossed to the window and closed the drapes with a brisk sweep of her arms. "Now we can switch on a real light."

Michael turned on the nearest lamp, on one of the nightstands. He opened the drawer beneath and stirred through the contents. "Condoms. Who did she think she was kidding?" He shut the drawer. "This may be the creepiest thing I've ever done."

"You've led a very sheltered life." Angus pulled a framed picture away from the wall and peered behind it.

Suki went to a jewelry armoire and lifted the top. "The creepiest thing I've ever done was on one of my shoots for *National Geographic.* I had to look through a crocodile's guts for our guide's watch."

"Gross," Michael said. "Why'd you have to do it? Did you lose a bet?"

Suki gave him a cold look. "Our guide would have done it himself, but it's hard with only one hand."

Angus went over to a small drop-front desk that stood against the wall. He lowered the front and pulled a stack of paper from a cubbyhole. "Credit card bills."

Suki got on her knees and looked under the bed. "Boxes." She slid a narrow black box out and opened the dusty lid. "Photographs. It's like I have a sixth sense."

"Listen!" Michael whispered.

They froze in place, Angus clutching a fistful of paper and Suki peering over the edge of the bed.

After a moment of silence, Michael got up, tiptoed to the window, and peered through the drapes. "Never mind. The wind has picked up, is all."

Angus expelled a held breath. "Grab a couple of those photo boxes and let's go to my room." He turned off the lamp and took the papers from the desk with him.

Once in Angus's room, Michael closed the door and put his box on the floor. He started to strip off his gloves.

"Best leave them on," Angus said.

"Okay." Michael sighed. "They're making my hands sweat."

"I'll try to remember to bring cotton photography gloves next time," Suki said. "They're a lot more comfortable." She put an open box of photos on the bed, sat cross-legged in front of it, and flipped rapidly through pictures.

Angus sat at the room's little desk with the credit card statements.

"These are all vacation shots," Suki said after a while, letting the last photo drop back into place. "What do you have, Michael?"

"The same. Cruises."

She clambered off the bed. "There was at least one more box farther under the bed. I'm going to trade these out." She stacked one box on top of the other and left the room.

"How are you doing, Angus?" Michael asked.

"Mmm . . ." Angus said absently. "The only thing of interest is Doreene's pattern of spending. She'd go months without paying anything more than the minimum, then suddenly pay the whole lot off. And there are a couple of times when she spent thousands of dollars on clothing or jewelry, only to return it the next week."

"Sounds like her income was pretty irregular. Any plastic surgery bills?"

Angus scanned another statement as Suki came back with a different box. "She went to a Dr. Mortimer every six months."

"Botox," Suki declared.

"And she spent five thousand dollars at Clinica Estética on her most recent trip to Brazil."

"Butt lift." Suki put the beat-up cardboard box on the floor. "This one is pretty dusty. I don't think I'll risk it on the bed."

"Thank you," Angus said. "I don't want to sneeze all night." He got up, credit card statements in hand. "I'll put these back."

Michael joined Suki on the floor as she unfolded the flaps of the box. It contained a hodgepodge of yellowed papers, photos, and memorabilia such as coasters and event tickets.

Michael removed a photo album covered in yellowed white satin and opened it. "Pictures from Doreene's wedding to Hank Gray. He looks just like that painting we saw at the gallery. Maureene really is good." He flipped through the stiff pages, then set it aside.

Suki opened a creased manila envelope and took out some older-looking photos. "Hey, here's a picture of Maureene with blond hair."

"Let me see." Michael took the photo from her outstretched hand. "Are you sure this isn't Doreene?"

"Yeah. Maureene has a slightly rounder jaw, and her eyelids droop a little, like she's hiding something. But the real tip-off is this." She handed him a second snapshot, then got to her feet.

Michael studied it. "Maureene holding a baby—presumably Lyndsay. Mom looks more worried than happy."

"Must have had a premonition," Suki said drily. "Let me see that again." She took it from him and scooped her camera off the bed on her way to the desk. After switching on a nearby lamp, she placed the photo on the desk, pressed the camera against the wall to keep it still, and took some pictures. She checked the result on her camera's digital screen, then flipped the snapshot over. "Whoa."

Michael looked up. "What?"

"Just a sec." Suki took another series of photos before handing the snapshot to Michael with the back side up. A neat penciled note in the corner read *Geneva, Switzerland.* Someone had scrawled *Bitch!* across it in black marker.

Angus returned in time to hear Michael give a low whistle. "Find something interesting?"

Michael extended his arm so Angus could take the picture. "Maureene and Lyndsay. After you've feasted your eyes on mother and child, check out the back."

Angus studied the photo for a moment, then flipped it over. His brows went up. "I can understand Doreene disliking Lyndsay when she was an obnoxious teen, but this suggests a long-standing grudge."

"It looks as though Doreene hated that Maureene had a kid," Michael said. "Do you suppose she couldn't get pregnant, and resented her sister for managing it?"

Angus shrugged. "Doreene never struck me as the maternal type, but this was a long time ago. Who knows what she was like?"

Michael took another snapshot from the box. "Check this out." He stood so they could all look at it.

The photo showed the twins as girls, seated side by side on top of a picnic table.

"They both have blond hair here," Suki said. "It must have gotten darker when they grew up."

"They look about sixteen in this picture," Angus said. "No question who's who, is there?"

"Nope," Michael said. "Doreene is the smiling one in the cute sundress, and Maureene is sitting there like a brick with a face."

Suki took the picture to the desk and photographed it. "Do you guys think Maureene might be a lesbian?"

They looked at her in surprise.

"I don't get a sexual vibe from her one way or the other," Suki said, bringing the picture back, "but look at her outfit in this shot—baggy pants and baggy sweater. Sixteen years old, hormones raging, and she's wearing clothes that say, 'I don't care about being attractive to men.' "

"She went on to have a child," Michael pointed out, "and she certainly seems fond of Enrico. Maybe she just didn't want to look like her sister."

"Or she was a late bloomer," Angus suggested.

"Yeah, maybe . . ." Suki said. "I still think there's something weird going on."

"That's why we're here," Angus said cheerfully. "What else is in that box?"

Michael knelt and rooted through some other photos. "Maureene holding toddler Lyndsay's hand. Still blond, and she looks happier. Doreene and Hank on a yacht with a bunch of rich people. Hey, look, Max is there, too!" Michael pointed with one yellow-gloved finger.

"Tan, rested, and ready to make deals," Angus observed, taking the photo. "I wonder which came first—working at Rothwell's or hanging out with moneyed folks?" He handed the picture to Suki.

The sound of a bark came from outside. Angus strode across the room and pulled the curtain aside slightly. "Reynaldo and Lyndsay are back."

"Shit." Suki knelt on the floor and quickly repacked the box. "Is there time to put this under the bed where I found it?" She took the camera from around her neck.

Angus looked out the window again. "Gigi is running around like she doesn't want to be caught, but I'd hurry."

Michael watched impatiently as Suki tucked in the box flaps. "No one's going to know it was like that."

"The police might." She picked up the box.

Angus looked over his shoulder at them. "They got her. They're almost to the house."

Michael picked up a paper that had slid partway under the bed. "You missed something!"

Suki glanced back from the doorway and shook her head. "No time. Just hide it somewhere."

Michael lifted the corner of the bedspread and stuffed the paper under it, then went into the hallway and listened for sounds from downstairs.

Angus tiptoed across the room to join Michael. As the sound of Lyndsay's voice floated up, they both looked down the hall toward Doreene's room.

Suki came out of the room a moment later. She picked up several loose ends of crime-scene tape and quickly stuck them to the door frame again. As creaking sounds came from the stairwell, she ran lightly down the hall and into Angus's room.

Michael swung the door closed behind her and slowly released the latch. The three of them stood silently, Suki holding her gloved hands over her mouth to quiet her breathing.

Footsteps traversed the hallway outside. "I don't think we're supposed to go in there," Reynaldo said.

Lyndsay's tone was gentle. "It's all right. I'm putting it right back where I found it, and anyway, the police don't care about a hair clip. In fact, you could probably move back in here. I could call Detective Kroger and ask, if you'd like."

"I don't want to be in that room!"

"Then where are you going to sleep?" Lyndsay asked. "If you don't feel comfortable asking those magazine people to leave, I could at least ask the two men to share a room."

"I will sleep downstairs, on the couch," Reynaldo said.

"You're too sweet, Rey. You need someone to stick up for you." There was the sound of a quick kiss. "Let me put this away and I'll be right back. Hold Gigi for me?"

Within a minute she had returned. "Let's find Lupita and ask her for some sheets and blankets. I might sleep here as well. It's crowded in that cottage, and I think Maureene and Enrico want some privacy."

Reynaldo laughed and said something inaudible to Angus and the others. A moment later, creaking sounds announced that he and Lyndsay were on their way downstairs.

Angus mimed holding a fishing pole. "She's reeling him in."

Michael pulled off his rubber gloves and waved his hands in the air to dry them. "Poor schmuck."

"Where's that paper you found on the floor?" Suki asked.

Michael pointed. "Under that corner of the bedspread."

Suki, still wearing gloves, retrieved the paper and unfolded it. "Photocopy of Lyndsay's birth certificate, signed by Maureene and with the space for the father's name left blank." She put it on the desk and photographed it. "I really don't feel like going back in that room after such a close call. What do you say I put this back tonight, when everyone is sleeping?"

"Fine with me," Angus said. "Don't get caught."

Twenty

Suki woke to the sound of her cell phone vibrating an alarm. She picked it up and silenced it with a finger before squinting at the time. One o'clock. She used the dim illumination to pull on her robe, which she had draped across the back of a chair.

Suki took Lyndsay's birth certificate from a pocket in her camera bag and went to the door, where she turned off her phone and dropped it into her robe pocket. She had discovered earlier that her bedroom door's hinges squeaked, so after turning the handle slowly, she jerked the door open a good two feet. It made only the slightest of noises.

She listened for several minutes, her eyes adjusting to the dark. Then she walked quietly down the hallway, sticking close to the wall. It took only minutes to go into Doreene's room, slide the box from beneath the bed, pull up the flaps enough to push the paper through, and slide it back.

Before Suki could straighten up, she heard a rustle behind her. She briefly considered trying to hide under the bed, but that was always harder than it sounded, and there was never a good excuse if you were caught.

She put a hand on the bed and stood, turning slowly as she did so.

The room appeared to be empty.

"Spooky," she muttered, then looked down as she heard a clicking sound move across the floor toward her.

Gigi appeared out of the gloom, walking oddly.

Suki squatted and saw that Gigi still wore the pink dress from earlier. She had apparently tried to paw it off, because the neckline now enclosed both her neck and one front leg.

Suki felt around the dog's belly until she located the Velcro fastening and pulled it apart.

Gigi ducked out of the dress and frisked around Suki, occasionally paddling the air with her front paws.

"Stupid Lyndsay." Suki had nothing against dressing a dog, but you didn't leave clothes on them indefinitely, any more than you would send a toddler to bed in shoes.

She bent and rubbed Gigi's head, then tossed the dress on Doreene's bed. "At least you'll be able to sleep now." She went to the door, only to hear Gigi run past her and down the hallway.

A faint whimper came from the darkness near the top of the stairs.

Suki took her phone out of her robe pocket and used it to light her way. She followed the clicking of Gigi's claws down the stairs and to the front door. Gigi stood in front of it, dancing on all four paws.

Suki waved her light around the foyer without much hope. "And still, there is no leash." Muttering further imprecations against Lyndsay, she put her phone in her pocket and untied the sash of her robe.

Gigi stayed reasonably still while Suki tied the sash around her collar. Holding the edges of her robe and the sash's end in one hand, she unlocked and opened the door.

Cool, damp air raised goose bumps on her skin, and a brisk wind blew the bottom of her robe open, exposing one bare hip.

Gigi ran ahead of her, pulling the sash taut and sniffing the ground busily. Suki followed, the grass damp under her bare feet. She hoped she didn't step on a slug or dog poop.

"This is a *great* spot," she whispered when they reached the corner of the house. "Wouldn't you love to go here?"

Gigi leaned against the leash, neck extended and nose working, clearly intent on making the most of her time outside.

Suki sighed and walked on.

Gigi darted this way and that. Finally she walked in a small circle, squatted, and did her business.

"Good girl," Suki said through a yawn.

They were close to the side door that led into the conservatory. Gigi headed for the stairs.

"We can try, but it's probably locked," Suki said. But when she went up the stairs and tried the door, it opened. They went in. Suki tried to lock the door behind her, but the wood had warped so that the dead bolt didn't line up with the lock plate anymore.

After the relative lightness of the conservatory, with its many windows, the kitchen was very dark. Suki picked up Gigi so she wouldn't step on her. She took out her phone and used its light to navigate her way through the house.

She was halfway back to the stairs when she heard low voices coming from somewhere to her right. Suki turned off her phone and tiptoed toward the voices. As she got closer, she realized it was Reynaldo and Lyndsay. She crept forward slowly, stroking Gigi's head to keep her quiet.

They were in the next room. Suki slowly peeked around the door frame.

A large couch sat in the middle of the room, facing several windows on the other side of the room. Two heads were visible over the back of the couch black blobs in the darkness. Lyndsay was speaking in a confidential tone.

"You should sell this house and travel. There's no reason for you to stay now." She sighed. "Poor Aunt Doreene. She and I didn't get to spend much time together, but I always sensed a kinship with her."

Lyndsay's head tilted toward Reynaldo. "It's strange, but now that she's gone, I almost feel her presence more—as though she's with me somehow."

"You are like her in so many ways," Reynaldo murmured. "Your beauty, your fire . . ."

Oh, hell no, Suki mouthed. She withdrew around the edge of the door and tiptoed quietly back toward the foyer. She turned on her phone when she judged that the light wouldn't be seen and picked up speed as she neared the foyer. Gigi's tail slapped against Suki's waist as she was bounced along.

Once Suki reached the safety of her room, she put Gigi on the bed. "Who's a good, quiet girl?" she murmured. "You are!" She untied the sash from Gigi's collar. "And who's going to pay for stealing my beret and being a terrible person in general? Lyndsay is!" She chucked Gigi under the chin. "Yes, she is!"

Gigi ran in a circle, then stuck her nose under the bedspread and rooted around playfully.

Suki tied her robe back together and pulled on her boots. Then she went into her bathroom, flicked on the light, and rooted through her makeup bag for the reddest lipstick she could find. She pocketed it and turned off the light.

Gigi jumped off the bed and followed her to the door. Suki stooped and put a palm up. "Stay."

Gigi ignored that and put her nose to the door.

"No." Suki moved Gigi away with one gentle foot and opened the door enough to slip through.

Once downstairs, she moved quickly and silently through the house to the conservatory. She opened the door to the outside and left it slightly open.

Suki walked around the side of the house, staying below the level of the windows. When she found what she thought was the correct room, she slowly raised her head and looked over the sill.

The dim light made it difficult to see much, but eventually she made out the shape of a couch and caught a hint of movement. Suki dropped below window level and took out the lipstick. She rubbed it across her left palm and fingers, then put it away one-handed.

Keeping the rest of her body below the window, she raised her hand and dragged her nails down the glass pane, gritting her teeth at the feel and sound. Then she groaned in what she hoped was a supernatural manner.

Alarmed voices came from inside the room, and a light switched on.

Suki raised her lipsticked hand and slapped it against the window glass, then pulled it slowly down, leaving a bloody-looking smear. She made sure to smudge her fingerprints on the dismount.

In the room, Lyndsay's scream was almost immediately drowned out by Reynaldo's.

Suki ran back to the conservatory door, holding her red hand away from her body so it wouldn't mark her robe. Once inside the house, she moved as quickly as she could toward her room.

She was halfway there when she saw light edge the doorway just ahead of her. She plastered herself against the wall.

A moment later, Michael and Angus ran through the doorway and past her. She darted through the doorway in the opposite direction.

Suki reached the foyer when she heard creaking on the staircase above. She hid in the shadow of a grandfather clock and watched as Lupita came downstairs in a terry cloth robe, holding the banister with one hand and crossing herself with the other.

Once Lupita's hurrying footsteps were inaudible, Suki ran upstairs to her room.

Gigi lay curled on the bed. She raised her head as Suki ran into the bathroom.

Suki dropped the lipstick in the toilet, then plucked it back out and took the lid off so it wouldn't float. She flushed both pieces out of sight.

Much of the lipstick from her hand was gone—left on the window—but there was still a fair amount left. She unspooled a couple of feet of toilet paper and scrubbed at it. "Thank goodness for moisture-drenched color," she muttered as it came off. She flushed the paper. A generous application of shampoo cleaned the rest of the stain from her hand.

She took off her robe, in case it had lipstick on it, and put on jeans and a T-shirt. Then she picked up Gigi and ran down the stairs with her.

The sound of excited voices led her to the room where she had seen Reynaldo and Lyndsay. Lights blazed inside.

Reynaldo paced the floor in a pair of flannel pants, raking a hand through his hair and describing what had happened to Lupita. Lyndsay sat on the couch in a brief nightie, contributing the occasional angry or frightened comment. Michael examined the window, wearing jeans and nothing else.

Angus paced the floor in slacks and yesterday's wrinkled shirt. He put his cell phone away and came over when he saw Suki.

"What's going on?" she asked breathlessly.

"Where have you been?" Lyndsay demanded.

"Outside," Suki said. "Something woke me up, and when I opened the door, Gigi was in the hallway doing a pee dance, so I put my clothes on and took her outside. Then I heard everyone making a racket and came in here."

"You didn't see anyone out there, did you?" Michael asked, coming over.

Suki put Gigi on the floor. "Huh-uh. What happened?"

"Lyndsay and Reynaldo were in here talking when they heard a strange noise outside."

"Not just a noise," Reynaldo said, his voice shaky. "It was groaning, like a soul in torment."

Angus nodded happily. "And then a bloody hand appeared at *that* window." He pointed dramatically.

Suki looked at the red imprint of her hand on the glass. It had turned out well. "Cool."

"The police are on their way," Angus said.

Michael put his hands on his hips. "I went outside and looked around the house, but I didn't hear or see anything."

Suki rested her hand on his bare shoulder. "You're very brave."

"Um, uh." Michael dropped his gaze to the floor. "I should get a shirt. It's cold in here."

"Would anyone like coffee?" Angus asked.

Lupita shook her head vehemently. "I am not going anywhere by myself."

"I'll go with you," Suki offered. "Come on."

They went to the kitchen, where Lupita got out coffee and filters.

Suki leaned against the counter. "Did you hear them scream?"

"I don't think so," Lupita said. "I woke up when people were running down the stairs. It shook my bed." She ran water in the coffeepot.

Suki's hands itched from being washed so aggressively. Rubbing at an itchy spot, she noticed a bit of red under two of her fingernails. She clasped her hands together, hiding the incriminating fingers. "Why aren't Maureene and Enrico here? I assume someone called the cottage, and that's what brought Lyndsay."

"No." Lupita scooped coffee into the machine with quick jerks of her wrist. "Lyndsay decided to sleep in the house tonight."

"Ah . . ." Suki said. "Where do you keep cups and saucers?"

Lupita pointed to a cupboard. "There." She turned on the coffeemaker.

Suki opened the cupboard and took out cups. "I thought there wouldn't be any more weird stuff after Doreene died."

"Spirits come back when they're betrayed." Lupita shook her head. "I didn't like Miss Doreene, but maybe she had reason to be the way she was. First her—" She broke off.

Suki set a stack of saucers on the counter and turned. "First her what?"

"Her husband," Lupita whispered. "Mr. Hank. And now this one."

"You think Hank had an affair?"

"I *know* he did."

"Did you walk in on them?" Suki asked. "Awkward."

"No, but I have seen the evidence." Lupita stared at the gurgling coffeemaker.

"What evidence?"

Lupita turned and focused on Suki as if realizing she was talking to someone other than herself. "Never mind."

"Was the painting the evidence?" Suki pressed. "Was that what all those paper bits were about? Something about an affair?"

"Never mind." Lupita pulled a tray from a lower cupboard and stacked the cups and saucers on it.

"At least Reynaldo waited until Doreene was dead," Suki said. "Probably," she amended.

Lupita put a ceramic coffeepot on the counter and bowed her head. "Marriage is sacred."

"Uh-huh," Suki said. "That must be why they make you sign a contract."

Lupita pointed to the refrigerator. "Will you get the milk?"

"Sure." Suki got out the milk and handed it to Lupita.

Lupita filled the pitcher, transferred the coffee to the ceramic pot, and put everything on a second tray, along with a sugar bowl.

Suki put a handful of spoons on the tray with the cups and saucers and picked it up. "I'll carry this one."

They walked back to the other room and put the trays on a table in front of the couch. Michael had put on a T-shirt, socks, and shoes.

As the others murmured thanks for the coffee, Suki said, "Lupita, do you have any sweetener that's not sugar?"

Lupita handed a cup and saucer to Lyndsay. "There is a pink bottle in the refrigerator door."

"Great." Suki turned toward the kitchen.

"Do you want me to come with you?" Lupita called.

"Nah, I'm fine."

Lyndsay called after her, "Bring it back with you!"

"You bet," Suki said. At the sound of cars pulling up outside the house, she broke into a trot.

Once in the kitchen, she ignored the fridge and went straight to the cabinet under the sink, rooting through it until she found some scouring powder. There was a vegetable brush next to the sink, and she used that and the powder to clean the last traces of lipstick from under her nails. She rinsed her hand and studied the results. "So much for my cuticles."

When she got back to the media room, carrying the pink bottle of sweetener, the room was full of cops.

In the wee hours of the morning, Detective Kroger looked even grayer than before. He took Reynaldo and Lyndsay away and questioned them separately. Now they were back in the room with everyone else, casting occasional glances at the handprint and looking exhausted.

Kroger was on his knees, measuring the handprint with a key chain tape measure, when a young officer approached him. He stood, grunting, and put the tape measure away. "Officer Madison."

"Maureene Pinter and Enrico Russo are on their way over, sir," Officer Madison said. "They say they didn't hear or see anything, but I told them you'd want to talk to them anyway." He held up a small sheet of clear plastic. A red smear decorated it. "Here's a sample of the handprint coloring. I bagged an additional sample."

Kroger took it. "Not blood, I assume?"

"Definitely not, sir," the officer responded.

"Ectoplasm, maybe," Angus offered from across the room. "It does have color, occasionally."

Kroger touched his finger to the edge of the plastic sheet where the red had been scraped up.

"I'd say it was crayon," Madison volunteered, "but it spreads too easily. Also, it has a slightly pleasant scent. Some kind of pastel, maybe? From a children's art set?"

Kroger rubbed the sample between two fingers and studied the result. "I'm pretty sure it's lipstick." He looked around the room. "I'm sure the women here won't mind if we take a look at their cosmetics, in the interest of clearing this up."

"Go right ahead," Lyndsay said.

"Mine is upstairs in my bathroom," Suki volunteered.

"I don't wear lipstick," Lupita said, "but you can check for yourselves."

Kroger pointed to another cop. "Go upstairs with Ms. Medina. After you've checked her things, she can go back to bed."

Lupita and the officer left.

Voices came from the hallway outside the room. Maureene and Enrico came in.

Maureene's gaze went immediately to her daughter. "Are you all right, Lyndsay?"

Lyndsay gave her a perfunctory smile. "Fine." Her gaze traveled to Enrico and she gave him a bigger smile.

Kroger consulted his notepad. "Neither of you heard or saw anything unusual tonight?"

They both shook their heads.

"Where is it?" Enrico asked.

Kroger pointed to the other side of the room. "On that window. Take a look and let me know if it means anything to you."

Enrico rested a hand on Maureene's back as they walked over to look at the handprint.

Kroger made a note and looked at Reynaldo. "I don't think there's much else we can do for now, Mr. Cruz. It is a little odd that we're dealing with lipstick. This seems like a kid's prank, and they usually use ketchup or paint—even that fake blood you get around Halloween. But you never know. Lipsticks fall out of cars, and kids are opportunists. One of them could have found it on the street and got the idea on the spot."

Reynaldo's hands were clasped tightly. "You will look at Doreene's makeup, too, yes?"

Kroger's brows rose momentarily. "Sure." He got to his feet and crossed the room to where Maureene and Enrico stood looking at the print. "Do either of you have any ideas about this?"

Enrico shrugged. "No."

"How about you, Ms. Pinter?" Kroger asked.

Maureene shook her head. "Doreene didn't usually wear red lip color. And she always wore glosses—said they made you look younger."

Kroger nodded. "All right. Ms. Pinter, we're checking all the women's lipsticks, just as a matter of form. Would you mind going back to your house with me briefly, to get it out of the way?"

"Of course not," Maureene said.

Kroger looked at the others. "If the rest of you can stay here, I should be back very quickly, and then we'll be out of your hair."

As Kroger and Maureene left, Enrico headed toward the sofa where Reynaldo and Lyndsay sat.

Angus went to the doorway. "Suki, Michael, can I talk to you for a moment?" He waved for them to join him in the hall. Once there, he murmured, "Maybe they'll say more with us out of the room." He leaned against the wall just outside the door and angled his head, the better to eavesdrop.

Inside, Lyndsay said, "It was probably a kid playing a prank."

Enrico's rumble wasn't as lighthearted. "Why were you sleeping here?"

"I got tired of the love seat after Maureene gave you the guest bed," Lyndsay said.

"How is a couch here better than a couch at your mother's?" Enrico asked.

"It's bigger, for one thing," Lyndsay snapped.

Reynaldo spoke. "Lyndsay did nothing to be ashamed of. I wanted someone to talk to—someone who knew Doreene."

"You don't need to protect me, Rey," Lyndsay broke in. "*I'm* the one who wanted to talk. Someone needed to tell Reynaldo to get away from this house."

"I'm happy to help Reynaldo get back to Brazil," Enrico said. "He knows that."

"Lyndsay, do you want me to go away?" Reynaldo sounded hurt.

"*Madre de Dios,* spare me," Enrico growled.

"It's not that I *want* you to go," Lyndsay said. "It's what's best for you. Find love again. Sell the house and the painting and travel."

"Wait just a minute—" Enrico said.

"Will you travel with me?" Reynaldo asked.

Lyndsay's response was gentle. "If you really want me to, I'd like that."

"You can't sell the painting!" Enrico said. "It rightly belongs to Maureene!"

"No, it belongs to Doreene's husband," Lyndsay said.

"And where is Maureene supposed to live if he sells the house?"

"My mother is a grown woman," Lyndsay said impatiently. "She'll figure it out."

"You are the most ungrateful child I have ever seen!" Enrico said. "Maureene has done nothing but try to help you your whole life—"

"You only think that because you weren't here." Lyndsay's voice was flat.

"It will all be okay, Enrico." Reynaldo sounded jubilant. "I will help Maureene just as she would have helped me."

Twenty-one

Michael and Angus waited with Suki outside her room while Officer Madison searched her makeup bag.

The officer came out and nodded to her. "Thanks for your cooperation."

"Happy to help," she said. "If you find out what brand that was, let me know. I liked the color."

He chuckled and went downstairs.

Angus rubbed his hands together. "Grab your camera, Suki, and let's take some pictures of that handprint."

Suki looked at his gleeful expression. "Could you guys come in here for a minute first?"

They followed her inside and she closed the door. "I thought I wasn't going to tell you this, but I guess I am. Weird."

"Tell us what?" Michael asked.

"I made the handprint," Suki said.

Angus's face fell.

"Are you crazy?" Michael glanced nervously at the door. "Why would you do that?" he whispered.

"Because Lyndsay is a *shit,*" Suki hissed ferociously. "She kept my beret and she was well on her way to convincing Reynaldo that she's Doreene, come back to life."

"That's Reynaldo's problem." Michael turned to Angus. "Is this *Tripping*'s policy now? To manufacture events?"

"Angus had nothing to do with this," Suki said fiercely. She looked at Angus, her expression penitent. "I'm sorry, Angus. I just wanted to make her pay, somehow."

Angus shook his head. "I understand the impulse, believe me, but Michael is right. Readers would abandon us in droves if word of this got out." He chewed his lip for a moment. "We'll have to leave it out of the article. Well, maybe not *leave it out,* since other publications will include it, but make it plain that we believe it was a prank as opposed to any real paranormal activity."

Michael looked from Angus to Suki. "I don't think either of you realize how serious this is. You're asking me to lie to the police."

"Oh, come on," Angus cajoled. "Journalists lie to the police all the time. It's called protecting their sources."

"Suki is not a source!"

Suki gave Michael a level look. "Fine. If it'll make things right, I'll tell the police I did it."

Angus's head whipped around. "You will not!"

Suki shrugged. "It's okay. I can probably talk my way out of an arrest, and you can fire me to show that the magazine wasn't involved."

"Bugger that." Angus turned to Michael. "*You're* fired. I need her more than you."

Michael rolled his eyes. "Fine. It's not as though—"

"If you fire Michael, I'll quit." Suki crossed her arms over her chest.

Michael looked at her in disbelief. "That doesn't even make sense! If anyone is going to quit—"

"Please don't leave, Suki," Angus begged. "If you do, Pendergast will start taking photos again. His finger was in so many shots, I had to change an article about zombies to one on giant worms."

Suki shook her head mulishly. "I'll stay as long as you don't fire Michael."

"No one has to *fire* me," Michael said loudly. "As I've been trying to *say*—"

"Eh-eh-eh!" Angus held up a hand. "Suki, you leave me no choice. Michael, you're bloody lucky she's willing to sacrifice herself to save your job. I'll see you two in the morning, and we'll consider the subject closed." He went to the door and opened it. "Disgraceful behavior, when we're supposed to be a team . . ." Muttering, he went down the hall and banged his bedroom door closed behind him.

Michael looked at Suki. "What just happened?"

She went to the open door. "I promise I will never fake a bloody handprint again." She glanced into the hall. "And I'll accidentally delete all my photos of it."

Michael looked uncertain. "You swear?"

Suki nodded. "Totally."

"Okay, then. I guess." He walked past her and out the open door. "But I'm pretty sure that conversation was supposed to turn out differently."

Angus closed his bedroom door and blew out a relieved breath. Maybe it would be better to go home now, before Michael found some other reason to quit. Not that they needed him, exactly. There were plenty of writer slash graphic designers out there, but Pendergast, the magazine's owner, wouldn't like having to find someone new.

Angus sat on a chair to remove his shoes and socks and noticed something white beneath the bed. He went over and pulled it out. It was Doreene's wedding album, from the box Suki had taken and then put back. He sat on the bed and flipped the pages. Doreene and the groom in a church. What had his name been? Hank. Angus flipped another page. Doreene and Hank in front of the minister.

Angus turned to the next page. Doreene and Hank in a garden, a crowd of well-wishers around them. A strong wind had pulled Doreene's dress taut between her legs and skinned the hair back from Hank's face.

Angus's mouth sagged open as he stared at the photo. Still holding the album, he ran into the hall, where he knocked urgently on Michael's door and then Suki's.

Michael stuck his head out of his room and spotted Angus in front of Suki's door. "I'm still happy to quit."

"Never mind that." Angus shook the photo album at Suki, who had opened her door. "C'mon, both of you. You have to see this."

They followed him into his room.

Angus held the album open in front of him. "Look at the picture on the right. See anyone you know?"

"Doreene and her husband," Michael said. "There's Maureene in the background."

Suki pulled the album from Angus's hands and stared at it. "Holy crap."

Angus smiled. "You see it, too?"

"See what?" Michael leaned over so he could see the page. "What do you see?"

Suki stabbed at the page. "Who is that?"

Michael studied the page. "Hank Gray."

Suki crooked her little finger and used it to cover the top of Hank Gray's head. "Now who is it?"

Michael took the album from her and gripped the covers. "It can't be, can it? Enrico Russo?"

Angus gave a satisfied nod. "Enrico Russo about thirty years ago. Subtract forty pounds, take away the tan, give him some hair and blue eyes instead of brown, and he's Doreene's dead husband, only *not dead*."

"Wow." Michael looked up. "Does this mean Reynaldo isn't Doreene's heir?"

"I hadn't gotten that far," Angus said, eyes widening. "I was still agog at the fact that Maureene had a child by her sister's husband."

Michael whistled. "That would explain why Doreene was so mean to both Maureene and Lyndsay."

Suki nodded. "Lupita told me she knew Doreene's husband had cheated on her. She said she'd seen the evidence."

"When did she say that?" Angus demanded. "And why are we only now hearing about it?"

"She told me when we were in the kitchen making coffee. There hasn't been a lot of opportunity to tell you before."

Michael looked at the picture again. "I wonder if Hank faked his own death to get away from the mess he'd made."

Suki tapped Doreene's image. "She must have collected life insurance on him. The insurance company could have sued her for fraud if Hank told them Doreene knew he wasn't dead. Do you suppose that's why she locked herself in the closet and took a bunch of pills? Because Hank threatened to tell?"

"'Give me the painting and no one has to know,'" Michael said. "Those were his exact words to Doreene."

Angus stared into space. "And now *we're* the only ones who know who he really is."

"Lupita knows." Suki grinned triumphantly. "I *told* you she knew how to fix Enrico's coffee."

"We have to tell Detective Kroger," Michael said.

"Yes, but not yet," Angus said. "Do you know how much this story would be worth to a tabloid magazine?"

Suki shook her head dismissively. "Not that much. None of these people are well-known outside of the art world."

"This is how people *become* well-known," Angus said. "By going off to Argentina and pretending to die. I know someone at *Star* magazine who would be quite interested in this story."

"Then you'd better call him fast," Michael said, "because I'm going downstairs to tell Detective Kroger about this."

Angus moved to block the door. "Now?"

"Yes, now! What if Hank came here to kill Doreene?"

"Leaving aside the fact that Doreene overdosed in a locked room, why on earth would Hank do that?"

"Because she wouldn't give him the painting," Michael said.

"But killing her didn't help Enrico—sorry, Hank—get the painting," Angus pointed out, "because Reynaldo is considered the legal heir. Hank *knew* that, because he was there when Reynaldo spilled the beans about their marriage."

"If Reynaldo is the only one between Hank and the painting, he might be in danger." Michael motioned for Angus to get away from the door. "Now move."

Angus grimaced. "Fine." He turned and pulled open the door.

"You kids have fun," Suki said through a yawn. "I'm going back to bed."

As Angus and Michael trooped downstairs, Angus said, "*I'll* tell Kroger. I'm the one who worked it out, after all."

"As long as someone tells him."

They found Officer Madison standing outside the closed door to the ballroom.

"Is Detective Kroger in there?" Angus asked.

"Yes, sir."

Michael bounced impatiently on his feet. "Tell him we have some vital information."

"Hush!" Angus said. "*I'm* going to tell him."

"I didn't say anything important," Michael said. "Anyway, it's not Kroger, it's just Officer Madison." He looked at the policeman. "No offense."

"None taken, sir. Detective Kroger told me he doesn't want to be disturbed unless it's a life-or-death situation. Is this a life-or-death situation?"

"No," Angus said.

"At least, probably not right away," Michael hedged.

"Then I'll tell him you want to see him as soon as he comes out," Officer Madison said.

"That'll be fine." Angus patted his pockets. "Must have left my phone upstairs."

Michael leaned against the wall and crossed his arms. "Go ahead and call your buddy at the *Star,* but can you really trust this person not to take the story and run?"

"Absolutely," Angus said. "He's an old friend." He trotted toward the stairs.

He was back ten minutes later.

Michael had found a chair and put it against the wall so he could sit while he waited. He looked up at Angus. "Well?"

"Apparently he doesn't work there anymore." Angus looked at Officer Madison. "Would you like a cup of coffee?"

"That's very kind, but I've already had three, sir."

"Can you tell me what time it is?"

Officer Madison checked his watch. "Three-thirty, sir."

Angus reached in his pants pocket and took out a business card. "Will you ask Detective Kroger to call me when he's free, please? Come on, Michael. We might as well get a few hours sleep."

Several hours later, Angus and Michael met on their way to the kitchen, where they found Lupita yawning into her hand. She had changed out of her bathrobe and wore her powder-blue uniform.

"I wondered if there was any coffee," Angus said.

"I just made a new pot." She filled a mug and gave it to him.

"Where is everyone?" Michael asked.

"Maureene took a cup of coffee back to her house, Enrico is in a meeting with Detective Kroger, and Lyndsay—"

"Wait, Enrico is *where*?" Michael asked.

Angus looked up from pouring cream in his coffee.

"In a meeting with Detective Kroger." Lupita handed Michael a mug of coffee.

Michael started to say something, but Angus caught his eye and shook his head slightly.

Angus picked up a spoon and stirred his coffee. "You know about Enrico, right, Lupita?"

"Know what?" Lupita asked warily.

"Who he used to be." Angus sipped his coffee, looking at her over the edge of his cup.

Lupita stepped closer. "You mean, like someone with a different name?"

Angus set his cup on the counter. "Someone with a different name who was very close to this family, in fact."

Lupita gave a little bounce. "You know, too!"

Angus lowered his voice. "We saw Doreene's wedding album."

"Does Lyndsay know who he really is?" Michael asked.

Lupita chewed her lip. "I don't know. He was gone before she was born."

"Didn't she ever look at family pictures?"

"Maybe when she was a girl," Lupita said, "but that was a long time ago, and why would Lyndsay pay attention to a dead uncle in a photograph?"

Angus nodded. "She probably wouldn't recognize him years later, looking so changed."

Lupita glanced toward the door to the rest of the house. "They've been in there half an hour."

"Do you think he might be telling Detective Kroger who he really is?" Michael asked.

Lupita looked surprised. "What else would he be saying?"

"He could be trying to put the blame for Doreene's death on Reynaldo," Michael said. "Lyndsay and Reynaldo were talking about selling the painting and the house and traveling together, which would leave Maureene without a place to live."

"No!" Lupita said.

"Sí." Michael took a sip of coffee. "Enrico doesn't need to confess his identity to separate Reynaldo from the inheritance. He could make up a story about how, when he moved his car that night, he saw Reynaldo's shadow against the curtain as he killed Doreene."

"I don't think there's a window in that closet," Lupita said.

Michael shrugged. "You know what I mean."

Lupita crossed her arms. "Reynaldo is stupid and wants money, but I don't think he would have killed Doreene." She moved her hands to her hips and looked at Michael. "Anyway, they said it was suicide."

"Or the spirits you saw that night," Angus offered.

Lupita shuddered and crossed herself.

Michael narrowed his eyes at Lupita. "Why didn't *you* tell Kroger that Enrico is Hank Gray?"

"And lose my job?" Lupita shook her head. "Everyone says Doreene took too many pills, and I believe them. She had the cancer."

Michael took a sip of coffee. "Well, if Enrico doesn't tell Kroger the truth, we will."

"*I* will." Angus raised his cup and smiled at Lupita. "Good coffee, by the way. I've been meaning to tell you that."

"Thank you."

They sipped in silence for a few minutes.

"I wonder what really happened to Enrico in Argentina," Michael mused. "Do you think Detective Kroger will tell us if we ask?"

"Enrico may not tell him," Angus said. "It might be up to the insurance company to demand that Hank Gray tell what happened in

Argentina. In the meantime, all Hank has to say is, 'I'm Doreene's husband and I'm not dead,' and Reynaldo gets absolutely hee haw."

Michael laughed. " 'Hee haw'?"

"It means *nothing*. Reynaldo gets nothing."

"If Reynaldo doesn't get the painting and the house, who will?" Lupita asked.

Michael looked at Angus. "I guess Hank would, unless Maureene wants to dispute that."

Suki came into the kitchen, her hair wet and spiky. "Hey, did you know Enrico had a meeting with Detective Kroger?"

Angus pushed away from the counter. " 'Had'?"

"Yeah." Suki took the cup of coffee Lupita handed her. "I ran into Kroger downstairs and told him Enrico was Hank, but he already knew."

"*I* was going to—" Angus's phone rang, and he answered it. "Yes. She just told me. No, that was it." He listened for a moment, then said good-bye and hung up. "Detective Kroger has asked Baumgartner to reexamine the will. In the meantime, they're taking Hank back to the station to ask him some questions."

Suki chortled. "I can't wait to see Lyndsay's face when she finds out Reynaldo is getting squat."

"Or *hee haw,* as the case may be." Michael smirked at Angus.

Maureene came in through the conservatory door. She hesitated when she saw them gathered there, then strode forward. "Enrico told me he was going to speak with Detective Kroger this morning. Does anyone know if they're still talking?" She fiddled with the twist tie on a plastic sleeve of bagels, her back to them.

"Hank went to the station with Kroger, to answer some questions," Suki said.

Maureene opened the cupboard and took out a plate. "They didn't arrest him, did they?"

"I didn't see any handcuffs," Suki said.

Angus cleared his throat. "I'm sure Mr. Gray is just helping them clear up a few things, but apparently the will is going to change. Mr. Baumgartner may be here later."

Maureene's shoulders relaxed slightly, and she turned to face them. "So you know. Does Lyndsay?"

Lupita shook her head. "She and Reynaldo went out earlier. I don't know where, but they left while Detective Kroger and Mr. Gray were still talking."

Maureene let out a breath that wasn't quite a sigh. She handed the plated bagel to Lupita. "Would you put some cream cheese and a tomato on this, please?"

Lupita nodded and took it.

Maureene leaned back against the counter and looked at the floor. "I had a dream about Doreene last night, before all this craziness started."

"Did you?" Angus asked. "The dead often speak to relatives through dreams."

Maureene nodded slowly. "We were sitting on the bed in her room, talking, like when we were kids. There wasn't any of this . . ." She waved a hand. "Tension, I guess you'd call it." She watched Lupita slice a tomato.

"Did you sense any emotions from her?" Angus asked gently. "Regret, perhaps, as to how things ended between you?"

Maureene gave a short laugh. "I wouldn't go that far. She kept pestering me about a secret spot. Something hidden."

"The missing collage pieces from the portrait?" Angus asked.

"Maybe." Maureene gave her head a frustrated shake. "I asked what she meant, but all she would say was 'secret spot' and 'something hidden,' over and over."

"Spirits seem to have a lot of trouble getting their message across," Michael said wryly. "Apparently dying really guts your vocabulary."

"Do you know of any secret compartments in the house?" Angus asked.

Maureene shook her head. "No, but I moved into the cottage when our stepfather died. Doreene might have found some hidey-hole after that, and never told me."

"Never told you while she was *alive,*" Angus said. "But she gave you a clue as to where to start looking—her bedroom, where the dream was set."

"I guess that makes sense," Maureene said. "Maybe I'll call the police and see if they want to look. I'm not ready to go through her things yet."

"We can do it if you'd like," Angus offered. "We're an objective party with no stake in the outcome, and Suki is a bit of a psychic."

"What?" Suki looked up from reading a cereal box.

"I *said,* you're a bit of a psychic," Angus repeated.

"Oh, right." Suki waggled the fingers of one hand in the air. "Woo."

Maureene pursed her lips thoughtfully. "I guess there's no harm in letting you look around, if you think it will do any good." She took the plate Lupita handed her. "Let me know if you find anything."

Angus lay a hand on her shoulder briefly. "Of course. And we'll be careful to put things back exactly as we found them. Can you think of anything else she said that might give us a clue?"

Maureene thought for a moment. "Not that she *said,* but she lit a cigarette, and Doreene never smoked when she was alive."

"Guess she figured now was the time to take it up," Michael said.

Angus put his empty cup in the sink. "Let's take a look, shall we?"

"Before breakfast?" Suki asked. "You know, my psychic thingie doesn't work right when I'm hungry."

"Are you sure about that?" Angus asked.

"Very sure," Suki said firmly.

Twenty-two

Lupita provided the staff of *Tripping* with a quick breakfast of cold cereal and toasted bagels. When they finished eating, they went upstairs.

Angus retrieved Doreene's wedding album from his bedroom. "Might as well put this back while we're at it."

They entered the still, scented air of Doreene's room. Angus pulled the box out from under the bed and returned the album. "Lift the mattress while I look under it, will you?" he asked Michael.

Michael went to the end of the bed and held the mattress up while Angus checked between it and the box springs.

"Nothing," Angus said.

Suki stood in the middle of the room, eyes closed. "Wooooo. Mmmmm."

"You don't have to pretend to be psychic for us," Michael said.

"Hey, if Angus is going to keep volunteering me for this gig, I want to have something worked up."

Angus chuckled. "The humming is good, but I've never heard a psychic say 'woo' before."

"That'll set me apart, then. It's all about branding." Suki went over to the dressing table, where she systematically looked through drawers and then pulled them out, checking their bottoms and the inside of the table itself.

While she did that, Michael looked behind pictures on the wall.

Angus examined the woodwork of the four-poster bed, then worked his way through the folds of its draperies. Letting the last curtain fall, he said, "What do you suppose it means that Doreene smoked in the dream?"

Michael straightened a picture. "Other than the fact that dreams don't make a lot of sense, nothing."

Suki went to the dresser and pulled open the top drawer. "She had cancer. Maybe she wanted Maureene to find her medical marijuana stash."

Michael stood in the middle of the room and gazed around. "Smoking. Fire." He pointed to the decorative mantel over the small fireplace. *"Fireplace."*

"Ooh, good idea!" Suki moved as if to join him.

"You stay right there," Michael said, going over to the fireplace. "You're always finding stuff." He took off his glasses and examined the carved mantel, then hooked his fingers under a center section and pulled. It came off in his hands with a scrape of wood on wood. "Eureka."

Suki and Angus hurried over to look.

A cavity of about three by six inches lay revealed. Michael put his hand inside and pulled out a folded half-sheet of paper.

"Remind me to give you a gold star," Angus said. "What's it say?"

"It isn't addressed to anyone. The signature says Doreene." Michael squinted at the page. "She didn't have the greatest handwriting."

Suki held out a hand. "I'm really good at reading difficult handwriting."

Michael turned slightly away from her. "I can do it." He read haltingly. " 'I'm sure you think I made the wrong choice, but I haven't. You may be my sister, but you have no right to question my decision. If

I wasn't confident that it was the right thing to do, I would have died rather than given up, but this was the right thing to do. Don't count on any financial help.'" He turned the paper over. "And that's it."

"A bit tetchier than your usual suicide note," Angus said, taking it from Michael.

"Maybe it's not really Doreene's writing," Suki said. "Hold on. I saw some notes on her dressing table." She came back with a scrap of paper. "Here. Looks like the packing list for a trip."

Angus compared the two. "It's the same handwriting—a little more rushed and emotional in the note, as you might expect." He pointed to an angry-looking scribble between *given* and *up*. "See where she made a mistake and almost gouged the paper scratching it out?"

"I can't believe she said, 'Don't count on any financial help,'" Michael said. "Leave it to Doreene to get in one last dig. Maybe Hank will share some of the inheritance with Maureene."

Suki leaned over so she could see the note in Angus's hand. "The language is weird. 'I would have died rather than given up.' It amounted to the same thing in the end, didn't it?"

Angus nodded thoughtfully. "She could have already taken the pills when she wrote this. If she was disoriented, that would explain why she hid the note instead of leaving it out for someone to find."

"Or this might have been a first draft," Michael suggested, "and she died before writing something else." He looked at Suki. "Were there any other notes on the dressing table?"

"Just a few reminders about appointments, plus blank scraps of paper—most of them torn off larger pieces, like this." She tapped the rough top edge of the note Michael had found.

"Just goes to show that a lot of debt can turn anyone into an environmentalist," Michael said. He reached into the space and felt around again. "There's nothing else."

They took the note downstairs and found Maureene in the conservatory, having another cup of coffee.

She read it silently, lips pressed together. Finally she lowered the note and rubbed at a furrow between her brows. "I almost wish you hadn't found this."

"Is that Doreene's signature?" Michael asked.

"Yes." She gave the piece of paper back to Angus. "I suppose you'd better take this to the police station."

"You don't want to take it?" Michael asked.

Maureene shook her head wearily. "I will if you insist, but I'm worn out with answering questions, and Kroger isn't going to like that the note was found because I had a dream. He gets this *look* whenever anything supernatural comes up." She glanced at Michael. "That's it exactly. You do a great impression."

"That's Michael's normal look," Suki said.

"We'll be happy to take it to the detective," Angus said.

"I appreciate that," Maureene said. "Just tell him I gave you permission to look around Doreene's room, and you ran across it."

"Do you want to make a copy first?" Michael asked. "You might not get it back for a while."

"No." Maureene closed her eyes briefly. "I don't need any reminders of how my sister felt, trust me."

The staff of *Tripping* went to the police station and met Maxwell Thorne coming out.

"What brings you here?" he asked them.

"We found what appears to be Doreene's suicide note," Angus said. "Ms. Pinter had a dream that led us to it."

Max's eyebrows rose. "Fascinating. Well, it's bound to help Enrico. Have you heard about that? Enrico is really Doreene Gray's ex-husband, Hank Gray!"

"We found out last night," Angus said. "Why are you here, if I may ask?"

"The portrait is still in the evidence room, and when I called and asked how they were storing it, they told me it was leaning against a wall, next to a blood-spattered card table and a mini-trampoline." He shook his head in amazement. "I suggested that if they didn't want to be sued, they might want to protect it a little more, so I brought the shipping box that Rothwell's made for it."

"Were you able to see the portrait?" Angus asked. "Has it changed any further?"

Max smiled. "I did see it, and it hasn't changed, luckily for the police. If there had been any damage . . ."

"Do you know if Hank Gray is still here?" Michael asked.

Max nodded. "I saw him waiting in a room, but I wasn't allowed to go in." He looked thoughtful. "You know, I met Hank several times when he and Doreene were still together, and I never would have recognized him. It's an amazing transformation."

"Do you have any idea what really happened in Argentina?" Angus asked.

"None whatsoever." Max glanced at his watch. "Do you think it would be all right to stop by the house and see how Maureene is?"

Angus nodded. "She might welcome the distraction."

"Especially if Lyndsay has come home," Michael put in. "Apparently she and Reynaldo left this morning before Hank made his big confession."

"So they don't know yet?" Max asked.

"I don't believe so," Angus said.

Max drew his breath in on a whistle. "You're certainly not short on excitement in that house." He lifted his hand. "If we don't see each other again before you leave, I hope everything goes well."

"Thanks," Angus said. "The same to you."

Inside, Angus handed his card to the officer behind the front desk. "Would you tell Detective Kroger that the people from *Tripping* magazine are here, and we've found what appears to be Doreene Gray's suicide note?"

The officer pushed a button on the phone and paged Detective Kroger.

Detective Kroger appeared about ten minutes later and took them to a room with enough chairs that they could all sit around a worn-looking table.

After they were settled, he held out his hand. "Let's see this note."

Angus gave it to him. "We found it in Doreene's room. Maureene gave us permission to look around."

"You should have asked me for permission."

"I'm very sorry," Angus said. "There seemed to be an understanding in the house that Doreene's death is considered a suicide."

"There's no official statement yet." Kroger looked at the note long enough to read it several times. "Where did you find this?"

"There was a hidden compartment in the mantelpiece, and the note was inside."

Kroger turned the note over, then back. "There's no salutation, and it looks as though something was torn off the top."

"We found a lot of torn-off paper on Doreene's dressing table," Angus said. "It appeared she was in the habit of using the blank parts of larger sheets as scrap paper."

Kroger grunted. "You'd think she'd want something more formal for the last letter she'd ever write. The language is kind of weird, too."

Angus nodded. "We wondered if she'd already taken the drugs and was starting to feel disoriented."

"I think she'd be more sleepy than disoriented, but I'll check with her doctor." Kroger put the note on the table and stared at it.

"We heard that Enrico told you that he's Hank Gray," Michael said.

Kroger's head came up quickly. "I meant to ask—how did you find out?"

Angus answered. "I found Doreene's wedding album while you were meeting with Enrico and recognized him in a photo. He's wearing brown contacts, right?"

Kroger nodded. "Now that you know, do you think he had anything to do with Doreene's death?"

"He certainly has more motive," Angus said. "Has anything changed in terms of his alibi?"

Kroger's mouth lifted on one side. "No, but it definitely changes his opportunity. Turns out the code to Doreene's locked room is the date of her wedding to Hank."

"Ah," Angus said. "That is suggestive."

"On the other hand, Hank's fingerprints weren't on the prescription bottle. Doreene's and a few of Reynaldo's, but not Hank or Maureene. Also, we got the results of a blood test back. It looks as though Ms. Gray had only a little more than a regular dose of painkillers in her system. I would have said it looked less like suicide and more like an accidental overdose until you turned up with this note." He flicked the paper.

"Are you going to release Hank Gray?" Michael asked.

Kroger nodded. "There's still no compelling reason to believe that Doreene Gray's death was anything but an accident."

Angus studied him. "What do *you* think?"

"I think it could go either way." Kroger tapped the note they'd brought in. "I wish stuff like this didn't keep turning up. People who commit suicide either don't write notes or they put them where people can find them. They don't hide them."

"Maybe they hide notes all the time, but you don't find them," Suki said.

Kroger stared at her.

Angus cleared his throat. "We had help finding this note. Maureene dreamed about Doreene last night. In the dream, Doreene sat in her bedroom and talked about something hidden. She also smoked a cigarette, but she wasn't a smoker in real life."

"Was the smoking a clue?" Kroger asked.

Michael lifted a hand. "Smoking, smoke, fire, fireplace. The note was hidden in the mantelpiece."

"Clever. Did Maureene figure that out?"

"No, I did."

"Good for you." Kroger checked his watch. "I'm taking Hank Gray back to the house in about forty-five minutes. Baumgartner is going to meet us there and tell everyone how this affects the will."

"Do Lyndsay and Reynaldo know they should be there?" Angus asked. "Apparently they left the house before Enrico revealed himself as Hank."

Kroger nodded. "Baumgartner told them to meet him there. He hasn't told them Enrico is Doreene's husband yet. Should be interesting." He picked up a stack of papers and fussed with them, straightening the edges. "Maybe I'll see you there."

"Was Kroger hinting that we should try to hear how the will changes?" Michael asked as Suki drove them back to the house. "I don't see how we can. It's a family matter, which is why they had it in the conservatory with the door shut. It's not like we can hide under the table."

Angus looked out the window thoughtfully. "What's the second room they'd most likely meet in?"

"The ballroom where Doreene had the press conference," Suki said. "It has a kind of circle of chairs and love seats."

Angus crossed his arms and nodded slowly. "Leave it to me."

There was a short silence.

"Leave what to you?" Michael asked.

"The room. Hearing the will." Angus rolled his eyes. "Do I have to spell everything out?"

"Yes!" Michael said. "You can't say something cryptic like that and expect us not to ask."

"I'm up for hiding under a table," Suki said, "but it has to have a long tablecloth or you're screwed."

Michael leaned between the two front seats. "Are you planning to make the conservatory uncomfortable somehow? You're not going to damage anything, are you, Angus?"

Angus gave him an affronted look. "I'm still thinking about it, all right? That's why I said 'leave it to me.' It's a general statement of intent." He looked out the window again. "Man."

Ten minutes later, they walked into the foyer of the house.

Suki heard the clatter of claws on hardwood and looked toward the stairs.

Gigi jumped down the last two steps and ran toward the closed door. She looked back at them, lifting one paw and then the other. Then she whined and scratched at the woodwork.

Suki stalked toward the front door. "I wonder when she was last taken out." She looked around the entryway. "And there's still no damn leash."

Angus came over and picked up the dog, who squirmed. "I'll take care of her."

"I don't *mind* doing it," Suki said, reaching for Gigi. "It just pisses me off that no one is caring for her."

"I know." He smiled and winked. *"Leave it to me."*

Suki lowered her arms. "Okay . . ."

Angus walked briskly through the house to the kitchen, carrying Gigi. The kitchen door was closed. He pushed it open cautiously.

Lupita turned from stacking cups on a tray and gave Angus a harried look. "I can't have the Chihuahuita in here right now. I almost stepped on her."

"That's fine," Angus said. "I'm on my way to take her outside, and thought you might have a leash." He looked down at the dog, who was squirming desperately. "And perhaps a small plastic bag."

Lupita disappeared into the pantry and came back with a produce bag and a length of clothesline. "Here."

The clothesline was fairly long. Angus threaded it through the loop on Gigi's collar and held on to both ends, not bothering to tie it. "Thanks."

He went through the conservatory and out the side door. Gigi ran ahead a little way, squatted, and peed copiously.

"What a good girl." Angus tucked the plastic bag in his jacket pocket and looked at his watch. "What do you say we take a brisk walk? Get things moving." He set off toward the street. Gigi, after a brief hesitation, caught up to him and frisked at his side.

They had walked perhaps a half-block when she took an interest in a grassy spot between the street and the sidewalk. Angus looked politely away as she walked in circles, back hunched.

When Gigi finished, he used the bag to pick up the mess. "At least they've been feeding you," he murmured.

They went back to the house and in the side door. A plate of sandwiches sat in the middle of the conservatory table. Gigi sniffed the air hungrily.

Angus took the plastic bag of dog poop from his pocket, untied the neck and rolled it down, then looked around the room. The sideboard had space beneath it.

He knelt and carefully pushed the open bag all the way under the sideboard. As he got to his feet, Gigi looked from Angus to the sideboard, her furry brow wrinkled.

"Sorry to damage your reputation," Angus murmured. He walked into the kitchen, where a coffee urn hissed and Lupita bustled around. "I'll keep the dog with me, shall I? Get her out of your way."

Lupita gave him a grateful look. "Thank you."

"No problema." Angus tugged lightly on the leash. "Come along, lass."

He went upstairs, checked to make sure Gigi had food and water in Doreene's room, then shut the dog in there. He went to his own room and got his laptop before tapping lightly on Michael and Suki's doors. They came out.

"Where's Gigi?" Suki asked.

"In Doreene's room, with food and water." Angus checked his watch again. "Both of you grab whatever you need to look like you're working and come with me. Michael, make sure you have your little recorder."

Angus led the way downstairs to the ballroom. He looked around, then went to a door in the wall and peered into the space beyond. "I think we can do better."

"What are you looking for?" Michael asked as he and Suki followed.

"A place to work quietly, just outside this room." Angus looked through another door. "This will do." He waved them through, into a dim hallway, and pulled the door to, leaving a gap of about an inch.

"What did you do to the conservatory?" Michael asked.

"Hid an open bag of dog crap under the sideboard. I only hope someone notices the smell *before* they start, or that's going to be one awkward meeting." Angus walked a few steps down the hall and looked into a doorway. "Here's a nice little sitting room. We'll set our things up as though we're working, and be able to run back here if anyone heads our way."

They turned on their computers and arranged them before going back to the hallway outside the ballroom. Angus peeked through the door, then backed away. "I think I hear people coming. Get settled."

Michael took his digital recorder out of his pants pocket, turned it on, and placed it carefully on the floor next to the door opening.

The sounds of conversation filtered in from the other room as the family settled themselves.

Angus angled his head so he could see through the opening without coming too close to it. Lupita crossed his vision, walking toward the back of the room with the coffee service on a tray.

Baumgartner and Detective Kroger came into view, bent toward each other in quiet conversation. Officer Madison followed them.

Angus watched Maureene and Hank sit in side-by-side armchairs, their backs to him. Lyndsay and Reynaldo settled on a love seat across from the older couple, and Lupita perched on the edge of a chair at the back of the circle.

Baumgartner sat down opposite Lupita and put his briefcase on his lap. "I have some new information that affects the outcome of the will for some of you."

Now that they were focused on the attorney, Angus moved nearer to the door. Michael bent and looked beneath him while Suki squatted on the floor.

Kroger stood outside the circle of furniture—behind Baumgartner, where he could see everyone's faces. Officer Madison stood beside him and unclipped a pad from his belt.

"Excuse me," Lyndsay said to Baumgartner, "but why are the police here?"

Kroger answered. "Today's information will help me fill in some of the blank spots in Ms. Gray's case file. I thought it would be quicker and easier to hear it firsthand, rather than take everyone through another round of questions."

There were murmurs of agreement.

Baumgartner took a stapled bunch of papers from his briefcase and flipped to the third page. "It has come to my attention that Doreene Gray's first husband is still alive."

"What?!" Reynaldo leaned forward as though he were about to rise.

Baumgartner went on. "Enrico Russo is actually Hank Gray."

Reynaldo and Lyndsay both stared at Hank. Reynaldo felt for Lyndsay's hand and gripped it.

Lyndsay turned to Maureene. "You had an affair with your *twin sister's husband*?"

Maureene said something too quiet for Angus to hear.

Lyndsay went on, her voice high and hard. "All this time, I've felt sorry for you—for us—because Aunt Doreene treated us badly, but I guess she had a good reason!"

Hank Gray stood, his powerful shoulders hunched. "You don't know the first thing about Doreene. Trust me, she doesn't deserve your sympathy."

Reynaldo shot to his feet. "*Traidor!* How can you say such a thing?"

Baumgartner raised his hands and patted the air. "This is not helping. Please take your seats and be quiet."

Hank and Reynaldo sat, eyeing each other angrily.

Baumgartner went on. "Mr. Gray, perhaps you could tell us the circumstances of your disappearance. It might help resolve some issues."

Hank looked to one side. "I didn't want to go to Argentina. Doreene and I hadn't been getting along for a while, and I hated the thought of spending every minute together." He expelled a breath through his nose. "But she'd already bought the plane tickets, so we went."

"After taking time to knock up my mother," Lyndsay said.

Hank looked at her, his expression unapologetic. "I've always loved Maureene. I dated her first, but Doreene treated life like it was an endless party, and that appealed to me when I was young. I was wrong."

"What happened in Argentina?" Baumgartner prompted.

Hank turned away from Lyndsay. "We were both good riders, so Doreene booked us an expert horse trek through the Andes—us, two guides, a cook, and a couple of extra horses to carry things." He sighed. "We argued—God, how we argued. By the third day, our guides were riding pretty far ahead. I'm sure they wanted to get away from the sound of our voices.

"We were at the top of a steep ridge when something made my horse shy. It threw me, and I fell over the edge. I remember lying on the ground with rocks raining down on top of me while fifty feet overhead, a thousand pounds of horse fought to keep from going over the cliff."

Officer Madison wrote frantically, eyebrows climbing up his forehead.

Hank went on. "Luckily, the horse didn't fall. Doreene called to me. I told her I was bruised all over and had a pretty good gouge in my leg where I'd come up against a sharp rock, but I was sure I could ride. She said she'd get the guides and they'd pull me up." He stopped and looked at the floor, a muscle in his jaw working.

"And?" Lyndsay demanded.

Hank met her glare. "And I didn't see her again until last week."

"Are you saying she never came back for you?" Lyndsay demanded.

"That's exactly what I'm saying."

"You're lying!" Reynaldo said. "My *princessa* would never do that!"

Hank gave a humorless laugh. "I didn't want to believe it, either. I lay there for two hours before I realized no one was coming back for me. So I stumbled down the mountain until I found a track. I followed it half the night, shivering from the cold, and finally ran into some gauchos. They didn't speak English, but they cleaned me up and took me to Mendoza, where I sold my watch for a lot less than it was worth.

"By the time I got back to Buenos Aires, the story about the American tourist who died on a horse trek was old news. The paper printed a picture of the place where I supposedly fell, and I can see why no one tried to retrieve my body. By the time Doreene arranged for a helicopter search, it seemed likeliest that I'd been eaten by animals."

Baumgartner looked up from writing a note. "You didn't tell people who you were?"

Hank's tone was wry. "I wasn't eager to go back to a wife who had left me to die. Who knew if she would be more determined the next time?" He paused. "Also, an experience like that makes you wonder about yourself. Someone hated me enough to leave me to die. I shouldn't have married one sister when I loved the other. I shouldn't have done a lot of things."

Detective Kroger broke the ensuing silence. "Ms. Gray brought your passport back with her. How did you manage to get a new identity?"

"Doreene and I had met a lot of people during our travels. One of them lived in Buenos Aires. He was very rich and, frankly, a little crazy. His gardener, Enrico Russo, had died a few months before I turned up, so this man bribed Russo's family to let me use his name and then found someone to make a set of papers."

"I suppose all that is possible," Kroger said, "but you were gone for *twenty-eight years.* Didn't you have family you wanted to see? And how did you make a living?"

"My parents are dead, and I'm not close to my brother," Hank said flatly. "The man who arranged for my identity let me live at his ranch in exchange for working around the place. I learned Portuguese, and gradually it dawned on me that I was happier where I was. Before I knew it, a year had gone by. I got a job with a company that imported goods from the U.S. and eventually became vice president. I fell in love with Argentina. There wasn't a compelling reason to come back."

Baumgartner smiled faintly. "But you did."

"When Internet alerts became a thing, I set one for Doreene's name. I figured that if she died before me, I'd come back to see what the situation was." Hank shifted restlessly, rubbing one hand over his mouth. "Instead, I read that Doreene was going to sell the portrait. The article also mentioned that Maureene had a daughter." He looked at Lyndsay again. "I had no idea you existed before then. I'm not sorry about a lot of things, but I am sorry I wasn't here to be your father."

Lyndsay stared at her lap.

Reynaldo put his arm around her shoulders and glared at Hank.

Maureene cleared her throat. "Does this mean Hank inherits the house and the painting?"

Baumgartner shook his head. "No."

Lyndsay and Reynaldo both looked up.

"No?" Maureene asked. "Isn't he still Doreene's husband, since they never divorced?"

"Yes, but the painting and the house are considered separate property, since they were deeded to Ms. Gray before the marriage," Baumgartner said. "And while those items might normally go to Mr. Gray by default, Ms. Gray's will specifically excludes him from inheriting them."

Hank's hands clenched, and his skin reddened under his tan.

Maureene stared at Baumgartner. "Doreene *wrote Hank out of her will?* Didn't that suggest to you that she knew he was still alive?"

Baumgartner shrugged. "His body was never recovered, so she might be excused for taking precautions."

"And it's not your job to ask those questions," Detective Kroger said drily.

"That, too." Baumgartner looked at Hank. "Given the circumstances, you could choose to contest the will."

"Never mind that," Hank said. "Who inherits now?"

"As Doreene's closest remaining family, Maureene Pinter does."

Lyndsay made an abrupt, bitter gesture and turned sideways on the love seat, away from her mother.

"In that case," Hank said, "I don't need to contest anything."

Maureene addressed Detective Kroger. "I don't mean to seem grasping, but do you have any idea when the portrait will be released from evidence so I can sell it? I do have a heavily mortgaged house and a housekeeper who needs paying."

Kroger rocked on his heels. "I'm not sure when we can release it. We have some new information we're working on."

"He means me," Hank said. "The key code to Doreene's locked room turned out to be our wedding anniversary. April 4, 1980."

"About that." Baumgartner turned his head and looked up at Detective Kroger. "I should point out that Ms. Gray used that date for most of her security codes. I told her it wasn't remotely secure."

"What do you mean, *most of her codes*?" Kroger asked.

"Safe deposit box, for example."

"And the ATM," Lupita added. "She used to send me to get money."

"She used the first three numbers for the padlocks on our luggage," Reynaldo said glumly.

Kroger made an exasperated face. "I'll see what I can do to hurry the portrait's release along." He turned and stalked toward the back of the room, taking his cell phone out of his pocket as he did so.

Baumgartner flipped through the files in his briefcase. "Ms. Pinter, now is as good a time as any to go over some paperwork and have you sign a few things, if you have time."

"Good idea." Maureene stood and looked around, then pointed directly at the door that shielded the *Tripping* staff from view. "There's a room through there with a table and chairs."

"Fine," Baumgartner said. "Let me just gather my things."

Angus and the others scrambled to get away from the door as quietly as possible, Michael darting back to snatch his digital recorder off the floor.

They tiptoed rapidly back to the room with their equipment, wincing at each creak of the floorboards.

Maureene opened the door to their room a few minutes later. "Oh! I didn't know you were in here."

Suki removed one of her audio earbuds. "Sorry, what did you say?"

Angus looked up from tapping on his computer's keys. "We were looking for someplace quiet where we could all work together, but it's not a problem to move." His laptop screen was turned away from the door, so Maureene couldn't see the device was still powering up.

Michael glanced at his watch and closed the lid of his laptop. "I have a phone call I need to make anyway."

Maureene stood aside as they went through the door.

Angus gave her a smile as he passed. "I hope we didn't disturb anyone. We had a rather heated discussion about pull quotes earlier."

"I never heard a thing," Maureene said.

"That's the beauty of these old houses. Thick walls." Angus nodded at the lawyer. "Mr. Baumgartner."

"Mr. MacGregor." Baumgartner gestured for Maureene to precede him, then shut the door behind them.

Angus went to the door through which they had eavesdropped and peeked through. "All clear." He pushed the door open. "I suppose I should go back to the conservatory and make sure the dog poop is taken care of."

Suki sighed. "I'll go let Gigi out of Doreene's room."

"I'm going to see if Detective Kroger is still around." Michael followed Suki toward the front of the house.

When they got to the foyer, Suki went upstairs and Michael went outside. He spotted Kroger sitting in his unmarked police car, cell phone to his ear.

Michael waited until Kroger had hung up, then strolled down the sidewalk next to the car and waved at him through the window.

Kroger opened his door and got out. "Did you need to talk to me?"

"Not *need,* no." Michael put his hands in his pockets. "So Maureene inherits after all."

Kroger chuckled. "Did you ask Lupita, or do you have the house wired?"

"We eavesdropped. Angus is old-school." Michael flicked a leaf off the hood of the car. "Are you bringing the portrait back?"

Kroger nodded. "I sent Madison to get it. If I tried to hold on to it, Ms. Pinter would get Baumgartner to hound us based on financial need, and I don't want the extra paperwork."

"So as far as the police are concerned, Doreene's death was either accidental or a suicide."

Kroger leaned against the side of the car. "The amount of painkillers in her system suggests she took one a little early or forgot and took an extra. She had cancer and a bad prognosis. She left something that could be construed as a suicide note. And finally, she was in a locked room."

Michael gave him a wry look. "With a key code that everyone in the household knew."

"Yeah . . ." Kroger crossed his arms, hunching slightly. "Sounds like they didn't know they knew."

"And while Doreene died in the locked room, the portrait magically changed."

Kroger made a face. "That's the part of the report I dread writing most. She must have pulled off all the crap and got rid of it somewhere." He glanced at Michael. "I don't imagine you guys will go with that explanation."

"Nooo. Our cover will probably say something like, 'Portrait of Doreene Gray—Possessed Painting Promised Youth, Delivered Death.'"

"Kind of long."

Michael shrugged. "Angus tends to be wordy."

Suki came out the front door with Gigi at the end of a curlicued lead. The little dog took a moment to sniff a weed.

"Is that a phone cord you're using as a leash?" Michael asked as Suki and the dog approached.

"Hey—at least I'm taking her on a walk, which is more than any of them do."

Gigi milled around Kroger's feet, sniffing his shoes.

"You in the market for a gently used Chihuahua?" Suki asked. "Only walked on Sundays by a little old lady."

Kroger grunted a laugh. "We already have two Shih Tzus, thanks."

They heard the front door shut and turned to see Angus coming down the walk.

He joined them. "I wondered where everyone had got to. Suki, is that a phone cord? There was a piece of clothesline on the dresser."

"I didn't see it."

Angus turned to Kroger. "So the painting is coming home and the case is closed?"

"Yeah."

Angus rubbed his hands together briskly. "This story is going to catapult *Tripping* into the ether. Bizarre happenings surround uncanny artwork. A rich socialite dies mysteriously. Shocking return of a supposedly dead spouse. The exotic young lover, disinherited."

"Exit, pursued by a bear," Michael said.

Angus's smile faded. "I do feel a bit sorry for Reynaldo. Do you think Maureene will help him get back to Brazil?"

Kroger raised his brows. "You don't think he'll stay here with the daughter?"

Suki gave a bark of laughter, startling Gigi. "Lyndsay will kick him to the curb now that he's broke."

Kroger nodded once. "Maybe the town will take up a collection for him." He pushed away from the car and looked down the block as a white van approached. "Here comes the portrait."

"That was quick," Michael said.

"It was already packed. Max Thorne came to the station with the shipping case and gave us hell about how we were storing it." Kroger sighed. "I'll be glad to be done with this case."

The van pulled up behind Kroger's car and parked next to the curb. Officer Madison got out and pointed the key fob at the van to unlock all the doors.

He and Detective Kroger walked to the back of the van and opened it. Madison climbed in. The crate lay on its side, and measured about six inches on a side larger than the painting's roughly two by two-and-a-half-feet dimensions. Madison raised the crate to sit on one end, then scooted it across the floor to the edge. Kroger held it steady while Madison jumped to the ground. They lifted it out together.

"Can someone get the door to the house?" Kroger called.

Michael trotted to the house and held open the door. Angus followed more slowly. Suki stayed back, making sure Gigi didn't get stepped on. When everyone else was inside, she picked up the dog and followed.

Kroger and the cop shuffled to the middle of the floor and carefully lowered the crate to sit on its edge.

Suki trotted past them and up the staircase, carrying Gigi.

"Where are you going?" Angus asked. "You'll miss it!"

"Camera!" Suki called down, already on the second landing.

Lupita came in, looking curious.

"Where's Ms. Pinter?" Detective Kroger asked her.

Lupita stared at the crate, her eyes narrowed. "Still with the lawyer, I think. I'll tell her it's here."

While they waited, Kroger examined the top of the crate. "I suppose Ms. Pinter will want to check the portrait for damage." He flipped up a couple of hasps. "These must be for padlocks."

Suki came running down the stairs, carrying a camera and tripod. She set them up in a few deft movements, powered on the camera, and flipped out the LCD screen. Then she picked up the camera, still staring at the screen, and moved around the room before settling on a spot.

Michael looked toward the interior of the house and saw Maureene and Baumgartner walking through the rooms toward them. "Here they come."

They waited in expectant silence until Maureene entered the room.

"Do you want to see it?" Detective Kroger asked.

"Yes, please." Maureene clasped her hands together and rubbed the fingers of one hand with the others.

Michael leaned toward Angus and whispered, "Someone should really approach this family about doing a reality TV show. All this scene lacks is a minor-key soundtrack, heavy on the drums."

"Shh," Angus said.

Kroger flipped back the hinged, wooden lid and looked inside. "Officer Madison."

"Do you want me to lift it out, sir?"

Kroger jerked his head toward the opening of the box.

Madison came over and looked into the crate, hands poised to grasp the portrait's edge. He looked up at Kroger instead, and blinked. "I saw him put it in the box, sir. I *helped*."

"Then where is it?" Kroger asked.

"Are you saying it's gone?" Maureene cried.

Everyone but Suki crowded around the shipping container, jockeying for a better view. Ridges of molded foam jutted from the inner sides of the crate, affixed to strips of Velcro. The space between them was empty.

Michael whipped out his digital recorder as everyone babbled questions. Then he gave his place to Suki, who had taken her camera off its tripod.

She held it over the crate while it flashed several times in succession.

Kroger winced and held up both hands, leaving his officer to grab the crate and steady it. "Everyone be quiet, please!" In the ensuing silence, he addressed Officer Madison. "When did you last see the painting?"

"Yesterday, sir. I accompanied Mr. Thorne to the evidence room."

"Good. Now tell me exactly what happened."

"He brought a protective bag, in addition to the crate. I held the bag while he put the painting in it. He slid the painting into the crate, which I held. He adjusted some of the foam pieces and closed the crate."

"And then both of you left."

"Yes, sir."

Kroger took a deep breath. "You didn't leave him alone in the room at any time?"

Officer Madison looked wounded. "No, sir."

Maureene broke in. "One of your people must have stolen it. Everyone knows how valuable it is."

"That is extremely unlikely." Kroger flipped the top of the crate closed, narrowly avoiding Officer Madison's fingers. "There's a security camera inside the evidence room. We'll be checking it." He turned to his officer. "Did you stop anywhere on your way here?"

Madison flushed red. "The van was low on gas, sir, so I stopped at a filling station. But I paid at the pump! I never left the van."

"We'll check their security footage, if they have any." Kroger thought for a moment. "You did *lock* the van, right?"

"It's an automatic lock, sir."

"And we're sure it's functioning correctly?"

Officer Madison looked panicky. "If you can hold this, sir, I'll check right now." He left the crate in Kroger's grip and trotted out the door.

Kroger caught Michael's eye. "Grab the other end of this, will you? Let's put it against that wall." He jerked his head toward the wall opposite the stairwell.

Michael stashed his recorder in his pocket and took the other side of the crate.

He and Kroger lifted it and leaned it carefully against the wall.

"You'll take fingerprints from that, right?" Maureene asked.

"From the metal parts," Kroger said, brushing off his hands. "But I doubt it will come to that. There's got to be some logical explanation." His dour expression lightened slightly. "Maybe Denton took the wrong crate out of the room. There's a ton of stuff in there, and things get moved around a lot."

Maureene looked relieved. "That must be it."

The front door opened and Lyndsay and Reynaldo came in.

"What's going on now?" Lyndsay demanded. "That policeman outside keeps starting and stopping a van and then running around to check the back doors." She caught sight of the crate and her mouth pursed as if she tasted something sour. "I see the portrait is back now that Reynaldo doesn't inherit."

Kroger looked at Maureene, as if hoping she would explain the situation. When she didn't say anything, he squared his shoulders slightly. "The painting isn't where we thought it was. We're—"

"You *lost* it?" Lyndsay's expression transformed from disbelief to rage.

Kroger went on, his voice a little overloud. "We're looking into the situation and expect to have it resolved shortly. There may have been a mix-up in the evidence room."

"Are you saying you got the painting confused with some *other* portrait of my aunt?" Lyndsay caught sight of the crate and went over to it. "Is it in here? Because I would love to see what you thought was the right painting." She lifted the lid and looked inside. "This is empty."

"That's the problem," Kroger said stiffly.

Lyndsay began to laugh. "Doreene kept that painting in a locked room that everyone knew the code to, for decades, and someone stole it while it was at the police station!"

"Perhaps it wasn't stolen," Angus said over her laughter. When all eyes were on him, he went on. "Perhaps with Doreene gone, it has been slowly disappearing."

Maureene pointed at him. "Get your things and get out."

"I understand that you're distraught," Angus began.

Maureene turned to Detective Kroger. "If they're not out in fifteen minutes, I want you to arrest them for trespassing."

Twenty-three

The staff of *Tripping* magazine trudged down the sidewalk, away from the house.

Michael tried to fasten the closure on his leather carry-on bag as they walked. "Couldn't resist, could you? Had to go for the dramatic statement."

"Ach, someone was bound to kick us out sooner or later," Angus said.

Suki glanced back and groaned.

"What?" Michael asked. He and Angus turned to look.

Framed in the front window, Gigi stood on the back of a chair, gazing out at them. As they watched, she lifted one paw.

Suki hung her head and turned away. "I'll call Kroger and tell him he has to get her out of there." Her voice was husky, and she cleared her throat as she walked on. "There's no way she can stay with those people. They're unfit."

"Eh, once she poops on the carpet a few times, they'll start taking her outside," Michael said.

"Or they'll put her outside and forget her," Suki said.

"I'm sure she'll be fine," Angus said. "Dogs are pretty resourceful."

Suki glared at him. "We're talking about an animal that weighs four pounds and has legs the size of twigs. If she has resources, I don't know where she's keeping them."

"I'll talk to Kroger as well," Angus said firmly. "If he doesn't help, we'll register a complaint with the local animal-protection service."

Suki unlocked the minivan's doors with the remote and stowed her photography equipment.

On the other side, Michael swung his bag onto the far seat before getting in. "So what do we do now? I'm talking about us, not the dog."

Angus took the front passenger seat. "We'll drive to the airport early tomorrow and put ourselves on the standby list."

Michael fastened his seat belt. "You don't want to try to fly out this evening?"

Angus shook his head. "We'll find a motel around here and drive to Seattle early tomorrow morning. That'll give us one more evening to scout around Port Townsend. I'd like to go back to Fort Worden. That was a wonderful, atmospheric place. Maybe it'll clear the bad taste out of our mouths."

Suki opened the driver's side door and got in. "Where to?"

"Start driving toward Fort Worden," Angus said. "We'll see what motels we pass along the way." He looked out the window. "I know this story has had its ups and downs, but it's going to put *Tripping* on the map, you'll see. We'll be credited in every book about paranormal activity from here on out."

"You don't think Kroger will find the painting?" Michael asked.

Angus made a scoffing noise. "You can't find what doesn't exist anymore."

They didn't see any motels on the way to Fort Worden, nor did they find any beyond it. Suki drove for ten minutes more, keeping to the main road, before pulling into the lot of a gardening supply store. "This isn't working. Let's see what we can find online."

They took out their phones and alternately searched the Internet and made calls.

Michael put his hand over the mouthpiece of his phone. "I've got one in Port Townsend proper if we don't mind sharing a room. It has two beds and a couch that folds out."

Angus looked at Suki.

"Fine with me," she said, starting the car. "Let's just book something so we can eat."

Angus dug out his wallet and handed Michael a credit card while Suki turned the car back toward Port Townsend.

The staff of *Tripping* sat in a vinyl-upholstered booth and discussed the painting's disappearance over dinner. Outside the restaurant's windows, a light rain speckled the gray waters of the Sound.

Michael squirted catsup onto his plate. "Angus, do you honestly believe the painting has vanished into thin air?"

Angus swallowed a bite of his fish po' boy. "Let's look at the evidence, shall we?" He counted points on his fingers. "Doreene feels pain when the painting is struck. Cryptic paper strips are found in the soup. There's a plague of slugs, and mysterious lights in the woods. Doreene dies in a locked room. With her death, the painting reverts to its youthful state. When the painting is removed from the house, it vanishes completely." He waggled his seven upraised fingers. "What part of *supernatural goings-on* do you not understand?"

"All of it." Michael picked up his pint glass of beer and took a swig. "The pain could have been a coincidence, or she might have faked it. The paper, slugs, lights—all of that could have been done by a person."

"And the painting's rejuvenation?" Angus asked. "You don't really believe someone could remove all those glued bits without leaving marks, do you?"

"I think that's more likely than that the portrait is actually magic,"

Michael said, "but it occurs to me that we're overlooking an important fact. Who painted the portrait?"

Angus gave him a suspicious look. "Maureene."

"That's right." Michael picked up a fry and pointed it at Angus. "And if she painted it once, why couldn't she paint it again?"

Suki turned from where she was staring out the window. "You think Maureene replaced the aged portrait with a new one?"

"Oh, please," Angus said. "No one knocks out an oil painting in one night. Even if Maureene could do such a thing, it wouldn't be dry. I think someone would have noticed that."

"First of all, we don't know the portrait they found in that closet *is* an oil painting," Michael said. "Now that it's gone, we may never know. Even if it was done in oil, Maureene might have painted it ages ago. Maybe she started out with two portraits, for some reason."

Angus frowned and put down his sandwich. "Then where is the first portrait?"

"I don't know."

"And why would Maureene take it?"

"To sell it? I don't know."

"Assuming Maureene did swap one painting for another, is she also responsible for Doreene's death?"

Michael held up both hands. "I don't know that, either."

Angus gave him a grumpy look. "I like my explanation better."

"I'm sure you do, but that doesn't make it true."

"Well, it's the only truth we have," Angus said, "because we're leaving tomorrow morning."

After they finished eating, they went to the restaurant's door and looked out through the glass. The rain had strengthened enough to bounce off the pavement.

Angus buttoned his coat. "Anyone got an umbrella?"

"I left mine in the car." Michael looked at Suki.

"Me, too," she said.

Angus opened the door, letting in a gust of cold, damp air. "At least it isn't far."

They ran to the car, Michael holding a hand above his glasses to shield them from the rain.

Once inside, Suki turned on the engine and let the defroster blow. "Are we still going to walk around Fort Worden?"

They stared out the windows at the dripping landscape.

"I think we have enough material without it," Angus said.

Michael nodded. "We're going to have trouble fitting everything in, really." He pulled the edge of his shirt from beneath his coat and used it to dry his glasses.

Suki checked her side mirror and pulled onto the street. "The motel it is, then."

The motel they had found dated to Port Townsend's Victorian heyday.

In their shared room, Michael pulled an upholstered armchair away from the wall and looked behind it. "There are no more outlets. I know these historic places are full of atmosphere, but they're not suited to three people all working on computers."

"Try the bathroom," Angus suggested.

"I'm not going to sit on the toilet to work. My butt would fall asleep." Michael turned and surveyed the wall against which Suki had stacked all her photo equipment. "Suki, isn't there anything you can unplug?"

Suki got up and checked her cell phone, which sat on one of the old-fashioned windowsills. "This is charged." She pulled the charger from the outlet, then looked outside, using one hand to shade the windowpane from the interior light. "Hey, it's stopped raining."

Angus looked at his watch and raised his eyebrows. "Would you believe, it's past midnight!"

Suki turned from the window. "Anyone want to go to Fort Worden? I had a couple of ideas for night shots of the battery."

"Now?" Michael asked. "Aren't we supposed to get up early tomorrow to go to the airport?"

"That's what coffee is for," Suki said. "Come on, it'll be fun."

Michael looked at Angus. "Won't the park be closed?"

"Officially, I suppose it is, but it's not as though they have a gate." Angus closed the lid of his laptop and stood. "Suki, can you do what you want in under an hour?"

Suki was already rummaging through her gear. "Forty minutes, tops."

They passed no one on the road that led to Fort Worden. Their headlights slid over rain-washed parked cars and wet leaves.

Michael tilted his head so he could look at the sky through his side window. "It's awfully dark, with all this cloud cover. What kind of shots are you hoping to get?"

"I want to see if the LEDs on our phones are bright enough to use as spotlights on the front of the battery. With the aperture opened up and a long exposure, we might get some cool effects."

"The phones will move if we just hold them," Michael said. "Don't we need to mount them on something to keep the front of the building from looking all smudgy?"

"I'm hoping for a certain amount of smudgy." As she turned into the entrance of the park, their headlights swept across the rhododendron garden, adding brief color to the darkness.

They passed the parade ground and made a right, driving past the Artillery Museum and park office, toward the beach and Admiralty Inlet.

"There are a few lights on inside Alexander's Castle," Michael observed.

"I wouldn't mind a night photo of that," Angus said.

Suki slowed the car to a crawl and looked up the hill toward the castle. "Maybe this road goes there." She turned left and drove slowly up a side street. The castle loomed ahead and to the right. A few lights burned inside, their glow barely revealing the brick crenellations that gave the building its name.

Suki pulled over to the side of the road and parked behind a few other cars, a good hundred feet back from the building. "Close enough. It could be park personnel in there, and I don't want to get kicked out."

"Good point. Try not to slam the car doors," Angus said as they unbuckled their seat belts.

"Michael," Suki said. "Pass me the tripod and the black bag with the blue zipper pull, will you?" She attached her camera to the tripod and they got out of the van.

As they walked up the road toward the building, Michael pointed at the castle. "Someone just crossed in front of a window in that upstairs room," he whispered.

"What were they wearing?" Angus whispered back.

Michael raised his brows. "Feeling voyeuristic?"

"Nothing wrong with that," Suki said, setting up her tripod.

Angus shook his head. "If the person you saw wore old-fashioned clothing, it might be a ghost."

"I don't think so," Michael said. "I'm pretty sure it was just a regular guy."

They all froze at the sound of a harsh scream, cut short.

"What the hell was that?" Michael whispered.

Angus was already loping toward the castle. He looked back and waved an arm for them to follow. Michael put his hand in his coat pocket and felt for his cell phone as he followed. Suki picked up her tripod and trotted after them.

The castle was essentially a three-story square tower, with windows on the first and second floors and small, one-story wings on either side. By the plainness of the exterior on this side, it appeared they were at the back of the building.

Suki and Michael joined Angus as he crouched at the corner of the structure, out of sight of the windows.

"Do you think we should call nine-one-one?" Michael whispered.

"Maybe," Suki murmured, "although it could be anything. I once heard someone scream like that when he passed a kidney stone."

"Let's see what the situation is first," Angus said. Crouching, he moved to one of two doors and quickly put his head up enough to see through the corner of the window. "Nothing." Still crouching, he walked to the second door and did the same thing. "Nothing here, either." At the sound of footsteps descending the inside stairs, he drew back, whispering, "Someone's coming!"

They hustled around the corner of the building, then peered around the edge.

The door opened. A man backed through it, holding another man under the arms and dragging him through. About five feet from the back of the building, the limp man suddenly pulled away, half-falling in his attempt to escape. The first man released him and grabbed at something tucked in the waistband of his pants. They heard a clicking noise, and the second man fell to the ground and screamed, the sound obviously muffled by something shoved in his mouth.

When the man on the ground had fallen silent, the first man spoke. "One battery can do that fifty times, and I have a spare in my pocket." The voice was Hank's. "Now get up."

The man on the ground groaned faintly and bent one knee in an attempt to rise.

Hank grabbed his arm and hauled him to his feet before letting go and stepping back a pace. "I can do this all night, or you can cooperate. I swear, I won't do anything to you afterward."

The other man, swaying, seemed to laugh through his gag.

"Don't be stupid. You'll keep quiet because if you go to the police, they'll know you stole it." Hank shoved the man toward the street and a dark car. "Now show me."

Angus and the others flattened themselves against the building as Hank made the other man get in the passenger's side of the car and crawl over to the driver's side. Then Hank got in the passenger's side and they left, the prisoner driving.

The glow of Michael's phone illuminated his hand. "I'm calling nine-one-one."

"Do it from the car," Suki said. "I'm going to follow them. The cops can't help if we don't know where they went."

"We don't need to follow," Michael panted as they ran to the minivan. "He's headed farther into the park. We can just park at the entrance to make sure they don't go anywhere."

"There are three entrances," Angus said, jerking open the van door and scrambling inside.

Suki didn't bother to put her tripod and camera in the back, but shoved the whole thing toward Michael, who wrestled the equipment into the space behind him.

Michael tapped on his phone's screen. "Okay, I'm calling."

Suki pulled into the street, keeping the van's headlights turned off. "Can anyone see them?" She sped up, leaning forward to peer through the front window.

"There!" Angus pointed. "They're turning left at that intersection."

"Got it." Suki sped up, made the turn, then slowed again, so as not to get too close. "Who's the guy on the Taser leash?"

Angus shook his head and started to reply, but Michael held up a hand and made a shushing noise.

"Yes," he said. "I'm in Fort Worden State Park, and we're following Hank Gray, who is . . . um . . . Well, he's taken someone captive with a Taser and is forcing that person to lead him to something. We're following them now." He paused. "Hold on." He spoke to Suki. "She says only follow them if you can do it without being noticed. They're sending someone." He addressed the phone again. "Can you send Detective

Kroger? He's been working on a case involving this person. Yes, I'll stay on the line."

Ahead, the car made another left and followed the coast road to the north.

Michael spoke quietly. "It must be Maxwell Thorne, don't you think? I know he said he moved to the hostel, but . . ." He trailed off.

Suki nodded. "The body looks too mature for Reynaldo. Hank must think he has the portrait."

Angus shook his head slightly. "None of this makes any sense."

The car ahead passed the first two parking lots next to the campground and turned into the last one, disappearing into the darkness.

Suki stopped the van on the road, choosing a spot partially shielded from the lot by a scrubby tree. She killed the engine and pulled the keys from the ignition. "Michael, point that phone up here, will you?"

Michael pointed the phone's face toward the overhead switches for the interior lights. Suki turned them off before opening her car door.

Angus grabbed the shoulder of her jacket. "What do you think you're doing?" he whispered.

Suki turned to look at him. "Following them, what do you think?"

"In the dark? On foot?" Angus shook his head. "He's bound to hear you tripping over tree branches and kicking rocks."

"Then maybe he'll think twice about killing Max, or whoever it is."

"With a handheld bug zapper? If he really wanted to kill someone, he'd have a gun."

"Guns aren't that easy to get," Michael said. "There are cliffs around here. Hank could shock him unconscious and roll him off."

"Give me that phone." Angus took it from Michael while still holding on to Suki. "Ms. Policewoman? Do you think we should follow this man now that he's on foot?" He looked at Suki. "She says *no.*"

Suki snatched the phone from his hand and threw it in the back of the car.

"Hey!" Michael protested.

"Angus, what is *wrong* with you?" Suki asked. "You're not one to stand by while someone is in danger."

"He doesn't want the cops to find the missing painting," Michael said, his voice chilly. "That's it, isn't it?"

"I'm only doing what the police told us to do," Angus protested. "Why call them if you're not going to take their advice?"

"Oh, *Angus.*" Suki's voice was full of disappointment.

Angus let go of her and raised his hands in surrender. "Fine. But if *Tripping* loses this story because of Jolting Jimmy out there, you'll have only yourselves to blame."

They got out of the car and tiptoed across the road to where they could see past the tree.

"Can you see anything?" Michael whispered as they stared in the direction the other car had gone.

"I can see what might be a car," Suki whispered, "or it might be a rock or a picnic table."

"They could be anywhere, after all that time we wasted talking," Michael said. "I'm going." He bent low and ran as quietly as possible down the sloped road to the parking area.

The others followed. They crossed the bare lot and found the empty car at the far end, where the asphalt ended and sloping, scrub-covered dunes began.

Michael looked back the way they had come. "Why aren't there any campers?"

"The boat festival ended this afternoon," Suki said. "I guess they left. Here's a path."

They walked up the sliding sand, weeds scratching at their pant legs. At the top, the concrete bulk of the battery was visible as a darker shape against the night sky.

They stopped and listened, but heard only the wind in the needles of the enormous firs overhead.

"Do you think Hank took him somewhere else?" Michael whispered.

They stiffened as a muffled shriek came from the building ahead. It echoed strangely.

"They're inside," Suki said. "Come on."

They crept across the graveled area in front of the building, their footsteps crunching slightly. It was darker beneath the concrete overhang of the second story. The doors that led to storage areas and from there to the tunnels were barely visible as pitch-black squares.

They slowly traversed the front, hands against the wall.

Suki, in the lead, felt a frantic tapping on her back. She turned.

"I think I hear something back the other way," Michael said, his voice a mere breath. He turned and ran into Angus, who grunted. Michael grabbed hold of his shoulders and turned him back the way they had come.

They crossed the center of the building and stopped at the first door on the other side. Slight sounds came from the pitch-black opening—the echo of footfalls on concrete, and the occasional grunt or groan.

Michael tugged at the other two until they were several feet to the side of the door. "You stay behind one of those trees and call the police again. I'll make a noise and see if I can lure him out. Then I'll tackle him or something."

"Or *something.*" Angus managed to pack a world of scorn into his murmur. "Have you ever been in a fight?"

Michael hesitated, then shook his head.

"Well, I have, many times. You two stay behind the trees and leave it to me. I'll give him the old Glasgow kiss."

"What?" Michael whispered.

"He means a head butt," Suki explained. "And why don't both of you stay behind the trees and let me handle this? You're looking at four years of kickboxing classes here."

They turned at the sound of approaching cars coming from the other side of the dune.

"The cops!" Suki whispered. "We'd better show them where to go."

"Good idea," Michael said.

Angus gave them both a little push. "Hurry. If we're lucky, Max hasn't broken down yet."

They found Detective Kroger and six officers at the head of the path. Kroger stationed police at the other entrances to the battery, to prevent escape, and then went inside with the remaining cops, their flashlight beams sweeping the walls.

He took up a position outside the tunnel entrance and accepted the bullhorn one of his officers held out to him. "COME OUT WITH—" Kroger jerked and lowered the bullhorn as echoes bounced around the concrete walls. "*Man,* that was loud."

From their place in the outer doorway, the *Tripping* staff removed their hands from their ears.

Kroger handed the bullhorn back to his officer and settled for shouting into the darkness. "Come out, Mr. Gray. Raise your hands above your head, fingers spread. We have every exit covered."

After perhaps fifteen seconds, they heard the sound of footsteps, and a light shone from the tunnel.

Kroger averted his face. "Point the light at the floor, Gray. Now."

The light dropped. A long, broken shadow preceded the men, and then Maxwell Thorne stumbled out of the tunnel. He held the gun-shaped Taser and its gathered wires in one hand. The leads ended in a bloody spot on his shirt. "Thank God." He tottered over to sit on the floor, his back against the wall.

As Hank Gray emerged, he raised his hands in the air. He wasn't wearing the brown contacts, and his blue eyes looked cold and sinister in the tanned surround of his face. "We were just having some fun, that's all. Max knows I would never really hurt him."

"Drop the flashlight and lie facedown on the floor," Kroger barked at him.

Hank obeyed, bending his knees and lowering himself awkwardly to the ground. At a nod from Kroger, one of the cops knelt on his back and handcuffed him, then searched him thoroughly as he read him his rights.

As Hank was hauled to his feet, he caught sight of Max. "Why don't you tell them, Max? Tell them it was just a little game."

Max pointed a trembling finger at him. "You're *crazy,* and I hope you rot in jail for a long time." His voice was weak.

Kroger nodded toward one of his officers. "Have the ambulance guys check Mr. Thorne." He turned to Max. "Afterward, Mr. Thorne, I'd like to see you at the station so I can ask you some questions."

"I'm happy to answer anything I can," Max said, "although I don't know if anyone can make sense out of this lunatic's actions."

Hank looked back from where he was being led to the outside door. "Don't believe him. He's lying." Still facing backward, his head smacked into a low-hanging concrete support. "Ow! Motherf—"

"Whoopsie," said the cop in charge of him. "You want to watch where you're going."

Twenty-four

Detective Kroger sat in the Port Townsend police station's interrogation room across a table from Hank Gray.

In a connecting room, Angus, Suki, and Michael watched the proceedings on a video monitor, accompanied by a policewoman.

"Why did you take Max into the gun battery?" Kroger asked Hank, for perhaps the thirtieth time.

Hank stared past him, stone-faced.

"You wanted him to show you something. You said he had stolen it. Do you think Maxwell Thorne has the portrait? He was having coffee while the van was in transit. He has a receipt with the time stamp and the waitress remembers him."

Hank remained silent.

Kroger tilted his head and studied him. "Maybe you think Thorne stole the painting from Ms. Gray the night she died, but he has the best alibi of any of you. He was at the Olympic Hostel with a bunch of rowdy kids. He helped make dinner. He played piano. Then he slept on the top bunk of a bunk bed, while the guy below stayed up most of the night texting his girlfriend back in Germany."

Hank continued to stare off to one side, his cuffed hands resting on the table. "Where's my lawyer?"

"I have no idea. Presumably Ms. Pinter is working on getting you one, but things take longer when it's the middle of the night. She has to wake people up. They have to get dressed and unlock their offices. Could someone else have stolen the painting? I'm prepared to believe that, but you have to give me something to work with."

Hank's gaze drifted to Kroger, and his lip curled. "Let me know when my lawyer arrives."

Outside the room, the policewoman's phone buzzed. She took it from the belt holster and checked the screen, then went into the room and showed it to Kroger.

Kroger pushed back his chair. "Think about cooperating, Mr. Gray. We'd be very glad to find that portrait."

The policewoman took up a position at the side of the room, one hand on her gun holster.

Kroger came out, leaving the door open. He gestured for Angus and the others to follow him down the hall. "They've brought Thorne in. Apparently he's okay, other than a couple of holes in his side where the Taser probes went in."

"Poor fellow," Angus said sympathetically. "It's pretty clear Hank Gray is a madman."

"I'd prefer it if he weren't," Kroger said, "but there's nothing in that gun battery. We also checked the video from the evidence room. It clearly shows Thorne putting the painting in the box. Officer Madison closed the lid, the two of them leaned it against the wall, and that's where it stayed until we took it out and put in the van."

"Does the van have video surveillance in it?" Michael asked.

Kroger's lips thinned. "No."

"Some kind of GPS tracker?"

"This isn't TV," Kroger said tightly. "It's just a van."

"But Officer Madison helped Max put the painting in the crate *and* he drove the van?" Michael asked.

"Yes."

Michael looked excited. "Did he and Maxwell talk about anything while they were in the evidence room?"

"Probably, but the surveillance camera doesn't have audio." Kroger narrowed his eyes. "What are you thinking?"

"What if, while they were in there, Max slipped the officer a note or a bunch of cash as a bribe to stop the van along the way? He got gas, right? How well do you know Officer Madison?"

"He's my nephew," Kroger said, "and the gas station is only about five blocks from this station, all on well-traveled streets. They'd be taking the painting out in front of anyone who happened to walk by." He sighed. "But I'll check and make sure Madison hasn't received any mysterious cash contributions."

Angus patted his shoulder. "You took every reasonable precaution, but you can't guard against supernatural vanishment. I think we have to accept that the portrait is gone forever."

"*You* may be able to accept that," Kroger said. "This station's insurance provider won't."

They turned a corner and Kroger led the way into his office, where he settled into his chair with a sigh.

Angus and Suki took the two guest chairs. Michael looked around for a third, then settled for leaning against the wall.

Kroger poked at some papers on his desk. "Someone will bring your transcribed statements to sign, and then you can leave."

Michael nodded absently. "Is someone keeping watch on the battery?"

Kroger looked up. "My guys went through every tunnel and looked in every room, and there's no painting anywhere. A bare concrete building doesn't have a lot of hiding places." He held up a hand. "And before you ask, they're checking the surrounding area, too."

Angus shook his head. “Stop pestering the man, Michael.” He turned to Kroger. “I wouldn’t spend too much time following up on the babblings of a lunatic.”

“Hey!” Michael said.

Angus rolled his eyes. “I’m talking about Hank. We don’t know that he was talking about the painting when he said Max stole something. He could have been talking about his favorite pillow or his left shoe. He’s clearly a nutter.”

Kroger smiled faintly. “Oh, I think he was talking about the portrait. We went through Thorne’s room at Alexander’s Castle. Someone had taken every picture down from the walls and pulled the canvases away from the frames. That’s in addition to tossing the contents of Thorne’s luggage, pulling the mattress off the box spring, and rolling back the rugs.”

Suki stirred in her chair. “I wonder why Hank didn’t say anything about Max to you guys.”

“Like what?” Kroger asked.

Suki pointed an accusing finger and lowered her voice. “Max stole the painting! He’s the bad guy!” She continued in her normal voice. “If Hank believes Max has the portrait, why not use the excuse that he’s trying to retrieve stolen goods? Instead, he makes up a bunch of crap about how they were playing a game.”

“That was *really* creepy,” Michael said.

Angus nodded in agreement.

Kroger thought for a moment. “The only explanation I can think of is that Mr. Gray doesn’t want us to find the painting. If we do, he can’t track it down and keep it.”

A policewoman came to the door, leading Maxwell Thorne.

He wore a fresh shirt but looked deeply weary, with pale skin and red-rimmed eyes. “You wanted to ask me some questions?”

Kroger stood. “How are you feeling, Mr. Thorne?”

“Like I need a lot of sleep and some trauma therapy.” Max’s voice was rough. He cleared his throat and addressed Angus and his staff. "I can't thank you enough. I really think he would have killed me."

Angus got up and gestured for Max to take his chair. "I'm just happy we were there to help."

Max sat, wincing slightly and angling his side away from the chair arm. He looked up at Angus. "Why were you at the fort? Were you following Hank for some reason?"

Angus shook his head. "Pure coincidence. Suki wanted to take some nighttime photographs of the fort. You must have a guardian angel."

"I must." Max turned to Kroger. "How can I help?"

Kroger took out a pad and consulted it. "How long have you known Hank Gray?"

Max thought for a moment. "I met him once or twice before he disappeared, when he and Doreene were still together. They hung out with a very wealthy European crowd." He smiled slightly. "The kind of people who splurge on art."

Kroger returned the smile. "Of course. You didn't recognize him when he showed up here?"

"No. I think he stayed out of my way, but it was also a very effective disguise."

Kroger nodded. "Hank said he knew you had stolen something. What was it?"

Max looked confused. "He didn't tell you? I assume it was Doreene's portrait, but I don't remember if he used those actual words."

"And did you tell him it was in the battery?"

Max nodded. "I chose that because it's right near the campground. I thought I'd have a better chance of someone hearing something through a tent wall than if they were inside a building. But it looked like they had all left. Then I thought that if I ran around the corner of a tunnel, I might be able to pull the Taser probes loose, but that didn't work, either." He shuddered slightly.

Kroger scribbled on his pad for a moment. "Can you think of other reasons Hank would target you? Some perceived motive for revenge?"

Max shook his head. "I've been racking my brains for something like that, but I can't think of a thing. I cultivated both Hank and Doreene as potential clients, but I don't think I paid her any attention that could have been misinterpreted. And he knew I was married, with a daughter."

"Mm-hmm." Kroger consulted the pad again. "You were in charge of the portrait's auction. Did Hank express any objections to that?"

"Not that I heard of, but he wasn't around when it was being set up."

"And when he did come on the scene, he didn't seem suspicious of you in any way?"

"Not until last night."

Michael raised his hand.

Kroger looked at him. "Did you notice something about Hank's behavior toward Mr. Thorne?"

Michael lowered his hand. "Um, not really. I wanted to ask Max a question."

"Go ahead," Max said.

"Why did you move back to Alexander's Castle? You had moved to the Olympic Hostel, right?"

Max gave him a sheepish smile. "I thought staying at the hostel would be fun, but they treated me like someone's dad, so I moved back. The castle has great views." He looked at Kroger. "It could have better locks."

"I'll tell the park service they should consider upgrading them." Kroger made a note on his pad and then looked up at Max. "Do you have the painting?"

Max gave a bemused shake of his head. "No."

"And you don't know why Hank Gray would think that you do have it?"

Max gave a bitter laugh. "No, but we're talking about a man who disappeared for almost thirty years and then showed up right before his wife died, in disguise. God knows what's going on in his head."

"Fair enough," Kroger said. "May I ask what your plans are?"

"I just want to get on a plane and go home, but I suppose I should get some sleep first." Max lifted a hand and rubbed his forehead. "It's going to be a little disturbing, going back to the room where I was tortured. Maybe I can find a hotel for what's left of the night."

"I think that's a good idea," Kroger said. "You can call here in the morning and ask someone to accompany you to Alexander's Castle to get your things."

"I think I'll take you up on that."

Kroger stood and came around his desk. "Thank you for your patience, Mr. Thorne, and for answering my questions. I'm very sorry you had such a terrible experience."

Max pushed himself to his feet and shook hands. "Without you, it would have been much worse." He turned to Angus. "Again, I'm so grateful." He reached in his pants pocket and took out a business card. "The next time any of you are in New York, please let me take you out to dinner."

Angus took the card. "Thank you. We're just glad you're all right."

Suki and Michael murmured agreement.

"I'll walk you out," Kroger said to Max, and they disappeared down the hall.

Michael quickly took the vacant chair. "I have to admit, he's pretty convincing."

"It's easy to be convincing when you're telling the truth." Angus jerked a thumb at Michael. "Out o' my chair."

Michael sighed and got up. "Why are you so reluctant to dig deeper into this?"

Angus sat and crossed his legs. "Because *Tripping* covers matters of paranormal interest. I'm not interested in anything else."

"Oh, come on, Angus," Suki said. "You were plenty interested when it came to Charlotte Baskerville."

"Charlotte Baskerville was in genuine danger," Angus said. "Plus, she was a nice old girl, whereas this lot is as unlovely a bunch of specimens as I've ever seen."

"Max is okay," Michael said, "assuming he's telling the truth, which I'm still not sure about."

"Reynaldo isn't that bad," Suki said, "even if he does hang around with a beret thief."

"All that may be," Angus said, "but none of them is in danger of dying."

"Doreene was," Michael said.

Angus gave him an affronted look. "Are you seriously suggesting we delay writing up the best story we've ever had to investigate the probable suicide of that poisonous old bitch? Who was *terminally ill,* I might add?"

Michael crossed his arms. "Well, when you put it *that* way."

After signing their statements at the police station, the staff of *Tripping* walked to their minivan, crossing squares of light from the station's windows. It was very quiet outside.

Michael took out his cell phone and glanced at the time. "Three-thirty in the morning," he said, his words barely intelligible through a giant yawn.

Suki stopped by the driver's side door and did some jumping jacks.

Angus groaned. "Is this really the time for calisthenics? I want to go to bed."

"You want me to be awake for the drive, don't you?" Suki pushed the button on the remote.

Michael slid open his door with a weary gesture. "It's not as though anyone will be on the road." He climbed into the van, rested his cheek on the seat back, and closed his eyes. "Two nights with hardly any sleep. I'm so tired, I'm almost queasy."

Angus grunted in agreement as Suki pulled onto the empty road. "At least we don't have to be up early. Our flight back to Colorado is scheduled for early evening."

"I've been thinking," Michael said. "I might pay to change my flight and stay longer."

Angus turned in his seat and looked back at Michael. "Why?"

Michael rolled his head to face forward. "It occurs to me that Reynaldo's story would make a great book. Young Brazilian sailor is plucked from a life of freedom on the ocean to become the dependent, land-locked lover of a wealthy older woman."

"Michael, you have a duty to *Tripping* magazine and this story," Angus said. "We need you back in Boulder."

"I can work from anywhere, so what's the problem?" Michael yawned again. "If Alexander's Castle is available, I'll stay there. Maybe I'll see a ghost—that should make you happy."

"You don't believe in ghosts!" Angus sputtered. "You just want to find that painting!"

Michael closed his eyes and rested his head again. "I can almost hear the spirit of John Alexander, moaning away in that Scottish accent about his faithless bride."

Angus turned to face the front. "When we get back, I'm going to have you sign such a contract, you'll need my permission to go to the John Alexander."

Twenty-five

At seven-thirty the next morning, Michael's cell phone vibrated an alarm from beneath his pillow. He took it out and dismissed the reminder before it could buzz again.

On the other bed, Angus snored gently.

Michael got up quietly and dressed.

Suki opened her eyes and looked at him from her bed on the fold-out sofa.

He put a finger to his lips, but she merely flapped a dismissive hand and rolled over.

Michael sneaked out of the hotel carrying his messenger bag, which he had packed the night before with his computer and digital recorder. Doreene's house, now Maureene's, was perhaps a third of a mile away. He walked, stopping only to get coffee at a café along the way.

Once at the house, he checked his watch. It was still a little before eight, but Angus might wake at any time, and who knew how long Reynaldo would stick around now that he was disinherited. Michael rapped on the door.

He heard barking after a few seconds. The sound came closer and settled on the other side of the door. "Hi, Gigi. It's me, Michael," he said, but she just barked harder.

A good three minutes passed before he felt the vibration of footsteps on the wooden floor.

Lyndsay's voice came from inside. "Would you *shut up*!" She opened the door.

Gigi darted out and into the yard, where she sniffed bushes.

"What do you want?" Lyndsay demanded of Michael. She wore a white satin robe with black flowers on it and looked beautiful, despite her sour expression and messy hair.

Michael smiled. "I'd like to talk to Reynaldo, if he's available."

"Why?"

"I want to discuss the possibility of helping him write a book about his experiences in the United States. Young sailor falls in love with a woman he meets on a boat, who then dies and leaves him without resources. That kind of thing. I think it has the makings of a bestseller."

Lyndsay chewed her lip thoughtfully. "Stay here." She retreated, shutting the door in his face.

"Your dog is still out here!" Michael called, but there was no answer.

He sat down on the step and whistled to Gigi. She approached cautiously, but eventually got close enough to let him pet her. Finally she rolled onto her back and accepted a stomach rub.

It was another five minutes before the door opened again.

Reynaldo stood there, looking boyishly sleepy and devastatingly handsome in jeans, a close-fitting red T-shirt, and leather sandals.

Lyndsay appeared behind him. "Don't agree to or sign *anything* without talking to me first."

An irritated expression passed over his face, but he nodded before coming outside.

Michael whistled to Gigi, who had withdrawn when he stood up.

"Come here." He picked her up when she got close and put her inside the house.

Reynaldo stuck his fingertips in his pockets and gave Michael a glum look. "The dog and I have a lot in common."

"Let's see if we can improve your situation," Michael said. "Do you want some coffee?"

Michael and Reynaldo sat in one of Port Townsend's cozy coffeehouses.

Reynaldo took a sip of his latte. "So, I tell you what happened, and you make it into a book."

Michael nodded. "And we share the money."

"How much money will you get?"

"Half," Michael said.

Reynaldo pouted. "But it is my story."

Michael smiled. "You can always write it yourself and keep all the profit."

Reynaldo took another sip. "How long before we would get the money?"

Michael leaned forward. "Remember, there's no guarantee we'll get any. With your help, I hope to write and organize the book in four to six months. If we can get a publisher to take it on, it'll be another year before it hits the shelves. Let's say two years, just to be safe."

"Two years?" Reynaldo exclaimed. "What will I live on in the meantime? Lyndsay is talking about moving to New York."

"I guess you'll have to find work," Michael said, "unless you can find someone else to pay your expenses."

"Can I live with you?" Reynaldo asked. "Then you would not have to travel to work with me."

"Possibly," Michael said. "But I can't afford to pay for your food and whatever. You'd still need a job, and Colorado isn't a big boat state."

At Reynaldo's blank look, he said, "It's right in the middle of the country—no ocean. Have you waited tables before?"

Reynaldo shook his head.

Michael tapped his fingers on the table. "You might be able to get modeling work in Denver. The thing is, there's a really good chance this book project could pay off, and what do you have to lose?"

Reynaldo stared at the tabletop. "I will think about it."

Angus and Suki sat at a table on the second floor of a waterfront restaurant. They had slept until half past nine and walked to a restaurant that served brunch.

A waitress took their order, casting frequent glances at Suki's gray shirt, the torn sides of which were laced together with electrical wire.

After the waitress left, Angus unwrapped his silverware, muttering as he did so. "I can't believe Michael. Of all the underhanded, ungrateful, unethical, sneaky—"

"Sneaky doesn't begin with *un*," Suki said.

Angus stopped muttering and stared at her.

"Plus, it has nothing to do with me." Suki gave Angus a distinctly chilly look. "Your misplaced anger is starting to get on my nerves."

Angus took a deep breath and laid his napkin over his lap. "You're absolutely right. I'm sorry." His lips turned up in a reasonable facsimile of a smile. "So. What do you do when you're not taking fantastic pictures for us?"

"Stuff." Suki used her head to gesture toward the other side of the restaurant. "Max Thorne and stupid Lyndsay just walked in."

Angus looked casually over his shoulder. "Sure enough."

Suki raised her brows at him. "Do you see what she has on her head?"

Angus watched Max usher Lyndsay into a corner booth. Lyndsay wore a saucy black raincoat and a black beret. "Some sort of hat."

"*My* hat." Suki spoke through gritted teeth. "What do you bet Max is hitting on her? Once, when I wore that hat, an Italian guy literally threw himself at my feet. We might have hooked up if he hadn't broken two fingers when they rammed into my boot."

"You're pretty enough to break men's fingers without a hat." Angus saw the waitress approaching with a tray. "Here's our food."

They ate in silence. Periodically either Angus or Suki glanced at the booth where Max and Lyndsay sat.

Max sat with his back to them, his posture changing gradually from casual to intense. He leaned over the table, making small, private gestures with his hands.

The bill came, and Angus gave the waitress the credit card provided by Pendergast, the orthodontist who funded *Tripping*. "Are you finished?" he asked Suki, who had left half her sandwich and was taking pictures of gulls outside the window.

"Sure." Suki powered off her camera, put it in her bag, and got up.

"Hang on," Angus said. "I still have to sign the check."

"I know. I'm just gonna go over and say 'hi' to Max and Lyndsay."

"Don't—" Angus reached to grab her, but she was too quick.

She glanced back and gave him an impish smile. "What? It would look weird if I ignored Max, what with us saving his life and all."

As she walked away, Angus looked around for the waitress, who still had his credit card.

She stood behind the cash register, chatting with the bartender.

Angus got up and went over to her. "I'm sorry, but we're in a bit of a hurry. If I could just sign that . . ." He held out his hand for the check.

"Oh, I'm sorry!" she said. "One second while I run it through the machine."

"That's fine. I should have told you," Angus said, looking over his shoulder.

Suki stood beside Max and Lyndsay's table. Max smiled up at her, looking casual and urbane. Lyndsay had taken off the beret. It sat on the seat next to her, with her purse.

The waitress handed Angus his bill and a pen. "Here you go. I hope you enjoyed your omelet."

"It was delicious, thank you." He scribbled a tip and his name, then strode across the room.

Suki looked up as he joined them. "Max is going to see if he can find Lyndsay a job at Rothwell's. Isn't that great?"

"Wonderful," Angus agreed.

"It's the least I can do for the family," Max said. "I feel somewhat responsible for the painting going missing. Maybe if I'd insisted on going with the van to pick it up, or hired a security detail . . ."

"Don't be silly, Max." Lyndsay patted his hand. "Anyway, we're better off without the painting. I just wish it hadn't had such a terrible effect on my father. The thing was clearly cursed."

Angus made a sympathetic tsking noise before asking, "Can we quote you about the curse?"

She looked at him coldly. "I'd rather you didn't."

Suki took her camera bag off her shoulder. "Do you mind if I put this on the table? It gets heavy."

"Go ahead," Max said.

Suki put down her bag. "Do you have a background in art, Lyndsay?"

"Just what I learned from my mother, mostly about portraits." She smiled at Max. "But I'm highly motivated."

Angus nodded. "I'm sure you'll do very well." He turned to Suki. "We should be going."

"Okay." Suki reached down and picked up her bag by the strap. "Good luck to both of you."

Max held out his hand to Angus. "Thanks again for helping me out last night. And if you're ever in New York . . ."

Angus nodded and shook his hand. "I'll be sure to look you

up." He took Lyndsay's hand. "Best of luck. I hope everything works out."

She smiled at him. "Me, too."

Angus turned to find Suki almost at the door. By the time he reached it, she was halfway down the steps to the street level. "What's the big rush?" he asked.

In answer, she lifted her hand over her head and waved the beret.

Angus caught up to her outside, on the sidewalk. "How did you do it?"

Suki glanced behind her, but kept a brisk pace. "I let my bag's strap dangle off Lyndsay's side of the table and scooped up the hat when I took it with me." She checked the street for traffic before crossing.

Angus glanced both ways and followed. "What would you have said if Lyndsay noticed the hat gone while you were still in the restaurant?"

"That it must have stuck to the Velcro on the bag's flap when I was standing next to the table."

"That's good," Angus said admiringly.

Suki suddenly pulled him into a nearby doorway. "Take a look at the car across the street and about a hundred feet ahead."

Angus peered around the edge of the wall. "What about it?"

"Maureene is sitting in it—staring at the restaurant we just left."

Angus narrowed his eyes. "I wonder if she's keeping an eye on Lyndsay."

"Or Max."

Angus withdrew and shrugged. "Either way, it's nothing to do with us."

Suki put her hands on her hips. "Really, Angus? We could be looking at the weirdest art heist of the decade. Are you sure you don't want to follow it?"

"Not when it's the paranormal story of the century. *Tripping* readers expect a certain kind of content."

"How many *Tripping* readers are we talking about?"

Angus fiddled with the zipper on his jacket. "Our subscription rate increased by thirty percent after the Baskerville story."

Suki folded her arms over her chest. "How *many,* Angus?"

Angus gave an irritated huff and met her eye. "A little over six hundred, but if we follow the mundane aspect of this story, we'll be in competition with every news publication out there."

"No we won't, because we're the only one with the inside scoop." Suki put an arm around Angus's shoulder. "Couldn't you expand the scope of the magazine to include the generally bizarre?"

"I don't know." Angus stared into space. "I could talk it over with Pendergast, I suppose."

"Why don't you do that. It's always good to have options." Suki peeked out again. "Max and Lyndsay just came out of the restaurant."

Angus leaned out enough to see around the corner.

Max and Lyndsay spoke for a moment. He leaned down and kissed her cheek before crossing the street to his car.

Lyndsay walked a few steps, only to stop and study a store window. She glanced sideways to watch Max's car drive away, then walked over to her mother's vehicle and knocked on the passenger-side window.

Maureene apparently rolled down the window, because Lyndsay leaned down and said something before pointing in the direction Max had gone. A few seconds later, Maureene pulled away from the curb and drove after him.

Lyndsay walked briskly in the other direction, which would take her back to her mother's house.

"Interesting," Angus murmured to Suki.

"What's interesting?" Michael said from behind them.

Angus jerked in surprise, and Suki gave a little yelp.

Angus turned. "Where have you been?"

"Meeting with Reynaldo," Michael said. "I wanted to get to him early, in case he had plans to take off."

"And does he?"

"Not yet." Michael leaned against the doorway's brick edge. "I pitched him my idea, and I think he's interested. I'll mention *Tripping* in the book, of course."

"Very gracious, I'm sure," Angus said drily.

Michael frowned. "It's good cross-promotion for *Tripping*, and I'm not infringing on your territory. There was nothing paranormal about Reynaldo's relationship with Doreene."

"That we *know* of," Angus said.

"If I run across anything supernatural, I promise not to write about it, okay?" Michael peered around the doorway in the direction they had been looking. "What were you doing when I got here?"

"Let's walk back to the hotel," Angus said. "We can talk on the way."

Twenty-six

Michael sat in the back of the minivan, hemmed in by their hastily packed luggage. "You know Alexander's Castle has only one bedroom, right? With one bed."

"I'm sure Suki and I can find something else at Fort Worden," Angus said. "Maybe in the officers' quarters."

"I thought you were set to go home." Michael leaned forward. "You don't have to keep watch on me. I'll finish the story for *Tripping* first."

"I have every confidence that you will," Angus said.

Michael sat back against his seat with a thump. "If I figure out what's really going on, I'm not going to hide it. The police will have to know."

"Of course," Angus said. "Did we hide anything from the police on the Baskerville story?"

"No, but you misled the public when it came to the article."

Angus turned in his seat. "We gave our readers what they wanted, and I don't remember misrepresenting any facts in that article."

"That's because you left out most of the facts!" Michael glared at him.

Angus glared back. "We are not *60 Minutes,* Michael. Our job is to entertain our readers. *They* know it, *I* know it, *Suki* knows it—"

"Sorry, what do I know?" Suki asked. "I wasn't listening."

Michael raised his voice. "That we're in the business of choosing how much to tell our readers, so they'll keep buying the magazine."

"Oh, right." Suki swung the minivan into the entrance of Fort Worden.

Angus went on. "The only person who doesn't seem to understand his job is you, Michael."

Michael raised both hands. "Fine. I'll write this story the way you want, and then I'm quitting."

Angus faced forward and stared out the car window. "Maybe that would be best."

"That's why I suggested it."

"Fine," Angus said.

"Fine."

Suki pulled the car to the side of the road in front of Alexander's Castle. "We're here, in case anyone is interested." She unclipped her seat belt. "Do you suppose Hank left anything behind? A couple of spare gags, maybe?"

"I'm going to take a walk." Michael got out and slid his door shut with unnecessary force.

Angus scrambled out and slammed his own door. "I'll come with you."

"Don't bother. We have nothing to talk about." Michael stalked off, hands in his pockets.

"It's just as well. I doubt I could hear anything over the sound of your self-righteousness!" Angus took a few long steps and caught up with him.

Still in the car, Suki reached back for her camera bag, which she had stowed behind her seat. She took out the camera and rested it on the frame of her open window. "Portrait of two assholes," she muttered, focusing on the two men walking rigidly away from her.

. . .

Michael walked swiftly, but Angus, who was slightly taller, had no difficulty in keeping up. They reached the coast road walking side by side. Michael turned left, toward Battery Kinzie and the lighthouse beyond.

They returned greetings from passing people as they trudged along: men and women carrying fishing poles, two boys with a plastic bag that dripped water. Still they walked, past the marine science center, a bleached and abandoned boat, and the first entrance to the parking lot for the campground.

Michael had studied a map of Fort Worden. Beyond the campground parking lots, a trail led from the road to Battery Vicars and from there to Battery Kinzie. He passed the final entrance to the parking lot and suppressed a smile when he heard a soft grunt of surprise from Angus.

Michael slowed his pace and kept an eye on the dunes to his left. A weedy path cut through the sand at the place where the road branched. He took it, changing direction so quickly that sand slopped over the side of his shoe.

Angus followed. "You heard what the police said. It's a concrete bunker. It's not as though the painting could be hidden under a floorboard."

"I just want to look. Being curious is part of the job, isn't it?"

The only answer was an unintelligible grumble.

They reached the broken edge of an asphalt walk and went on to find a low concrete building set down into the ground. It was smaller than Kinzie, with a battered white sign that read THOMAS VICARS affixed to its front.

Angus paused at the top of some concrete stairs. "Don't you want to take a look?"

Michael kept walking. "Not really."

"Suit yourself," Angus muttered, and went down the stairs.

Michael continued on and found his way to the side of Battery Kinzie. He walked around to the front to study it. As he recalled, at least one of the huge iron hatches was affixed to the concrete wall so it couldn't be closed. Had the cops checked behind it?

He peered behind all the hatches. Nothing. The room beyond was dim. He went inside, checking his jacket pocket for his cell phone.

Max and Hank had emerged from the tunnel at the back of this room. Assuming Max *had* hidden the painting here, would he have led Hank to the correct tunnel? Maybe, if Hank had broken his spirit enough.

Michael found himself tiptoeing as he moved to the back of the room. He stopped at the tunnel entrance and listened.

Faint noises came from the darkness beyond, like stone scraping across stone. The hair rose on the back of Michael's neck, and he looked over his shoulder. Should he get Angus? If he left, whoever it was might get away.

Michael took out his cell phone and sent a quick text to Suki and Angus. *At Kinzie. Hear something. Going in tunnel.* He pressed send and switched the phone to silent. He held it to his side, allowing only the faintest illumination to escape, and stepped into the tunnel.

Angus felt the buzz of his phone and took it out. "Oh, for crying out loud," he muttered, reading the message. He trotted up the cement stairs of Battery Vicars.

Michael walked as quietly as possible along the damp floor of the tunnel. It made a right-angle turn ahead. A faint light came from the opening beyond. He heard a woman grunt, and then the sound of shoes stumbling.

Michael turned the corner and saw a small shape run toward him, accompanied by the sound of claws on concrete. Lyndsay stood just beyond, barely visible in the gloom.

"Grab her!" Lyndsay yelled.

Michael bent and managed to grab Gigi's leash as it slithered past. As he rose, his peripheral vision caught what looked like a piece of driftwood swinging toward the side of his head. It was too late to duck.

Angus pelted down the stairs that led to the ground level of Battery Kinzie, the metal handrail rough under his palm. He could hear a high-pitched racket up ahead, as if someone were yelling hysterically. As he hit bottom, he saw Lyndsay poke her head out of one of the ground-floor rooms and look both ways.

"What's going on?" Angus called. "Is it Max?"

"Yes!" Lyndsay yelled. "Hurry! They're fighting!"

Angus ran across the front of the battery. Lyndsay stood just inside the door. Her hands and dress were dirty, and she was frantically disentangling a gnarled piece of driftwood from what looked like a black plastic trash bag.

She got it loose and thrust the wood at him, yelling to be heard over the ear-splitting racket coming from the back of the room. "Take this!"

Angus grabbed the stick from her and ran to the entrance of the tunnel. Now that the echoes were fewer, he realized that what he had thought was yelling was barking. He glanced back at the door, but Lyndsay was gone.

Angus took out his cell phone and used the light to navigate, holding it in his left hand while he kept his improvised club raised high in his right. He almost tripped over Michael, who was pushing himself off the wet floor with one hand. Gigi barked hysterically by his elbow, her leash trapped beneath his side.

Angus dropped his stick and grabbed Michael under one armpit, but the narrow confines of the tunnel made it difficult to haul him upright.

Michael shook his head and squirmed from Angus's grip. "I can do it. Just shut her up, will you?"

Angus reached for Gigi.

She made a token snap at the air by his hand, but allowed him to pick her up.

He held her in one arm and stroked her head with one finger. "Hush."

Michael staggered to his feet and leaned against the wall. "Where's Lyndsay?"

"Outside, hopefully calling for help." Angus aimed his phone back and forth, nervously checking either end of the tunnel. "Where's Max?"

"Max?" Michael lifted a hand to his head and winced as he touched it. "I never saw Max, but I'm pretty sure Lyndsay *hit* me." He caught sight of the piece of wood Angus had dropped on the floor. "With that, I think."

"Why on earth would she hit you?" Angus asked.

"That part's kind of fuzzy, but if I had to guess, I'd say it has something to do with the painting. Was she carrying anything when you saw her?"

"She had a plastic bag. I thought it was trash." Angus tugged on Michael's sleeve. "Can you walk?"

"Yeah." Michael picked up the stick and followed Angus a little groggily. "Take my advice and don't go around corners headfirst."

Angus led the way into the anteroom. "Don't forget to duck," he said as they passed beneath the concrete buttress that crossed the ceiling.

"*Now* you tell me." Michael followed him outside, blinking in the weak sunlight. Patches of dark muck splotched his cheek, and one side of his clothes was dark with water where he had lain on the tunnel floor.

Suki came running down the path toward them, sand spraying under her feet. She came to a halt in front of Michael and her eyes widened. "What happened to you?"

"Lyndsay walloped him over the head with that stick," Angus said. "You didn't see her, did you?"

"I *thought* that was her car that passed me going the other way."

Michael dropped the piece of driftwood and patted his pockets gingerly. "I must have dropped my phone somewhere in the tunnel. Someone else is going to have to call the police."

Angus handed Gigi to Suki and dialed 911 on his phone.

"Look at me," Suki said to Michael. "I want to make sure your pupils are the same size."

Michael squinted at her, struggling not to blink. From her place on Suki's arm, Gigi tilted her head at him.

"They look okay to me," Suki said. "You don't have a gooshy spot on your skull, do you? Any nausea?"

Michael probed the side of his head, grimacing in pain. "Just a big lump and a hell of a headache."

Suki patted him on the arm. "You're okay. Walk it off."

Angus waved them into silence as he spoke into his phone. "This is Angus MacGregor. Please tell Detective Kroger that Maureene Pinter's daughter, Lyndsay, assaulted one of my staff at the Kinzie Battery and then took off in her car." He paused. "She was armed with a stick, but she doesn't have it anymore. I have no idea where she was going. No, I can't stay on the line." He tapped the screen and hung up. "Let's go."

"Hospital or police station?" Suki asked.

"Do you need the hospital?" Angus asked Michael.

"I don't think so."

"Then let's go to Maureene's house," Angus said.

"Are we going to tell Lyndsay's mom on her?" Suki asked as they walked to the car. "Cool."

"I'm hoping to find Lyndsay and ask her a few blunt questions."

Michael opened his car door. "I thought you didn't want the painting's disappearance debunked."

"Maybe not," Angus said, "but I take exception to someone bashing one of my reporters over the head. We don't want that kind of behavior to catch on."

Angus and Michael told Suki what had happened as she drove through the park. When they reached the main road, she put on more speed.

Michael closed his eyes and clenched his teeth as the car leaned into a turn. "I want to catch Lyndsay more than anyone, but can you slow down a little? The G forces aren't doing my brain any good."

"Sorry." Suki lessened her pressure slightly on the gas pedal. "Angus, you said Lyndsay had a trash bag in addition to the stick?"

"I can't say for sure if it was a bag, but it was that kind of plastic." Angus scanned the other cars on the road as they drove. "It wasn't the size of the painting."

"A painting doesn't have to include a frame," Michael reminded him. "It's basically a piece of canvas."

"Then I suppose that could have been it," Angus said. "Honestly, it looked as though Lyndsay had picked up the stick from some trash, looking for a weapon, and the bag came with it."

"Did you notice the plastic lying around when you left?" Suki asked.

Angus shook his head. "I didn't notice much of anything, except how bad Michael looked."

Michael sat up a little in the backseat. "Here's what I'm thinking. Lyndsay gets into town the evening of the night Doreene dies. Like anyone in the family, she could have known what code Doreene used. She sneaks upstairs and opens the locked room. Maybe Doreene is already dead, or maybe Doreene wakes up, groggy from her pills, and goes in there after her. Lyndsay holds some clothes over her aunt's face to suffocate her and steals the painting."

"What about Reynaldo?" Angus asked. "He was sleeping beside Doreene."

"He and Lyndsay could have been in it together. In fact, Lyndsay might have met Reynaldo anywhere and sent him to meet up with Doreene in Brazil!"

"That leaves out the rejuvenated portrait that was in the room," Angus said.

"Lyndsay must have had her mother paint a replacement portrait," Michael said. "They were all in it together."

"And where is the replacement portrait now?" Angus asked. "Is the police department also part of this caper? Turn here."

"I don't know where the other painting is," Michael said, groaning as they took the turn.

"And where does Max fit into things?" Suki pulled up to the curb in front of the house.

"It's just a working theory, okay?" Michael said.

Gigi had been sitting in Angus's lap, but he picked her up in preparation for getting out of the car. "Let's not go in with a bunch of accusations. We'll ask where Lyndsay is because we found her dog. Don't let on that we're suspicious of anything."

"Michael might want to clean himself up, in that case," Suki said.

Michael brushed at the crud on his face, causing a shower of black flakes to fall on his lap. "Better?"

"Just stand at the back," Suki said.

They got out and went to the front door, where Angus pressed the doorbell and then knocked.

After a few seconds, Lupita opened the door.

Angus smiled and raised Gigi slightly. "Look who we found wandering around lost."

"The Chihuahuita! I wondered where she was." Lupita stepped aside. "Go ahead and put her inside."

Angus continued to hold the dog. "She's acting a little strange, like she might have been grazed by a car or eaten something bad. Is Lyndsay here?"

Lupita shook her head. "I haven't seen her since early morning. She came in the kitchen to tell me she was going out to breakfast." Lupita leaned out the door and scanned the street, then pointed. "Her car is still here."

The others turned. Sure enough, Lyndsay's car sat between two others, perhaps a half block in front of where they had parked.

Suki leaned toward Angus and murmured, "I'm going to see if the hood is warm." She jumped off the step and trotted down the street.

Angus smiled at Lupita. "So you haven't seen Lyndsay since this morning?"

Lupita shook her head.

"What about Reynaldo?" Michael asked.

"I saw him leave with his gym bag just a little bit ago." Lupita's gaze shifted to the street, where a police car slowed as it neared the house. *"Dios mio, la policia."* She gave Angus a fearful look. "No one is dead, are they?"

"Not as far as we know," Angus said.

Suki ran back to the house in time to greet Detective Kroger as he got out of the car. They walked to the house together, heads bent in conversation.

Angus and Michael parted to let the detective through. He came to a stop in front of Lupita. "Do you know the location of Lyndsay Waring?"

"No," Lupita said, her voice trembling.

"How about Reynaldo Cruz?"

"I think he's at the gym."

"She says Reynaldo left a little bit ago," Angus volunteered, "carrying a gym bag."

"Did he say that's where he was going?" Kroger asked Lupita. "Did you talk to him?"

Lupita twisted her hands together. "I was upstairs cleaning and heard the front door close, so I looked out the window and saw him. That's all."

"What gym does he go to?" Kroger asked, taking out his phone.

"The one on Monroe Street, I think," Lupita said. "I saw him come out of there once."

"Would he have driven or walked?"

"Walked. He didn't know how to drive, and anyway, there is Doreene's car." Lupita pointed down the street in the other direction.

Kroger went back to his car, cell phone to his ear. He opened the door and sat, then leaned over to twiddle the radio.

"What's going on?" Lupita asked.

Angus started to answer.

Michael cut him off. "We shouldn't say anything." He looked at Suki. "Was Lyndsay's car still warm?"

"Oh, yeah."

They waited as Kroger had several animated conversations.

Finally he came back. "There's no sign of either of them."

"What about Maxwell Thorne?" Michael asked. "He has a car. Could he have picked them up?"

Kroger seemed to notice Michael's grubby clothes and face for the first time. "Are you okay? I heard you got hit in the head."

"It's just a headache and a lump," Michael said.

Kroger nodded. "When I left the station, Maxwell Thorne had just gone to Alexander's Castle with one of my officers to pack up his things. I imagine he's there now."

"Can you check and make sure?" Michael asked.

Kroger took his phone out, typed in a text message, and waited a bit. "He's still there. I don't think he has anything to do with this."

Michael chewed his lip. "Max had breakfast with Lyndsay this morning. She said he was going to try to find her a job."

"Don't forget Maureene," Suki said. "She was sitting outside the restaurant in her car, watching the place. Lyndsay came out, said good-bye to Max, then went over to the car and talked to her mother. They might be on the run together."

"We know where Maureene Pinter is," Kroger said calmly.

"Where?" Michael asked.

"At Fort Worden." He smiled. "She appears to be following Maxwell Thorne."

Angus blew out a frustrated breath. "It's like a Pink Panther movie. All we need is the man in a gorilla suit."

Michael looked at Kroger. "Hank Gray isn't out on bail, is he? He has a car."

Kroger shook his head. "Hank is still locked up. Why are you asking about people besides Lyndsay?"

"Because Lyndsay's car is over there," Michael pointed, "so presumably she needs someone to help her get out of town with the painting."

Kroger's brows rose. "You think she has the portrait?"

Michael nodded. "One of them, anyway."

Twenty-seven

They went back to Battery Kinzie with Detective Kroger, who wanted a description of what had happened.

Angus pointed to the piece of wood Michael had left on the ground in front of the building. "Here's the stick Lyndsay used on Michael."

Kroger put on gloves and picked up the piece of driftwood, which was about three feet long. "That had to hurt."

"It still hurts." Michael led the way into the room, ducking under the concrete. "Can I borrow your phone?" he asked Suki. "We need some light."

Suki got out her phone and tapped the screen a few times until it lit up brightly.

Michael took it from her outstretched hand and stepped into the tunnel's dark opening. "This way."

They walked in single file, Michael first, then Kroger, then Suki and Angus.

Michael turned a corner and stopped. "Here's where I fell." He scanned the floor with the light, stopping when he saw a pale square next to the wall. "There's my phone." He picked it up and pressed something. The screen lit up. "Still works."

"What's that up ahead?" Kroger asked, pointing.

Michael aimed both phones farther down the tunnel, creating weird, angular shadows. "Looks like a rock."

They moved forward in a tight bunch, Suki and Angus trying to see over the shoulders of the two men in front.

It was a broken piece of cement block.

Kroger stared at it. "I'm pretty sure that wasn't there when we searched the place before."

"Kids might have brought it in," Angus suggested.

"It's about where Lyndsay was standing." Michael shone light on top of the cement hunk. "Look. There are streaks of mud on top, like she stood on it for some reason." He swept the light up to the ceiling.

The concrete walls of the tunnel were black with mold and grime—except for two pale marks on either side, near the top, where something rough had scraped the concrete clean.

Kroger pushed carefully past Michael and stood on top of the cement chunk. He raised the piece of driftwood he still carried and held it near the top of the tunnel, where it lined up with the pale marks. "I'll be damned."

Suki raised her camera and took photos of the ceiling and the cement block.

Michael winced as the flash went off. "Lyndsay could have covered the canvas portrait in a black plastic bag and folded it around the stick. Then she wedged the stick at the top of the tunnel."

"Wait a minute," Angus said. "*Max* is the one who told Hank that the portrait was in the tunnel, and *Max* is the one who had breakfast with Lyndsay this morning, not long before she came here. He could have told her where the painting was and asked her to get it because he knew Maureene was watching him."

"That would make sense," Kroger said, "except that he has a great alibi for the night the portrait changed—or was stolen and replaced.

We'll keep an eye on him, but I don't like to bring people in on the basis of coincidence."

"Is it possible Lyndsay was *hiding* the portrait instead of retrieving it?" Michael asked. "Since the police have already searched here, she might have thought it was the last place anyone would look. Then I interrupted her, so she hit me and took off."

Kroger nodded thoughtfully. "Another possibility." He reached into his pocket, took out another pair of latex gloves, and held them out. "Can someone put these on and carry the cement block outside?"

Angus carried the block to Kroger's car, where he put it on the floor with a thump. He took off the gloves and tossed them in as well.

Kroger took a sheet of plastic from a kit in the trunk and wrapped the stick before laying it across the backseat. "I'm surprised they haven't found Lyndsay or Reynaldo yet," he said, checking his phone for messages. "There are very few roads off this peninsula, and we have people watching them. I also told the guys at the Jefferson County airport to keep an eye out for her."

"What about boats?" Suki asked.

Kroger nodded. "I alerted the ferry stations, too."

"No, I mean regular boats," Suki said. "All those big cruisers that came here for the boat festival. Some of them go a long way, right?"

Kroger stared at her for a moment, then raised his phone and tapped frantically at the screen.

"Do they even go through customs?" Suki wondered aloud.

Kroger went to the front of the car, still holding his cell phone to his ear. "Ships have been leaving that marina all morning. I could kick myself." He opened the driver's door of the police car and slid in. "It's Kroger," he said, paying sudden attention to his phone. "Call the Point Hudson harbor master and find out what boats left in the last hour and a half." He tossed the phone on the passenger seat and started the car.

"Wait!" Michael leaned against the door, clutching his small pocket notebook. "Reynaldo met some friends at the festival. They were in the middle of a big trip and asked if he could crew for them."

Kroger looked up at him. "Do you know the name of the ship?"

"I wrote it down." Michael flipped pages. "The *Rachel Diana.*" He stepped away from the car as Kroger put it into gear. A moment later, the police cruiser sped out of the parking lot and back toward town.

Suki followed Kroger as best she could and parked on Water Street, not too far from the marina. She and Angus got out of the van and ran toward the dock.

"Do you think Michael will get some kind of public-service citation?" Suki panted.

"God, I hope not," Angus said. "He's arrogant enough as it is." He looked back to where Michael trotted gingerly behind them, one hand to his head as if to keep it from falling off. "Come along, Michael!"

Michael grimaced and made a shooing gesture, to signal they shouldn't wait.

"He'll catch up," Angus said.

They found Detective Kroger standing at the end of the dock, along with a leather-skinned woman with short white hair, who stared out at the water through a pair of binoculars. She looked around sixty, and wore jeans and a canvas jacket.

"Do boats have to clear customs?" Suki asked Kroger as she and Angus came to a stop beside him.

The woman lowered her binoculars. "Not on the way out."

Kroger made the introductions. "Suki Oota, Angus MacGregor, this is the harbor master, Karen Cullough. Karen, these are the people from the magazine."

Michael joined them in time to have his hand shaken. "Did you find them?"

Cullough resumed staring at the water. "The Coast Guard is bringing the *Rachel Diana* in now."

"Did you tell them not to let anyone throw anything overboard?" Michael asked.

Cullough's mouth quirked. "They know that, trust me." She lowered the binoculars and turned. "We might as well go inside. It'll be another thirty minutes, motoring."

Cullough led the way inside a two-story L-shaped building. A balcony ran the length of the back side, and windows ran all along the top floor.

"Have a seat." She gestured to a table. "I'll get some coffee."

Kroger and the *Tripping* crew sat as Cullough went over to a coffeemaker that sat on top of a file cabinet.

A meticulously drawn boat plan lay on the table. Michael slid it carefully to one side. "This looks complicated."

Kroger glanced at the drawing. "That's a kayak."

"Oh."

Cullough came back with three paper cups on a tray, plus sugar and cream. "To be fair, it's a very nice kayak. Five kinds of wood. Do you boat, son?"

Michael shook his head. "I've often thought it would be nice."

She chortled. "You could call it nice. It's also expensive, time-consuming, and dangerous. But spend enough time on the water, and the water gets in your blood." She passed out the cups. "I know the people who own the *Rachel Diana*. Sissy and Paul. I hope they're not in any trouble."

Kroger blew on his coffee. "I doubt they're involved, but don't say anything when they get here, Karen. You might think you're doing them a favor, but if they get confused and say something they don't mean, it could make things worse for them."

She sipped her coffee. "Noted."

Eventually the ships arrived, the *Rachel Diana* nosing into the marina while the Coast Guard ship blocked the entrance behind her.

Officer Madison had joined the group waiting on the dock. He and Detective Kroger walked down the pier toward the two Coast Guard officers who stood on board the captive ship. "Permission to come aboard?" Kroger asked.

One of the Coast Guard men unclipped a line and waved the police onto the *Rachel Diana*'s deck.

The staff of *Tripping* had been asked to wait at the Maritime Center.

Suki put a telephoto lens on her camera and set up her tripod on the top floor, behind a huge window. "This would be way better if someone had a sword between his teeth," she said, eye to the lens.

"What are they doing?" Angus asked.

"Kroger and the other cop went into a cabiny sort of thing. Here comes someone. It's not Reynaldo or Lyndsay."

"Must be the owners," Michael said.

Suki tweaked her lens slightly. "Man, those Coast Guards are buff."

"Are you looking at the right boat?" Michael asked.

"Of course I am. Oh, there they are. Reynaldo and Lyndsay." Suki held her finger down on the shutter. The camera whirred as it took multiple frames.

"Are they carrying anything?" Angus asked.

"No." Suki's grin spread beneath the camera. "But Kroger is. It looks like a rolled-up canvas."

Detective Kroger sat in the interrogation room once more while the staff of *Tripping* magazine watched through the video monitor.

Reynaldo sat across the table from Kroger, his face drawn and fearful.

Detective Kroger paged through a sheaf of papers. "I have to tell you, Mr. Cruz, your situation is not good. You married a rich older woman, and shortly afterward, she died mysteriously." He looked at

Reynaldo over the top of the paper. "Only Doreene wasn't really your wife, was she?"

"I thought we were married." Reynaldo's voice was barely audible.

Kroger flipped to another sheet and shook his head. "You fled the country with stolen artwork and a woman. Lyndsay Waring says you tricked her into getting on the *Rachel Diana*. Even if you had nothing to do with Doreene's death, you and your friends could face kidnapping charges."

"Kidnapping?" Reynaldo's voice was loud and clear now. "I told Lyndsay I had friends who could take me home to Brazil. I asked her to go with me, and at first she said no." Reynaldo's voice became increasingly bitter, and his hands came up to gesture wildly. "This morning, Lyndsay calls and says now she wants to go. She tells me she has the portrait, and we can sell it in Brazil."

"How did you explain that to your friends?"

"I didn't!" Reynaldo was adamant. "They knew *nothing*."

"Then how did you explain that you needed to leave right away?"

"I didn't have to! After the will changed, I told Paul and Sissy that I might need to work for them. They were only here because they were waiting to hear from me." He ran a hand through his hair and gave a choking laugh. "When Lyndsay called and wanted to go, I thought, *I am so lucky.*"

Lyndsay Waring sat across from Detective Kroger at the interrogation table, the front of her sundress marked with dirt from Battery Kinzie.

Kroger leaned back in his chair. "Reynaldo says you called and told him you had the painting."

"Does Reynaldo know he should wait for a lawyer?" Lyndsay bit out.

"He says you were planning to find a buyer overseas."

Lyndsay leaned forward. "He's *lying*. I had no idea the painting was on board that ship or that those people were planning to go on a long trip. Reynaldo asked me to take a little cruise with him and his friends, and I said yes. That's *it.*"

Kroger consulted his legal pad, which he held upright, so Lyndsay couldn't see it. "What's your relationship to Maxwell Thorne?"

"He's a friend of my mother's. That's the only relationship we have."

"Thorne said he might find you a job. Did that job include stealing the painting? Did you have to kill your aunt to do it?"

Lyndsay put both hands on the table. "I didn't kill anyone, and I didn't steal anything!" Her anger suddenly faded, and her lower lip trembled. "I'm not talking to anyone without a lawyer."

"You can certainly do that." Kroger smiled sadly. "Of course, lawyers don't want you to talk to the police, even if it might help. They want to go to court and rack up fees." He looked at his notes. "Let's review what the jury is going to hear. You came into town, and your aunt died. You immediately started a romance with your dead aunt's husband, who was supposed to inherit her very valuable painting. When he didn't inherit, you wound up on a boat with the stolen painting, leaving the country."

Lyndsay began to sob.

Kroger leaned forward. "This is your chance to help yourself, Lyndsay. What really happened the night Doreene died?"

"I don't know! I wasn't there!" She buried her face in her hands.

Kroger's phone buzzed on the table. He picked it up and looked at the display. "Think about what I've said, Ms. Waring. I'll be back in a while."

He went through the door and entered the room where Angus and the others waited. "Come on. Evidence says they have something I should see. Maybe you'll know something about it."

Doreene Gray's altered portrait lay faceup on a table, its grotesque features staring at the ceiling.

One of Kroger's officers, a woman in her midthirties, leaned over the canvas with a magnifying glass and a pair of tweezers.

Kroger greeted her by saying, "I hope you're not doing something the insurance people won't like, Officer Denton."

"I think we're okay," she said, looking up. "This painting hasn't been handled gently. A whole section of pasted-on paper has lifted, possibly from humidity in the gun battery."

"We think the painting was also wrapped around a piece of driftwood."

"That wouldn't help it any." She handed him the magnifying glass.

Kroger took it and bent over the painting. "What am I looking for?"

Denton used the tweezers to lift a shiny flap of glued-together paper. With the other hand, she shone a flashlight on the surface it revealed. "See the handwritten section, underneath the flap?"

Kroger tilted his head and read aloud. "'I didn't mean for it to happen. He fell overboard and was so drunk and angry, I was afraid it would be worse than usual. I got the oars out and kept moving the boat away, hoping he would calm down. Eventually he went under and didn't come back up.'" He raised his head and looked at Angus and the others. "Does that mean anything to you?"

Angus nodded. "Doreene and Maureene's stepfather went out in a boat and drowned." He looked at Michael. "How old were they when that happened?"

"Eighteen," Michael said. "Someone told us he was an abusive drunk."

Officer Denton put down the tweezers and flashlight. "I have something else you should see, sir." She picked up a file folder from the table and took out the top sheet. "Take a look at this." She handed it to Kroger and resumed her place with tweezers and flashlight.

Kroger held the sheet of paper in one hand and compared it to the writing on the painting. Then he straightened. "Have someone bring her in, please."

"Yes, sir." Officer Denton put down her tools and left the room.

Angus had been chewing his thumbnail. He dropped his hand and cleared his throat. "What is it? What are you looking at?"

Kroger looked up from the sheet of paper. "Maureene Pinter's statement, taken the night of her sister's death. It looks like a match for the handwriting on this painting."

Detective Kroger and Maureene Pinter sat on either side of the interrogation table, the painting between them.

Kroger lifted the flap and read the text beneath. "You wrote that, didn't you? About your stepfather."

Maureene stared down at the portrait. She appeared to have aged several years in the last few days.

In the next room, Suki kept her gaze on the video monitor. "You think she'll go crazy, right here in front of us?"

"What a terrible thing to say," Angus chided. "Poor thing. She was very young, with no one to turn to. I can't believe they'd actually prosecute after all this time."

Michael shifted on his molded plastic chair. "There's no statute of limitations on murder."

"Yeah, but *is* it murder?" Suki asked. "I mean, if she was afraid of what her drunk stepfather would do, is keeping away basically self-defense?"

"Shh . . ." Angus said. "I think she's going to say something."

In the next room, Maureene slowly raised her head. "I don't know anything about this. My sister must have written it."

Detective Kroger folded his hands on the table. "You wrote a confession, and your sister cut it up and pasted it onto your portrait of her."

Maureene turned her face to one side and gazed at the blank wall.

"Doreene blackmailed you for years and years," Kroger went on. "You supported her in exchange for keeping your secret, didn't you?"

Maureene shook her head slightly, but said nothing.

"But then she decided to sell the portrait." Kroger continued his calm, flat recital. "You didn't want anyone to know what you had done, so you unlocked the room with the code she used for everything. You took the portrait with your confession and replaced it with a copy of the original."

"I never left my cottage that night," Maureene said quietly.

"Then your daughter, Lyndsay, did it," Kroger said.

Maureene's head swung around. Her sudden animation was as startling as if a statue had come to life. "She did *not*."

In the monitoring room, Suki whispered a quiet "Dude."

Kroger didn't change position. "Lyndsay and Reynaldo must have known each other before he came here with Doreene. Lyndsay sneaked into the room while Reynaldo lay next to Doreene, and together they stole the painting and killed your sister."

Two spots of red burned on Maureene's otherwise white face. "That's a lie!"

Kroger lifted his brows. "Is it? Then how did your daughter wind up with the painting? Why were she and Reynaldo fleeing the country together in possession of the painting? Why did she—"

"Shut up!" Maureene shouted. She pressed a hand over her mouth and squeezed her eyes shut.

"All right." Kroger leaned back in his chair and folded his hands on the table. "You talk. Because if you don't, Lyndsay is going to be tried for murder and theft."

Maureene took a deep, shuddering breath and opened her eyes. "I want to speak to Hank Gray. Alone."

Someone brought a spare chair to the interrogation room, and Officer Denton brought Hank Gray in.

Hank sat next to Detective Kroger and smiled wistfully at Maureene.

A ring of gray stubble grew on his usually shaved scalp, like a monk's tonsure.

Maureene looked from Hank to Kroger, an expression of irritation on her features.

Kroger shook his head. "You can't talk to him alone. Sorry."

Maureene sighed and turned away for a moment. Then she addressed Hank. "They think Lyndsay stole the portrait and killed Doreene."

Hank turned to Kroger, his heavy features angry.

Kroger nodded. "She and Reynaldo were leaving the country with the portrait. It doesn't look good for either of them."

"How can anyone call it murder?" Hank demanded. "The coroner said Doreene took an overdose of pills!"

"Even if a jury decides that's the case, Lyndsay and Reynaldo were on the scene and didn't call an ambulance," Kroger said. "That's criminal negligence. A conviction for that and theft could result in a long sentence."

Hank and Maureene exchanged a look. Hank opened his mouth to say something.

Maureene held up a hand to stop him. She took a deep breath. "Lyndsay couldn't have stolen the portrait because legally, it's hers."

Hank turned away.

Kroger shook his head. "I see what you're trying to do, Ms. Pinter, but you can't abdicate your inheritance in favor of your daughter. The theft of the painting is a crime against the estate."

Maureene gave a tremulous smile. "There is no crime, because you can't steal from yourself. Lyndsay is not my daughter. She's Doreene's."

In the monitoring room, Suki threw herself against her chair's back, causing it to tip backward to an alarming degree. "Dude!"

Michael scribbled frantically in his small notebook.

Angus shook his head in disbelief. "Amazing."

• • •

Kroger recovered his equanimity with an obvious effort. "Does Lyndsay know that Doreene is really her mother?"

Maureene had looked bemused at Kroger's obvious shock, but now she sobered. "No."

Kroger turned to Hank. "Did you?"

Hank nodded. "Maureene told me when I came back. She thought it was only fair that I know."

"Wouldn't it be only fair to tell Lyndsay, as well?" Kroger asked.

"It would have been cruel," Maureene said. "Doreene got pregnant shortly before she and Hank left for their trip to Argentina. She didn't tell him, and I could tell she wasn't overjoyed about having a child. But when she came back without Hank and told me she wasn't going to keep the baby, I couldn't believe it." Maureene shook her head. "I knew their marriage was in trouble, but I thought she would want to keep the last vestige of her lost husband."

Hank snorted. "I wasn't lost. Doreene knew exactly where I was."

Maureene acknowledged his remark with a grim smile before going on. "I went to Switzerland to be with my sister during the last months of her pregnancy." Her gaze dropped to the table. "Hank and I were close before Doreene took an interest in him, but my stepfather . . ."

Hank reached across the table and took her hand.

Maureene gripped his and continued. "I couldn't bring myself to have intimate contact with a man, but I also couldn't bear the thought of Hank's child going to a stranger. The orphanage had a policy. If a mother changed her mind within two weeks, she could take her baby back. So I bleached my hair and pretended to be Doreene. Doreene was already vacationing in Spain. She didn't know I'd claimed Lyndsay as my own until months later."

"But what about the birth certificate?" Kroger asked. "It must have had Doreene's name as the mother."

Maureene shrugged. "Correction fluid and photocopies. Doctors and schools understand that it's hard to get originals from another country. Once Lyndsay was old enough for the family resemblance to show, it was even less of an issue."

Kroger frowned. "Wait a minute . . . Do you have proof that Lyndsay is Doreene's daughter?"

"Do you remember the letter the magazine people found hidden in the mantelpiece?"

"Doreene's suicide note?"

Maureene gave a brief nod. "I put it there. It was the bottom half of a letter Doreene sent me after a mutual friend congratulated her on her new niece. What Doreene actually wrote was, 'If I wasn't confident that this was the right decision, I would have died rather than given her up'. I scratched out the word *her* and tore off the top part of the letter, but I still have it. That should be enough proof." She released Hank's hand with a pat and sat back.

Kroger rubbed his forehead, then looked at Maureene with new determination. "All that may be true, but the fact is, Lyndsay didn't know she was Doreene's heir. She and Reynaldo took that portrait, and they left Doreene for dead in a locked room." He pointed at Maureene. "And you were part of it. You must have painted the portrait that was left in the original's place."

Maureene gave Hank a look that was half-question, half-plea.

Kroger turned to look at him. "Is there something you want to tell me?"

Hank put his joined hands on the table and stared at them for a moment before replying. "It was my idea."

"What was?"

"Everything. You have to understand, Maureene and I were always close." Hank's voice broke, but he recovered and went on. "The night before Doreene and I left for Argentina, I went to Maureene's cottage. We got a little drunk and started to talk about the horrible things Doreene had done over the years. Maureene told me about her stepfather. How, immediately after his death, she wrote down what happened on the night he drowned. Doreene took that journal and pasted pieces on the portrait over the years." He smiled wryly at Maureene. "I liked to imagine you were a little relieved at my death, since it meant one less person knew."

Maureene gave a choked laugh. "Don't be stupid."

Hank went on. "A couple of weeks ago, I got an Internet alert with news of Doreene. When I read that she was going to sell the portrait, I knew what that could mean for Maureene, so I came back to see if I could help. But when I confronted Doreene, she refused to stop the sale. So Maureene and I worked on Reynaldo."

"Did you tell him who you were?" Kroger asked Hank.

"Not at first."

"Then what do you mean, you *worked* on him?"

Maureene answered. "Even though he'd sailed all over, Reynaldo was still very provincial and superstitious. I thought maybe we could scare him enough that he would take the portrait and destroy it. I did things like putting paper strips with scary words in the soup, hoping he might find a way to destroy the painting. But no matter what I did, it wasn't enough, so we decided to tell him who Enrico really was."

Hank nodded. "Maureene found some photos of Doreene and me together. We showed them to Reynaldo and told him that Doreene had lied to him. I threatened to tell her lawyer that he wasn't her real husband." He fell silent.

"We gave Reynaldo a choice," Maureene said. "If he helped us steal the painting, we would pay his way back to Brazil or let him remain Doreene's husband, so he would inherit when she died. Either way. All we wanted was the portrait."

"But why did you need Reynaldo at all?" Kroger asked. "If everyone knew the code to the room, why didn't you just take the painting when no one was looking?"

Hank and Maureene exchanged a rueful look.

"Doreene made such a big deal out of the locked room," Hank said. "It never occurred to us she might use that old code. We hoped Reynaldo knew the combination, but he didn't."

Maureene nodded. "But he did have an idea. Reynaldo told us that Doreene's evening medicine made her so groggy, they could have a whole conversation in bed, even sex, and she wouldn't remember the next day."

Hank took a deep breath. "That night, Reynaldo got up and let me in the bedroom. I didn't trust him to do it alone, so I stood behind the curtains while he shook Doreene awake. He told her the house was on fire and they needed to get the portrait. She staggered over and opened the door, and he went inside." Hank stopped.

Kroger looked from Hank to Maureene and back again. "So? What happened next?"

"The painting wasn't there," Hank said.

Kroger raised his fists to his temples. "I don't believe this."

"Reynaldo went in," Hank said. "Then he came out and said, 'The portrait is gone.' "

In the monitoring room, Angus pumped his fist. "Yessss!"

Hank continued. "I went in the closet to help look. We were checking the walls when we realized we didn't know where Doreene was." He rubbed a hand over his mouth and shook his head slightly. "She had fallen facedown among the clothes and was not moving."

"Suffocation?" Kroger asked.

Hank shrugged. "You saw the coroner's report, I didn't. Reynaldo gave her mouth-to-mouth resuscitation, but it didn't work." He shook his head. "If the painting was gone and Doreene was alive, it was simple theft. But if the painting was gone and Doreene was dead, then it looked like murder. We had a problem."

"You could say that," Kroger said.

Hank gave him a sour look.

Maureene took up the story. "I had originally painted two versions of the portrait. I showed the one I liked best, but they were very similar. After Doreene's third cosmetic surgery, I offered to exchange the youthful portrait for the one she had modified. It was pretty hideous by that time. I argued that having the portrait appear young again would do so much for my career that I could give her even more money. She wouldn't do it."

Kroger turned to Hank. "Go back to what happened the night Doreene died."

"I went to Maureene and told her Doreene was dead," Hank said. "We put the young-looking portrait in place of the one that had been stolen. Everyone thought there was something supernatural about it anyway. We figured it was our one chance."

Maureene looked at Kroger intently. "The important thing is, Lyndsay had nothing to with Doreene's death. Nothing."

"Okay." Kroger nodded, a little manically. "I get that. But are you also telling me that you don't know who took the altered painting?"

Hank's expression darkened. "It had to be Max. When Doreene and I were in Europe, we heard things about him. How, if you were rich in art but poor in cash, you should call Max. He could arrange things so you could keep your art but also get money, either by selling someone a forgery or by declaring the piece stolen."

"Are you saying Max and Doreene collaborated on insurance fraud?" Kroger looked up at the sound of banging on the door to the room. *"What?"*

The door opened. Michael, Suki, and Angus spilled into the room, followed by the police officer who had been at the monitors with them.

"I know how Max could have taken the portrait!" Michael yelled.

Angus grabbed his shoulder and tried to pull him back. "You do not! Remember, I saved your life!"

Michael turned to look at him. "You did not."

"You were unconscious, facedown in the water. If I hadn't rolled you over, you would have drowned."

"Right," Michael said sarcastically. "I was getting up before you came barging in. I know, because you almost ran into my head."

Kroger held up one hand toward Angus. With his other, he pointed to Michael. "Tell me what you think happened."

Michael came over and leaned on the end of the table. "The day before Doreene died, Max came to measure the painting for the shipping crate, remember?"

Kroger nodded.

"Doreene had a bunch of clothes piled on her bed, for charity," Michael went on. "One of the things was a fur coat, and Max commented that his assistant would love to have it, and Doreene handed it over."

Kroger nodded. "Okay."

"You don't see it?" Michael grinned. "The painting was *wrapped in the coat.*"

Gasps and exclamations filled the room.

Michael nodded happily, his grin almost splitting his face. "Maureene was standing right there, but Doreene knew her sister didn't wear fur. She gave Max the painting in front of all of us."

"Good Lord," Angus said.

"When Doreene died so soon after she gave him the painting," Michael went on, "Max must have freaked out and hidden it in the gun battery. He probably figured the police would watch him even more after Hank's stunt, so he asked Lyndsay to retrieve the painting for him. I'm sure he offered to pay her, but she decided to keep the portrait and take it to Brazil to sell."

Kroger took out his cell phone. "I'm not sure we can prove Max was involved, but it's worth bringing him in." He dialed a number and waited, drumming his fingers on the table. "Hello? Any idea where Max Thorne is? Well, call the airlines and find out *what* flight. If the plane hasn't left, have them delay him." He hung up. "Thorne left Port Townsend about an hour ago, presumably for the Seattle airport." Kroger started for the door, but turned back and addressed Michael.

"You don't have any ideas about the second painting, do you? The second, young-looking one that disappeared from the van?"

Michael bumped his closed hand against his mouth and stared into space. "I don't know how that was done." His hand hovered at chin level. "Max bought a painting of a boat for his daughter. He had the gallery package it for shipping, but said he was going to take it on the plane with him." Michael looked up, clearly excited. "If Max *did* somehow get the second, young-looking portrait of Doreene, he could hide it behind the boat painting!"

Kroger groaned. "In that case, he could ship it straight to a buyer, rather than risk airport security and X-rays. We may be too late. On the other hand, if he doesn't have a buyer, he might still have it with him." He looked at the staff of *Tripping*. "You guys want to go on a little trip?"

Twenty-eight

Detective Kroger had a friend with a Cessna 206. Charter planes were not allowed to fly into the Seattle-Tacoma airport, so they flew to Boeing Field. From there, it was only a fifteen-minute cab ride to Sea-Tac.

"I'm only taking you as a favor, you understand," Kroger told Angus, Michael, and Suki on the way there. "You've been very helpful."

"I try," Michael said.

"Yes, we do," Angus said.

"Sea-Tac confirms that Thorne has already been through security," Kroger continued, "so at least there's no question of him being armed. Still, stay back and don't get in the way."

"Can I take pictures?" Suki asked.

Kroger considered this. "Can you do video?"

"Of course."

"Video is harder to manipulate, so we might be able to use it for evidence. Go ahead, but be discreet. And for God's sake, don't say anything about working for a magazine. The Seattle police would never let me hear the end of it."

. . .

A TSA agent met Detective Kroger and the staff of *Tripping* at Sea-Tac Airport and introduced himself as Agent Robert Hanley. After checking their IDs, Hanley led them through an unmarked door and set a rapid pace down a series of corridors.

"Did Max Thorne bring a big, flat box to the airport?" Kroger asked Hanley's back.

"He checked something as luggage," Hanley said. "They're unloading the plane now."

Kroger grimaced. "Sorry about that."

The TSA man glanced back and smiled. "Don't be. It's worth it for the chance of getting all up in Interpol's face." His smile disappeared. "That's my personal feeling, you understand, and not anything endorsed by TSA or Homeland Security." He faced forward and pushed open a door. "Here we are."

Maxwell Thorne sat in one of two gray chairs at a scratched, plastic-topped table, reading a magazine. Two TSA officers stood guard—one beside the door, one behind Max.

As Kroger and the *Tripping* crew filed in, Max let the magazine drop. "Detective Kroger. And friends."

"Hello, Mr. Thorne," Kroger said. "Mr. MacGregor, why don't you and your staff wait over there?" He nodded to a corner of the room.

Angus and his staff did as directed. Suki stood halfway behind Angus and powered up the camera that hung around her neck. She looked up to see Max leaning to one side so he could see her.

He smiled mockingly. "Come to film my beating?" The smile disappeared as he turned to Kroger. "Maybe you can tell me why I'm being held with no explanation."

Kroger walked to the table and draped his trench coat over the empty chair. He sat down facing Max, and rested his arms on the table.

"We found Lyndsay Waring and Reynaldo Cruz hiding on a boat, trying to smuggle Doreene Gray's portrait out of the country."

Thorne's brows shot up, and his angry look faded. "Well done, detective! Is the portrait in good condition?"

"It's been better," Kroger said.

A thump sounded from the hall outside as something knocked against the wall near the door.

Hanley opened the door.

A man in a blue jumpsuit stood in the hallway with a metal cart of the sort found at lumberyards. A familiar wooden crate sat upright on it, held in place by straps. "Sorry about that," the man said. "It's kind of tight out here."

Kroger looked at the crate, then at Max. "Wait a minute . . . Isn't that the shipping crate from the van?"

"Didn't it go back to the evidence room?" Michael asked.

Kroger shook his head. "It should have, but we were convinced we had the wrong crate, so we dusted the hasps for prints at the house and left it there. Things were a little hectic, if you recall."

Max folded his arms across his chest. "Those crates cost several hundred dollars to make, and Rothwell's will want it back." He gave Kroger a wry look. "And after all, you weren't using it."

The man rolled the cart past the table and into the open space beyond, then stopped and rested a hand on the top of the crate. "You want me to open it?"

Max frowned. "That painting is a gift for my daughter, and it's very carefully packed."

Agent Hanley gave him a look. "Unlock the padlock, sir."

Max sighed. "If you insist." He got up and took a set of keys from his pocket as he walked over to the crate. He opened the padlock, then removed it from the hasp. "Please be careful when you take it out."

As the man who had brought the cart undid the straps, Hanley approached Max and held out his hand. "I'll take that padlock, sir."

Max gave it to him.

Hanley gestured for Max to move. "Stand against that wall, please, sir."

Max raised both hands in an exaggerated gesture of surrender and stepped over to the wall, next to one of the other agents.

Detective Kroger opened the crate's lid and reached inside. After getting a grip with both hands, he pulled out a framed painting enclosed in a white, pressed-fiber bag.

Everyone was silent as the detective took the painting to the table. He set it on one edge, untaped the bag, and carefully pulled it off.

It was the ship picture Max had bought in the gallery.

"I don't know what else you expected," Max said.

Kroger frowned. "Somebody spread that bag on the table."

Hanley obliged.

Kroger laid the painting facedown on the protective bag. A smooth sheet of brown paper covered the back, its edges glued to the frame. Kroger picked at the paper's edge. "What's the best way to get this off?"

Max shrugged. "You can rip it off like a kid at Christmas, as far as I'm concerned. It's just cosmetic."

"Use this." Hanley reached into his pocket and took out a Swiss Army knife.

Kroger pulled out one of the knife's blades and slit the paper all the way around its perimeter. He gave back the knife and pulled the paper off the frame.

The back of the painting lay revealed, its canvas edges stapled taut around a wooden stretcher.

Kroger looked at Michael. "Now what?"

"Take it out of the frame and pry the staples off."

"Wait just a minute." Max took a step toward the table but was stopped by Hanley's arm across his chest. "Taking the canvas off the stretchers is not good for the paint. It can crack or flake."

"That's a risk we're going to have to take." Kroger turned to the man with the cart. "Excuse me . . ."

"Dave," the man provided.

"Dave. Can you get me a medium-sized, flathead screwdriver?"

Dave lifted a clanking canvas bag from the cart and set it on the table. "You'll want a pair of bent-nosed pliers, too."

Max leaned over Hanley's outstretched arm. "If you tell me what you're looking for, maybe I can help."

"We're looking for the portrait of Doreene Gray," Kroger said. He pried up the first staple.

Max made an exasperated noise. "You said Lyndsay and Reynaldo had it when you caught them. Did you lose it already?"

"They had the first portrait, yes." Kroger tossed a staple on the table. It made a slight metallic sound as it bounced. "Now we're looking for the second portrait—the one that disappeared from the van."

"There were *two* portraits?" Max said.

"Yup." Kroger pried up a second staple and froze as the canvas made a slight cracking noise.

Max groaned. "I'm going to file a claim against your department, Detective Kroger." He waved an arm to take in the TSA agents. "Against everybody here. You're damaging my property."

Hanley smiled. "I'll make sure to pass your message on to the head of Homeland Security."

Kroger pulled all the staples from one side of the canvas, then carefully pulled the stiff, bent edge of the painting away from the stretcher. "Hmm."

"Can you see anything?" Michael asked. "Is there a second canvas?"

Kroger pulled the canvas out farther and peered at the underside. His mouth twisted to one side. "Nope. It's just one painting."

Michael went over to him. "Let me see." He lifted the canvas up and examined the edge of the painting. Then he lay it flat again. He took the screwdriver from Kroger's hand and removed three more staples from a second side.

Max crossed his arms over his chest and looked at the painting glumly. "You might as well take it off completely. It'll have to be restretched, and who knows what that will do to the impasto." He glared at Kroger. "And who is going to pay for all this?"

Kroger looked at Michael and raised his brows. "That's a good question."

Michael peered under the canvas again before straightening. "Did you check out the officer who drove the van?" He cleared his throat. "Your nephew?"

Kroger nodded. "He hasn't gotten any sudden cash windfalls that we can tell." He crossed his arms. "And his mother vouches for his good character."

Michael made an apologetic face.

"And before you ask," Kroger went on, "we searched the entire van. Took all the panels off, inside and out."

"And you searched it *right after* the painting went missing?" Michael asked. "Not the next day or anything?"

Kroger nodded slowly. "Right after."

Michael looked into space, drumming his fingers.

"Do you *mind*?" Max pointed to where Michael's fingers drummed on the surface of the painting.

Michael looked down. "Sorry." He lifted his hand.

Max turned to Suki, who still had a camera trained on them. "I hope you're getting all this. I'm going to want it for court."

She gave him a thumbs-up.

Michael went to the crate, which leaned against one of the railings on either side of the cart. He reached into the interior, pulled out a foam pad with a scritch of Velcro, and tossed it on the floor. He did the same with the rest of thc pads.

Kroger rubbed his forehead as he watched. "We checked the inside of the box."

Michael turned on his cell phone's light and aimed it inside the foam-free crate. Squinting, he angled both the phone and his head in several directions. Finally he examined the outside of the crate.

"What are you looking for?" Kroger asked.

Michael straightened. "Can we take the crate apart?"

Max shook his head in apparent disbelief. "You're going to damage the painting *and* the box it came in? Did I do something to piss off the government?"

Michael pointed to the crate. "This has double walls."

Kroger frowned. "The surveillance camera in the evidence room didn't show Max doing any major woodworking."

Max spoke, his tone weary. "There's padding between the two layers of plywood. It absorbs shock and acts as a buffer against temperature changes. Also, if something were to break the outer layer of plywood, the painting would still be protected."

Dave joined Michael at the crate. He squatted and ran his fingertips over the screw heads. "Nice work. These are glued and screwed."

Michael put one arm inside the crate, pressing his cheek against the edge so he could reach the very bottom. Suddenly he lifted his head and sneezed. He sniffed the opening of the box. "I smell contact cement."

"As the man told you, it's glued together," Max said.

Dave shook his head. "You don't want contact cement for this. Wood glue is what you want."

"They probably used whatever would dry quickest," Max said. "Doreene decided to ship the painting on very short notice, and it had to be custom made."

Michael smiled. "When you measured the portrait, you jokingly complimented Maureene on using a standard canvas size. If it was standard, why would you have to custom-build anything? Rothwell's should have bunches of crates that size lying around." Michael patted the crate. "But I do think this one is special."

Dave went to the canvas bag and took out a large cordless drill. "I can take the screws out and use a pry bar to break the glued sections apart. *Or,* I can get a Sawzall up here and cut one end of that puppy right off. You just say the word."

Detective Kroger turned and studied Maxwell Thorne.

Max's air of outraged irritation had vanished. Two lines appeared on either side of his mouth.

Kroger leaned back in his chair and clasped his hands behind his head. "Let's try the pry bar first."

Once the screws were removed, Dave took a hammer and chisel and gouged a hole in the seam between two sides of the crate. He laid the crate flat, put the toe of his boot in the open end to hold it still, and levered with the pry bar.

Michael watched intently. "Of course, the painting could be in the other side."

"Or neither," Angus said. "I still think it dissolved into the ether after Doreene died."

Max gave Angus a sour look.

Angus returned it. "If anyone should be backing me up on this, it's you."

Suki circled the crate, camera trained on it. As the plywood began to splinter and separate, she licked her lips.

Agent Hanley leaned toward Kroger. "Is the photographer part of your department?"

"Freelance," Kroger said.

"I think I'll ask for a card." Hanley angled his head toward Michael. "What about Sherlock Holmes over there?"

Kroger uncrossed his legs and crossed them the other way. "Consultant."

Hanley lowered his voice further. "And the big guy with the funny accent?"

Kroger glanced at Angus, who chose that moment to ask one of the TSA agents if he had ever seen a ghost at the airport, late at night. "My uncle, from out of town," Kroger said. "He really wanted to watch me work."

Hanley nodded. "That's nice."

The plywood side of the crate came up with a sudden crunch of splintering wood. Dave reached down and wrenched the broken side free. "Well, would you look at that."

A wrapped canvas rested in the hollow side of the crate. Detective Kroger stepped across the broken plywood and picked it up. A few foam spacers fell to the floor.

He took it over to the table and removed the bag. The portrait of Doreene Gray smiled serenely up at them.

Twenty-nine

"That was a nice piece of detective work," Kroger told Michael, back in his office. They had returned to Port Townsend and stowed both the painting and Maxwell Thorne in locked rooms.

Michael's smile held more than a touch of smugness. "It was just a matter of realizing that if the painting was put in the crate, and no one removed it on the trip between the police station and the house, then it must *still be* in the crate."

"Plus, you smelled contact cement," Suki said. "How did that work, exactly?"

"It was like an illusionist's trick," Michael explained. "Remember, the crate had double walls. One of the inside walls wasn't attached. Before Max took the crate to the police station, he applied some contact cement to the loose wall's edges and some on the inside of the box, where the wall was supposed to go. But when he put the wall back in the crate, he shoved it over to the opposite side, against the inner wall."

"Just think," Angus said with false brightness. "If Thorne had used odor-free poster stickum, we might still have a story."

Kroger gave him an incredulous look. "You don't call this a story?"

"Not *Tripping*'s kind of story," Angus said.

Michael grinned at Kroger. "He's going to fire me."

Kroger gave Angus a stern look. "You're going to fire him for cooperating with the police? If I had solved this on my own and found out you withheld information, I'd arrest you as accessories."

Angus waved a negligent hand. "Michael's only joking. I wouldn't fire him." When Kroger turned away, he glared at Michael.

"What do you think will happen to everyone?" Suki asked. "Maureene, Hank, Reynaldo, and Lyndsay. Max."

"We should be able to get Max on the theft of the second painting, no problem." Kroger blew out a breath. "The first one, maybe not. As for the others, it's hard to say. Maureene will probably get off pretty easy. She wasn't in the house when Doreene died, and as for the death of her stepfather . . . She was young, he was a drunk who sexually abused her—I'm guessing probation, maybe some court-ordered counseling."

"What about Hank and Reynaldo?" Angus asked.

"That's trickier," Kroger said, leaning back in his chair. "It's conceivable the state might try for a verdict of criminal negligence, but it would be tough to get, especially since the victim's sister will presumably be on their side. Reynaldo may just be deported, since his marriage to Doreene wasn't legal and he isn't a U.S. citizen. It turns out Hank made a lot of money in Argentina, so he can hire a good defense. I wouldn't be surprised if he helps Maureene and Reynaldo with their legal fees, too."

"And Lyndsay?" Suki asked.

Kroger gave a low whistle and shook his head. "What a mess that is."

"Does she know Doreene was actually her mother?" Angus asked.

"Not yet," Kroger said. "She may find out from her attorney first. I suppose Lyndsay could claim she somehow knew Doreene was her mother, so there was no question of theft. Given that she inherits everything anyway, a judge might decide it's not worthwhile to try the case. I'm just guessing, you understand." He looked at Michael. "I'm assuming you want to press charges against her for hitting you on the head?"

Michael gave an exaggerated nod. "*Oh,* yeah."

Suki smiled. "That's my boy."

"Assault, then," Kroger said. "That's something."

Everyone sat in thoughtful silence for a few seconds.

Angus looked at his watch. "I checked flights earlier, and there are still seats on one of today's flights out of Seattle." He stood. "If we leave right this minute, we might be able to catch it."

Kroger got up to shake their hands. "It's been a real pleasure. If you're ever in Port Townsend again, let me know. Michael, have you ever considered joining the force?"

Michael chuckled. "I'm pretty determined to make it as a writer, but this has definitely been a thrill. Thanks for letting us help."

"Any time."

They left the brick building. Outside, the sun shone brightly, and a fresh breeze blew.

"It's a good thing you're firing me," Michael said as they walked to the minivan. "I'll need all my time if Reynaldo lets me work on his book. That story's even better now."

Angus strolled across the parking lot, hands in his jacket pockets. "You're not fired."

Suki smiled as she unlocked the minivan with the remote.

Michael ran in front of Angus and looked back at him. "What do you mean I'm not fired?"

"It's too early to go into details," Angus said, opening his car door, "but Suki said something that made me think the magazine could be a bit more inclusive."

Michael got in the backseat and tapped Suki's shoulder. "What? What did you say?"

Suki turned to look out the back window and reversed the car. "I don't remember exactly."

Michael slumped in his seat and buckled his seat belt. "Oh, I get it." He gave the back of Angus's head a bitter look. "It's in my contract that I can't sell any story *Tripping* covers, even if I quit first. What are you going to do, Angus, include a one-inch sidebar about Doreene in the next issue, so I can't benefit from it?"

"Certainly not," Angus huffed. "I'm not a punitive man. I think we should serialize the whole story. Afterward, you can integrate those articles into a book."

"With lots of photos," Suki added.

"Of course," Angus said. "Michael, you'll write it as a *Tripping* employee, but I'm sure we can come to some agreement on remuneration." He glanced in the rearview mirror and smiled. "I think that's fair. After all, you wouldn't have been here to see it all happen if it weren't for *Tripping*."

"Unbelievable." Michael shook his head and stared out the window. "Hey, Suki, this isn't the way out of town."

Suki turned the wheel and drove up a hill, toward the bluff above the shore. "I just need to make one quick stop."

Angus looked at his watch. "There really isn't time if we're going to make that plane. Can't you use the bathroom at the airport?"

"I don't have to pee. I'm going to get Gigi."

Angus stared at her. "You can't mean to take that dog with us."

Suki kept her gaze on the road. "There's no one to take care of her. The whole family is in jail."

"I'm sure Lupita will make sure she's okay," Michael said.

Suki shook her head irritably. "Lupita doesn't know the first thing about dogs, let alone Chihuahuas. Chis have a soft spot on their heads, are prone to luxating patellas, and walking them with a regular collar and leash can damage their tracheas. You're supposed to use a harness."

Angus raised his brows. "Been doing a little Internet research, have we?"

"No," Suki said. "My mom . . ."

"What?" Michael asked, when she didn't continue.

"My mom breeds long-haired Chis, okay?" Suki blurted. "I grew up with Mr. Toughie, Sugar Mole, and Sissy May Twinkletoes—Twito for short. They were all champions."

Michael burst into disbelieving laughter.

"Shut up! They made more money than you do." Suki stopped in front of Doreene's house and shoved open her car door. "I'll be back." She lifted a hand to show she had the car keys, then slammed her door shut and stomped down the walk, the buckles on her black boots jingling.

Angus caught Michael's eye in the mirror. "Do you suppose Mr. Toughie influenced her taste in clothes?"

They broke into renewed laughter.

Michael finally stopped laughing enough to speak. "We're never going to make that flight now. Do you suppose Detective Kroger is grateful enough to put us up for the night?"

"There's a good chance." Angus looked out the window. "I heard him say he thinks of me as an uncle."

"Really?" Michael wiped his eyes and chuckled one last time. "That's nice."

Portrait of Doreene Gray—Mysterious Painting Baffles Police!

If you could walk through the mist-wreathed streets of Port Townsend, Washington, enter the police station, and pass through the locked door of the evidence room, you would see two portraits hanging side by side. One depicts a laughing girl, the other an age-raddled hag, yet these pictures are of the same woman: a jet-setting socialite who left her husband for dead, blackmailed her twin sister, and abandoned her daughter at a Swiss orphanage—Doreene Gray.

When Ms. Gray cajoled the staff of Tripping *magazine into staying at her home, we had no idea of the frightening events that would test our nerve: diabolical messages that appeared in our soup as we ate it, a maid terrorized by skeletal lights in the woods, and a still-unexplained plague of slugs. Despite all this, we persisted in our search for the truth.*

What we found was stranger than anyone had imagined.

(continued on page 4)